Praise for Stanley

"A hero of American letters, a great artist, a stylist without peer."
—Tim O'Brien

"Stanley Elkin's imagination should be declared a national landmark."
—Paul Auster

"Pushing the envelope has always been Stanley Elkin's
stock-in-trade . . . If we didn't have him to read, we'd need to invent him.
But we couldn't come close."
—Richard Ford

"Funnier than Bellow, more single-minded than Roth, more irreverent
than Malamud. . . . His prose is always a delight, a reminder
of fiction's power to enthrall."
—*New York Newsday*

"*A Bad Man* comes breathtakingly close to rivaling Malamud's *The
Fixer* and Kafka's *The Castle* in its richly ironic black humor, its
oppressive ambience of pervasive menace; and, even more important,
its capacity to make us care what happens next."
—*National Observer*

"Stanley Elkin is such a down-to-earth and funny writer that
how smart he is sneaks up on you."
—John Casey

"One of our most original voices."
—John Irving

"Here again is the ferocious Elkin genius, elevated this time to even higher
powers of astonishment. All writers have contempt and hatred for death,
but Elkin's comic shocks stand against death more than Dostoyevsky
knew how to imagine. And the language, the language!"
—Cynthia Ozick

Other Books by Stanley Elkin

a bad man

Stanley Elkin

Introduction by David C. Dougherty

Dalkey Archive Press

First published by Random House, 1967
Copyright © 1965, 1967 by Stanley Elkin
Introduction © 2003 by David C. Dougherty

First Dalkey Archive edition, 2003

Library of Congress Cataloging-in-Publication Data

Elkin, Stanley, 1930-1995
    A bad man / Stanley Elkin ; introduction by David C. Dougherty.— 1st
Dalkey Archive ed.
        p. cm.
    ISBN 1-56478-332-4 (alk. paper)
        1. Department stores—Fiction. 2. Prisoners—Fiction. 3. Prisons—Fiction.
    I. Title.

PS3555.L47B33 2003
813'.54—dc21

                                                        2003055101

Partially funded by grants from the Lannan Foundation and the Illinois Arts Council, a state agency.

Dalkey Archive Press books are published by the Center for Book Culture, a nonprofit organization.

www.centerforbookculture.org

Printed on permanent/durable acid-free paper and bound in the United States of America.

For Joan
And for her brother Bernard

Acknowledgement

The author wishes to express his thanks to the
John Simon Guggenheim Memorial Foundation
and to Washington University for their support.

INTRODUCTION

Meeting Bad Men

Readers encountering the comic, eccentric, eclectic, exotic genius of Stanley Elkin for the first time could choose no better point of entry than *A Bad Man*. Others familiar with Elkin's work will find or rediscover in this, his second novel, confirmation of the belief that Elkin is among the most important fiction-makers of the second half of the twentieth century, even if the literary historians and critics haven't quite caught up with his authentic originality. For Elkin is a writer with a distinctive voice, a vision that challenges our preconceptions of what life and writing are supposed to be about, and a sense of humor that surpasses all the comic writers of his generation. Although Elkin often groused about scholars' categorizing him as a comic writer, he is funnier more often than any serious writer of his time—or most other times.

Between these covers readers will find all the signatures of Elkin's unique genius, including his characteristic rhetorical riffs that remind us of Cannonball Adderley on the tenor sax, but the book is somewhat less "difficult" to grasp than many of his subsequent novels, such as *The Dick Gibson Show, The Franchiser, The Magic Kingdom,* or Elkin's personal favorite, *George Mills*. Readers with traditional expectations about plot, setting, and character development should encounter little difficulty in following the journey of Leo Feldman, the ostensible "bad man" of the title, from his arrest through his adventures in a prison like none this side of *Alice in Wonderland* to the kangaroo court that ends his sentence.

At the same time, Elkin gently pushes the envelope of every familiar modernist and postmodernist convention in this novel. The plot employs an arbitrary chronological organization around the year of Feldman's incarceration, a time frame reminiscent of the one-day organizations of two great high-modernist novels, Virginia Woolf's *Mrs. Dalloway* and James Joyce's *Ulysses*. Because of this seemingly arbitrary chronological frame, Elkin subtly manifests the intense pressure time has for Feldman as an inmate, as opposed to the illusion of timelessness he sometimes had on the outside, when he was an opportunist and businessman. Similarly, Feldman's increasing sense of the pressure of time during his incarceration contrasts with his nemesis the warden's relative freedom from such pressures. Central to the warden's confidence is that he has all the time he'll need to accomplish whatever design he has in mind for Feldman, and one key element of the novel's plot is the unfolding of that design. Moreover, like Woolf and Joyce, Elkin employs frequent flashbacks to tell stories of Feldman's past, those experiences that shaped him to become the entrepreneur and convict he is. We do not, however, get comparable background information for Warden Fisher to explain how he evolved into a manic, obsessive, keeper of bad men. When the prison narrative requires historical background, readers learn about Leo's relationship with his crazed father Isidore, his strained relationships with his wife Lilly and son Billy, his experiences as an entrepreneur who built a department store out of a jobber's position, and some good luck during World War II. We also learn about his mistreatment of his unfortunately-named friends, Victman, Freedman, and Dedman.

Elkin later regretted that he gave in to the temptation to use allegorical names for these important supporting characters when names suggesting verisimilitude might have better served his narrative interests. The three associates never come alive as characters in their own right, but rather as extensions of Feldman's voracious ego, the central theme of the narrative. In effect themselves manifestations of the lengths to which Feldman will go to discover and explore his character, these men represent personality types: Victman the frustrated marketing genius, Freedman the professional corrupted by his willingness to bend rules to meet the needs of a friend and patient, Dedman the schmuck/loser who really needed nothing so much as a buddy. By contrast, Elkin never had any reason to regret the symbolic naming of his two central characters. Elkin's mother was born "Tootsie" Feldman, a name the young writer employed for the protagonists of several early stories, notably "In the

Alley." While he was writing *A Bad Man,* the appropriateness of this name, suggesting a "felled man," occurred to him. In fact, the novel's genesis traces to an anecdote Elkin's St. Louis friend, author and lawyer Al Lebwoitz, told him about a middle-class lawyer sentenced to a term in prison. Elkin became intrigued by the notion of the adjustment in worldview such a sentence would require of a white-collar criminal, then added the crucial detail that Feldman is technically innocent of the crime for which he's incarcerated—he is, as Elkin was fond of saying, "convicted of his character."

The name of Feldman's antagonist, Warden Fisher, deliberately echoes the "Fisher King" of grail myth and archetypal romance, the wounded authority figure who must be made whole by the quest hero in order for the land to recover its order and vitality. Twice the warden calls himself a "fisher of bad men," his zeal suggesting ironically the passivity of the Fisher King in romance, who awaits the healing touch of the quest hero, as well as the New Testament promise that Christ would make his disciples "fishers of men" (Matthew 4:19). This evangelical obligation transforms into fanaticism in the warden's desire to root out and segregate all the bad men in his prison. One of several paradoxes in the character of this, Elkin's first great antagonist, is that the warden is an evangelist for the ordinary, a man who passionately believes in the suppression of all passions. One of many grand rhetorical moments in *A Bad Man* occurs at Warden's Assembly, sort of a mandatory convocation for cons. The warden's obsession with bad men—not all prisoners, readers will find out, are bad men, and the warden gets to decide who is and who is not a bad man—launches him into a religious zeal reminiscent of a fundamentalist Christian revival:

> Men with pencils, scholars of this place, ministers of my administration—hear me. Explain to them. Speak what I tell you. The tongues of Pentecost are upon me, and I would teach you prison business. [. . .] I am calling for the infusion of the sacerdotal spirit! I need inquisitors' hearts! You must be—you must be *malleus maleficarum,* hammers of witches, punishers and pummelers in God's long cause. You must be warden's familiars. We shall share the power of the keys. Despoil, confiscate, make citizen's arrests. You know what needs to be done.

This rich infusion of allusions, phrases, and clauses from religious tradition, especially from the language of the Inquisition and the Salem Witch-Hunts of the late seventeenth century, suggests that we are hearing a man who, through his rhetoric, is paradoxically charismatic, in the manner of Joseph McCarthy, Adolf Hitler, Mao Tse-tung, and the countless demagogues who created so much misery throughout the twentieth century, and those thugs and word-slingers who continue to make life wretched for their people during the twenty-first. So very often, the protocol of demagoguery is the isolation of a group or type of persons for persecution and scapegoating. Clearly, the warden (the novel was written a decade after the House Un-American Activities Committee Hearings and the McCarthy witch-hunts of the 1950s) plans to demonize all the bad men to create an artificial community among the other prisoners and thereby assert psychological control over the majority of the prisoners and political control over the bad men.

The landscape of this novel is almost as strange and exotic as its inhabitants are. In some ways, the prison is an extension of the warden's personality, but its surreal landscape resembles the work of Salvadore Dal , Franz Kafka, Lewis Carroll, and Monty Python. Whereas actual prisons are usually rectangular, functional structures, this one resembles a labyrinth. Corridors seem to lead nowhere, but all passages ultimately lead to the center of the prison, the Warden's Quarters, which appear to be directly over the execution chamber. While writing the novel, Elkin toured the Walpole, Massachusetts, correctional facility as research toward the setting, but he quickly concluded that the imaginary prison is far more functional to his themes than any effort to describe an actual building might be. His invention would be a prison of the mind, perhaps resembling the troubling engravings of Giovanni Battista Piranesi, whose images from the 1740s anticipate modern surrealism in *Carceri d'Invenzione* (literally, "prison of the mind"). To achieve this Elkin created a structure lacking distinct shape or boundaries—in the first chapter, the deputy taking Feldman to the slammer makes ominous suggestions about the mass of the facility, implying that one can never know just when one is inside or outside—a prison that contains the body and ensnares the mind, that ultimately absorbs the soul. In such a prison, mad bad men cultivate mad obsessions. Ed Slipper absurdly seeks to become the oldest living convict and hungrily gathers news of the deaths of the few older inmates in America. This obsession the warden nurtures, for it symbolizes a broken soul.

Moreover, *A Bad Man* contains its own microsystem that reveals much about Elkin's challenge to his readers as well as the literary and cultural conventions central to the novel's larger themes. When the warden puts Feldman in charge of the prison canteen, the entrepreneur immediately reverses the prisoners' (his customers') expectations. Prisoners come to the canteen to buy postage for appeals and letters home, but Feldman presses on them exotic stamps that have no practical value. He removes the cigarettes, shaving cream, and other items prisoners would be likely to want, and stocks his shelves with unappetizing candies, shoetrees, and a guava-flavored soft drink that tastes like bubble gum. Obviously, Feldman is creating conditions that force the marketer to improvise and innovate. Anyone can sell customers what they want, but only a master salesman can sell someone a good or service (s)he doesn't want. And for Feldman, as owner of a department store or as operator of a prison canteen, selling is power; to make the sale is to assert dominion. In one of Elkin's many brilliant puns, Feldman announces that "I am master of all I purvey." Of course his real mastery is over the person to whom he purveys something, whether shoetree, bedspread, or abortion.

While he recalls transforming the basement of his department store from the cliché bargain-basement to a clearinghouse for the forbidden, the illegal, and the socially excluded, Feldman remembers discovering an excitement and power that intensified his life, that made it matter. Before that time, the merchant had been, despite his material success, bored, even depressed, playing cruel mind-games with his wife and son just to stay mildly interested in ordinary domestic life. In a related flashback, Feldman recalls visiting a country fair in Indiana, where as a callow youth he experienced all the attractions—hot dogs, rides, games of chance, exhibits, pornographic displays—concluding from each experience, "nothing special there." So it was with legitimate vending. How tough is it, after all, to sell something to a customer who has come into a store expecting to buy something? But as he discovers the possibilities in the basement of his store for prying into the secret lives of his customers, of finding the unspeakable need and figuring out how to meet it, Feldman feels animated as he has not for many years. He considers his creation of the basement the "great serendipity" of his career, a vocation not in vending but in energizing his life though the power of anticipating, meeting, and transforming a repressed desire: "It hadn't ever been profit that had driven him, but the idea of the sale itself, his way of bearing down upon the world." And he is never as wholly alive as the time a paranoid political cultist comes to the basement seeking ammunition and weapons to fight the conspiracy of "the Mistaken" (meaning mainstream

America?). For the seller, this is the master test—to meet a difficult need, unaware of the possible implications of the sale he's making. As Feldman thinks, hardly suppressing his glee, "This is it. *This* is."

This redirecting the customers' expectations in the basement and in the prison canteen is moreover a paradigm for the thematic and popular-culture centers at which *A Bad Man* operates. In one of the novel's more subtle allusions, Feldman mutters that he's unwilling to assume the hero's role the prisoners seem eager to impose on him: "What am I, a hero? Spartacus? They had him covered. They had him." *Spartacus* was Stanley Kubrick's brilliant 1960 saga of the slave rebellion in ancient Rome. Coincidentally, Elkin had himself performed a bit part in a film about Cleopatra while he lived in Rome writing *Boswell: A Modern Comedy*. But as Elkin knew, *Spartacus* employed the sword-and-sandal genre to critique the imperialist values implicitly endorsed by such films. Its hero, a slave sold as a gladiator, led a peasants' rebellion that came precariously close to toppling the new Roman Empire. This was the first of a substantial series of books and films in which, as in *A Bad Man*, the prison becomes a symbol for the power of any oppressive society and the forces that administer it.

This trope, prison as a symbol for the power of government or society to control or coerce the thoughts and feelings of its citizens, constitutes a cultural motif of the 1960s, one to which Elkin's novel offers an original and challenging variant. For all these films and books, from *Spartacus* through *Cool Hand Luke*, from Bernard Malamud's *The Fixer* (which Elkin reviewed) to Ken Kesey's *One Flew Over the Cuckoo's Nest*, soften the impact of the prison-as-symbol motif by representing the hero as evolving toward a meaningful role as champion of the oppressed, and in that role, achieving transcendent meaning through death. With heavy-handed symbolism, the hero of *Cool Hand Luke* morphs into a modern Christ-figure, suppressing his own interest in order to take on the system, and to defy, on behalf of his fellow prisoners, a cruel prison captain, unforgettably played by Strother Martin, who in his ordinariness, incipient cruelty, and zealous rooting out of men like Luke Jackson, very much resembles Elkin's Fisher. Similarly heavy-handed in its symbolism, *One Flew Over the Cuckoo's Nest* represents Randle Patrick McMurphy as a synthesis of Dionysus and Christ. He imports wine, sex, and song into the sterile asylum environment, but he leads twelve disciples to the sea and lies down on a cross-shaped table for shock treatments. Eventually, McMurphy reluctantly abandons his temporary role as self-serving conformist to take on the burden of defiance for men too weak to stand up for themselves, and attacks the Big Nurse (the warden's equivalent in cruelty, zeal, and determination to impose a monotonous order at the cost of individuality). The trope of prison as symbol usually invokes the compensating illusion that defiant prisoners are ennobled when they redirect their energies to serving the needs of their fellow inmates, and that their defeat is ultimately sacrificial.

In this important way, *A Bad Man* challenges the assumptions implicit in the genre out of which it grows. Although Feldman takes a brief stab at being a confessor to the other prisoners, at learning their secret crimes and lusts, he quickly becomes bored with that and cruelly attacks a moronic inmate who comes to him with his story. Feldman's response is deliberate and vicious—"*Stupid! . . . You thing!*"—and thus ends Feldman's effort at being the messianic prisoner. Like McMurphy and Cool Hand Luke, he tries, once he understands the full extent of the warden/nurse/captain's control over him, to become a model prisoner in order to placate the System by being docile—as Elkin calls it in *The Rabbi of Lud*, "lying doggo."

Whereas all the other 1960s prison heroes enact the decade's cultural myth of communal rebellion, completing themselves only by means of acting, even sacrificing, for a larger community, Feldman experiments with and rejects this role. Much as he resisted "The Conventional Wisdom" (the title of a wonderful Elkin novella) on the outside, refusing to heed the strategies of the marketing whiz Victman, or the advice of a developer who recommends suburban expansion and possible relocation (history has definitely proved the developer correct), Feldman and his creator challenge our convictions about what the prison literature trope means. We do not get the comforting illusion that manic imprisonment by ruthless authority apparently answering to no check or balance will eventually transform the renegade to the rebel, the criminal to the unwilling saint. This is among the most important pop culture and serious-literature myths of the 1960s. As Feldman resists the conventional wisdom, so does Elkin. His brush with what Hamlet called "the insolence of office" (Elkin quotes or paraphrases *Hamlet* several times in the novel, suggesting comic contrasts as well as the melancholy Dane's habit of introspection and solitary reflection) leads Feldman not to engagement in his fellow inmates' needs, but to a defiant search for the meaning of himself. He recognizes early in the process that this is a no-exit strategy, that the warden has absolute power and that Fisher will compel the other inmates to destroy Feldman. But he persists in demanding that he will collect every element of his existence, including his death. This demand for authenticity is prefigured in Feldman's eerie night in the electric chair, then completed in his kangaroo trial.

Thus Elkin gives readers a reversal of what the literary and cinematic conventions of the decade led consumers to expect. Instead of a defiant hero whose defeat is a communal victory, he gives us an anti-hero—who could consider Feldman a "hero" after reading about his mistreatments of Victman, Dedman, Lilly (his wife) and Billy (his mentally challenged son), and his secretary Silvia Lane? With Elkin's blessing, Al Lebowitz wrote the following jacket copy for the first edition: *"What if all the barbarians had not been destroyed? Suppose, just suppose, one survived, one made it, one flourished?"* By deploying the most outré metaphor of the novel, Feldman's homunculus, Elkin suggests that the compassionate, heroic character beneath the cruel exterior, the prevailing cultural myth of the decade, is a possibility that never materialized, a comforting cliché that never came into being. During his long dialogue with the homunculus (literally a "little man," or a "dwarf") while he's in solitary, the "scaled-down schema of waxing Feldman" tells its "greater frater" that "I would have done things differently. I would have taken better care." This "fossilized potential" is the man Feldman might have become, an ordinary man with ordinary values, perhaps a variation on the model of Oliver B's father, the successful developer to whose advice Feldman refuses to listen.

The several allusions to the movies, including the reference to *Spartacus* mentioned earlier, suggest one final unique dimension of this funny, uncompromising novel. It was often considered as a film script, but the film was never made. One Christmas season Philip Yourdain flew the entire Elkin family to Madrid to discuss making a film of the novel, and he took an option in 1968. He inquired about Broadway director Alan Schnieder's interest in making this as his first film and planned to produce it in 1969, but the project languished. There was some talk of actor Robert Shaw's taking the title role. And other options were taken in the next two decades. What a shame that no Hollywood producer has had the inspiration and cojones to follow through on such a project. If ever there was a novel waiting to be filmed, it's *A Bad Man*, a novel structured around a visual metaphor. The great scenes, such as Warden's Assembly, the visit to Billy's school, the "Diaspora in Indiana" created by Leo's mad father, Leo's morning walk through his legitimate store to get to the basement, the kangaroo court, and the night in the electric chair, challenge the director's creativity and ambition.

Even the greatest director, however, could not hope to capture the rhythms of Elkin's prose, the bravura of his rhetoric. Between these covers lie treasures of Elkin's incomparable prose and his unpredictable, uncompromising vision, the work of one of America's unacknowledged comic masters. Enjoy.

David C. Dougherty
2003

a bad man

1

One day a young man in an almost brimless fedora burst into the office where Feldman was dictating a letter to his secretary. He pointed a gun and said, "Reach, the jig is up, Feldman." They were working in front of Feldman's safe, where his department store's daily receipts were kept. The secretary, whose name was Miss Lane, immediately pressed a button on an underledge of Feldman's desk, and loud bells rang.

"That will bring the police before there's time to open the safe," she announced in the dinging din. But Feldman, who until this time had been sitting in his chair, elbows on the desk, his cheeks pushed into his palms in a position of concentration, slowly began to raise his arms.

"I'm afraid I shan't require your services for a while, Miss Lane," Feldman shouted.

"One false move," the young man said, "and I'll plug you."

"You've got me covered," Feldman admitted.

Miss Lane looked from one to the other. "What is this?" she demanded.

"It's the jig," Feldman explained. "It's up."

He was sentenced to a year in the penitentiary.

It was in the western part of the state, in the mountains, where he had never been who went East for vacations, to a shore, or who had been to Las Vegas for the shows, and twice to Europe for a month, and to the Caribbean on cruises with clothes from Sportswear.

It was not in a town, or near one, and there were no direct connections between Feldman's city and the prison, three hundred miles away.

After his sentencing, a deputy came to him in his cell. "Tomorrow we're going on a train ride," he said.

Feldman didn't sleep. Except for the few hours when he had been arrested, it was the first evening he had ever spent in a jail. He still wore the fresh blue businessman's suit the buyer had brought him from Men's Clothing. He wondered if he would be handcuffed. (He remembered a pair of specially wrought silver handcuffs he had once had made up for the sheriff.)

In the morning the deputy came. He was carrying a large suitcase. "Right-or left-handed?" he said.

"Pardon?"

"Left-handed or right-handed?"

"I'm right-handed."

The deputy studied him for a moment. "It's on your record. I could check."

"I'm right-handed. I am."

"Put out your right hand." He locked up his wrist.

"You've scratched my watch."

The deputy smiled. "Tell you what. I'll give you a fiver for that. They won't let you keep it. You can use the money in the canteen."

"I have money."

The deputy grinned. "They'll take it away," he said. "Afraid of bribes. You can keep up to five dollars. I'm giving you top dollar."

"Take the watch," Feldman said.

The deputy slipped the watch from his wrist and put it in a pocket of his suit coat.

"Where's my five dollars?"

"Listen to me," the deputy said. "You *are* green. They take everything away. They don't give any receipts. Afraid of forgery. There are guys up there could forge a fingerprint. The state'd be in hock to the cons up to its ears if they gave out receipts. With no claim you never get anything back. You should have left everything behind. They should tell you that. I don't know why they don't tell you that."

Feldman nodded. The other loop of the handcuff swung

against the coins in his pocket. The empty handcuff felt like some strangely weighted sleeve he had not yet buttoned.

"Even change," the deputy said. "Listen to me. It's too late for you to do anything about it now. Try to complain. You can't complain against a custom. You know? So listen to me, give me your wallet. You probably got cards, pictures. I'll keep the money and send the wallet to your people. Why should those guys up there get it? They're mostly single men up there. I've got a family. Listen to me."

"All right," Feldman said.

The deputy took the wallet Feldman handed him. He looked familiarly at the photographs and cards. "You want to know something funny? My wife has a charge account at your store." He ripped the cash out of the wallet. "She needs a new dress. You may get some of this back."

"The rich get richer," Feldman said.

"Here's a buck for the watch," the deputy said. He shoved the bill behind the handkerchief in Feldman's breast pocket. "We'll go in a minute," he said. He leaned down, picked up the suitcase he had brought with him into the cell, and heaved it up onto Feldman's cot. He opened the grip and took out a strange leather harness which he fitted over his jacket. "Buckle me up in the back," he told Feldman. "Okay, your right hand again." He took the empty handcuff and fitted it through a metal ring that hung from a short chain attached to the harness. "Latest crimes-topper. Both hands free," the deputy explained. "Close the suit-case," he commanded.

Feldman shut the suitcase clumsily with his left hand. He felt leashed.

"You carry that," the deputy said. "Wait a minute." He took a chain from his pocket and looped it quickly and intricately around Feldman's left wrist and through the handle of the suit-case. He locked the chain. "Okay," he said, "now we can go."

Feldman strained against the suitcase. "Nothing in there but my pajamas and a change of underwear. The suitcase is weighted, that's why it's so heavy," the deputy said.

In the train Feldman was told to take the aisle seat. The dep-uty would not unlock his left hand. He pressed a button on the armrest and pushed his seat back. "Long ride," he said. "Say," he said, looking at Feldman maneuvering the heavy suitcase stiffly with his locked left arm, his body twisted, "you don't have to be so uncomfortable. Why don't you shove your seat back? Here, I'll do it." He leaned across Feldman's stomach and found the button on the armrest. "Now lean back." Feldman pushed against the seat. "Hard," the deputy said. *"Hard."* Feldman shook his head. "Busted," the deputy said, and leaned back against his own seat.

"We could find other seats," Feldman said.

"No, don't bother," the deputy said. "The train doesn't go straight through. We have to change in a couple of hours. It doesn't pay." He smiled. "Say," he said, "look at that. There's somebody in a mighty hurry. Look at that guy come."

A man in a black suit was running along the station platform.

"Freedman," Feldman said.

"What's that? You know him?"

"It's Freedman," Feldman said.

"Come to tell you goodbye," the deputy said. "That's nice." He lifted the window. "In here, Freedman," the deputy called. He turned and smiled at Feldman.

In a moment the door at the end of the car was pulled open and Dr. Freedman came in. He rushed up to them. "Deputy," he said, "Feldman. May I?" He pulled roughly against the seat in front of Feldman and turned it around. He sat down in the empty seat, facing Feldman. "So you're going on a journey. I'd shake your hand, but—" He pointed at the handcuff.

"Mr. Feldman's on his way to penitentiary, Mr. Freedman," the deputy said.

"Ah, to penitentiary. Yes, I read about that. To penitentiary, is it? Crime does not pay, hey, Feldman? Well well well. What do you know?"

"Get away from me, Freedman," Feldman said.

"Tch tch tch. I have a ticket. Here it is. To . . . Enden. Yes. You go perhaps further. But that's where I leave you, where you leave me. But of course if the deputy objects I'll find some other seat at once. *Do* you object, Deputy?"

"No sir, Mr. Freedman, I sure don't. It's nice to have the company."

"Thank you. Personally, I too find that the company of honest men is welcome, but my friend Feldman here has things to think about, perhaps. I hope our chatter don't disturb him. He's not well, you know. I was his doctor, did you know that? Yes, indeed. *I know his condition!*"

"Is that so?" asked the deputy.

"Oh yes. He has a condition. A remarkable one."

"Freedman—"

"Medical science is still in its infancy. As a doctor I admit it. It hasn't even begun to understand the strange ways in which life works."

"Freedman—" Feldman said again.

"You know, Deputy, seeing him attached to you like that is very striking, very unsettling." He looked at Feldman. "You can imagine my surprise, Feldman, when I came into this car and I saw the bonds by which you are forged to the deputy here. Knowing your history—"

"What's that, Dr. Freedman?" the deputy asked.

"Well, it's very strange. Years ago, when we were on terms, I made an x-ray. There was a shadow—by his heart. A strange thing. At least four inches. Lying across his heart."

"*Freedman*—" Feldman said, straining forward.

"Now, now," the deputy said. "You behave yourself. You're in custody now. This isn't any department store. As far as you're concerned, this railroad train's already your prison. That makes you a con. Now unless you want to find out right here what we can do to cons who don't shape up, you better start acting like a con."

"A homunculus," Freedman said.

Feldman groaned and the deputy grabbed at the handcuff and jerked it sharply. "You be quiet," he said.

"I didn't know, of course, until I had had him x-rayed again. Oh, many times. I'm still not absolutely sure, but there, between the sternal ribs, and lying across his heart's superior vena cava and aorta—a homunculus, perfectly shaped. About four inches. A fetus. There, of course, from prenatal times. He was probably meant to be a twin, but something happened. Some early Feldmanic aggrandizement, and the fetus froze there. It couldn't have been four inches at birth. Something that large would have killed him. It must have been alive inside him—God knows how. But Feldman killed it off, didn't you, Feldman?"

"Why didn't you take it out?" the deputy asked.

"Well, I wanted to. He wouldn't let me. It's very dangerous even now. It's probably petrified by this time. If his heart should enlarge, if he should have an attack, or perhaps even a heavy blow in the chest, the homunculus could penetrate the heart and kill him."

The train moved out slowly and Feldman felt an exceptional urgency in his bowels.

"You ought to have that taken care of," the deputy said. "You don't let a thing like that go."

Suddenly Feldman leaned forward. "How do you know?" he asked Freedman. "How do you know?"

"You saw the x-rays. You saw them," Freedman said. "What do you think, I painted them myself?"

"It's too strange," Feldman said. "A fetus is curled. This is straight."

"Why balk at that? Everything's strange," Freedman said. "You know, Deputy, the fact is, I thought at first it was an extra rib—something. But I'm certain now it's what I said. There was a case in New York State—That's why I was so surprised to see Feldman here attached to you like this."

"Can you see the head and arms?"

"Indistinctly, Deputy, indistinctly," Freedman said.

"It's too much for me," the deputy said. "Excuse me a minute, Doctor. Come along, Feldman."

They went forward to the toilet, Feldman pulling the weighted suitcase behind him terribly. Once inside, he tried to lift it up onto the washstand. It must weigh a hundred pounds, he thought. The deputy watched him tugging at the case and smiled. Feldman felt something wrench in his arm, but at last he was able to swing the heavy case up onto the sink. It teetered dangerously and he moved against it to keep it from falling.

"Now, now," the deputy said, "is that a way? You think the railroad wants you scratching its sinks? Anyway, how do you expect me to sit down and take my crap with you all the way over there?"

"Unlock me," Feldman said.

"Well, I can't do that," the deputy said. "The custody code in this state says that any prisoner being transported to the penitentiary must be bound to his custodian at all times. Now you've rested enough. You get that suitcase down from there and you come over here." With both hands he pulled on his harness, and Feldman stumbled and fell to his knees. The grip fell from the washstand against Feldman's leg.

The deputy undid his trousers and let them fall to the floor. He pushed his drawers down. He sat on the toilet seat, and Feldman was pulled toward him at the level of the man's stomach.

"What are you looking away for? Don't you ever move yours? Don't you look away from me like that. You think you're better than I am? *Don't you look away, I said!*"

Feldman turned his head to the deputy. He started to gag.

"Maybe you're uncomfortable," the deputy said. "Maybe you'd be more comfortable if you could rest your head in my lap. You uncomfortable?"

"No." Feldman said. "I'm comfortable."

"Well, if you're uncomfortable you just put your head down. And you better not be sick on me. You understand?" Feldman swayed dizzily against the deputy. "Hey," the deputy said, "I think you like this. I think you think it ain't so bad. A man gets used to everything. That'll stand you in good stead where you're going. That'll be a point in your favor up there." Feldman pulled away again.

"Well, I'm done, I guess," the deputy said in a few moments. "How about you? Do you have to go?"

"No."

"Don't be embarrassed now."

"No," Feldman said, "I don't have to."

At Enden they had to change trains.

"So this is Enden," Freedman said. "It isn't much, but I'm glad I saw it. I've still got some time before I make my connection back to the city. I'll walk along with you."

"Dr. Freedman, it was nice to have your company," the deputy said. "Say goodbye to him, Feldman. You won't be seeing your friend for some time."

"Maybe I'll come out to visit," Freedman said.

Freedman and the deputy shook hands.

"Oh, and listen," Freedman said to the deputy, "don't forget what I told you. A homunculus. Petrified. Over the heart. A heavy blow in the chest. Tell them. *Tell the convicts.*" He crossed the tracks and walked beside them toward their train. Three cars ahead a porter stood waiting for them. Near the vestibule where they were to board the train, Freedman moved suddenly in front of Feldman and the deputy. He went up on the little metal step and from there to the lower stair of the train and looked up into the vestibule.

"Ah," he said, "Victman." He held onto the railing and leaned backwards as Feldman and the deputy came up. "Look, Feldman," he called, "it's Victman."

They had to change trains once more. In the foothills of the great dark mountain range which climbed like tiered chaos to the gray penitentiary. There Victman left them, and Dedman took his place.

In the night Feldman whispered to the deputy. "I have to go," he said.

"Sure, Feldman, in a minute, when this game is finished." Dedman and the deputy were playing cards.

"Please," Feldman said, "now. I have to go."

"You know the rules. I can't unlock you. I asked before if you had to go. Have a little patience, please."

The deputy won the game and sat back comfortably. "Some revenge, Dedman?" he said. "I believe a man is entitled to revenge." He dealt the cards, and they played for another hour.

Feldman urinated in his suit. The deputy and Dedman watched the darkening, spreading stain.

"That's more like it," the deputy said.

2

There was an old Packard touring car waiting for them at the station.

The deputy had fallen asleep; Feldman had to wake him. Dedman had disappeared. Before they left the train the deputy unlocked Feldman's handcuff and the chain that wrapped his wrist. He moved him down the steps and into the back seat of the car. It was very dark.

"You're where they shoot to kill now, Feldman," the deputy said.

The driver laughed sourly and the deputy closed Feldman's door and walked around the car and got into the front seat next to him.

When they had ridden for almost an hour—Feldman could see the tan twist of dirt road as the car's head lamps swept the sudden inclines and turns of the arbitrary mountain—he asked how far it was to the penitentiary.

"Hell," the deputy said, "you've been in it since the train went through that tunnel just after dark. It's *all* penitentiary. It's a whole country of penitentiary we got up here."

"It's four miles from where we are now to the second wall," the driver said.

In twenty minutes Feldman saw a ring of lights, towers, walls.

"That's her," the deputy said.

9

The car stopped. Feldman guessed they had come to a gate, though he could see no passage through the solid wall.

"Out," the deputy said. "Nothing wider than a man gets through that wall. There's no back-of-the-laundry-truck escapes around here."

The driver opened a metal door, and they walked single file, Feldman in the middle, through a sort of narrow ceilingless passageway that curved and angled every few feet. Along the wide tops of the walls strolled men with rifles. Feldman looked up at them. "Head down, you," a guard called. Every hundred feet or so was another metal door, which opened as they came to it.

"Maximum security," the deputy said.

"Maximum insecurity," said the driver.

They came to a final door, which opened onto a big yard lighted with stands of arc lamps, bright as an infield. Across from him, about two hundred yards away, in an area not affected by the lights, he could see the outlines of buildings like the silhouette of city skylines in old comic strips. They took him to one of these buildings—all stone; he could see no joints; it was as though the building had been sculpted out of solid rock—and the deputy prodded him up the stairs.

"You'll have your interview with the warden here," the deputy said.

Feldman looked at his wrist for marks that might have been left by the chain. He was certain the deputy had abused him, that the business of the suitcase had been his own invention. There was something in the Constitution about cruel and unusual punishment. There was a slight redness about his left wrist but no swelling. He was a little disappointed. If he got the chance—he would study the warden carefully; didn't they have to be college graduates?—he would report the deputy anyway.

They took him to an office on the second floor.

Feldman was surprised. For all the apparent solidity of the outside of the building, the inside seemed extremely vulnerable. There was a lot of wood. He could smell furniture polish. The old, oiled stairs creaked as they climbed them. It was like the inside of an old public school. There were even drinking fountains in the hall.

"You wait here," the deputy said. He opened a door—it could have been to the principal's office; Feldman looked for the American flag—and pushed him inside.

"The warden doesn't want anyone around when he talks to

a con," the deputy said. "I'm sacking out. The driver's your guard now. He'll be right outside." He closed the door and left the room. Feldman waited a few minutes and opened the door. A few things the driver had said made him think he might be approachable.

The driver was sitting in a chair, a machine gun in his lap. "I'm no friend of yours," he said. "Get back in there."

Feldman sat down to wait. I'm probably on television, he thought. They're watching me this minute. Strangely, he felt more comfortable. If everything was just a strategy he could deal with them. Just don't let them touch me, he thought. He fell asleep. Let them watch me sleep, he dreamed.

When he woke up he expected to see the warden standing over him. It was not impossible, he felt, that the warden could even turn out to be the deputy. But when he opened his eyes no one was there, and he knew that there were no one-way mirrors, no hidden microphones, and was more frightened than at any time since he had been arrested. I'm in trouble, he thought, I'm really in trouble.

He began to pray.

"Troublemaker," he prayed, "keep me alive. Things are done that mustn't be done to me. Have a heart. If the question is can I take it, the answer is no. Regularity is what I know best. I have contributed to the world's gloom, I acknowledge that. But I have always picked on victims. Victims are used to it. Irregularity is what *they* know best. They don't even feel it. I feel it. It gives me the creeps."

He finished his prayer, and still seated, looked around the office. It was past midnight. He might have hours to wait yet. "You wait here," the deputy had said. Was it a stratagem? They file you paper-thin with expectation and anxiety. I expect nothing. I'll take what comes. He folded his arms across his chest, trying to look detached. It would be best, he thought, if he could sleep again. A sleeping man had a terrific advantage in a contest of this sort. It would invariably rattle whoever came to shake him awake. "You see what I think of you?" a sleeping man said to the shaker.

But he wasn't sleepy. He was too cold. It's the altitude, Feldman thought. At night you need a coat up here even in summer. He looked down at his suit and stroked his sleeve. It was lucky he believed in appearances. ("A *heavy* material," he had told the buyer. "In this heat?" "What should I wear in that courtroom, a luau shirt?") A man of conservative, executive substance, silver-templed, and tan for a Jew. Never split a Republican ticket in my life, gentlemen.

The door opened and Feldman looked up. A man stood in the doorway for a moment and then moved behind the desk and sat down. He had some papers with him which he examined as if they contained information with which he was already familiar, using them easily but with a certain disappointment.

Feldman watched the warden, if this *was* the warden. (Already he had begun to do what all strangers in new situations do—attribute to others exalted rank, seeing in each comfortable face an executive, a person of importance.) He was a man of about Feldman's age, perhaps a little younger. Feldman guessed they were the same height, though the warden was not as heavy. What struck him most was the man's face. It seemed conventional, not unintelligent so much as not intelligent. It was, even at midnight, smooth—not recently shaved, just smooth—as though lacking the vitality to grow hair. Its ruddiness could probably be accounted for by the heavy sun striking at this altitude through the thin atmosphere. He might have been one of the salesmen who called at his store. Feldman had hoped, he realized now, for someone mysterious, a little magical. He saw, looking at the warden's face, that it would be a long year.

"Is it all right with you if I open a window? It's a little stuffy in here," the man said.

"I'm cold," Feldman said.

"I'm sorry," the warden said, getting up. "I have to open the window." He opened it and came around the front of the desk to where Feldman was sitting.

"Mr. Feldman," he said, "I'm Warden Fisher, a fisher of bad men."

Feldman stood up to shake hands. The warden turned away and went back to stand by the open window.

"Be seated, please," the warden said. "In this first interview I like to get the man's justification."

"Sir?"

"Why are you here?"

"They say I'm guilty."

"Are you?"

Feldman answered carefully. There was some question of an appeal, of getting his case reopened. Probably there was a tape recorder going someplace. The warden was trying to disarm him. "No, of course not," he said, undisarmed.

The warden smiled. "I've never had an affirmative answer to that question." Feldman, disarmed, at one with all the robbers, bums, murderers and liars in the place, felt he needed an initiative.

"You may want me to put this in writing later," he said, "but I feel I have certain legitimate complaints about the way I was treated coming up here."

The warden frowned, but Feldman went on. He explained about his watch and the money. Telling it, he knew he sounded like a fool. He didn't mind. It added, he felt, to an impression of innocence. "I have reason to suspect, too, that the deputy took money from certain enemies of mine in exchange for showing me off to them in my humiliation."

The warden nodded. "Go on," he said.

Feldman felt the warden was bored by the story, but he couldn't stop. When he came to the part about the toilet he tried to get outrage into his voice. Somehow it sounded spurious. He finished lamely with an allusion to the final proddings and shoves.

"Is there anything else?" the warden asked.

"No sir," Feldman said.

"Do you have any proof? Would Dedman or Freedman or Victman testify to any of this?"

Feldman admitted they probably wouldn't. "I'm not lying though," he added helplessly.

The warden opened a second window. "The deputy's a pig," he said suddenly. "He ought to be in prison. Without proof, however—"

Feldman shrugged sympathetically.

"He ought to be in prison too, I mean," the warden said, turning to Feldman.

"I'm innocent," Feldman said mechanically.

"All right," the warden said, "that's enough."

It was. He regretted having spoken. He didn't know what it was tonight. Every action he had taken had been ultimately cooperative. It was a consequence of being on the defensive. Feldman knew how easy it was to accuse. That was the trick the warden had been playing on him. He had to assert himself before it was too late. If he had the nerve it would be a good idea to push the warden, to run behind his desk and sit in his chair. Then he seized on the idea of silence. To speak, even to speak in accusation was, in a way, to fawn. Let the warden make the mistakes, he thought. Mum's the word. He folded his arms.

"It's easy for me to believe you've been wronged," the warden was saying. A trap. Shut up. Forewarned is forearmed. "There are enough bad men in the world. We all have our turn as their victims."

Not me, Feldman thought.

"What I want to know," the warden said, "is what you've done."

Feldman said nothing.

"Answer me," the warden said.

"I've done nothing."

"All right," the warden shouted, "I said that's enough. Since you've been here you've spoken only of your own injuries. Granted! What else?"

It was no contest. He wasn't free to remain silent. The thing to do was to yield, to throw himself not on the warden's mercy but on his will. He wants words, Feldman thought, I'll give him words. He wants guilt? Let there be guilt.

"It says in that paper on your desk what I did," Feldman said hoarsely. "It says I did favors."

"What else?"

"That I was a middleman, a caterer. That they came to me. That I didn't even have to advertise. Ethical. Like a doctor."

"This is nothing," the warden said. "You're wasting time."

"All right. I filled needs. Like a pharmacist doing prescriptions. Did you ever know anyone like me? The hell. A woman needed an abortion, I found a doctor. A couple needed a kid, I found a bastard. A punk a fix, I found a pusher. I was in research."

The warden shuddered.

"Wait," Feldman said, "you haven't heard anything. In my basement. In my store. In a special room. Under the counter. I've found whores, and I've found pimps for whores. You don't see it on the shelf? Ask. You have peculiar tastes? Feldman has a friend. What I said about the doctor and the pharmacist—that's wrong. I was like a fence. I was a moral fence. That's what it *says* I did." He stopped talking. "One more thing," he said in a moment, looking around, "this isn't a confession." He raised his voice. "Warden Fisher wanted me to talk, so I'm talking. I'm just repeating in my own words what's written in his paper. None of it is true."

The warden stared at him.

"That last takes care of your tape recorders," Feldman told

him. "And if you're thinking of clipping it just before I added that, let me point out that I wasn't speaking in my natural voice."

The warden shook his head.

"I never took a penny," Feldman whispered.

"I can't hear you," the warden said.

I nev-er took a pen-ny, he mouthed. "I did favors. I helped people. The whole case against me turns on whether I accepted money. I never did. And if you want to know my justification, it was for fun I did it," he told him softly.

He spoke again in his normal voice. "According to your records, Warden, I accepted money from a Mrs. Jerome Herbert for arranging an interview with a judge who was to hear a case against her husband. Mrs. Herbert had a charge account at my store. We had just installed a new billing system. She received an unitemized bill for five hundred dollars, which she paid with a personal check made out to me. God knows what she bought from me for five hundred dollars, but it wasn't an interview with any judge. God knows, too, why she would pay an unitemized bill or why she would make the check out to me, but that's what happened. That's why I'm here now. It was the machine's mistake."

"I smell you," the warden said quietly.

"What?" Feldman asked. "What's that?"

"I smell you."

The pee, Feldman thought, embarrassed. He looked down at his pants and touched one palm of his trouser leg. It was still damp. The altitude—pee didn't dry. That deputy bastard.

"I told you," Feldman said, "you want evidence? There's evidence. Send my piss to your crime lab."

The warden moved suddenly and grabbed Feldman's trousers, bunching the damp material in his fist, squeezing it. "That," he said, "that's nothing. I smell *you*."

"What do you mean?" Feldman said, genuinely angry. "What kind of thing is that to say? What kind of way is that for a warden to talk? The deputy was ignorant, but you're supposed to know better. I won't be insulted by you, by someone in authority. I'm warning you. I have plenty of friends in this state."

"You still think this is a game, don't you?" the warden said. "You still think some philosophical cat and mouse is going on here. You bad clown, you wicked fool with your nonsensical impersonations and your miming and your boastful confessions. You bad, silly man, this is no game. Can you understand? You're here for a year in this state's licensed penitentiary, and it's no game.

There are no tape recorders. When I want you to confess I'll have you beaten up and you'll confess. Do you understand?"

"Yes sir," Feldman said quietly.

" 'Yes sir,' " the warden mocked. "You don't understand yet, do you, actor? You still want me to say what's always said. All right. 'You play ball with us, we'll play ball with you.' All right. But don't let that be any comfort to you. There aren't any prizes for playing ball with us. I don't care about your mind, and I promise no one will lay a finger on your soul. It's your ass that belongs to us, Feldman. You want it back, stay out of trouble. Do the routines. Learn to think about your laundry. Keep your cell clean. Don't put more on your tray than you can eat. Look forward to the movies. Make no noise after ten o'clock. Learn a trade. Try out for the teams. Pray for the condemned."

Feldman's heart turned. He felt the homunculus riding it twist.

"Stand up," the warden commanded.

He stood slowly, forcing himself to look at the warden.

"There are some good men here," the warden said. "I don't want them corrupted by you."

He watched the warden glumly.

"I don't expect to see you again. Do you understand me? If we have business it's to be conducted through a procedurally constituted chain of command, and the probability is I'll initiate it. No more midnight meetings with the warden, actor." He started to cough. "Get out," he said. "Your stench gags me."

3

Feldman's cell was ten feet wide and a dozen deep, about the size of the room in his father's house when he was a boy. This struck him at once, and since he noticed that the cells varied in dimension, and even in their basic shapes, he wondered if perhaps this information had not also been in his records, and if putting him there had not been meant as some subtle lesson.

When he knew him better he asked his cellmate, a man named Bisch, what his room had been like as a child.

"Like a kitchen," Bisch said. "I slept by the stove." The man was tall—Feldman thought of him at first as a mountaineer—with grayish bushy hair that tufted up from his temples. Everything he did he did slowly, moving deliberately to tasks with the loose moodiness of an athlete stepping up to a mark. He had great pulling-and-tearing power in his long dark hands. Feldman was afraid of him. A strangler, he thought, a chopper, a choker.

Bisch had not even looked up, though he was awake, when Feldman was brought in, or when, moments later, Feldman urinated, splashing loudly, in the lidless toilet. They were awake together for hours that night, and though Feldman coughed and shivered, catching cold, the man said nothing.

Maybe there's a ritual, Feldman thought. Maybe a new prisoner is supposed to introduce himself and announce his crime.

17

"Feldman's the name, favors the game," he said to himself experimentally. "Feldman, not guilty. Machine error."

It was, at first, like being in a hospital. What they all had in common was not their crime or their back luck or their contempt. Being locked up was their mutual disease, but because he was the most recent arrival he thought of himself as the sickest, the one with the greatest distance to travel to recovery, the most to lose. It did not matter that many of these men would never, as he would in a year, see the outside again. They were used to it. To judge by appearances, they were habitual criminals or men for whom being inside a prison was somehow a relief. Later he would look for the one called Pop, the one whom age made spotless, harmless, a saint by weary default of health and ego. Who volunteered to remain there always, who would be dangerous only if let loose, and then just long enough to get back, who would plan his last crime against society with the precision of a scientist and the knowledge of a Blackstone or a Coke, who knew even as he picked the lock or jimmied the window just how long he'd get, where to go till they caught him—only enjoying that much freedom, the two weeks like a sailor's shore leave it would take to catch him. Nervous even in the local jail, wondering as he awaited trial if he had done enough to discount their mercy, their solicitude for his white hairs, his years, and calm only when pronounced guilty, and serene only back in the penitentiary. There was no such man.

He did not really wonder very much about the other men, however. He gave them his thoughts when he was with them in the dining hall or as he watched them from his cell, exercising in the prison yard—because of his cold they allowed him to remain inside, though he saw no doctor—but most of the time he could think of no one but himself, again like a man coming into a hospital.

As he began to feel better—now he was counterfeiting his cough—he worried about what to do with his time. During the daily hour of free time, he left his cell to see the library, as he had gone, too, to the swimming pool and gymnasium and crafts hall, as he had gone to *all* the facilities, hearing of them and finding them greedily, as on ocean liners he had taken his preliminary inspections of the ship, going into each of its salons and bays, only to decide, finally, on lunch in his cabin, or to sit for long hours in a deck chair.

He recalled his initial tours of their grounds when his son was a small boy and they had first moved to their house in the private suburb. In the back, set a good distance from the house and closed in by a low wall, was a large patio. One night Lilly had made supper out there—big steaks like great meaty South Americas, long fat cobs of corn, potatoes like brown, warm rocks, pale yellow butter, sour cream, rye bread, deep wet lakes of cream soda. Afterwards she went back into the house to do the dishes.

Feldman laid down along the wide top of one of the patio walls and stared up at the just dark sky. One bright star blazed directly above him.

"Come here, Billy," he said to his son. The boy came and Feldman touched his cheek. "Bring Daddy a pillow from the house," he said. When his son came back with the pillow, Feldman pulled him up on his stomach. "I'll be *your* pillow." He pulled him gently along his body. "Be careful," he said, "don't hurt me with your head." Billy snuggled against Feldman. "Let's look up at the night sky," Feldman said. "I'll give you all the stars you can count."

The boy counted four pale stars and the bright one Feldman had seen when he first lay down.

"No you don't," Feldman said, "that bright one is mine."

"You said I could have all of them," Billy said.

"Not the bright one."

"What makes that star so bright?"

"It's closer." He thought about light years.

"Is that one Mars?"

"Mars is a planet," Feldman said. "It's red."

"I can't see it."

"It's not out yet." Feldman had never seen Mars.

"What's a planet? Is a planet a star?"

"There are nine planets," Feldman said. "Earth is a planet. And Mars. There's Jupiter, and Saturn. Saturn has rings." I've never been able to see the damn things, Feldman thought irritably. "Uranus is another planet." He couldn't think of the names of the other four. Maybe there were just two more. He couldn't remember. He was pretty sure there weren't just five. So much for the night sky.

"I tell you what," Feldman said, "I'll trade you your four stars for my bright one."

"All right," his son said.

"Done," Feldman said. By this time more stars had appeared.

Feldman counted off eleven. "Those eleven stars are mine," he said. "Daddy has fifteen, Billy has one."

"That's not fair."

"Look alive then."

"I'm mixed up," his son said.

Feldman had hoped that as the sky grew darker one of his stars would outshine his son's, but it hadn't happened. He saw that he had to get the bright star back from the kid. "Billy," he said, "I'll give you that new star for your star." There wasn't any new star, but Feldman pointed vaguely into the heavens.

"No," Billy said.

"Billy, I think that new star is a planet."

"How do you know?"

"It looks like a planet."

Billy looked into the sky.

"All right," he said.

"It's an even trade," Feldman said. "I get the bright star."

"All right," Billy said. After that, Feldman grew tired of the game and made his son get up.

"Billy has no sense of values," he told his wife later. "He doesn't have any idea how to do business. I killed him. You can tell him anything."

It bothered him, however, that he didn't know anything about the stars except how to trade them. The next week he brought home a high-powered telescope from Cameras, but he never learned how to focus it properly.

He saw at once on his tour of the prison that he would never use the gymnasium or the pool or go back to the crafts hall. But Jesus, he thought, remembering the warmth of his son's body, what's a man like me doing in prison?

In the mornings a bell rang at 6:30, and the men had twenty minutes to dress and shave and clean their cells.

His cellmate had told him the first morning that Feldman would have to clean the toilet and that he would do the sink himself.

"Why don't we draw straws?" Feldman asked cheerfully.

"I already drew straws," the man said. "You do the crapper."

It's my new concern with shit, Feldman thought darkly. Some gesture must have revealed his repugnance, for a man directly across from him stood at the front of his cell, watching as Feldman, still in his blue suit, scrubbed the inside of the bowl, flushing it constantly as he worked. The man said nothing, but Feldman could hear him come forward each morning he kneeled into position above the toilet.

One day Feldman watched as the man cleaned *his* toilet. That ended it—their caged inefficacy must have seemed as ridiculous to the man as it did to him, as if contempt without the possibility of blows and wounds was too wasteful, too extravagant. Perhaps it was for this reason that though arguments between men in the same cell were frequent and violent, conversations between cells were for the most part gentle. If their impotence taught them tolerance, it taught Feldman that the emotions were the first to go. There was comfort in this. Was that good?

Was it even true? He was still suffering from the warden's avowal that he was a bad man, his proclaimed nostril knowledge of his soul. (And Feldman was a man used to hatred. There had been competitors, people who worked for him, even some people who had loved him who yielded to hatred at the last. Too many men had bad hearts, ulcers; nail biters and strainers to piss, they wasted their substance, dissipating in envy and worry and grudge everything they had. The Ten Commandments were good hygiene, the Sermon on the Mount an apple a day. Victman was his enemy, Dedman was, Freedman, but was he theirs? He was as indifferent to their loathing as he was to the mechanical blessings of beggars he gave quarters to in the streets.) The warden's hatred was different. It was the hatred of someone who didn't have to hate him, hatred that flowed from strength rather than weakness, choice rather than injury, and it was disturbing to him, and confusing.

What was there bad enough to hate? There was nothing. Being uncomfortable maybe. He thought of winded boys in shorts he had seen in the park, racing against themselves, their faces inhuman, distorted, their lungs bursting; of hedge-clippers, mowers of lawns, weekend washers of cars, of husbands and fathers around their own dinner tables on hot summer evenings with their jackets on—of all the volunteers for pain, chippers-in for suffering, *tzouris*-chasers there were in the world, of all the men and women who out of propriety refused second helpings, other people's last cigarettes, candy, tips, favors, of every abstainer and ascetic and celibate who celebrated some baseless principle of thinness and hunger and lack. You can have it, Feldman thought, you can have not having.

Yet the certainty of the warden's contempt was alarming. Forget it, he told himself, the man's a jerk, a man on a mountain with an upper hand. But he could not see him—in the first week he saw him twice more—without offering up some travesty of surrender, without waving some not understood white flag in his face.

One afternoon the warden stopped by Feldman's cell. "Why isn't this man out with the others?" he asked the guard.

"He says he's sick, sir."

"How are you, Warden?" Feldman asked compulsively.

The warden, of course, turned and walked on without answering.

Then, during Warden's Rounds, he came into their cellblock again. Feldman, excited, went to the bars to watch him. He noticed that the warden would stop before certain cells but not before others, and he understood at once that the cells he bypassed contained other bad men.

The warden came up to his cell. "How are you getting on?" he asked.

"About the same, sir," Feldman said hurriedly. "Thank you."

"I was talking to Bisch," the warden said, and backed off as if struck.

It's an act, Feldman thought angrily, it's an act.

But he was not at all sure that it was.

It had been more than a week, and they hadn't bothered him. For three days his cold, which had never been bad, was better. One day he stopped his shammed cough. Momentarily he expected word from the officials, a command to appear at one of the prison shops. Perhaps they were waiting until he had his prison clothes. (He still wore his blue suit.) It was possible that they had run out of uniforms—loose, grayish sweat suits—for in the dining room and from his window overlooking the exercise yard he would occasionally spot others who still wore their street clothes too.

So far he had had little contact with the other prisoners. His cellmate continued to ignore him (though from time to time, Feldman caught him eyeing him from his cot), and in the dining hall it was forbidden to speak. It was strange to sit there while food traveled noiselessly about the table: baskets of bread, bowls of scrawny fruit, platters of grayish vegetables and plates of thin, disreputable meat—apparently floating in sourceless, graceless flux, from one prisoner to the other. Initially Feldman was grateful for the enforced silence—he had feared harassment—but after a few days he began to regret it. He himself had been a bully at dinner tables, pushing and pulling conversation out of his guests like an old bored king. In restaurants he picked up checks to pay for the privilege.

Now his fear was that no command would come, and he realized that his overtures to the warden had been probably meant to provoke one. It was surprising to think of, but he had never expected, after his arrest, to be let off. In a way he had actually been anticipating jail. He had missed the army, had never lived in a dormitory. His knowledge of large groups of men had been limited to the locker rooms of country clubs, but even there, in the carpeted corridors and shower rooms, with the tall, colorful bottles of hair oils stacked on the marble washstands like thick liqueurs behind a bar, he had sensed undertones of violence and truth. He did not want camaraderie; he wanted men: to be thrust among them, to see what would happen to him among them, to see what they would be like unencumbered by wives and kids and jobs they cared about—to see, finally, if they would be like himself.

And still he waited—for prison clothes, for Bisch to talk to him, for a command. He spent most of his time lying on his cot alone in his cell—Bisch did not return until evening—and he could not have told himself that night what he had been thinking of that day. He thought, he supposed, of what men think of in the waiting rooms of train stations, or standing in lines, or driving on turnpikes.

He was a man in jail for a crime that technically he had not committed. And that made him a victim. Yet he did not feel like a victim, nor even particularly wronged. He did not find himself, as he supposed many here did, waiting expectantly for communiqués from his lawyers. He did not even particularly believe in his appeal, nor in second chances generally. Though he was a man who usually made first moves, there was a vast inertia in him which made it difficult for him to believe in changes, revolutions, upsettings, rectifications, undoings.

"Nothing doing," he said aloud. It was as hard to get started on himself as it was to learn about the stars. (He wondered what was written about him in those records they kept.) In this prison,

in this small cell no bigger than the rooms where he had slept out
his childhood, guilt came as hard as righteousness.

When Feldman was not on his cot or in the dining hall, he
was at his window watching the exercise yard. There, in the early
afternoon, the men came randomly from the different buildings
about the enormous yard to walk beneath the guns of the guards.
Most moved about talking quietly in small groups, seemingly conspiratorial clusters. But others—even two floors above, Feldman
sensed their ruthless energy—might almost have been men
splashing naked in lakes. It excited him to watch them. Frequently
one would bolt forward in a sudden passionate run. It was pa-
thetic to see him turned by a wall or have to pull abruptly up as
he came near the others. Another might stop where he was to
jump violently in place for a few moments. One man was constantly winding up in frantic arcs, but nothing came out of his
hand when he threw. And certain others would sink abruptly to
their knees as though hit by bullets and then roll about on the
ground.

The first time this happened Feldman looked instinctively to
the guards who, though they had seen all that Feldman had, continued their careless, placid patrols along the walls. They did not
seem to regard as important the sudden screams that tore from
the throats of a few of the men like great flags of pain. Only later
did Feldman realize that the guards never watched the groups at
all, but concentrated instead on the seven or eight he had noticed.

They were, like himself, men in street clothes.

"We're in business," Feldman said softly. "Now. Now it
comes."

4

It did.

Two days later when Feldman returned from his noon meal there was a brown paper parcel on his cot. He unwrapped it quickly. Inside was a blue suit like the one he wore but of a vastly cheaper quality. He understood that these were to be his prison clothes. The thick rich wool of the original had been vulgarized into a thin cotton blend, but the color and cut and shape were enough like his own that except for the feel Feldman suspected that even he couldn't tell them apart.

"The crooks," he said, "they forged a suit."

He tried it on. There was no mirror, but he knew something was wrong. He felt oddly unbalanced, almost as if he had just put on new eyeglasses. When he walked across the cell he was aware from how it felt—coming suddenly up against a trouser leg with his thigh, or feeling a shoulder slip slightly from under a plank of cloth, experiencing as he moved in it an almost orchestrated series of tugs, clingings, pulls and slacknesses—that it was not so much a copy of his suit as a clever parody of it.

He handled the pearl-gray buttons on the jacket. They were just too small for the buttonholes, which were just too large. On the sleeves, buttons big as watch crystals were sewn in a crooked line. He shoved one hand into a trouser pocket, blunting his fin-

25

gers against its incredibly shallow bottom. On the other side the pocket was as deep as a third pants leg.

He found one of Bisch's pencils and wrote a note to the warden:

I may be a bad man, but I am not a clown.

This he gave to a guard, requesting that it be shown to the warden.

Within an hour he had a reply:

Don't be ridiculous. Every bad man is a clown. All evil is a joke. And vice versa. Don't send me notes; we are not pen pals.

The guard came into the cell and confiscated Bisch's pencils.

"They're not mine," Feldman said worriedly. "They're Bisch's. He'll kill me."

The guard shrugged and took the pencils.

That very night Bisch wanted to write a letter. "Where's my pencil?" he asked darkly.

"The guard took your pencils," Feldman said. It was the first conversation they had had since Feldman suggested that they draw straws.

"The guard's got his own pencil," Bisch said, grabbing Feldman's suit. "He gets them from Supply."

It was very quiet. The men in the other cells had stopped talking. Feldman could sense them straining to listen. He thought of himself at the window.

"Where's my pencil?" Bisch roared.

"Look," Feldman said. "I've got a big department store. How would you like new pencils? A whole bunch of them." Bisch loosened his hold on Feldman's collar. He seemed interested. "And maybe a nice pencil box with special drawers?" Feldman said quickly, following up his advantage.

"Crayons?"

"Sure, crayons. Absolutely. Crayons."

"Scissors?"

"You bet, scissors. Scissors it is."

"Shit," Bisch said, "they'd never let me have scissors in here." He grabbed the suit again.

"No, no," Feldman said, "these are blunt scissors. For a child."

"What do you mean for a child?"

"No, not for a child. I don't mean for a child. But a child could use them. *Safety* scissors! Look, for God's sake, don't touch me. I didn't take your pencil. I used it for a minute to write a note. We're cellmates. Guys in the same cell use each other's pencils. I wrote a note to the warden and he got sore and the guard took them."

"What'd you say in the note?" Bisch asked. "Was it about me? If it was about me—"

"I swear it wasn't. Of course not. It was about me. I swear to God."

"What'd you say?"

"What difference does it make?"

"It *was* about me." He pulled Feldman closer to him.

"No," Feldman said, terrified. "It was about me."

"What did you say?"

"That I'm not a clown," he said helplessly.

Suddenly there was laughter. The big hands released Feldman's suit, and he sank weakly to the cot. All the men in the cellblock were laughing. Some guards had come in. They were laughing too. Bisch, choking, had tears in his eyes. He sat down heavily on the cot and wrapped his big arms around Feldman's shoulders.

"*That I'm not a clown,*" he sputtered between fits of laughter. Inspired, he let go of Feldman's shoulders and began to button the buttons of his suit coat. They tumbled out of the wide buttonholes.

"Pleased to meet you," Bisch said when he had regained control of himself, "I'm your tailor."

There was a second burst of laughter, like a round of applause.

Feldman slumped backwards, falling against his pillow.

"ALL RIGHT, LIGHTS OUT!"

Feldman lay in the dark with Bisch beside him. The man was still giggling. Feldman moved against the wall.

Bisch stood up and turned Feldman on his back. He leaned down and patted Feldman's chest and went back to his own cot.

He knows about the homunculus. They're going to kill me.

Feldman knew he had to get away from them. He was astonished to be contemplating escape. No, he thought. Solitary confinement, he thought. Could he be alone for a year? To stay alive? He'd be Robinson Crusoe. He would wait until Bisch was asleep. He could use his shoe. Heavy blows across the bridge of Bisch's nose. Against the temples. Under the jaw, on the throat. What am I thinking of? he thought. They'd add to my sentence. Then it would be two years. Every few years they'd get me to do something else. I'd be here forever. That's what he wants.

He meant the warden. It was amazing. They knew everything about him. Feldman was the trade they'd learned. Some warden. Some penologist. Some Fisher of bad men. Remote control. Brothers' keepers. Con against con. King Con.

He remembered how the warden had by-passed certain cells. Bad men were in them. How many were there? What was up? He had to talk to them. He had to get to the men in the street clothes. Who was he kidding? What am I, a hero? Spartacus? They had him. They had him covered.

He grieved for the year. In a strange way, to lose freedom meant to become visible—to ignore inspiration, always to have second thoughts. It was to live with the passions down, to move through the world like someone sick whom the first cigar, binge, fuck could kill. Finally—oh God, this was astonishing, terrifying—it was to be *good*. They had surfaced him, materialized him—Feldman flushers. He was their man in the blue fool suit. Under surveillance. Under. And before, who was he? A cat burglar, a man in carpet slippers, Boston Blackie, Jimmy Valentine. In what did happiness subsist? In darkness.

All at once Feldman missed his home. He remembered the wine-dark carpets and thought of the master bedroom with its silken bed. He remembered the mahogany apparatus on which he hung his clothes when he took them off, the built-in trays for cuff links, studs. He sighed for the master toilet, the glassed shower, the cunning lights. He thought of the long curves of pale blue sofas, of Thermopane picture windows wide as walls, of the clean white margins of his Ping-pong table, its crisp green net. He thought of his color television set, his air conditioning, his stereo, of the clipped turf that was his lawn. He wept for lost comfort and missed his wife.

Oh, Lilly, Lilly, Lilly. He wondered if he would ever see her again. Oh, Lilly, he thought, almost praying, I swear, never again will I betray you. He tried to remember her face, and got a sudden fix on a beautiful girl. It was Barbara, in his wife's car pool. He strained and brought up Marlene. He saw Joyce in Curtains, Olive in Cosmetics, Harriet in Ladies' Leather. He saw his models, his buyers, one or two of the high school girls who worked part-time in Sporting Goods because he liked to watch them stretch the bows. He saw Miss Lane. But where was Lilly? All right, he thought fiercely—*Lilly. Come on. Come on, Lilly!* Lilly was tough, but maybe piece by piece he could do it.

Her glasses came to him first—gold-rimmed. Then he could see doctors' bills, organs she'd had removed, surgical bandages, the cream-color crisscross of hernia tape. Now he had her—the wide lap, the thick thighs she couldn't remember to close, the monstrous tits. It was Lilly! It was Lilly, goddamnit! *But where was Miss Lane?*

5

For the first twelve years they fled the minion. They hid
from it in Maine, in Vermont, in Pennsylvania, in Ohio,
in Indiana. Once his father had seen a film of ranchers in
Montana, but they never got that far. At last they came to southern Illinois' Little Egypt.

His father rebuilt his peddler's wagon for a fifth time, nailing
the old lumber with the old nails. "Test it, test it," his father said,
and Feldman climbed inside, stretching out on his back in the
gentile sun, the goyish heat. His father stepped inside the long
handles. "Old clothes," he called, "rags, first-born Jews." A
woman stood on her porch and stared at them. "Go inside, lady,"
Feldman's father said, "it's only a rehearsal. Out, kid."

Feldman sprang from the wagon. "What a leap, what a
jump," his father said. "Soon I ride in the wagon, you get a good
offer and you sell me." He stooped and picked up the paintbursh
and threw it to his son. "Paint for the hicks a sign. In English
make a legend: ISIDORE FELDMAN AND SON." His father
watched him make the letters. "It's very strange," he said, "I have
forgotten how to write English. But I can still read it, so no tricks."
When Feldman had finished, his father took the brush saying,
"And now I will do the same in Hebrew on the other side. For
the Talmudic scholars of southern Illinois." His son climbed into
the wagon and lay back against the planks with their faded, flak-

30

ing legends, the thick Hebrew letters like the tips of ancient, heavy keys. "This afternoon it dries, and tomorrow it is opening day in America."

His father was insane. For five years Feldman had been old enough to recognize this; for three years he had been old enough to toy with the idea of escaping; for two weeks he had been brave enough to try. But he had hesitated, and for a week he had realized with despair that he loved his father.

They had rented a house. It was like all the houses they had ever lived in. "Look at it," his father said, climbing up on the porch. "White frame." He touched the wood. "Steps. A railing. A swing. Here, when you're old enough, you'll court Americans in that swing. And *screen* doors. Look, look, Leo, at the *screen* doors. A far cry from the East Side. No screen doors on the East Side. Smell the flowers. I wish I knew their names. Get the American girls in the swing to tell you their names. That way, if they die, we will know what seeds to ask for. Good. Then it's settled."

While the paint was drying they walked in the town. His father showed him the feed store, the courthouse, the tavern. They went inside and Feldman's father drank a beer and spoke with the bartender. "Neighbor," his father said, "a Jew is a luxury that God affords Himself. He is not serious when He makes a Jew. He is only playing. Look, you got a wife?"

"Sure," the man said uneasily.

"Tell her today you met Feldman and Son." He leaned across the bar and winked. "If a Jew wants to get ahead," he whispered, "he must get ahead of the other Jews. He must go where there are no Jews. A Jew is a novelty." He turned to his son. "Tell the neighbor our word," he said.

"Please, Papa," Feldman said, embarrassed.

"In the first place, papa me no papas, pop me no pops. This is America. Dad me a dad. Father me a father. Now—the word."

"Diaspora," Feldman said.

"Louder, please."

"Diaspora," he said again.

"Diaspora, delicious."

The bartender stared at them.

"Explain. Tell the fellow."

"It means dispersion," Feldman said.

"It *says* dispersion, and it *means* dispersion," his father said. "I tell you, ours is a destiny of emergency. How do you like that? You see me sitting here fulfilling God's will. I bring God's will to the Midwest. I don't lift a finger. I have dispersed. Soon the kid is older, *he* disperses. Scatter, He said." He looked around the tavern significantly, and going to the front window, made an oval in the Venetian blinds for his face and peered out. "To the ends of the earth. Yes, Lord." He rushed back to the bar. "Who owns the big store here?" he asked suddenly.

"That would be Peterson," the bartender said.

"Peterson, perfect."

The bartender started to move away, but Feldman's father reached across the bar and held his elbow. "The jewelry store? Quickly."

"Mr. Stitt."

"Stitt, stupendous."

"Come, Father," Feldman said.

"There's no *shul*, no Jew?" his father said.

"I don't know none, mister."

"Know none, nice." He stood up. At the door he turned to all of them in the tavern. Huge men in faded overalls looked down at him from enormous stools. "Farmers, townsmen—*friends:* I am your new neighbor, Isidore Feldman, the peddler. In the last phase of the Diaspora. I have come to the end of the trail in your cornfields. I can go no further. Here I hope to do business when the pushcart dries. I have scouted the community and can see that there is a crying need for a ragman. The old-clothes industry is not so hot here either. Never mind, we will grow together. Tell the wife. Meanwhile, look for me in the street!"

Going home, his father, elated, taught him the calls as they walked along. "Not 'rags,' not 'old clothes.' What are you, an announcer on the radio? You're in a street! Say 'regs, all cloze.' Shout it. Sing it. I want to hear steerage, Ellis Island in that throat. I'll give you the pitch. Ready, begin: *Rugs, oil cloths!* Wait, stop the music. *Greenhorn*, you're supposed to be a greenhorn! What, you never saw the Statue of Liberty through the fringes of a prayer shawl?"

He hadn't and neither had his father.

"All right, from the top. *Rocks, ill clots.* Better, beautiful, very nice, you have a flair."

"*Rex, wild clits*," Feldman sang out. A hick stared at him from behind a lawn mower. He could smell preserves in the air.

"Terrific," Feldman's father shouted, " 'wild clits' is very good. We'll make our way. I *feel* it. *I* know it's a depression, once I built a railroad, made it run. *I* know this is Illinois, America. *I* know the rubble is not the destruction of the second temple, but just today's ashes Never *mind!* We are traveling Jews in the latest phase of the new Diaspora. We will be terr*ific.*"

He stopped and pulled his son close to him. "Listen, if anything happens you'll need wisdom. I can't help you. Father's a fathead. Dad's a dope. But in lieu of wisdom—*cunning.* These are bad times—bad, *dreckish,* phooey! But bad times make a bullish market for cunning. I'm no Red. From me you don't hear 'from each according to his ability, to each according to his need.' From me you hear 'from them to me.' I know the world. I *know* it. I fight it one day at a time. This is your father speaking. This is advice.

"*Rogues, wooled clouds,*" he roared down the American street.

So they sold and sold. "It's the big sellout," his father said. "What did you sell today?" he would ask people he met in the street. "Trade, traffic, barter, exchange, deal, peddle, purvey," he called ecstatically to the house fronts.

They'd go into Woolworth's—Woolworth's was one of his father's chief suppliers; "My wholesaler," he'd say—and his father would gasp at the abundances there, the tiers of goods, the full shelves, the boxes on high platforms lining the walls. "Commodities," he'd sigh. "Things. Thing City." Staring like a stricken poet at an ideal beauty. "Some operation you've got here," he said to the girl who sold the clusters of chocolate peanuts. He stared passionately at the penny weighing machine, the Foot-Eze machine. "Nothing for something," he groaned jealously.

He turned to his son. "The beggars. Ah, the beggars and cripples. The men who sit armless and stumpless on a spread-out sheet of newspaper with the pencils in their caps. They have it made. *They* do. Take the nickel and keep the pencil! Delicious, delightful! The freaks stashed in cages, getting *gelt* for a gape. My son, my son, forgive me your health, your arms and your legs, your size and strong breathing, your unblemished skin. I chain you forever to invoice and lading, to rate of exchange, to wholesale, to cost." He'd wink. "Sell seconds," he'd say, "irregulars. Sell damaged and smoke-stained and fire-torn things. Sell the marred and impaired, the defective and soiled. Sell remnants, remainders, the used and the odd lot. Sell broken sets. That's where the money is."

He would pick up a pair of ladies' panties from the lingerie counter. "Look, look at the craftsmanship," he'd say distastefully, plunging his big hand inside and splaying his fingers in the silky seat, "the crotchmanship." He'd snap the elastic. "No sag, no give," he'd say to the startled salesgirl. "Give me give, the second-rate. Schlock, give me. They're doing some wonderful things in Japan.

"*Because*," he'd say, explaining, "where's the contest in sound merchandise? You sell a sound piece of merchandise, what's the big deal? Demand has nothing to do with good business, not *good* business. Need, who needs it? In England—come closer, miss, you'll enjoy this—they have a slang term for selling. 'Flogging,' they call it. Flogging, fantastic. But that's it, that's it exactly. Beating, whipping. Every sale a scourge. Sell me envelopes."

"That's the stationery counter. Aisle four."

"You hear, Leo? A *stationary* counter. Wonderful, wonderful. Not like with us with the wheels on the wagon, the rolling Diaspora. What a thing it is to be a gentile! A goy, gorgeous!"

He leaned across the counter and took the girl's hands in his own. He moved with her like this to the break in the counter and pulled her toward him gently. They were like sedate figures in an old dance.

"It's not my department," the girl objected.

"You drive a hard bargain," his father said. "It's a pleasure to do business with you."

"No, really—listen—"

"Envelopes, forty. One pack, wide white. Here's the quarter. It's a flog. Now, please, beat me a box pencils."

Then, incredibly, he would sell the envelopes. One at a time. He would go into the office of the farm agent. "Have you written Mother this week?" he might ask, and sell him an envelope for two cents.

"What have you got for us today, Isidore?" an old man would call from the bench at the courthouse. His father sold him an envelope.

He lived by sufferance, his son saw. His father saw too. "They owe me," he explained. "Fuck them."

Little children suffered him. He would stride up to them in their games in the schoolyard. Perhaps he would intercept the ball, running after it clumsily, knees high, awry, hugging it ineptly. Holding it high. "Want to buy a ball?" he shouted. The children laughed. "What did *you* sell today?" Leering awfully, asking Helen, a girl in his son's class, eleven and breasted, eleven and haired. The children roared and touched each other.

"What have you got for us today, Isidore?" a child yelled. It was what the old men called.

He tossed the ball aside, pushing it as a girl would, and reached into his pocket. "*White,*" he whispered, pulling a crayon from the pocket, holding it out to them, a waxy wand. "White!"

"I'll tell you about white. White," he'd say, his loose, enormous lids heavy, slack wrappings for his eyes, "is the first thing. White is light, great God's let was, void's null. You can't go wrong with white. You wouldn't be sorry you took white. Ask your teacher, you don't believe me. It reflects to the eye all the colors in the solar spectrum. How do you like that? This is the *solar* spectrum I'm talking about, not your small-time local stuff. You take the white—the blue, yellow, red and green go with it. Some white! A nickel for the rainbow, I'm closing it out."

"What could you do with it?" a boy asked.

"Color an elephant and sell it," his father said. "Put up a flag. Tell a lie. Ah, kid, you know too much. You've seen the truth. It's the color of excuse and burden. I've got a nerve. You're too young. Why should I saddle you with white? But have you got a big brother maybe? Nah, nah, it's a grownup's color. Buy better brown. Go green, green's grand. You want green? Here—" He stuck his hand into his pocket and without looking pulled out a green crayon. The boy gasped and moved back. "No? Still thinking about the white? Naughty kid, you grow up too fast today. White-hot for white, are you? All right, you win, I *said* white for sale and I *meant* white for sale. White sale here. *All right, who wants it?*"

A boy offered three cents, another four. A child said a nickel. He sold it to a girl for six.

"Done," he said, and took the money and reached back into his pocket. His eyes were closed. "*Purple,*" he said.

They lived on what his father earned from the sales. Maybe fifteen dollars came into the house in a week, and although it was the Depression his son felt poor. Perhaps he would have felt poor no matter what his father earned, for all he needed to remind him of their strange penury was one sight of his father at his card table in what would normally be the parlor. (A card table and chairs in the American Home; they had brought the Diaspora into the front room.) It was the counting house of a madman. On the table, on the chairs, on the floor—there were only the card table and two chairs for furniture—were the queer, changed products and by-products, the neo-junk his father dealt in. There were stamped lead soldiers, reheated on the kitchen stove and bent into positions of agony, decapitated, arms torn from the lead sides, the torsos and heads and limbs in mass cigar-box graves. His father would sell these as "a limited edition, a special series from the losing side" ("An educational toy," he explained to the children. "What, you think it's all victories and parades and boys home on furlough? This is why they *give* medals. A head is two cents, an arm a penny. It's supply and demand"). There were four identical decks of Bicycle cards into which his father had inserted extra aces, kings, queens. These he carried in an inside pocket of his coat and took with him into the pool hall for soft interviews with the high school boys ("Everybody needs a head start in life. You, fool, how would you keep up otherwise?"). There were single sheets torn from calendars ("April," he called in February, "just out. Get your April here"). There were collections of pressed flowers, leaves ("The kids need this stuff for school"). There was a shapeless heap of dull rags, a great disreputable mound of the permanently soiled and scarred, of slips that might have been pulled from corpses in auto wrecks, of shorts that could have come from dying men, sheets ripped from fatal childbeds, straps pulled from brassieres—the mutilated and abused and dishonored. Shards from things of the self, the rags of rage they seemed. Or as if they grew there, in the room, use's crop. "Stuff, stuff," his father said, climbing the rags, wading into them as one might wade into a mound of autumn's felled debris. "Someday you'll wear a suit from this." There were old magazines, chapters from books, broken pencils, bladders from ruined pens, eraser ends in small piles, cork scraped from the inside of bottle caps, ballistical shapes of tinfoil, the worn straps from watches, wires, strings, ropes, broken glass—things' nubbins.

"*Splinters,*" his father said, "there's a fortune in splinters."

"*Where's the fortune in splinters already?*" his father said. Looking at the collection, the card table, the two chairs, the room which for all its clutter seemed barren. "Look alive there. Your father, the merchant prince, is talking. What, you think I'll live forever? We're in a crisis situation, I tell you. I have brought the Diaspora this far and no further. Though I'll tell you the truth, even now things fly outward, my arms and my heart, pulling to scatter. I don't want to go, I don't want to go. There are horses inside me and they are stampeding. Run, run for the doctor. Get cowboys with ropes. Talk to me. *Talk!*"

"What do you want me to say?" his son asked.

"Yielder, head bower, say what you mean."

The boy didn't know what he meant.

"It's not moving, it's not moving," his father moaned. "Business is terrible. Are you hungry?"

"No."

"Are you cold?"

"No."

"Nevertheless, business is terrible. It stinks, business." He brushed a pile of canceled stamps from the table. "Everything is vendible. It *must* be. That's religion. Your father is a deeply religious man. He believes in vendibility. To date, however, he has failed to move the unsalable thing. The bottom has dropped out of his market look out below."

They lived like this for three years.

For three years he was on the verge of fleeing his father. What prevented him now was not love (love goes, he thought) so much as an illusion that the Diaspora *had* brought him to an end of the earth, an edge of the world. For all that there were telephone poles about him, newspapers, machines, cars, neon in the windows of the taverns, he seemed to live in a world that might have been charted on an old map, the spiky spines of serpents rising like waves from wine-dark seas, personified zephyrs mump-cheeked and fierce—a distant Praetorianed land, unamiable and harsh. There might have been monkeys in its trees, burning bushes in its summers. He lived in a constant fear of miracles that could go against him. The wide waters of the Ohio and the Mississippi that he had seen meld from a bluff just below Cairo, Illinois, would have turned red in an instant had he entered them, split once and drowned him had he taken flight. There was the turtle death beyond, he vaguely felt, and so, like one who has come safely through danger to a given clearing, he feared to go on or to retrace his steps. He was content to stay still.

Content but embarrassed.

His father was famous now, and they seemed to live under the special dispensation of their neighbors. "I would make them eat the Jew," he would confide defiantly.

Like anyone famous, however, they lived like captives. (He didn't really mean "they"; surprisingly, he was untouched—a captive's captive.) It must have been a task even for his father to have always to come up to the mark of his madness. Once he bored them he was through. It was what had happened in Vermont, in Maine, elsewhere. Once he repeated himself—not the pattern; the pattern was immune, classic—it would be over. "There's a fortune in eccentricity, a fortune. I'm *alive*," his father said in honest wonder, weird pride. "It's no joke, it costs to live. Consumers, we're consumers. Hence our mortality. I consume, therefore I am." He would smile. "*I hate them*," he'd say. "They don't buy enough. Read Shylock. What a wisdom! That was some Diaspora they had there in Venice."

It was not hate, but something darker. Contempt. But not for him. For him there were, even at thirteen and fourteen and fifteen, pinches, hugs, squeezes. They slept together in the same bed ("It cuts coal costs. It develops the heart"). Awakened in the declining night with a rough kiss ("Come, chicken, cluck cluck cluck. If you cannot tell me, hold me"). Whispers, declarations, manifestoes in the just unhearing ear. Bedtime stories: "Your mother was a gentile and one of my best customers. I laid her in my first wagon by pots and by pans and you were born and she died. You think I hate you, you think so? You think I hate you, you took away my *shicksa* and a good customer? Nah, nah, treasure, I love you. She would have slowed down the Diaspora. We had a truck, and she couldn't read the road maps. Wake up, I'll tell you the meaning of life. Can you hear me? Are you listening? This is rich." (At first he was terrified, but gradually he accommodated to madness, so that madness made no difference and words were like melodies, all speech as meaningless as tunes. He lied, even today. He said what he wanted, whatever occurred to him. Talk is cheap, talk is cheap.) "Get what there is and turn it over quick. Dump and dump, mark down and close out. Have specials, my dear. The thing in life is to sell, but if no one will buy, listen, listen, *give* it away! Flee the minion. Be naked. Travel light. Because there will come catastrophe. Every night expect the flood, the earthquake, the fire, and think of the stock. Be in a position to lose nothing by it when the bombs fall. But what oh what shall be done with the unsalable thing?"

Madness made no difference. It was like living by the railroad tracks. After a while you didn't hear the trains. His father's status there, a harmless, astonishing madman, provided him with a curious immunity. As the boy became indifferent to his father, so the town became indifferent to the boy, each making an accommodation to what did not matter. It was not, however, that madness made sense to him. It was just that since he'd grown up with madness, nothing made sense. (His father might even be right about things; he was probably right). He had been raised by wolves, he saw; a growl was a high enough rhetoric. But he could not be made himself. Perhaps he did not have the energy for obsession. He had lived so close to another's passion, his own would have been redundant. "You have a locked heart," his father told him. Perhaps, perhaps he did. But now if he failed to abandon him ("When do you go?" his father sometimes asked. "When do you embark, entrain, enbus? When do you have the shoes resoled for the long voyage out? And what's to be done with the unsalable thing?"), it was not a sudden reloving, and it was no longer fear. The seas had long since been scraped of their dragons; no turtle death lay waiting for him. The Diaspora had been disposed of, and the tricky double sense that he lived a somehow old-timey life in a strange world. It was *his* world; he was, by having served his time in it, its naturalized citizen. He had never seen a tenement, a subway, a tall building. As far as he knew he had never seen a Jew except for his father. What was strange about there being a cannon on the courthouse lawn, or a sheriff who wore a star on his shirt? What was strange about anything? Life was these things too. Life was anything, anything at all. Things were of a piece.

He went to a county fair and ate a hot dog. (Nothing strange *there*, he thought.) He chewed cotton candy. He looked at pigs, stared at cows. He came into a hall of 4-H exhibits. Joan Stizek had hooked a rug; Helen Prish had sewn a dress; Mary Stellamancy had put up tomatoes. He knew these girls. They said, "How are you, Leo?" when they saw him. (Nothing strange *there*.)

He went outside and walked up the Midway. A man in a booth called him over. "Drop the ring over the block and take home a prize," he said. He showed him how easy it was. "Three tosses for a dime."

"The blocks are magnets," he said. "There are tiny magnets in the rings. You control the fields by pressing a button under the counter. I couldn't win. There's nothing strange."

"Beat it, kid," the man said. "Get out of here."

"I am my papa's son," he said.

A woman extended three darts. "Bust two balloons and win a prize."

"Insufficient volume of air. The darts glance off harmlessly. My father told me," he said.

"I'll guess your birthday," a man said.

"It's fifteen cents. You miss and give a prize worth five. Dad warned me."

"Odds or evens," a man said, snapping two fingers from a fist.

He hesitated. "It's a trick," he said, and walked away.

A sign said: LIVE! NAKED ARTIST'S MODEL! He handed fifty cents to a man in a wide felt hat and went inside a tent. A woman sat naked in a chair.

"Three times around the chair at an eight-foot distance at a reasonable pace. No stalling," a man standing inside the entrance said. "You get to give her one direction for a pose. Where's your pencil? Nobody goes around the chair without a pencil."

"I haven't got one," he said.

"Here," the man said. "I rent pencils. Give a dime."

"Nobody said anything about a pencil," he said. "It's a gyp."

"The sign says '*Artist's* Model,' don't it? How you going to draw her without a pencil?" He narrowed his eyes and made himself taller. "If you ain't an artist what are you doing in here? Or are you some jerk pervert?"

Feldman's son put his hand in his pocket. "Green," he said, showing a crayon from the inventory. "I work in green crayon."

"Where's your paper?" the man said. "Paper's a nickel."

"I don't have paper," he admitted.

"Here, Rembrandt," the man said. He held out a sheet of ringed, lined notebook paper.

"Are we related," Feldman's son asked, handing him a nickel.

He joined a sparse circle of men walking around the woman in a loose shuffle.

The man at the entrance flap called directions. "Speed it up there, New Overalls."

"Hold your left tit and point your finger at the nipple," a man in a brown jacket said.

"That's your third trip, Yellow Shoes. Get out of the line," called the man at the entrance. "*Eight-foot distance*, Green Crayon. I told you once."

"Spread your legs."

"Boy, oh boy, I got to keep watching you artists, don't I, Bow Tie?" the man said. "You already said she should grab her behind with both hands. One pose, *one* pose. Put the pencil in the hat, Yellow Shoes. You just rented that."

"Spread your legs," Feldman's son said. Nothing strange there, he thought.

"Keep it moving, keep it moving. You're falling behind, Brown Jacket."

He left the tent, still holding the unused sheet of notebook paper that had cost him a nickel.

There was an ox-pulling contest. He found a seat in the stands near the judge's platform and stared at the beasts. Beneath him several disqualified teams of oxen had been unyoked and sprawled like Sphinxes, their legs and haunches disappearing into their bodies, lush and fat and opulent. He gazed at the behinds of standing animals, seeing their round ball-less patches, slitted like electric sockets. They leaned together in the great wooden yokes, patient, almost professional.

"The load is eight thousand-five hundred pounds," the announcer said, drawling easily, familiarly, a vague first-name hint in his voice. "Joe Huncher's matched yellows at the sled for a try, Joe leading. Willy Stoop making the hitch. Move those boys back there, William. Just a little more. A *little* more. You did it, William. Clean hitch."

The man jumped aside as the oxen stamped jerkily backwards, moving at a sharp left angle to their hitch.

"Gee, gee there, you." The leader slapped an ox across the poll with his hat. He beat against the beast's muzzle. "Gee, you. Gee, gee."

"Turn them, Joseph. Walk them around. Those lads are excited," the announcer said.

The leader looked up toward the announcer and said something Feldman's son couldn't hear. The announcer's easy laugh came over the loudspeaker. He laughed along with him. I'm a hick, he thought. I'm a hick too. I'm a Jewish hick. What's so strange? He leaned back and brushed against a woman's knee behind him. " 'Scuse me, Miz Johnson," he said, not recognizing her.

"Hmph," she said.

Spread your legs, he thought. Touch your right tit with your left instep.

The oxen were in line now and the farmer stepped back. "Gee-*up*," he yelled, waving his hat at them. "Gee-UP!" The animals stepped forward powerfully, taking up the slack on their chain harness: They strained at the heavy sled, stumbling, their muscles jumping suddenly under their thick flesh. "Gee-*UP!* Whoosh whoosh whoosh whoosh whoosh, whoosh whoosh whoosh whoosh whoosh!" The burdened sled nine feet forward in the dirt.

The crowd applauded, Feldman's son clapping with them.

"Thataway, William, good work there, Joe," he called. Hey,

Willy, yo, Jo, he wanted to call aloud. Hey hey. Hi yo. Hee hee. Yo yo. Hey hi yo hee ho! Whoosh, boys. Whoosh whoosh whoosh whoosh whoosh.

"I thought I saw William spit there, Joe. No fair greasing the runners," the announcer said.

Feldman's son laughed.

"All right, folks," the announcer said, "next up's a pair of brown Swiss from the Stubb-Logan farm over county in Leeds. That's George Stubb up front, Mr. Gumm at the hitch. You been feeding them roosters, George? They look to me like they did some growing since the last pull."

At 9,500 pounds only Huncher and Stoop and the Leggings brothers were still in the contest. The matched yellows, his favorites because they were the crowd's, were unable to move the sled even after three trys.

He applauded as Joe Huncher led the team away. He leaned forward and cupping his hands shouted down at them: "That was near five tons on that sled there, Joseph. Hose those boys down now, William. Hose those boys down." Stoop waved vaguely toward the unfamiliar voice, and Feldman's son smiled. "A man works up a sweat doing that kind of pulling," he said to his neighbor.

The Leggings brothers led their oxen, sleek and black as massive seals, toward the sled to make the hitch. They maneuvered them back carefully and one brother slapped the ring solidly onto the peg.

"Come," the other brother commanded. "Come. Come. Come." The two beasts struggled viciously forward. It seemed they would strangle themselves against the yoke. They stretched their necks; their bodies queerly lengthened. There was a moment of furious stasis when Feldman's son thought that either the chain must break or the beasts themselves snap back against the sled, breaking their legs. Then he saw the thick wooden runners scrape briefly sideways, and the animals dragged the load five feet.

The announcer called the brothers up to collect their prize.

"Just a minute. Hold your oxes," a voice called. It was his father, standing in front of the judge's stand looking up. "Your Honor," he called, "Your Honor."

The crowd recognized him, laughing. The boy heard his father's name repeated like a rumor up and down the grandstands.

"What is it?" the announcer asked over the loudspeaker.

"Your Honor," Feldman said, "the contest ain't over."

"Of course it's over. What do you mean it's not over?"

It sounded like a routine. The son wondered if it was. "It's part of the show," he turned around and told the woman behind him. "It's part of the show, Miz Johnson."

"Now what's the meaning of this interruption, Isidore?" the announcer asked.

Yeah, Izidore, what? the son thought. Vat iz diz?

"These Leggings brothers are waiting for their check," said the announcer.

"It's not fair," Feldman shouted. "Anyway, the little one pushed from behind." The crowd roared. "Let it stand, but give a man a chance, Your Honor."

"What are you saying, Isidore? You mean you want to be in the contest too?"

His father flexed his arm, and the crowd laughed harder than before.

"Do you folks think Isidore Feldman here should take his turn?" They cheered. "All right, Isidore, let's see what you can do then," the announcer said.

Feldman walked past the sled and looked at it for a moment but did not stop. "Cement," he called roughly, pointing to the massive blocks chain-belted to the sled. "Cement for sale. Cash and carry."

"Make your hitch there, Isidore," the announcer called. He seemed annoyed. The son had an idea now it might not be an act.

Alarmingly, Feldman suddenly began to run. As he ran he shouted up to them, blowing out his phrases in gasps. "Wait, wait—while you're here—I've got—something to show you." He ran across the small stadium and pushed open a gate in the low wall. Feldman's son recognized the wagon, piled incredibly high. His father placed himself inside the long wood handles and bent far forward, like one in a storm. A tarpaulin had been spread over the load, so that it looked like a mountain. He seemed heroic. The people gasped as the wheels began slowly to turn and the wagon, the mountain inside it, began to move. He came steadily forward. "Talk about strength," he intoned as he came, "heavy as earth, terrible tons, see how I pull it, drag it along, I break all the records, an ant of a man, prudent as squirrel, thrifty as greed, they'll be a winter, who'll make me warm?"

He brought the wagon to rest a few feet from the grandstand and straightened up. He turned around, and grabbing one corner of the tarpaulin, pulled at it fiercely. "Ladies and gentlemen," he announced, shouting, *"THE INVENTORY!"*

"Things," he called, "things here. Things as they are. Thingamabobs and thingamajigs, dinguses and whatsits. Whatdayacallits, whatchamacallits. Gadgets and gewgaws. Kits and caboodle. Stuff. Stuff here!" He stood beside the pile, studying it. "What's to be done with the unsalable thing?" He pulled at his sleeve like one reaching into dishwater for a sunken spoon and slipped his hand with gingerly gentleness into the center of the pile. "Teakettle," he said. He pulled out a teakettle.

"We will trade together," he said seriously. He advanced to the railing at the foot of the stands, the small kettle swinging like a censer before him. "Diaspora," he called. "America, Midwest, Bible Belt, corn country, county fairgrounds, grandstand. Last stop for the Diaspora, everyone off." He recognized his son in the stands and winked hugely. "All right," he said, "I just blew in on the trade winds, and I'm hot see, and dusty see, and I'm smelling of profit and smelling of loss, and it's heady stuff, heady. I could probably use a shower and a good night's sleep, but business is business and a deal is a deal." He held out the kettle. "All right," he said, "This from the East. All from the East, where commerce begins. Consumers, consumers, purchasers, folks. I bring the bazaar. I've spared no expense. Down from the mountains, over the deserts, up from the seas. On the hump of a camel, the back of an ass. All right. Here is the kettle, who drinks the tea?" He leaped over the low rail and rushed into the stands. "Buy," he demanded, "buy, damnit, *buy, I say!*" He chose a farmer and thrust the kettle into the man's hand. He waited. The man tried to give the kettle back, but Feldman's father wouldn't take it; he folded his arms and dodged, bobbing and weaving like a boxer. "Pay up," he shouted, "a deal is a deal." The man made one more attempt to give it back. "All sales final," his father said. "Read your contract." At last the man, embarrassed, dug into his overalls and gave him a coin. His father held it up for the crowd to see. "Object's no money," he said scornfully. Passing his son, he took the sheet of notebook paper the boy still held. He sold it, then returned to the wagon. "Come," he said over his shoulder. "Come. Come. Come." Several followed him.

Again and again Feldman dipped into his pile. He pulled things out, handling, caressing, rubbing value into everything he touched. He signaled them closer. "Come," he called to those still in the stands. "Come. Come. Come." One by one they left the stands to crowd round his wagon. In ten minutes only his son was still in the stands. His father climbed into the wagon and yelled to the announcer. "I win, Your Honor." He indicated the large crowd beneath him that he had brought from the stands. He pointed suddenly to his son. "I can't move that item," he confessed.

He disappeared behind his inventory. "I've got the goods," he shouted, "and that ain't bad." In half an hour the pile had diminished, and his father, still in the wagon, seemed to have grown taller. He waved to his son. "Are you learning anything?" he called to him over the heads of the crowd.

Gradually the people began to drift away. There were still two or three things unsold, and Feldman reached down and held a man's arm. "Wait," he roared, "where are you going? You think I'm through with you? This is winter I'm talking about. This is the cold, sad solstice. Just because the sun is shining over us now, you think it's stuck up there? You take too much for granted. You buy something, you hear me?" He bent down and picked up a carved, heavy leg from an old dining-room table. "Here," he said. "A wonderful club. For your enemies. You got enemies? No? Then build a table over it and invite your friends to supper."

Finally there was nothing left to sell and the people had all gone. His father still stood in the wagon, tall, forlorn as a giant. The oxen passed beside him, led by their owners. "What's to be done with the unsalable thing?" Feldman crooned.

His son, in the stands, stared at him without moving. "What *is* the unsalable thing?" he called.

"The unsalable thing? My God, don't you know?"

"No."

"No?"

"You never told me."

They were shouting to each other.

"I didn't?"

"Not once."

"Never?"

"No."

"I had to tell you? You couldn't guess?"

"I never bothered."

"Some son."

"Well?"

"Well what? What well?"

"What is it?"

"What is what?"

"The unsalable thing."

"It's me," he said.

A year later his father began to cough. The boy was always with him now on the wagon. During the choking, heavy seizures, brought on, it seemed, by the swelling, passionate spiels themselves, his son would take over the cries, shouting madder and madder things into the streets. The cough grew worse; it would begin as soon as he started to speak.

Feldman went to the doctor. "It's cancer," he told his son. "I'm dying."

"Can he operate?"

His father shook his head. "It's terminal." He coughed.

"Terminal," his son repeated the word.

"Sure," his father said, coughing so that he could hardly be understood. "Last stop for the Diaspora. Everyone off."

The boy went to the doctor and conferred with him.

Three months later, when the old man died, his son got in touch with the doctor. They argued some more, but it was no use. The doctor, on behalf of the tiny hospital, could offer him only fifteen dollars for the body.

6

"Where are *you* going?" the guard asked.

"I've been sick in my cell, and I never got an assignment. I was told that I had to see a guard."

"Plubo. You have to see Plubo."

"Yes. Him."

"Where's your pass? You can't get through here without a pass."

"Where do I get a pass?"

"The Fink makes out the passes in this wing. Or the warden if he's around."

"Where do I find the Fink?"

"Through that door." He pointed down a long corridor.

Feldman began to walk toward it.

"Wait a minute, you."

"What is it?"

"You'll need a permission slip to get a pass from the Fink. The Fink is only a trusty. He can't write one up on his own authority."

"Where do I get a permission slip?"

"From a guard."

Feldman waited.

"Oh, *I* can't give you one if that's what you think. You get permission slips from pencil men. There have to be rules," he said.

"Where do I find a pencil man?"

"Return to your cell. Don't you know anything? The pencil man is the counter."

Oh, he thought. There were major counts four times a day when a bell rang and the prisoners had to freeze, as in a fairy tale or a child's game. Minor counts occurred every half-hour, when a guard came through carrying a clipboard. He was the counter, the pencil man. Feldman went back to his cell. He found out he had just missed the pencil man and would have to wait twenty-five minutes for the next one.

He lay down on his cot to wait, but he fell asleep. When he woke he called out to some convicts playing Monopoly in the corridor. "Has the pencil man been through?"

"Ten minutes ago," a man said.

Feldman sat up and waited for the next pencil man. When he saw him he called out at once.

"Thirty-eight," the pencil man said. "Remind me. I stopped at thirty-eight. What is it?"

Feldman explained what he needed.

He showed the permission slip to the Fink, and the Fink gave him a pass. Feldman started to walk off.

"Hold it, smart guy."

"What?"

"Let's have that permission slip back. That has to be destroyed. Got any cigarettes?"

"Yes."

"Give us four smokes. What are they, plain-tipped or filters?"

"Filter."

"Give us *six* smokes, and I'll let you keep the permission slip."

"I don't need it."

"You don't need it now, but suppose you need it later? Suppose that? Suppose you miss your pencil man and have to wait half an hour?"

Feldman nodded.

"You see?" the Fink said. "You can never find a pencil man when you need one."

"But the slip is dated."

"Only the quarter. It's the loophole. There's got to be rules and there's got to be loopholes. You don't know anything about this place, do you?"

"I guess not," Feldman said.

"That's all right," the Fink said. "Some of the lifers don't know much more than you do. The oldest lifers are still learning. Not even the warden knows everything about it."

Feldman gave him the cigarettes.

The Fink winked. "At lunch rub it in the butter."

"Why?"

"It preserves it. Otherwise the permission slip gets all yellow and wrinkled. You grease it down, that won't happen."

"Oh."

"Usually I get a couple more cigarettes for that tip."

"I see."

"It's not part of the service."

"I gave you my last cigarettes."

"Better yet. You owe me. In this place always get a guy to owe you."

"I see. All right. I owe you two cigarettes."

"Four," the Fink said.

"Why four?"

"For the second tip. Get a guy to owe you."

Feldman presented the pass that the Fink had made out for him to the guard. Saying nothing, the man unlocked the door. He was in a part of the prison he did not remember having been in before. Offices opened onto a long central corridor. He wondered if the warden's office was in this building.

He knocked at a door marked "Personnel." "Come in," a voice called, and he opened the door. "You want *Inmate* Personnel," a man said harshly.

At Inmate Personnel there was no answer and he had turned to go when the door opened. A large ruddy-faced man with white hair stood inside. He had loosened the knot on his tie, and his shirt collar was open. His jacket had been carelessly placed across the back of a chair.

"Hi ya," the man said expansively.

"I'm looking for Major Plubo, sir," Feldman said. (The guards' ratings were astonishing. Feldman had never seen one below the rank of captain. The guard who had directed him to the pencil man was a lieutenant colonel. The pencil man himself had been a one-star general.)

"I'm Plubo. Call me Plubo. I figure an officer earns his respect or he doesn't deserve it. What good does it do me if you call me 'sir' to my face and something else behind my back? Isn't that right, sir?"

"I was told to see you for an assignment."

"That was a question. You have to answer a question. I asked, sir, if this business of saying 'sir' isn't finally meaningless unless it's earned."

"I guess that's right, Mr. Plubo," Feldman said.

"And you can drop the 'Mister,' sir. Plubo's good enough. Titles aren't that important to me. There's just man and man. Don't you feel that, sir?"

"Yes, Plubo. I feel that."

"Of course you do, sir."

"You don't have to call me 'sir' either, Plubo," Feldman said uneasily.

"Well, you see, sir, I respect you. That's why I do that. I *already* respect you. It's a voluntary thing."

Uh oh, Feldman thought. Uh oh, uh, oh. Not for nothing were people in jails. Even the guards. Jail was where the extortion was. A place of forced gifts, hidden taxes, tariffed hearts. You paid through the nose, and it was difficult to breathe. But if that was what he wanted, Feldman could stir him with 'sirs.' He would pay the sir tax. There would be no sir cease. And in a way, 'sirs' *were* earned. Robbery was hard work, and Feldman *did* respect him. As he respected many people here. Hats off to the strong-arm guys. Wide berths to the breakers and enterers. He was learning to send along the best regards of his suspicion and fear.

"Sir," he said, "I've been ill since I came here—in my cell—and though I wanted to work, sir, though I wanted to pull my own weight, it was impossible until just now. And then I didn't have a prison uniform, sir, and as I say, sir, I've been sick in my cell—"

"Sick in your soul, you say." Plubo winked at him.

Feldman, at a loss, smiled.

"That's more like it," Plubo said. "Time out. This is off the record, mate. Time out. *You're lying. You're a liar.* That's all right. There has to be lies and there has to be truth. You're doing fine now. Go ahead. Eat more shit. . . . You were ill? And?"

"I didn't get an assignment."

"Well now, you want an assignment, is that it?"

"Yes sir."

Plubo reached behind him and slipped into his jacket. He buttoned the gold buttons. He did the button at his neck and tightened his tie. "Well," he said, "well. What experience have you had, Mr.—"

"Feldman, sir."

"What experience have you had, Mr. Feldman? (Is this tie straight? There has to be straight ties and there has to be stains in the underwear.) Have you ever made any license plates?"

"No sir."

"How about molds for manhole covers, have you poured any of those?"

"No sir."

"Stop signs? 'Busses Must Halt at Railroad Crossings, Open Doors and Blow Horn'? 'Caution—S Curve'?"

"No sir," Feldman said.

"Well now," Plubo said. "That's all right. Don't be nervous. We'll find something for you. *I* know. Have you bristled brushes?"

"Sir, I owned a department store."

"Well, if you'll forgive me, Feldman, we don't have much demand for that kind of experience in here. Stand up straight a moment. Turn around."

Feldman did what he was told.

"You're a pretty big fella, aren't you?" Plubo said.

"I'm heavy, yes," Feldman said. "I've always eaten all I've wanted of the things I've liked."

"Yes," Plubo said. "Of course you have. Have you played much sports?"

"No sir," Feldman said. "I haven't lived very physically."

Plubo considered him, and then came around from behind his desk. "Let me feel those arms," he said. He squeezed Feldman's arms, digging hard into the flabby biceps. He put both hands around Feldman's left arm and increased the pressure steadily.

He knows, Feldman thought. He knows about the homunculus.

Plubo let go of Feldman's arm. "A man your size, I see you on the football field," he said ominously. "No? You don't think so?"

Feldman rubbed his arm.

Plubo had seated himself behind his desk again. He put on his glasses and studied some papers. "Report to the canteen," he said. "*Dismissed.*" He hissed the word contemptuously. "Jerk," he said, "jerk clerk. Bad man. You make me sick—you and your comfortable kind. All the bad men in here are clerks. Like you. They're not in the foundries, not in the shops. None of them. They'd be a danger to themselves, to others. Glutton. Pig. Sedentary piece of shit. *You're dismissed, I said!*"

Feldman turned to go.

"You salute me, you jerk clerk jerk. And you say 'Thank you, Major Plubo, sir.' "

"Thank you, Major Plubo, sir," Feldman said. He was terrified.

"We've got your number," Plubo shouted as Feldman closed the door. "We've got your number, and it's zero. It's nothing. Jerk clerk, clerk jerk. *Nothing!*"

Feldman, breathless, stood beyond Plubo's door and cursed the surreal. Well, it was *cheap*, he thought.

Calm again, he asked a guard to unlock the door for him, but the man wouldn't let him back into the other wing until he had gotten another pass. For a pass he needed another permission slip. He was afraid to show the permission slip he already had; he didn't know if it was valid in this wing. He waited twenty minutes for a pencil man to get another one.

"Not on *this* side," the pencil man said angrily when Feldman told him what he wanted. "On this side you get permission slips from the opposite number."

"I don't understand," Feldman said.

"Who'd you just see?"

"Major Plubo."

"Major Plubo is in charge of Inmate Personnel. His opposite number is Major Joyce in Personnel. Rap three times and jiggle the doorknob twice so he'll know what you're there for."

Feldman nodded.

"It's a cross-check. There's got to be cross-checks. Otherwise a con could float around in here indefinitely without ever reporting to the man he's been given the pass to see. It's an angle."

"There's got to be curves and there's got to be angles," Feldman said ardently. He understood. The place was not surreal; it was a place of vicious, plodding *sequiturs*, though not even the oldest lifers fully understood it, not even the warden.

7

"I'll explain the operation," Manfred Sky told him when he reported to the canteen. "Mr. Flesh is my assistant. And Walls here is in charge of stock. You're his assistant."

Feldman nodded. Walls was arranging packages of gum in a pyramid.

"You had a department store on the outside. That's very impressive."

Feldman shrugged.

"No," Manfred Sky said, "it's nice. Hey, Walls, this guy had a big department store on the outside. What do you think about that?"

Walls whistled.

"You had a thing like that going for you," Harold Flesh said, "and *still* you had to fuck around. It don't make sense."

"Leave him alone, Harold," Sky said. "You don't know anything about it. Maybe he was framed. Were you framed, Leo?"

"In a way," Feldman said.

"You see, Harold? In a way he was framed. Don't be so quick to jump to conclusions."

"He's got a blue suit on," Walls said.

"I look at the man, not the suit," Sky said. Sky was wearing a dark suit with white, thickish, diagonal pin stripes. The pin stripes were not straight, but abruptly angled like bolts of lightning in a comic strip. It was difficult to look at him.

"*Still*," Walls said. Walls wore a bright pink polo shirt and Bermuda shorts. They seemed perfectly normal except that there were neither buttons nor zipper on his open fly. It was difficult to look at him too.

"The operation," Harold Flesh said impatiently. There seemed nothing unusual about his apparel. He wore the grayish sweat suit that was the normal prison uniform. Catching Feldman's glance, Flesh spoke irritably. "It's cashmere. All right?"

"I beg your pardon?"

"It's cashmere. My uniform. And like yours it don't fit. All right? Satisfied?"

"We just look funny," Walls said, "but Harold *smells* funny. When he sweats—the cashmere—it's terrible."

"Shut up, Walls," Flesh said.

"I was just telling him," Walls said defensively. "He'd find out anyway," he added.

"All right," Sky said, "all right, let's settle down here. Let's not kill each other. Let's leave that to the authorities who get paid for it. Come on, Leo here wants to know about the operation."

"I pile the chewing gum, that's the operation," Walls said. "I make it in neat stacks." He giggled, and Flesh walked over and knocked his pyramid down.

Feldman, surprised, heard Manfred Sky laugh. "Come on," Manfred Sky said—he was still laughing—"what kind of impression do you guys think you're making?" He turned to Feldman. "Tell them the impression they're making."

"It's an impression," Feldman said neutrally.

"Mind your business," Walls said from the floor. He was gathering up the gum that Flesh had tumbled. "I ain't making any impressions on nobody, you fat bastard. How do you know you ain't making an impression on *me*? How do you know that? The truth is you are. I'm down here on my hands and knees, picking up chewing gum, and there's a draft in my crotch, and you're making an impression on *me*. It's not a good one."

"Walls," Sky said.

"It's not a good one, Manfred. A blue suit is a blue suit."

"All right, all right," Sky said. Harold Flesh had drifted off toward the rear of the canteen—it seemed to be several converted four-man cells—and was thumbing through inventory slips. "I'm going to explain the operation if it kills me," Manfred Sky said.

Feldman, who was uneasy, wished he would begin. He

looked as wide-eyed as he dared at Manfred Sky.

"First of all," Sky said, "you've got to imagine it's a gigantic, permanent depression, and everyone's on relief. Everyone. That's this place. These guys don't have any money. They use prison chits. The state pays them three-fifty a month, after taxes, for the work they do here. Almost everybody gets the same."

"Some get more?" Feldman asked, surprised.

"Some get less," Sky said. "You do, I do. All the bad men."

"That's not fair," Feldman said. "That's not legal."

"It's for our costumes," Harold Flesh said, plucking at his cashmere sweat shirt. "They dock us for the labor and the special material. They get another five dollars from the outside if their family comes up with it. It's credited to their accounts. I suppose you won't have any trouble about that if you've got a department store."

"That's right," Walls said, "in the department-store department he's all fixed."

"You're a clown, Walls," Harold Flesh said.

"You're a clown too, Harold. We're all clowns."

"I won't go on with it, okay?" Sky said dramatically. "I'll stop right there."

"No, Manfred, tell him," Walls said.

"No. You guys want to crap around, crap around. Go on. I'll just sit here with my mouth shut."

"The conniver in conniptions," Harold Flesh said.

"The dissimulator digusted," Walls said.

"The piker piqued," Harold Flesh said.

"That's enough," Sky told them. He turned to Feldman. "I cheated the poor," he said. "I nickeled-and-dimed them. Widows and grandpas, the old and the sick. I reduced the reduced."

"Oh Christ," Flesh said, bored, "explain the operation, Sky."

"This *is* the operation," Sky cried, wheeling. "What do you think? This *is* the operation. There are fortunes in doom and dread. Look," he said, staring at Feldman, holding him, "during the war—"

"We've heard all this, Manfred," Flesh said.

"During the war—everything I touched. *Gold!* The things I sold. Amulets. To send to their boys so they wouldn't be hurt. And privilege. I made my collections. Like the insurance man I went around from scared door to scared door. I sold a policy to the parents, the wives—Prisoner-of-War Insurance, ten dollars a week. People are stupid, *they* don't know. They think, when they've nothing, that things are controlled. They believe in our money. Theirs only buys bread, but ours can buy fate. I told them I worked through the international Red Cross, that their boys would be safe as long as they paid. They couldn't afford not to believe me. That's where the money is. Where people gamble because they can't afford to take the chance."

Sky closed his eyes. "Ah," he said heavily, "I never had any confidence in my generation. I thought we'd lose the war. I'm here today because we won."

"This all came out at the trial," Walls said wearily.

Sky opened his eyes. "Well," he said, suddenly cheerful, "forgive and forget, let bygones be bygones."

"Guilty as charged," Walls said.

Flesh—the tough one, Feldman guessed—snickered.

"All right," Sky said, "you keep the accounts. Is that okay?"

"Whatever you say," Feldman said.

"I say Freedman," Walls said suddenly.

"I say Victman," Flesh said.

"All right," Sky said, "I say Dedman!"

8

Feldman lay on his cot, thinking: Uh oh, uh oh, uh oh.
Across the cell, Bisch farted in his sleep.
It was the bad man deal, Feldman thought. They
would give him the business, like the Duke of West Point. What
a place, he thought. Thieves, he thought, safe-crackers, bookies,
guys who jump cars. Pickpockets, he thought. Larcenists and ar-
sonists and murderers in all degrees. Rapers, embezzlers, hit-and-
run drivers. Fencers and inciters to riot. Bagmen, wheelmen, fixers
and bribers. Kidnappers, he thought, counterfeiters, short-
changers, pushers and pimps. Menslaughterers, drunken drivers,
and guys who didn't give fair measure. Jack-offs. Disturbers of
the peace. Vandals. Scoff laws. Bad sports.
The homunculus seemed to stretch in its death. Pain flared
briefly at his heart.
Blackmail, he thought. The perfect crime.
He paced the cell like a benched athlete stalking the sidelines,
stalking the game.

Ed Slipper was the oldest inmate in the penitentiary, the
fourth oldest inmate in the country. Two years before, he had been
only the seventeenth oldest prisoner, but the succeeding winters
had been hard. Many of the old-timers had died and Ed had
moved rapidly up the list. "You watch my smoke now," he would

say to the men gathered about the television set in the recreation room as the announcer on the screen stood before the weather map and spoke of storms developing in the northwest, of cold spells in their ninth day, their tenth, their eleventh.

"Did you hear that, Ed?" a prisoner said one evening as Feldman, on a break, sat watching television. "Thirty-eight below in Medicine Bow, Wyoming."

"Shit," the old man said, "that's unimportant. That's a fucking wasteland up there. There's no prison, no jail even. All that place is is a ton of ice and a thermometer. Nobody never died of the cold in Medicine Bow, Wyoming. You tell me what the cloud cover is in Leavenworth, Kansas, in Atlanta, Georgia, in Baton Rouge, Louisiana. Then I'll listen."

Feldman remembered the old man when he saw him the next night at the canteen. Walls was in the infirmary, and Feldman had taken his place behind the candy counter.

"Have you got the chocolate-covered cherries?" the old man asked.

Feldman pushed a box toward him.

"That's a quarter," Sky said. "You got the chits for it, Ed?"

"Aw Sky," Ed Slipper said, "it's not but a week till payday."

"You know the rules. No credit:"

"I only got ten cents."

"Try the licorice."

"Sky, you bastard, I ain't eaten the licorice since Cupid was warden here in '37. I'm the fourth oldest inmate in this damn country, and I ain't got the teeth for no licorice."

Sky shrugged. "Get your warden pal to help you out," he said.

"Your ass, Sky," Slipper said. He took a small Hershey bar without nuts and a cylinder of cherry Life Savers. "Home brew," he explained to Feldman. "I have to do that sometimes." He gave him the last of his chits and turned away forlornly.

Later that evening Feldman, by-passing the pencil man, used the permission slip the Fink had given him for the cigarettes. The new Fink on duty in his cellblock gave him a pass for it, and he showed this to the guard.

"It is important?" the guard wanted to know. "I ask because you're entitled to only two round trips in a quarter. You've already had one this quarter."

"I didn't know that," said Feldman, troubled. "When is the next quarter?"

"The warden declares the quarters," the guard said. "No one knows."

What a place, Feldman thought uneasily. A guilt factory.

"It keeps it interesting," the guard said.

"Sure," Feldman said.

"There's got to be calm and there's got to be excitement," the guard said as Feldman moved off.

He passed Warden Fisher in the corridor, but the man did not return his nod.

He found the old man. His room was in the wooden, school-building structure which Feldman had first entered when he came to the penitentiary. With its armchair and wooden bed and small bedside table and single lamp, it looked like a room in a wicked hotel. There were no bars on the window. Slipper lay on top of the bed—there was a thin green linen bedspread across it—eating his candy. "You like my room, kid?" he asked.

"It's nice," Feldman said.

The old man laughed. "Sure," he said, "it's wonderful. I'm eighty-seven years old. How long you in for? You a lifer?"

"No," Feldman said, "I'm only here for one year."

The old man seemed relieved. "Well, they give shorter sentences nowadays," he said. "Except in the South. Hell, even in the South you don't hear that ninety-nine years plus seven any more. Them other three old guys—they're in the South. It's no accident those bastards are still alive. Balmy breezes, clear skies. Goddamn South. I have to be twice as strong to last out the winter. You heard any weather reports? And more humane parole laws too. Don't forget that. I'm the last. Fourth to last. A young man today don't stand a chance of breaking our records. You noticed, didn't you, you had to get a guard to unlock this chickenshit room? I demanded that lock. I don't want no favors. I'm no martyr, but I didn't do what they said I did. Hell, I don't even remember what they said I did. There are innocent men in this place, don't kid yourself."

"I know," Feldman said.

"What? You? Don't kid yourself."

"Couldn't you get out?" Feldman asked. "Your age? A parole?"

"No, I can't. No. I can't get out. I *could* of got out. Cupid was working on it. But I'm a bad man. That's what that new warden says. You should have seen *my* outfit. I wore one. But the doctor said I'd get sick, and they gave me this. This room too. And the soft job. Trusty. It's the jerk's own rule. After seventy-five every con is a trusty. Age has its privileges, he says. It's *Chinese*, he says. Shit. Don't do me no favors. Why are *you* here?"

"To do you a favor," Feldman said. He went to the side of the old man's bed. His Hershey bar had been broken into little squares. On each chocolate square he had placed a cherry Life Saver. "You shouldn't have to eat that," Feldman said.

Slipper shrugged. "You make do in this life, kid," he said.

Feldman pulled a long thin box of chocolate-covered cherries from the pocket of his suit. "Here," he said.

"You bastard," the old man said, taking the candy.

"I keep the accounts," Feldman said. "At the canteen."

"You got a swell job," the old man said glumly. "I got a swell room, and you got a swell job. We're doing terrific."

"I keep the accounts," Feldman repeated, trying to keep the excitement out of his voice. Here we go, he thought. Here we go and here we come. Out of retirement. In from lunch. Business as usual. He stared pitilessly down at his customer, the old man on the bed, struggling to sit up, his face radiant with suspicion, seeming, looking, sniffing, a victim *manqué*. He was just an old man, proud only of an oblique statistical distinction. It was enough. You make do in this life, kid, Feldman thought. But circuitously, he cautioned. "Whoever it was died sometime in 1945," Feldman said. He glanced down briefly at the note he had made on the box of candy. "February or March," he said casually. She, probably. We'll say 'she,' old-timer. And we'll say 'died.' Love goes, people forget, but we'll give you the benefit of the doubt and we'll say 'died.' She died in February or March of 1945 and you haven't had your five dollars a month from that time to this. I keep the accounts."

"It was my sister," the old man said.

"I'm sorry for your trouble," Feldman said. "So I thought: It's been almost twenty years, and in twenty years there's time to break any habit."

"Is there?" the old man said. "Is there?"

"*Any* habit. And don't give me *that*, old man. This is twenty years I'm talking about. You weren't such an old man then. You didn't have the habit of your old age then. You were just a seasoned con with years until your seventy-fifth birthday."

"I was innocent then too," the old man said petulantly.

"*You listen to me*," Feldman commanded. "So I thought: Twenty years ago it was cigarettes, an extra pint of milk, an occasional cigar maybe. The candy is as recent as your grudge, as your age and your obsession with it. Maybe it dates from your being declared an ancestor. I'll bet it does. You're never too old, old man. Sky says there's a fortune in dread, that doom's a gold mine. Doom is peanuts. Obsession—*that's* where the money is. There's a king's ransom in other people's dreams."

"What are you talking about?" the man protested. "I don't know what you're talking about."

Feldman lifted the tiny chocolate wafers with their cherry Life Savers from the bedside table. They seemed like hors d'oeuvres for a children's party. He dropped them into the wastebasket. "I've written my lawyer," he said. "There will be five dollars in your account by Thursday."

"What is this?" Ed Slipper said. "You think you can buy an old man for five dollars?"

"No," Feldman said, "you don't understand. This would be five dollars a month. *Every* month. You're going to live forever. You'll be rich."

"No sale," the old man said.

"That's not your decision."

"Whose is it you think?"

"Mine. The money accumulates no matter what you do. Every month—five dollars. All sales final."

"I'll return it. I won't touch it."

Feldman laughed at him. "Then I don't know my man," he said affably.

The old man groaned. "*I'll* touch it. I always touch everything."

"It's your sweet tooth, Ed," Feldman said.

"I liked stuff."

"All you criminals do, Ed. You all do."

"I couldn't see why I should have to be the one to go without."

"You're on the staff then, Ed. I've put you on the staff welcome aboard."

"What do I have to do?" Slipper asked dully.

"Whatever comes up," Feldman said. "You're a trusty. What's your work?"

"I'm in Administration. I clean up the offices."

"I want my file," Feldman told him.

The old man looked at him as if he were crazy. "Your *file*?"

"I'll give you four days," Feldman said.

The man stared.

"All right, say six. What's the matter, don't you think you can do it?"

The old man smiled.

"Sure you can," Feldman said excitedly. "You old dog. Let's see those fingers. Spry. Pretty spry, flexible, strong still. Spry old man. Thank your sweet tooth." He pointed to the candy. "Expensive tastes are a blessing, hey, old man? That's crap about dissipation. Indulgence is the thing to keep a guy in condition. Afford, afford and enjoy. Meaning of life, money in the bank. Live soft, live long. Hope those bastards down South never find out." Feldman clapped the old man's shoulder. "I'm a good boss. A good boss doesn't rub it in. We'll get along, _you'll_ see. That's right, eat, eat your chocolate cherries. Goodnight now. Suck, chew. Sweet dreams. Goodnight, kid."

Feldman started back toward his cell, almost happy. It sets a man up, he thought, it sets a man up to get away with something.

He didn't see Warden Fisher approaching until they were almost abreast of each other. He decided to cut him.

"Hold it there," the warden said as Feldman passed. "What are you doing in here?"

Feldman showed him the permission slip he had gotten from the opposite number. The warden took it and tore it up without looking at it.

"That's my permission slip," Feldman said. "I need that to show the guard to get my pass."

The warden stuffed the pieces of the permission slip into his pocket. "Why are you in these halls without a permission slip?" he demanded.

"I _had_ a permission slip. You tore it up. Hey," he said, "what is this?"

The warden smiled broadly and winked at Feldman.

Feldman blinked back, startled. He has to take care of me, Feldman thought. He _has_ to. He's the warden. It's civil service.

The warden turned to go. Feldman started after him and held his elbow. "There have to be rules," he insisted crazily.

The warden turned on him suddenly, shaking his elbow loose from Feldman's grasp. _"Yes,"_ he said, "there _have_ to be rules. It had grease on it! _Your permission slip had grease on it!"_

"No," Feldman said, "no. It didn't. You've got the pieces in your pocket. See if it did."

"Not this one," the warden said, tapping his pocket. "This

one is just the wages of sin. The *other* one. The one you gave the
Fink tonight. I look at the permission slips and I see the grease
on them and then I have you guys. *Grease. Grease.* You bad men
are all the same. You live in grease."

I wish I were seventy-five years old, Feldman thought.

"Privilege!" The warden almost spit the word. "I hate that
word. Angles, cut corners—there's nothing else in your geometry,
is there?"

Feldman stared at him.

"The Finks change daily. Didn't you think of that? Corner-
cutter, didn't you think of that? I change my Finks daily."

Like sheets in a hotel, Feldman thought.

"What did you have to give him? Cigarettes? Probably cigarettes. Two? Three?"

Six, Feldman thought. I've been screwed.

"You're a laughingstock, Feldman. Evil is clumsy, funny. Get
back to your cell."

The guard would stop him. He would be put on report. "I
request a permission slip, sir," Feldman said.

"You've already had two this quarter," the warden said.

"I'm entitled to a round trip."

It was hopeless. There was something wrong somewhere. He
had cheated, but someplace it had all been canceled out, and now
they were cutting corners on him.

The warden considered Feldman for a moment and then took
a pad of fresh permission slips from his pocket. He wrote one out.
"Here," he said magnanimously. "The warden declares the quarters."

Feldman hesitated. It would be charged as his first permission
slip of the new quarter. He would be forever one half a round
trip behind—maybe a whole trip. He couldn't think. You had to
be a Philadelphia lawyer to serve time here.

"Go on," the warden said, "take it." He held out the slip to
Feldman. "There are more than four quarters," he explained. "The
warden declares the quarters, and the warden declares how many
quarters there will be."

Feldman took the slip in a daze.

"Candy?" the warden asked.

"I beg your pardon?"

"Candy, wasn't it? Chocolate-covered cherries?"

Feldman feared for his life.

"No, no," the warden said, "there's no magic, I'm no magician. It's attention to detail, endless attention to detail. That's why crime doesn't pay. Crime is a detail-evasion technique. It's pushing, pulling, the physics of force. You have the blackjacks, the shivs, the machine guns and bombs. We have them too, of course, but mostly for show. We have *investigators*, the crime lab. We have the laws and the rules, don't you see? We keep the records and have the radios and the alarm systems and the TV over the teller's cage. We have the cells and the jails and the institutions. We have the speed zones and the traffic signals and the alternate-side-of-the-street parking regulations. We have the magnified maps of the city, the pins in the colored neighborhoods. We have the beats and patrols. We have the system. Virtue is system, honor is order. God is design, grace is a covenant, a contract and codicils, what's down there in writing."

"Cops," Feldman said softly, as if to himself, "cops twisting arms, hitting where it doesn't show."

"What, are you kidding me? Fire with fire. That's nothing," the warden said.

"Punishment."

"Sure, why not?" the warden asked.

"I have to be back in my cell by ten," Feldman said nervously. It was another rule. He looked at the clock on the wall. "I've only got five minutes," he said. He turned to go, but the warden stopped him. He winked again at Feldman.

"Hey," the warden called. "THIS IS THE WARDEN," he shouted.

"Yes, Warden, what is it?" a voice down the corridor called back.

"Is that a guard there?" the warden yelled.

"Yes sir. What is it?"

"THIS IS THE WARDEN. IT'S NINE-THIRTY. GOT THAT?"

"Yes, Warden," the guard answered.

"Now we can talk," the warden said, smiling at Feldman.

"The rules are for me," Feldman said. "Is that it?"

"The rules are for everybody. Somebody has to make them up," he said quietly.

Feldman wondered if it was an apology. He looked at the warden and knew it wasn't. He thought of the year ahead, of the rules. He was lonely. What he missed, he supposed, was the comfort of his old indifference when nothing counted and madness was all there was. Now there was a difference. It was because he counted; his *life* counted. It always had. How could it be? It didn't make sense.

"So," the warden said comfortably, "it was the chocolate-covered cherries." He regarded Feldman intensely, with a swift, inexplicable ardor. "Stop to figure. Corner-cutter, clown, stop to figure a minute. Who do you suppose stocks that canteen, decides the items and proportions? Who fixes the prices? Didn't you know? Didn't you even know that? It's the texture that gets these old men—the thick syrup, the fruit, smooth, bright as a prize, the dark chocolate soft as meat. I know the chemistry of old men, their sweet greeds. It's detail, Feldman, painstaking attention to dependency. I have to know who's vulnerable here."

Feldman felt his heart scratched by the homunculus.

"So," the warden said, "what was the bargain? What did you make him do for you? What's *your* dependency? Speak up. I'll order it for the canteen on the next requisition. No? It doesn't come in a box? Wait, wait, you've still got your teeth. What did you make that old man—my trusty, *my* trusty, Feldman—promise you? This is the warden speaking."

"I needed a man," Feldman said hoarsely.

The warden stared at him. "Fool," he said.

Feldman added his losses—twenty-five cents for the candy, the money for the stamp on the letter to his lawyer, the five dollars it was too late to stop, his valuable time at eight and a third cents a day, say another two cents. It was as Sky said. It was the Depression.

9

One morning when Feldman could not endure the thought of being in the prison, or of going to his job in the canteen, or of fencing one more time with the guards and trusties and pencil men, or of having to cope one more day with the elaborate rules of the community, complex and arbitrary as the laws of a boxed game, he chose to remain in his cell. It would cost him. It was bad time and did not count toward the fulfillment of his sentence. He lay on his cot, seething. The idea that it *was* costing him, that in several months he would have to relive this day, made him furious. He couldn't afford his holiday. Ah, he was a sucker, he thought angrily. The shame and guilt he felt came from his recognition of how futile it is to defy one's poverty.

He heard someone humming tunelessly and looked up. It was a prisoner on his hands and knees. The man pushed a scrub brush before him and pulled a pail. He crawled along like a chipper pilgrim, scrubbing forcefully with the brush. Feldman stared at his soapy hands and at the brush, its thick, plain wooden handle like something baked in an oven.

The man paused for a moment and raised his sweat shirt to wipe his face. "Whew," he said, "whew," and saw Feldman. He dipped into the pail. "Son-of-a-bitching brown soap," he said, holding it up for Feldman to see. "What the hell's wrong with

you guys in Seven Block? In Five, where I'm from, we get Tide,
Glo, all the latest products. Brown soap's for prison ivy, clap. It's
medicine. It ain't no more effective on floors than fucking spit. It's
your maintenance screw, Jerrold. I told Dean I wouldn't be able
to get along with him." He looked at the floor. "Who does this
floor anyway? Who's Crew in here? I hope he gets better soon,
so's I can go back to Five. Who is he?"

Feldman shook his head.

"Me neither," the man said. "The guy wouldn't last ten
minutes in Five. He'd be thrown the hell off Crew like *that*. Dean
doesn't take no shit. You know Dean?"

Feldman shook his head again.

"Chief of Crew in Five. The best maintenance screw in this
place, I don't care *who* you work for. He works us hard as hell.
When I first come with him I thought: Why, you son of a bitch,
I'd like to get you on the outside sometime. But that was just to
see if we could take it—he was testing. You play ball with Dean,
Dean'll play ball with you. That guy ain't put me on report once
in fourteen years."

"You've got it made," Feldman said.

"But let him catch me talking to you like this, he'd kick his
boot so high up my ass I'd be three days crapping it out," the
man said, chuckling.

"He kicks you?"

"Hell yes, he kicks me. Dean's *old* school. But he won't kick
a man unless that man's disappointed him."

"Fair enough," Feldman said.

"A guy has to bug out once in a while, though," the man
said. "Dean knows that."

"It's human nature," Feldman said.

"I don't care how hard a worker a man is," the man said.
"There's more to life than scrubbing floors." He stood up. "Let
me go get my rinse water." He disappeared and Feldman lay
down again on the cot.

"Our detail picks up the supplies for all the other crews."
Feldman looked around. The man was rubbing the bars of Feldman's cell with a cloth.

"It's treated," he explained, showing Feldman a dark purple-
stained cloth. "It's yellow in the tube. *Ferr-all.* It turns that color
on the cloth. It's a chemical. I seen Dean use it on his pistol barrel
once. He let me borrow it to try on the bars."

Feldman winced at the odor.

"It stands to reason. They got the same base. It works too. Look at that. He showed Feldman the bar he had been working on. The dark iron bristled with light. "I wanted you to see that because you work in the canteen."

"You know that"

"Sure. You're Feldman. I'm pleased to meet you. I'm Lurie." He pushed his hand and wrist through the bar, and Feldman shook it. "It's my forearms," Lurie said apologetically, "they're too big. I can't get them all the way through. It's from scrubbing." Feldman released Lurie's big, clean hand.

"Excuse the stink," the man said. "It's this stuff, the Ferr-all. I don't mind it, but I guess you've got to get used to it." Feldman smelled his hand. It smelled ferrous, dense, like the odor of pistol barrels. The bars had such an odor too, of pistol barrels, spears, chains, the blades of knives.

"It's too expensive for the state to buy for the inmates. They just get it for the guards. The men use it for their armor. I was the one first found out it works on bars. I told Dean, and he took it up with Requisitions. I'm glad I ran into you. If you stocked it in the canteen the men would buy it and do their cells. You see how it shined up this bar? And it wouldn't take that much effort. Three, four times a year tops, that's all it takes. It makes a difference."

"I don't have the authority," Feldman said.

"I know that," Lurie said. "But you could talk to the men. You're in a position. If enough guys wanted it, the warden would stock it." He put his face close to the bars and lowered his voice. "You know what would happen if a few guys started treating their bars? Pretty soon it would become mandatory. For the uniformity. *That's what happens*," he whispered. "They'd make it a rule." Feldman sat down on his cot. "Some of these soreheads would grouse. Sure. What the hell? Cons. But it makes a difference."

"I'll see what I can do," Feldman said.

"It's all I ask," the man said. "Here, as long as I started, let me do the rest of these. Then I'll slip the tube through and you can do the bars over the window."

Lurie rubbed the bars. They gleamed. They stank. It smelled like a munitions dump, a metal butcher shop. "I was telling you," he said as he worked, "we pick up the supplies for all the crews. In '57, during that railroad strike when the trains weren't rolling, it was a pigpen around here. There was even a comment in the paper: 'It isn't a pen, it's a pigpen.' That was printed right in the paper. Well, there weren't any supplies. After a while we were trying to keep this place clean just with water. There wasn't any antiseptic, nothing. (And your cons are dirtier than your Honest Johns anyway. It's not just the way they live, it's the way they are.) The infirmary was filling up. Well, Dean picked me and another guy, and we drove seventy-five miles into Melbourne to pick up some emergency supplies. The warden wanted Shipman's crew to go, but old Dean said, 'Fuck Shipman's crew. Does Shipman's crew take the stuff off the cars down to the depot when the stock is rolling? Does Shipman's crew wind the toilet paper after a riot?' You should've heard him. This was one screw talking about another screw in front of the warden. But Dean stands up for his boys, and the warden went along. So we got our ride in the deuce and a half all the way into Melbourne. I asked Dean if I could drive, and he let me for fourteen miles. Well, the part I wanted to tell you about is this. We picked up the stuff in a big supermarket. I pushed one cart, and Millman the other. And Dean come along behind us with the shotgun. You should've seen them housewives. We scared them whores right out of their panties. 'It's a stickup,' Millman would tell them, and one time he reached right into this whore's cart who'd got the last box of Duz and took it right away from her. I'd take the ammonia bottles and hold them up with the top unscrewed and I'd turn to Millman. 'Do you think this wine will go good with dinner, dear?' I'd ask him. 'Delicious,' Millman would say. Even Dean had to laugh. It was something." He paused, chuckling. "You ever been in one of them supermarkets?" he asked Feldman.

"Yes."

"*They* got the products, *Gleam, Oxydol, Shine, Spic and Span,* Jesus. I don't see how they keep them all straight. Dean let us take one of everything just to sample. You know what we done? We give Shipman's crew all the pansy, perfumy kind." Lurie laughed. "You should of seen. They had a time, those bastards, trying to get this place clean with all that shit the broads use on their cruddy underwear. That must have been something. I got down on the floor where Shipman's crew works, and it smelled like some fucking cunt-castle. *Jesus!*"

Feldman stretched out on his cot.

"Sick?" Lurie asked him.

"Yes."

"Go on sick call?"

"I'm taking care of it myself."

"That's it," Lurie said. "Stay away from these sawbones. A man with your history. They wouldn't be allowed to patch a tire on the outside. I haven't gone on sick call since Brunner left. He was terrific. He really knew medicine. He was a genius."

Feldman had wearied of the man's incredible loyalties, his fierce spites. This was prison, he thought. In his office there were a million ways to defend against bores. He could make a telephone call, go to lunch early, plan a trip, have an appointment, get off a letter. There were things to do with his hands. He remembered filling his water carafe, taking a cigar from a humidor that played "Smoke Gets in Your Eyes," lighting it with a lighter shaped like a cash register (you punched No Sale), adjusting the Venetian blinds, slanting the sun in a visitor's eyes. Or the toys—the absurd executive toys: the gold Yo-Yo's on silken strings, the pointless machines with visible moving parts, the kaleidoscopic paperweights, the office golf (he only played golf in the office), the tiny TV set on which he caught the noon news. There were conferences, committee work (he was a downtown merchant, public-spirited, the inventor of the Free Friday Bus Ride and the Shopper's Nursery Service in the public park). And there was his basement. But here he could not even pull down a shade or open the window. He lived in a cage, bored as a beast.

Lurie was still talking. Feldman had a thought, a wish so clear and incisive it could almost have been an idea. He wanted Lurie to die. He wished desperately that this bore might be suddenly seized with something angry and irrevocable, that he would disintegrate! But he had thick forearms and hadn't gone on sick call since Brunner. A collapse was unlikely, but Feldman knew that if he had a gun and the opportunity to get away with it, he would kill Lurie. It didn't surprise him. It was the system which shaped these thoughts. It did not provide for the splendid half and quarter measures of freedom—executive toys and committees and the heft of a paperweight in the palm of your hand and the rest.

Suddenly Feldman stood up and dropped his trousers and went to the toilet between the two cots. He squatted on it and strained and stared at Lurie. The man continued to rub the bars. Feldman might have been doing nothing more private or offensive than biting his nails. I don't know, he thought, this would have cleared them out back at the office. He sat hopelessly, beginning, despite himself, to nod as Lurie talked.

"Cancer," Lurie was saying, "the big one. That's what they

finally diagnosed. After all that time. So he's finally lying there—
my cellmate—in the infirmary. They ain't doing nothing to clean
it out of him. Too late, they told him. What do these guys care?
You know something? This is a guy that always worried about
himself. He kept up. He used to drive me nuts with his grousing.
You know those seven danger signals they're always talking
about? My friend had a match cover that listed them, and he had
four out of the seven. Four out of the seven danger signals, when
only one's enough. He went to the infirmary each time he'd get
a new danger signal, but they didn't know it was cancer until his
third danger signal. That's the kind of doctor they got over there
in that infirmary. He's laying there now. Last week a guy on infirmary crew fucked up and got thrown in solitary, and Dean
fixed it so I could clean my friend's room. It tore me up. He was
a strong guy, my friend. He's nothing now. He told me he's up
to six of the seven danger signals. He laughed about it."

Feldman flushed the toilet.

"Listen," Lurie said, "if you're sick you probably don't feel
like getting the bars over your window. You can do it later, or—
I'll tell you what—I'll come back sometime when your cell is open
and do it for you myself."

Suddenly, irrationally, Feldman was moved. "Thank you," he
said. He wanted to cry. I'm crazy, he thought. They've driven me
crazy.

"No, it's nothing," Lurie said. "You can see yourself what a
difference it makes."

"It's very nice," Feldman said. "I've got the shiniest bars in
my cellblock."

"It makes a difference."

"It certainly does."

"I enjoyed talking to you," Lurie said.

"I enjoyed talking to *you*."

"It's a terrible thing to say, but it makes the day go faster
when I run into a sick con."

Feldman nodded.

"This ain't fun," Lurie said.

"No," Feldman said.

"Scrubbing's no deal."

"No," Feldman said, "I guess not."

"Even when you got a crew chief like Dean."

The man folded his rag and pushed it up the sleeve of his
sweat suit, where it lay on the thick ridge of muscle along his big

forearms like the handkerchief of a gentlewoman. "Everybody's got troubles," he said.

Feldman decided to eat his lunch with the men.

Tables with large black numbers painted on their tops were assigned them, and twice each month everyone was given a new number corresponding to one of the tables. They had to carry this number with them and show it to the dining-hall official if he asked to see it. The men had their special friends, of course, and sometimes moved beside them regardless of their assigned numbers. It was a major offense if they could not justify their seating, but they often took the risk. The dining-hall official moved arbitrarily among the tables, spot-checking.

Feldman, studying the men as they took their trays and moved silently to seats, could tell, just as surely as the dining-hall official, from the gestures and nudges and shufflings, which men were falsifying their assignments. It was queer how men properly assigned to a place noiselessly submitted to those who would force them in turn to seek false positions. To break silence if one was being pushed away from one's proper place was permitted, of course, but such an action was considered a betrayal by the men and was severely punished by them. And since to scuffle openly in the dining hall was an even more serious offense than either sitting at an unassigned table or breaking silence, the displaced and expelled stalked nervously under the eyes of the official toward some hopefully unassigned space. (There were several such spaces: "free spaces" deliberately kept open by the warden; the unoccupied seats of the sick, of men on special-duty rosters, of men brooding in their cells.) Usually, so suspicious did they look, an official did not spot-check in vain, although the man caught was more frequently the moved than the mover. The official, silent himself, would tap a man on the left shoulder, and *all* the men at the table, so no con at the right table could slip his number to an interloper, had to place face up in a vacant corner of their trays the laminated plastic numbers they were forced to carry.

Occasionally there was an attempt to divert an official. Taking circuitous routes among the tables, prisoners might deliberately try to seem suspicious so as to make a fool of a guard, or to serve some friend actually counterfeiting a table assignment as a decoy. The men did not seem to understand that they were serving the warden's ends and not their own when they played these jokes, by bringing astute and astuter officials into the dining hall. The beauty of the warden's system did not escape Feldman, however. Like many other rules in the prison it seemed unbeatable, and provided the warden with still another means of testing the convicts. ("It accomplishes several things," the warden later told Feldman. "For one, it exposes the queers. It gives me an insight into who might be planning an escape. It speeds up meals. It saves the state money. The men grab their trays and move on to their seats rapidly so as not to be shouldered out of the way. They take less food on their trays.") They might have tried to *trade numbers*, Feldman thought, but they were a disorganized bunch, and this never seemed to occur to them. They relied instead on risk and chance. Yet Feldman was aware of the astonishing fact that it was love—the conspirators, the escape-planners, could always meet in holes and corners; the rules, if they had to contend only with the plotters, would have forced them to plot elsewhere—which made the system work, that there would always be those who would take the risks.

Reckless, reckless people, he thought contemptuously as a new man, obviously an intruder, moved into place beside him. It was a stunning fact, he thought, that whoever the man's friend was, he would not even be able to talk to him. Watching the man's eyes, Feldman spotted the friend. The new man looked at him with something like love, and the friend smiled briefly and looked down at his tray shyly.

The others at the table were as conscious as Feldman of the friendship. They smiled openly, fondly, as at lovers who have overcome difficulties and earned a sympathy which costs no one anything. Indeed, Feldman himself felt a fillip of kindredness and had a sense of being at table at a resort, or aboard ship.

So they sat, each man conscious of the number that gave him the right to be there, but each with a little viciousness in reserve, his self-righteousness underwritten by the fact that he could produce his number on demand. However, the viciousness may have been softened by the jeopardy of the intruder and regard for his lover's boldness, they would, if the need arose, have dissolved in a moment the accidental community which that boldness had made manifest, and brought guiltlessly and quickly to bear their detachment, even the man who had inspired the risk, the surprised friend like the obligationless guest of honor at a party.

Feldman was aware that the enforced silence made the companionship of the two friends somehow deeper, more meaningful.

They all felt it. They felt, too, all the significance of the pair's proximity and were charged with a kind of sympathetic giddiness, a sense of the glowingly unstated, of the imminent. It was just as if someone they did not hear stood behind their backs, or as if, in the dark, they could sense the nearness of walls, the presence of furniture.

Then something happened that had never happened.

"The Talking Lamp is lit," a voice said suddenly over the loud-speaker, startling them. It was Warden Fisher.

"How did you know where I was? I haven't seen you since the new assignments," the friend said.

"I was behind you in the line last night, Joseph. Are you angry?"

"Of course I'm not angry," Joseph said. "But you took a risk. You could have gotten us both into trouble."

"I didn't think about that, Joseph," the man said gloomily. Then he brightened. "But isn't it wonderful?" he asked, reaching across the table. "We can talk. It's a miracle."

"No. You mustn't touch me, Bob."

Feldman wondered how the other men took this. He looked around the table, but no one seemed interested in the pair any longer. They were more concerned with the warden's announcement, clearly puzzled by the opportunity to talk in the dining hall. They contained themselves, halting in their silences, like inexperienced people asked to give their opinions into a microphone. Then, gradually, they found things to say.

A man leaned toward Feldman and spoke in a low voice. "I thought it was *you* he come to see, Feldman. It surprised me."

"No, of course not. I don't know him."

The man laughed, and Feldman was conscious suddenly of hips touching his on the crowded bench, conscious of shoulders brushing his own, conscious of hands lifting spoons, conscious of men's tongues. Under the table someone stroked his thigh.

"Stop it."

"Sure," a man said, winking. "You're not my type."

"Feldman isn't anyone's type," Joseph said.

Feldman couldn't eat with them. (I'll starve, he thought, thinking of the dozens of meals he had still to eat with these men.) Undeclared, in the silence, their friendship—their love—had a certain dignity, and even the imagined possibility of their acts together had a built-in innocence: the allowance one made for life under difficulties, life against odds. Talking, they seemed grotesque. What lay behind it all was more of the same, importunateness, rough will. Probably Joseph did not even care for Bob.

"How long has it been, old-timer," one man asked a trusty Feldman had seen in his own cellblock, "since the Talking Lamp's been lit?"

"Not in my time," the old man said. He turned to the man on Feldman's right. "You ever know it to happen, Bob?"

"Once," Bob said. "When Fisher had been here a year," he said. "Isn't that right, Joseph?"

"It was on the first anniversary of Fisher's system," Joseph said.

Feldman, frightened, perceived something complex and astonishing: Bob and Joseph had been softened. They confronted him, he realized, not as men but as *changed* men. Feldman saw that very plainly. They might have been old acquaintances with whom he had lost contact for twenty years and suddenly saw again in their acquired differences as in a costume. These softened men had once been dangrous. The length of their terms here proved the violence of their crimes. It meant that if love was what lay behind the efficiency of the warden's vicious system and made that system work, then it was viciousness that ultimately made love work. Character tumbled, and even *these* men could not finally hang on to themselves. They'd had the tenaciousness of murderers, of men who took guns in their hands and pulled triggers. But even these—they were talking quietly now, courting sedately—hard cases had proved malleable in the end. Appetite died last; *nobody* lost his sweet tooth. It was the most nearly immortal attribute of men. As a businessman, Feldman was impressed by the warden's techniques (What an operation this is, he thought), but as a man he was terrified. Oh, men's troubles, he thought; that warden, he'll get me too.

That evening he asked Bisch about his life. For all his apparent formidableness, his cellmate was a gentle man (After all, Feldman thought, he's a tailor, he makes men's clothes), and he began to talk about his life as if he had only been waiting to be asked. Telling Feldman of his troubles, the gloomy man seemed to brighten. Feldman remembered the expression. He had seen it before, in his basement when people had come to him for his favors. He had not wanted their stories—only their demands, the swooped desperation of their terrible solutions. But nothing could keep them from talking. They became debaters, makers of speeches, articulating grievances as if they had been statements of policy, listing troubles like logicians posting reasons. On their faces too he had seen the same queer gaiety, the high hilarity of their justifications. It was not gaiety, of course, or even nervousness, but a kind of awe, as if, hearing what they said themselves, they were not so much touched by their griefs as impressed by them. They smiled as they spoke. It was the smile anterior to sin. Priests never saw that smile, policemen didn't. All confessions were bawled, whined, whispered from trance. Trouble only sounded bold, choppy with detail like the breathless report of a messenger from a burning city.

"She had this infection," Bisch said. "In her face. She'd get a fever. A hundred. A hundred one. It would swell. My wife's beautiful face. The gums drained. In her sleep. One night she almost choked on it. It stank. I made her pillows in my shop. She slept sitting up. She wouldn't let me sleep with her. She was ashamed of the way she smelled. I would wipe her lips in her sleep with a tissue. I flushed it down the toilet. I wanted her to think she was getting better. But I couldn't wipe the taste out of her mouth.

"The doctor said if was sinus. That's what they treated her for. But it wasn't sinus. They gave her tests. All the tests. She was always in pain. She said it was like having cuts inside her mouth. Then they said she had to have all her teeth out. What was she—twenty-eight? She didn't want to. They weren't even sure, she said. It changed the face. She had a very beautiful face. The muscles collapse. Something happens to the jaw, the lips. The expression is different. It looks like spite.

"But I made her do it, and it was terrible for her. She was a beautiful woman.

"But she was right. It didn't make any difference. She still had the fever after they pulled the teeth. They said it would go down when the gums stopped draining, but the gums didn't stop draining. It was as if there was a fire inside her somewhere and they couldn't find it. They couldn't do anything.

"Her jaw was too small. The teeth they made her didn't fit. I got her others. She couldn't wear them. She said what difference did it make. I tried to kiss her, but she wouldn't let me. We didn't sleep together any more. One night I went to wipe her lips and I bent down to kiss her while she slept. It was soft—her mouth. I never felt anything like that before. It was as if there was just this soft skin over her and she was empty inside. I threw up. It was awful. I still taste my wife's mouth.

"She couldn't forgive me. She was always crying. I made her

beautiful dresses. I always made her beautiful dresses, but these were even more beautiful. She wouldn't wear them. She thought I was laughing at her. Laughing at her—*Jesus!*"

He killed her, Feldman thought. The poison flowed from the high ground of her fever and he couldn't stand it and he killed her. He looked away from Bisch's shining eyes. Why, he's like a soldier, he thought. He serves his trouble. Feldman shuddered and nodded helplessly.

Bisch sighed, observing him.

Ghost stories, Feldman thought.

He went to the television room, where he saw a documentary on migrant workers and their families and a situation comedy about a little boy with divorced parents who goes to visit his father or mother on alternate weeks in the series. Feldman had seen the program before. The kid, obsessed, conspired to bring his mother and father together again, and tonight he shammed infantile paralysis. The news program reported white reprisals in Philadelphia for the attack of two fifteen-year-old Negroes on a nun. It told of cold war and plane crash and storm. Today the President, after a flying trip covering eight states, had declared seven new disaster areas. The governors in the Midwest had asked for only five. *He* knows, Feldman thought. He returned to his cell. Bisch, asleep, was groaning in a dream. Feldman wondered if he should wake him, wipe his lips.

Until now Feldman had tried to ignore his fellow convicts. He feared them, of course. They were hostile men and seemed to know more about him than he wished. The famous grapevine, he thought, and imagined a sort of demonic pony express. It's all that talking out of the side of the mouth (he fancied a great hoarse chain of whispered intimacies). What was astonishing was their accuracy. Because they were accustomed to conspiracy's low tones nothing was lost, and because they had no imagination nothing was distorted. So he kept out of their way.

Now, however, he was interested. Appalled by their horror stories, he wondered about them. (Wondering about them, he wondered about himself. *Is this character?* he thought.) He had none of their desire to gossip. Yet he discovered a quality in himself that he had been unaware of before. Surprised at their unhappiness—*how* unhappy? *why* unhappy? weren't *all* men happy?—he wished now to know about other men, to ask them questions.

He thought it would be difficult, but it was easy. People were willing, even eager, to talk. There was in them, he supposed, a respect for his wealth, his differences from them. Then they were losers, and losers were accustomed to talking about themselves. They spilled the beans and exposed the linen to guidance counselors, juvenile parole officers, social workers, free psychologists, free psychiatrists, sob-sister reporters, and at last to their court-appointed lawyers. They would mourn to anyone who might help them, to anyone not in trouble who might get them out of trouble. Open not to advice but to miracle, they rattled away in any ear.

So he made it his business to find out about them. With their permission he peeked into their moneyless wallets, stared fascinated through the yellowing plastic windows at wives and fathers and sweethearts and mothers and sisters and sons and daughters, the human background of even the loneliest men. (Staring, he thought: Everyone has been photographed, everyone in the world; everyone, smiling, posing, has made the small, poor holiday before a camera, thinking: Catch me, hold me, keep me.) How thin they all were. Even in pictures, which normally added pounds, these people seemed light, foreign and a little like Indians. They looked to have frailty's toughness and wiry strength, but they would not last, he knew. The children had the sharp vision of the poor, their clever legs. They could see long distances down alleys and run quickly through city streets, making fools of their pursuers, but they would not last either. What attracted Feldman most were the women—thin, hard-armed, hard-breasted, and with babushkas on their heads. Yesterday's B-girls and waitresses and bench workers and bruised daughters, foulmouthed, pitiful and without pity, their suspicion misplaced and their trust too. Kid-slappers, Feldman thought, smokers in bed, drinkers in taverns while the apartment is burning, runners amok. Whew, whew, he thought, tricky in bed, tricky, tricky, too much for me— *I* wouldn't last—clawers of ass and pullers of hair and suckers of cock.

"What is your wife doing, now that you're in jail?" Feldman, looking up from the picture, asked Coney.

"Tricks," Coney said gloomily.

"Ah, a magician." (I'll *bet*, he thought, seeing the girl's grim mouth and long nails. He suspected palmed hatpins, bold kicks to the groin, all the rough whore's holds. He thought of Lilly, who had no trade and knew no tricks and couldn't take a punch. He thought of Lilly's dull loneliness.)

"How does your family make out?" he asked Maze, in the cell across from his.

"On relief," Maze said. "On A.D.C. On Community Chest."

"I'm a very big taxpayer in this state," Feldman said thoughtfully.

He saw a picture of a big boy in one of those double strollers for twins.

"My kid is sick," Butt said, "he needs an operation on his back. He can't move his legs, and the nurse at the clinic says he has to get fresh air so he'll be strong enough if we ever get the money for his operation. We live on the third floor, and my wife has to carry him up the stairs. She ain't strong and he weighs a hundred pounds and we have to move into a building which has an elevator if he's ever to get enough fresh air and sunshine. We ain't got the rent for that kind of building. They're asking a hundred dollars. She's moved his bed next to the window, but the night air gives him a sore throat."

"We need a wagon," Clock said. "It'll be spring and the phone books come out, and my wife can deliver them but we don't have a wagon. She used to get five cents a book, but in the last election the townships all merged and the book is much thicker. They'd give her a dime if she just had a wagon. The wagon she used was stolen last year, but it wasn't no good for it was too small. She needs a new big one—an American Cart. They're twenty-eight bucks, and she ain't got the dough. If she just had the wagon she was promised the job."

"I've—" Feldman said.

"Flo doesn't drive," McAlperin said. "She never learned how and the car's up on blocks. There's no one to teach her, and lessons are high. She ain't got the nerve, to tell you the truth. Her first husband died—he was creamed by a truck. But *if* she could drive she could get a good job. Selling cosmetics, or maybe those books. You make a commission, they pay very well. They're crying for help, and Flo would be good. People all like her, she knows how to talk. Presentable too, attractive and neat. Now she's a waitress, but that's not for her. If she just learned to drive she'd be better off. The car could come down. It's not good for a car to be idle like that. I don't like the idea of her being out late, waiting on tables and talking to men. You know how men are, what they want from a girl. If she'd just learn to drive she could sell door to door, talking with housewives and doing some good. Getting those books into their homes. If she'd just learn to drive."

"I've got—" Feldman said.

"It's like this," Munce said, "my wife saw this ad on the side of a bus. For finishing high school on home-study plan. A place in Chicago, and in her spare time she does all the lessons; they come through the mail. But she can't buy the books that they want her to read—biology, English, big books and dear. What makes it so bad is she can't get a card, or she'd go to the library and take them all out. But I've got a record, and that nixes the deal. Of course she could read them right there at the desk; they'd let her do that, but she'd have to stand up. She might use her sister's, but that girl's a bitch. They ain't spoke for years, and my wife is too proud. If they only made up she could borrow the card and take out the books and study at home and get a diploma and then a good job."

"I've got—" Feldman said.

"My daughter's fifteen," Case said, "and don't know I'm here. We told her a lie to save her the shame. She just had turned six when they took me to jail. I made an arrangement with an old friend of mine, a guy off in Europe—Fred Bolton's his name. Fred was a pal that I knew from the block. Smart as a whip, we knew he'd go far. A scholar, you know, but a regular guy. He won all the prizes and went off to Yale, where they paid his tuition and gave him free board. He got his degree and then left the States. He writes to my daughter and signs himself me. For years Fred has done this—a letter a month and often a gift. Once perfume from Paris and leather from Spain. She thinks we're divorced, but she's proud of her dad. But Fred has sclerosis and now he may die. There's one chance in a million—you see, they're not sure. It might just be a nerve. Fred always was jumpy, even in school. So they've taken a test and we're waiting to hear. They've sent it to Brocher, a big man in the field. But Brocher's in Russia, he defected last year. And Fred writes these books that the Communists hate. They might *want* him to die—then what will I do? Who'll write my daughter? Who'll save her the shame? How can we tell her I'm supposed to be dead? A girl needs a father—she's only fifteen, and though she don't see me it keeps up her heart. If only they'll let Brocher look at the tests—if only they'll tell him, okay, go ahead. Then if only the tests turn out to be good and they locate the nerve that's bothering Fred, they can probably treat it, and in time he'll get well—then maybe in time he can write her again."

"I've got—" Feldman said.

"And send her those gifts, those prizes she loves—"

"I've got—" Feldman said, "the picture."

"They say you listen," a convict said to Feldman one evening, moving beside him.

Feldman had another image of the grapevine, pendent with talk, with talk about talk. "I've heard a few," he said noncommittally, not looking up.

"I want to tell," the convict said.

They were just outside the shower stalls, sitting on the benches that ran along the walls of what might have been a locker room if this had not been a penitentiary. Feldman was undressing. The room was damp, the stone floors clammy, mucoid. He remembered his own carpeted bathroom, the cut-glass decanters with their bright sour-balls of bubble bath, and he felt like crying. (It was the toilet he missed most. He thought of his golden hamper. It was really beautiful, a piece of furniture practically. He thought of it stuffed with white shirts hardly soiled—he loved the generous reckless act of throwing shirts into the dirty clothes. The memory of his shower almost brought tears to his eyes. There were long rubber treads built right into the smooth tile floor of the shower stall. One wall was clear glass, much sexier than the milky glass of your ordinary shower. There were recesses along another wall for shampoos, soaps, rinses, and there were roll-out men's and ladies' razors on nylon cords that worked on the principle of a window shade. There were marvelous flexible tubes that pulled out of the wall, and cunning, splendid brushes and a nozzle complicated and delicate as something in a Roman fountain. The dancing waters, Feldman thought.)

"I'm Hover."

"Pipe racks," Feldman said, thinking aloud of the prison's crude plumbing. "Drainpipes with rain water trickling out," he said.

"I want to tell," Hover said.

"Listen," Feldman said, looking up at a naked man. "I don't want to hear about it." He had not recognized Hover's name. Now he placed him. The man had a legendary stupidity; he was someone the others tormented without mercy. Feldman had never been alone with him before.

Hover was an illiterate, but more than that he *knew* nothing, understood nothing. He was almost without memory. In the dining hall it was only with difficulty that he was able to match the number he was given with the one on his table. Several times Feldman had seen him, confused by the oversize numbers painted on the tables, hand his number to a prisoner to read it for him. Hover seemed to know the prisoner might lead him astray, and his expression at these surrenders was one of hope and terror. Feldman had heard that the man could not even recognize his own cell and had to be pushed into it each night. His cellmate beat him because he could not remember to flush the toilet. He could do no work, of course, and he usually wandered aimlessly through the corridors, lost, uncomprehending, unable to distinguish between the prisoners and the guards. He probably did not even know that he was in a prison, let alone why. (He used to walk into grocery stores when he was hungry and take fruit from the bins and eat it on the spot, the juice of oranges and lemons dripping down his hairless chest. Or he would bite into breads, and after someone had shown him what was inside an egg, crush it in his mouth. He could not button a shirt, but someone had taught him to put on a jacket, and someone else had gotten him a pair of flyless elastic pants. It was these clothes he wore in the prison.) Incredibly, he had not been placed into an institution for the insane. Feldman was sure the warden had asked for him, though he did not understand the strategics of it yet.

Hover moved closer to Feldman on the bench. He reached out and touched Feldman's thigh.

"You mustn't do that," Feldman said, standing up.

"I want to tell," Hover said indistinctly.

Ignoring him, Feldman moved into the shower room, and Hover followed. He stopped just inside and stared while Feldman adjusted the taps of a shower and moved under it. Hover was saying something, but he could not make it out in the big, resonant room. He could see that Hover was excited; the man pointed to the shower above his head and frowned.

"You have to turn it on," Feldman said. "Turn it on. Turn on the water," he shouted. "Wait. Here, I'll do it for you." He walked over to Hover, but the man jumped back clumsily, raising his fists in an obscure gesture of anger and fear.

"Hot," he shouted, "hot." He started to bring down his fists on Feldman's shoulders, but Feldman pushed him away. He had no coordination, and his reactions were so slow that one might have done almost anything to him.

Hover stumbled awkwardly backwards. "What's wrong with you?" Feldman demanded. "Did you think I was going to scald you? Is that what the others do to you?"

"Hot," Hover whined. "Hot. Hot."

"It's not hot," Feldman said, turning on the water. "Here. Feel it yourself. Put your hand out."

"Hot," he said, shaking his head.

"No," Feldman said. "Tepid. Tepid." He stuck his hand beneath the forceless spray.

"Hot," Hover said again.

"All right," Feldman said, "so it's hot. Leave me alone then."

He moved back under his own shower and began to soap himself. Hover still stood in the doorway, watching him. "Go on," Feldman said. "Get away from me, you dummy." He was made uneasy by the man; it was like being observed by a brute, Feldman turned his back, but it was no better; his neck and spine began to prickle. (Once his son had brought a cat home, and Feldman had not been able to eat while the animal was in the house.) He turned back to face Hover. "Go on," he said, "go away from me." He was beginning to panic. He cupped his hands and threw water at Hover. The man screamed. (At the fairgrounds, as a boy, he had gone to a cattle show. One brute, on its straw, in its own piss and dung, had bellowed meaninglessly. Thick yellow saliva hung in drooled strings from its mouth. He had wanted to smash its face with a club.) Feldman threw more water; Hover screamed again, and Feldman went for him.

"Why are you screaming?" he shouted. *"Why are you screaming?"* Why are you afraid of the water? I'm going to put you under it, you son of a bitch, and *show* you."

Hover yelled and tried to move away, but backed into a corner. His abjectness enraged Feldman, and he wrapped his arms around the man and pulled at him violently. In his confusion and terror Hover could not distinguish between resistance and its opposite; he fell heavily against Feldman, seeming deliberately to rush him. The two fled backwards over the slippery floor, and Feldman bruised his back against the tap. In his pain he punched Hover's face as hard as he could. The man brought his hands slowly to his head, and Feldman smashed at his belly. This defenselessness enraged Feldman even more and he struck out at will, clipping Hover's ears and chest and neck, hitting him with great, round swinging blows.

"*Stupid*," Feldman screamed. "*You thing!*"

Hover slipped to the floor and buried his head in his arms. Feldman, above him, desired to kick him in the groin, to smash his useless head. Oh my God, he thought suddenly, terrified, *that's the strategics!*

He leaned against the dun-colored tiles, panting. I'm sorry, he thought. I'm so sorry. He looked again at Hover, collapsed on the floor, and knew he must apologize, must try to find some language outside of language that would make Hover understand. He squatted down beside the man, his long scrotum brushing the back of Hover's outstretched hand as he grasped his shoulders gently. He had fallen beneath the shower and sat sprawled and somnolent in the warm water.

"Hover," Feldman said quietly, "Hover."

But Hover had already forgotten the blows, and he looked up at Feldman with a question he could never ask.

Feldman—thinking trouble was something outside, like a sudden freeze or extended drought; or something mechanical, like fouled ropes or defective brakes; or something inside and mechanical, like a broken tooth or cholesterol deposits—met the bad man Herbert Mix.

Mix winked. Feldman tried to brush past him.

"It takes one to know one," Mix said.

"Excuse me," Feldman said, "I'm on Warden's Business." It was the phrase for official errands. On Warden's Business a convict could go anywhere, even places forbidden to trusties, and no one was to interfere with him. Feldman carried a small warden's flag the size of a pocket handkerchief, folded and hidden inside his suit coat. Theoretically, he could approach a guard, show him the flag and ask to be conducted outside the walls. It was, however, the most serious offense in the prison, punishable by irrevocable loss of parole, for a convict on Warden's Business to deflect that business to his own ends, and a few men, accused of using the flag to effect an escape, had actually been killed on these errands. (The death penalty in the state had not been imposed for eight years, but the men feared assassination by the guards. It had happened that men who had induced enmities in a guard had sometimes been shot and then had a warden's flag planted on their persons. It was necessary for the guard to produce supporting testimony that the convict had used Warden's Business to attempt an escape, but everyone knew the guards were thick as thieves. Indeed, it was not impossible to get another convict to back up the guard's story, for just as there were prisoner mentalities among the guards, there were guard mentalities among the prisoners.)

Because there was always a threat to the life of anyone on Warden's Business—the men speculated that at all times there was always some guard plotting against the life of some prisoner; several prisoners actually claimed to have been approached by guards and obliquely invited to join with them in vendettas against their fellow convicts—only two kinds of men were ever sent on these errands: men who were generally liked by the guards, and men whom the warden felt he could afford to lose— the bad men themselves. Complexities of timing and circumstances, and the difficulties implicit in the conspiratorial nature of an assassination, reduced the chance of death to little more than an outside possibility, as subject to thin contingency as a trip at night, say, on an unfamiliar highway in an automobile that requires some slight mechanical adjustment. Still, the possibility was there, and it troubled Feldman.

"I'll walk with you," Mix said. He showed Feldman a pass and winked again. It was probably a phony. (Feldman himself had been careful to obtain a pass to show to the guards in case he was stopped. Only one pass remained to him now for the new quarter, but he was proud of his caution. Most men would simply have flashed their warden's flag in a guard's face.) Feldman didn't answer Mix, and quickened his pace, sorry now he had told the man he was on Warden's Business. (Manfred Sky had said it was a good idea to let people know if they started to interfere with you.) "I don't blame you," Mix said. "It's like a time bomb ticking away in there. Where you carrying it?"

"In my pocket," Feldman said. "Please."

"Why don't you take it out and blow your nose in it? That's what I'd do."

"Please," Feldman said, "I want to get this over with as quickly as possible."

"You're not *very* nervous, are you?" They had come into the exercise yard. "Hey, fellas," Mix called, "Feldman here is on Warden's Business."

A few of the men laughed. One, off by himself, approached on hearing Feldman's name. "I'm up for parole," he said, "in two or three months. I'm up for parole and ain't learned a trade. They made me a trusty as soon as I came. A trusty's no *good*, I told them right then. The work's not connected with anything real, it doesn't prepare me for outside the walls. Then learn to be honest, they told me, instead. I begged to do printing, but one lung is weak—the dyes and the filings no good for my health. I asked at the foundry, they turned me away. What the hell kind of deal is that for a man?"

"Not now," Feldman said.

"So now I'm all honest but don't know a trade, and up for parole in two or three—"

"Please," Feldman said, "*not now.*"

Mix shoved the man away. "Warden's Business," he said. They came up to a guard. "Feldman is on Warden's Business, Officer," Mix said. He winked at the guard. "If you want to kill him, I'm your witness."

"Are you on Warden's Business, Feldman?" the guard asked.

"Yes sir," Feldman said. He decided not to show the guard his warden's flag until he was asked. He knew he wouldn't be shot if he didn't show it. The guard didn't ask to see the flag, and they passed through a door leading from the exercise yard back into the main building.

"You don't like me shooting off my big mouth, do you?" Mix said. "You don't even like me walking along with you like this, right?"

Feldman said nothing.

There was a guard at the end of the corridor by a barred gate leading to the administrative offices.

"I asked you a question," Mix said.

"All right," Feldman said, "I'm a little nervous."

"Stop here a minute," Mix said.

Feldman looked up ahead at the guard and thought he recognized him. He stopped.

"Give me something," Mix said. "Make a deal."

Feldman stared at him.

"Give way, give way," Mix said in a subdued voice. He was a pale man, and as he spoke he troubled to smile. He would trouble to smile, Feldman suspected, even at Hover. "You guys who don't give way," he said, "who hold on tight. Boy, every son of a bitch I ever met holds on tight. What am I supposed to do, jump overboard? Fuck that noise. You know what I'm here for? You know why I'm in this maximum-security rathole with the kooks and the killers and the kid-buggers and all the rest of you big time assholes? I'm a hat, coat and umbrella man. I work restaurants and theaters. Let me tell you, intermission is my busy season, ha ha. I steal from parked cars. Shit, everybody's got an out. The restaurants have little signs, the garages do: 'Not Responsible,' blah blah. Only I'm responsible. Outless as the stinking dead. Who ever saw Mix's sign? 'Herb Mix Isn't Responsible for Stealing Your Lousy Umbrella, Lady. Watch Your Frigging Hat, Sir. Do Not Blame Herb Mix.' Well, I figure it different. I'm as entitled as any man born. You own a department store; I don't. Who's responsible for *that* little oversight? Why ain't I rich, President, King? Why ain't there broads lined up to kiss me? Where's mine? Where does it say *I* have to be unhappy? Come on, come on, I've even got an ulcer. Everything I eat turns to poison."

"What do you want?" Feldman asked.

"I don't fix prices," Mix said. "This is a new line with me. You don't think the crappy fence would ask me what *I* thought a thing was worth."

Feldman tried to remember if he and the guard had had any dealings. In the early days he had made certain mistakes, but surely the guards took into account a man's newness.

"From the look on your face," Mix said, "I'd say you know that feller. He's got a quick temper. Look at that fucking red hair under his cap. That old Irishman sure hates the Jews."

"All right," Feldman said, "say what you want or leave me alone."

"I'm a bad man," Mix said. Feldman waited for him to go on. It was true, he thought; he could not make demands. He could only sneer his griefs and object and schnorr around for reasons. "I'm a bad man," Mix said again, "and a heavy smoker, and I like my candy and my stick of gum, and most of the guys around here have radios and I don't. Where's *my* five bucks a month from the outside that the rest of you get? Is it my fault my old man's a prick and pretends I ain't alive? I've got expenses too, you know. And because I'm a bad man and still paying for this jerk suit"— he pointed to his costume, a satire on the new blends, which, dimly phosphorescent, shone on his pale wrists like fishskin— "I'm docked a buck a month in canteen chits."

"I'm a bad man too," Feldman said. "They dock me."

"Fifty cents a month," Mix said, ignoring him. "I could have asked for a buck."

"It's ridiculous for me to buy you off at all. Why should that guard kill me?"

"He's seen your record," Mix said. "He knows all about you."

That was true, Feldman thought. He was wondering if he should offer Mix a quarter.

"Give me a dime," Mix pleaded. "For two months."

"You haven't sense, Mix," Feldman said. He turned away from him.

"I'll tell," Mix said. "I swear it."

"I know that," Feldman said quietly. He cupped his hands over his mouth. "Guard," he called suddenly. "Guard. *Guard.*"

"What's that racket?" the guard yelled.

"Hey, what is this?" Mix said.

"I'm on Warden's Business," Feldman shouted. "I'm Feldman the bad man and I'm on Warden's Business." He took out the warden's flag and waved it furiously. "Feldman the bad man coming through here on Warden's Business," he called. "Feldman the bad man on his way to Records and Forms in the supply wing, to pick up requisitions for the canteen. No more requisitions in the canteen," he yelled. Some civilians and other prison officials from the administrative offices stared at him from beyond the barred gate. Feldman continued to wave his flag and shout. "Feldman the bad man on Warden's Business for Lieutenant Crease. Feldman the bad man on Get the Requisitions from Records and Forms in the Supply Wing Business. Coming through."

"Cut out that screaming," the guard roared.

Feldman marched toward him, waving his flag.

"All right, all right, I see it. Go on the hell through." He unlocked the gate, and Feldman marched through. He looked back over his shoulder and winked at Mix, but the troubled man had turned away.

In trouble. These were the words of Feldman's dream. He awoke. He sat up. *In trouble.* As *in atmosphere.* Or *in China.* It was an ambience, a dimension. Sure, he thought, the turd dimension. Something in nature. Something inside and mechanical. Something inside and not mechanical at all. Doom, he thought, the house struck by lightning, the wooden leg in flames, the poisoned heart.

Then why, he thought, why am I smiling?

He had been awakened by a noise. Was someone escaping? Was a cell open? Had a prisoner thrust his hands through the bars to catch a guard's throat? Would he be made to run with them? He listened.

There was only the breathing in all the cells. It was a sustained, continuous sigh, the men's breath going and coming like hissed, sibilant wind. Somewhere down the cellblock he heard a toilet flush. Someone wrenched up phlegm from a sour throat. In their sleep men turned uncomfortably on their narrow cots. Rolling, they groaned. He heard farts, coughs, the clipped, telescoped declarations of dreamed speech. No one was escaping. All cells were locked. They were cornered, all of them. No one could get in.

He lay back down again and tried to sleep. How long had he been there? Two months, three? Would they really let him out in only a year? They had to. That was the law.

"Who's up?" a voice asked suddenly, timidly. "Is someone up?"

The words were clear; they had not sounded like a sleeper's mutterings.

"Is there someone awake in here?" It sounded as if the man were testing, like a soldier poking with his rifle into the rooms and corners of an empty farmhouse.

Feldman remained silent. Why am I smiling? he thought.

"Dear God," the voice said. The speaker, someone two or three cells away from Feldman, had slipped out of his cot. Apparently he was on his knees. "Forgive my mistakes, God. Help me to think of a plan to get out of this place."

Then another voice spoke. "Dear God, forgive and forget. Wipe the slate. I need a chance. Give a guy a chance."

Another: "God in Heaven," the voice said, "see the children get an education."

Men were awake throughout the long, dark cell-block.

"Get the rat who squealed, who turned state's evidence, Lord."

"Dearest Jesus of my soul, give me courage."

"Give me brains, God."

"I want to go back to Kansas."

"Make me lucky."

"Dear God, look after my wife. See she stays true."

"My kids, God."

"Kill my enemies, Lord."

"Please, help my mother to forget me."

"Help me to learn a trade, Lord."

"Dear God, please make the parole board see things my way."

"Help me, God, to give up smoking."

"To get ahead."

"Dear Jesus, I can't stop thinking about women. Help me to forget women. Make me queer."

"Dear God in highest Heaven, let me win."

"Place."

"Show."

"Grant that society sees fit to abolish capital punishment, Lord."

"Teach me to get along with others."

"I need a drink bad, Lord."

"Dear God, give our leaders the wisdom and strength they need to guide us through these troubled times."

"Keep China from developing the capability to deliver The Bomb, sweet Jesus."

"Keep my daughter off the streets. Don't let her run with a fast crowd."

"Show me, Lord, how to commit the perfect crime."

"Dearest Lord, don't let them discover where the money's hidden."

"Gentle the guards, Jesus."

"Sweet Jesus, protector of my soul, fix my life."

"Amen."

"Amen. Amen."

"Amen."

Feldman smiled. His joy was immense.

In his dream he had left his cot too. He was on his knees. Like the goyim. He felt he owed it. He was very grateful. "For having escaped the second-rate life," he prayed; "for having lived detached as someone with a stuffed nose, for my sound limbs and the absence of pain, for my power, for my hundred-and ten-thousand-dollar home in a good neighborhood, for the tips on the market, for my gold hamper and all the dirty shirts in it, for my big car and good taste, for the perfect fits and silk suits, for my never having been in battle or bitten by beasts; for these things and for others, for the steaks I've eaten and the deals I've closed, for the games I've won and the things I've gotten away with, for my thick carpets and my central air conditioning, for the good life and the last laugh—Father, I thank Thee.

"Amen."

10

A short time after his monthly physical Feldman received a note from the warden:

Your weight is good, your lungs are clear, your specimen sparkles like a trout stream. But slow down. I tell you for your own good. You're too nervous. You'll never make it. The doctor is very concerned, and so am I. I'm no killer—that's your department. I'm just a custodian, a sort of curator, and it grieves my collector heart if I have to lose one of you guys. You're terrified. Of what? Of what, Feldman? You make your own problems. If I thought it was guilt—guilt's good, guilt's healthy, but your kind of guilt isn't honest. It doesn't do anybody any good. It's diffused, unfocused. Anyway, slow down, play ball, calm down. Life is ordinary, Feldman.

Fisher

P.S. Here are the basic rules of this place. I'll just sketch them in for you. I won't be very particular, because you're probably already familiar with the particular stuff. (We have an expression: "You bad men can't see the ropes for the loopholes.")

1. Lights out at 10 o'clock. The day begins (adjusted, of course, to seasonal dawn) at 6:30. That means you can get eight and a half hours' sleep if you work it right. Bankers don't get

91

that much, ship's captains don't. Guys who have lumberyards in Ohio get less. Actually, it's an hour more of sack time—this is supported by many sociological studies—than is put in by the average U.S. citizen. Penologists are beginning to think that a greater sleepload is a very important factor in rehabilitation, an aggressive dream life being a major element in holding down violence. (Also, if it's carried over into the outside would, it gives you jerks less man-hours on the streets.)

2. Keep a neat cell. There's no real complaint here.

3. Silence at meals. Sit at your assigned table. There's no real complaint here.

4. You already know the mechanics of permission slips and passes and so forth, so I won't go into that here except to say that it's to a man's benefit to learn to live with nuisance. Accustom yourself to it. It is easier for a camel to pass through the eye of a needle than for an annoyed man to enter into Heaven.

5. Work. THIS IS MOST IMPORTANT! I can't emphasize this too much. Develop a good work ethic. The most difficult thing you will have to face up to here is the problem of sharpening your work ethic in the absence of a profit motive. But this is very important. I assure you, Feldman, if you can overcome your qualms in this area the world will absolutely open up for you. You will begin to understand how ordinary life is. What do you need here that isn't provided? Food? We give you food. Shelter ditto. Likewise plumbing. If you need an operation or an aspirin tablet, ask and it shall be given. What's left? Movies? We show subsistence-level movies once a week. Live with an edge on. I don't say suffer. Repress, repress. Have Spartan sensibilities. Be always a little uncomfortable. Then, when pain comes—and how often does it come? real pain is very rare—it won't matter so much. I've already said more than is necessary. (I don't owe you anything.) Work hard at your job. You're in the canteen. These men have a limited amount of money to spend. Still, you're a merchandiser. See what you can do to improve business in your department. Let's make that more positive. I want to see improvement over last month's figures, or else!

6. Sex. There's no complaint here. I'm no prude. I don't know what your tastes are and I don't want to know. What's okay by consenting adults is okay by me.

7. Free time. This is up to you. You can read, play sports, work in the model shop—whatever. It's a good idea, however, to make a friend. Many of the men here develop lasting relationships that enrich their lives. Now I know that you've been listening to several of these men recently and letting them tell you about their troubles. All I can say is, that isn't exactly what I mean. You were selfish there, Feldman. You did that out of morbid, unhealthy curiosity and to achieve a basis of comparison for your own comfort. That must stop. (Some of them were putting you on, anyway.) Life is ordinary. Mine is, his is, yours is. I could give you literally hundreds of examples that come readily to mind, but right here on my desk now is the file of Rudolph Held. Held is in this prison for arson. (You've probably seen him. Rudy's the trusty who runs the projector.) Now you might think that arson is a sick, dramatic, extraordinary crime, and for some perhaps it is, but Rudy gets no hard-ons from setting fires. He doesn't wet his pants when he hears a siren. Rudy's a looter. He starts a fire and is there on the scene when it takes. He's always been very athletic, fast, a champion sprinter in high school, and a superb broken-field runner. However, Rudy didn't have the opportunity of going on to college to develop these interests. He might conceivably have been offered athletic scholarships, but his father died when he was very young—of a perfectly ordinary coronary—and he had to remain with his mother and support her. Actually, he didn't even finish high school, need was so pressing. Well, this was the Depression, and there wasn't much work available for a boy like Rudy. He found a job delivering groceries in a wealthy part of town, but then his mother became ill—these things happen— and he needed extra money for an operation. He remembered those wealthy homes and the valuable things he had seen in them. What was more natural for a loyal, dutiful boy than to think of stealing them in order to obtain money for his mom's operation? But how could a kid delivering groceries, limited mostly to the kitchen, grab anything of value? He knew he'd have to go back at night, to break and to enter. In a wealthy home there are always plenty of people around—servants, guests. It was too risky. (Again, self-preservation is a perfectly normal, ordinary motivation in human beings.) If it was to do himself or his mother any good he had to find some sure-fire way of getting into these homes and stealing the stuff. He asked himself: under what conditions will it seem normal to force your way into a home that is not your own? And the answer came—

perfectly rational, perfectly normal: when that house is on fire and it looks like you're going in to save someone! *So Rudy would start a fire and then bust through a window and go in and take what he needed. He made so much noise he was actually responsible for saving many lives, and then, with his God-given talent for broken-field running—and what's more natural than making use of your talents?—he'd dodge around in the flames and burning rooms, grabbing up whatever he needed. So you see? When you understand the background, there's a reason for everything. Nothing is strange. Consecutive, the world is consecutive. It's rational. Life is ordinary.*

You'll be getting another examination in a month. If you're no better then, stronger measures will have to be taken.

Fisher

Sure it's ordinary, Feldman thought, awakened the next morning by the flash of sun on the bright mirror surfaces of the bars Lurie had shined. Sure it's ordinary, he thought, plunging his arm deep into the toilet bowl to polish it. He looked up and down the long line of cells. Men sat on the sides of their cots, their shoulders slumped, their heads in their hands. Sure it is.

"Good morning, fellas," he said to the cellblock at large, to the murderers and robbers of banks, "how'd you sleep?"

"Stow it, big mouth," warned a convict in another cell. "Watch your step, pig creep. Fuck with me and I'll get you on your way through the foundry to deposit the chits. I'll crack your skull with a shovel and stuff your body into furnace six."

"These things happen," Feldman said.

He would give the warden his way. When in jail, he thought. It was a matter of indifference to him. Life *was* ordinary. Only what happens to *you*, he thought, not entirely clear what he meant. Then he thought: My crime, one of them, was that I thought the world itself was happening to me. And when it didn't, I tried to make it happen. Ah, he thought, like the other bad man—like Mix.

That warden, he thought, shuddering, he'll pull me apart. The thing to do is to play ball. The warden was a great man. As great a man as he had encountered. As great as his father. Greater. To use his health like that, to scare him into docility! The man used the character of the opposition. To fright he applied fear, to greed dreams of surfeit, to courage (the complicated possibilities of his system of silence in the dining hall) encouragement. It was important to know what he thought of you. Feldman remembered his file. What *was* in it? Ed Slipper had let him down. Slipper had been in the infirmary nine days. Had the warden anything to do with that? Incommunicado. When he was there for his physical, Feldman had bribed an orderly to get a report on him.

Higher purposes. He was all higher purposes, the warden. Feldman knew *that*, and the warden knew he knew. That probably explained the warden's note, the explanations that explained nothing, the warden's fear that Feldman was on to something. (Sure, fear. The son of a bitch was on the run. You didn't understand fear that well without having known a fair amount of it yourself. You couldn't manipulate greed unless you'd been there.) Then—he had come a long way today—this: he's one too. The warden. *He's a bad man too!*

Maybe. Higher purposes. Nobody understood the prison. Rules, exceptions to rules. The world as tightrope. Feldman didn't know. Does he want me to understand? Does he not want me to understand?

Anyway, okay. The warden said be calm. He'd be calm. He *was* calm. There were certain dentists you could trust. They said, "This won't hurt you," and it didn't. That was no guarantee you wouldn't die from pain on the way home, but you knew you were safe just then. That's how he felt. Safer, for the time being at least, than at any time since he'd come. That's why he had spoken out his greeting like that. He was pretty happy. What couldn't he do now that he was safe for a while?

"Bisch," he told his cellmate, "watch my smoke."

The first thing he did was to get Wall's power of attorney. Then he got Flesh's. Sky's was more difficult. "Authority isn't authority until it's deputed," Feldman said. "Responsibility doesn't mean anything until it's delegated."

"I'm in charge of the operation," Manfred Sky said sullenly.

"I *know* that, Manfred. *I* know that. Listen to me a minute. Did you ever see a general?"

"What is this? Why rake over the past? Just because I once sold phony Prisoner-of-War Insurance—"

Feldman had forgotten about the man's war experience. He didn't believe for a minute in Sky's sore spot, but understood that it was fashionable just then in the prison for bad men to assume long, penitent faces, to "make warden's mouths," as the phrase had it. (He had thought it a chink in the warden's armor when he realized that the man would settle for insincerity, but he had been quickly straightened out about that in Warden's Assembly. "*Forms*, gentlemen," the warden had roared over the convicts' forced applause and cheers, "civilization is *forms*." There was even some talk that the warden would soon reinstitute an experimental measure that had been abandoned shortly before Feldman's arrival. When the practice was in force, a convict encountering a guard in the corridor had to greet the guard formally, inquire after his health, and his family's if he had one. Then the guard had to do the same for the convict. Each was required to offer some minor complaint, some small concern—these didn't have to be real—for the other to be solicitous about. The system had been discontinued, Feldman understood, because the prisoners were helpless to project a believable insincerity.)

"Did you ever see a general?" Feldman repeated. "Did he carry an M-one? Was he issued a trenching tool? Did he, except on formal occasions, wear as many ribbons as his driver, say? Manfred, I've *seen* a general. I sat with one across a conference table when the store was promoting defense bonds for the government. He had assistants—captains, majors, a full colonel. Manfred, those junior officers looked *Toyland* next to this fellow. Do you understand? West Point cadets, senior prom, Flirtation Walk. They looked like men who had never done anything more military than hold a sword above some R.O.T.C. lieutenant and his pretty bride. But that general, that general was a *dream* of power! In a khaki uniform, very plain, unribboned, almost a business suit. He deputed his messkit, Manfred, he delegated his knapsack. Just the stars on each shoulder like awry stick pins, like something in a brown firmament. He looked like the United States sitting there. He never opened his mouth. This was a complicated thing. I had lawyers from my staff; he had his judge-advocate people. I was asking concessions for the space. Many things had to be worked out. Decisions. He never said a word. With the eyes, everything with the eyes. He never made a sound. Well, that's an exaggeration. I was sitting across from him and I heard this faint hum. Like a generator or a transformer. Oh, the power in that man. Don't kid yourself, Manfred. He was in charge of his operation too."

"Wow," Manfred Sky said.

"I ask for your power of attorney, Manfred. Give me your hand on this."

"Why? What's in it for you?"

"*Me?*" Feldman said, "I'm a *workhorse*, Manfred, a *grind*. Feldman the fetcher, the rough and tumbler. This is true, Manfred. I have no executive gifts. I haven't the gift of silence. Hear how I talk. It's a failing."

Flesh and Walls were listening. Feldman had simply promised them he would do their work.

"How about it, Manfred?"

"Well, I don't know."

"Look, Flesh, look, Walls. Look at Manfred. With the eyes, everything with the eyes."

"Well, I don't know," Manfred said.

"What would you say to a *bribe*, Sky?"

"Done," Sky said.

Then Feldman took down the chewing-gum displays. Walls, who had taken some trouble with the arrangement of these, objected. "Wait," Feldman told him, "you'll see."

He cleared away the toothpaste tubes. He had Flesh hide the cigarettes, and he removed the shaving creams and aerosol deodorants. He stood back critically and looked at the shelves. "My God," he said, "the candy!"

"Wait, I'll get it," Walls said.

"Never mind," Feldman said, "I will."

He took away the famous kinds and allowed those he had never heard of to remain. He was very discriminating. There were seventeen boxes of Licorice Brittle, two dozen tubes of Flower Balls. Rose, Gardenia, Gray Orchid, Pine—some of the other flavors. He gave prominent space to some curious unwrapped bars of hardened confectioners' sugar. They had precisely the texture and taste of the candy sockets that support the candles on a child's birthday cake. They had jelly centers. Not by bread alone, Feldman thought.

He opened the soft-drink cooler and peered inside. He removed the Coke and Pepsi Cola and 7Up and all the fruit flavors except guava. He held up a bottle of bright mauvish liquid. There was no label. He read the cap. "Fleer's," it said. Hits the spot, Feldman thought, and returned it to the cooler.

Then he picked through the tray of combs, leaving out only the wide, eight- and ten-inch ones and removing all the tightly toothed pocket combs. These he placed in a large cardboard box into which he had already put writing paper, packets of envelopes, ball-point pens and all the number-two pencils. He covered the box and shoved it under the counter out of sight. He found a single box of number four hard-lead pencils, and these he built in a rectangular construction on the top of the counter.

He discovered some shoetrees, which he hung on a tall revolving razor-blade stand from which he had first removed all the double-edged blades. (He allowed a few packages of odd-shaped injector blades to be displayed.) He arranged the greeting cards, first transferring to the cardboard box all those cards whose messages of sympathy or celebration seemed rather ordinary. He was left with a small, curious assortment: "Get Well Soon, Stepmother"; "Bon Voyage, Cousin Pat"; "Best Wishes for the April Primary"; "Too Bad Your Dog Was Run Over"; "Welcome Back to Civilian Life, General"; "Congratulations, Comrade, on the Success of Your Strike!"

He took away all the Kleenex and white pocket handkerchiefs, substituting five carefully folded floral-pattern babushkas the men sent as gifts. There were other gift items: three travelling clocks, a portable iron and several umbrellas. Then, in a massive ziggurat, he arranged six dozen bottles of suntan lotion that had arrived yesterday by mistake. He stood back to appraise what he had done. "How do you like it?" he asked Manfred. Sky stared at him.

The canteen opened for an hour and five minutes in the afternoon. (The scheduling of canteen hours was among the more complicated arrangements at the prison. This was Thursday. On Thursday those men who hadn't taken their free hour at ten in the morning on Monday could take it with an increment of five minutes at two-thirty in the afternoon.)

A convict holding an envelope came up to the wire cage behind which Feldman was waiting. "Give me a stamp," he said.

"Certainly," Feldman said. He took a special-delivery stamp from the special drawer he had prepared and slipped it to the man through the opening in the cage. "Thirty cents, please," he said politely.

"Not this," the man said, "a *stamp*. A regular stamp. A nickel stamp."

"All out," Feldman explained.

"What do you mean all out? I want to send a letter."

Feldman glanced down at the stamp the convict had just returned to him. "They deliver it any hour of the day or night with this," he said. "This is one of the best stamps there is."

"I don't want it delivered any hour of the day or night. It's a letter to my mother. I say I'm feeling fine and that I'm glad Uncle had a nice time in Philadelphia."

Feldman nodded sympathetically.

"Look," the man said, "have you got an air-mail stamp? I'll send it air-mail."

"All out," Feldman said. He considered the problem for a minute. "*I* know," he said suddenly. "Do you know anyone in Europe?"

"Why?"

"Well, if you know someone in Europe, I could sell you an overseas air letter for eleven cents. You write your mother the air letter, and your pal in Europe redirects it to your mom. If he does it right away, she'll have it in under two weeks."

"I don't know nobody in Europe," the man said.

"*Asia.* These air letters go to Asia too. It takes a little longer, but—"

"I never been to Asia. I don't know nobody in Asia. Just give me the goddamned special-delivery."

"Coming right up," Feldman said sweetly.

The next customer, a young man, wanted a stamp too. He was holding some documents. They looked important. Probably they were legal forms he was sending to his lawyer.

Feldman shook his head sadly. "I've only got this cent-and-a-quarter precanceled job for nonprofit organizations," he said.

The young man made some private calculations. "Well, give me seven of them. That'd make more than the eight cents it costs for an air-mail."

"Gee, I've got only one left. There's not much call for them."

"What would happen if I put a cent-and-a-quarter stamp on this?"

"You'd have to send it open, unsealed," Feldman said expertly. "It goes surface mail. Rail, bus, that sort of thing."

"These are important confidential papers," the convict said. "My appeal rides on this."

"Uh huh," Feldman said.

"They have to go out today."

"Do you know anybody in Europe?"

Finally the man had to take his chances. He stuffed the papers into the envelope and started to lick it.

"Unh unh, unh, uhn," Feldman warned, waving his finger.

"I forgot," the man said. He handed the unsealed envelope to Feldman reluctantly, anxious and very doubtful. Feldman dropped it cheerfully into the mailbag.

"How about a drink?" Feldman asked. "To relax you."

"All right," the convict said. "A Coke."

"All out. Here," Feldman said, "try this. Just got in a shipment. A new taste sensation." He extended an open bottle of the mauve soda pop.

The young man took a few swallows. "It tastes like bubble gum," he said.

"That's what they're drinking today," Feldman said. "The kids. They're doing the twist and drinking bubble-gum soda."

"Yeah."

"Say," Feldman said, "if that appeal comes through, you'll be getting out soon."

The young man looked troubled again. "Maybe you'd better give me back my letter," he said. "Maybe my friend has a stamp."

"You *kidding*" Feldman said. "You kidding me? That's a federal rap, buddy. Me tamper with the mails? I'm not sticking *my* hand into that mail bag. What, are you kidding? That's *federal.*"

"Well, let me back there. I'll do it."

"I can't," Feldman said. "You never heard of an accessory? Forty-two percent of the guys *in* here are accessories. Besides, I can't let unauthorized personnel back here. That would be an infraction of prison decorum. Jesus, the Feds would want me, and the warden would want me too."

"Well, what about me?" the convict said. "I already *committed* a federal offense."

"You did?"

"I'm not a nonprofit organization," the man said gloomily.

"I didn't hear that," Feldman said. "You never said it, and I didn't hear it." He looked at Sky and Flesh and Walis. "You guys are witnesses. I didn't know. To me he looked nonprofit." He turned back to the young man. "Look, relax. Try to see the bright side. Maybe the papers *won't* fall out. Maybe the transportation strike will be over soon. They're not too far apart. The President is sending an arbitrator in a private plane. As soon as the fog lifts. If your appeal goes through you'll be out soon."

"In a few months," the young man said doubtfully.

"What have you done about your shoes?" Feldman asked.

"What shoes?"

"Your *shoes*," Feldman said. "That you came in with."

"I don't know. They took them away."

"Well, certainly they did. They hold them down in wardrobe for when you get out. Were they new?"

"I don't remember. Yes. I got them just before I was framed."

"I see."

"They were Italian."

"I see."

"They didn't have laces."

"Oh?"

"They had these little gold zippers."

"They sound very nice," Feldman said.

"They were comfortable. Very light," he said wistfully.

"Soft leather," Feldman said.

"Yeah. Very soft."

"That's too bad."

"Why? They were very comfortable."

"No, I mean soft leather collapses. It doesn't hold its shape."

"Oh."

"Shoetrees would save them," Feldman said. "Of course the wardrobe guard doesn't tell you that when he takes your shoes. Sure, he's looking out for himself. He tries to save himself a little work. What does the wardrobe guard care? A man gets out and his shoes are shot. It's a goddamn fucking pity."

The young man pulled on his soda. When Feldman hooked his finger at him he leaned forward.

"Get a pair of shoetrees," Feldman said confidentially. "What is it, a three-dollar investment? If you're talking about the style I think you're talking about, you'd be protecting something worth many times more."

"They cost twenty-five bucks."

"There, you see?" Feldman's face became very serious. "Save your shoes," he said slowly. He might have been a dentist warning schoolchildren about their teeth. He reached behind his back, detached a shoetree from the razor-blade stand, brought it around his body quickly and slapped it with a smart, ringing clap into his palm. Startled, the young man jumped back. Feldman's eyes were closed. *"What is it preserves in this world that decays? Where age always withers and time's never stayed?"* The young man stared at him. Feldman opened his eyes. "What, friend, do the ancients say makes perfect?"

The convict shook his head.

"Come on," Feldman said, "this is basic. What do the ancients say makes perfect? *Practice*, that's what. Practice. Practice does. Do, re, mi, fa, sol, la, ti, do. Practice. 'Peter Piper picked a peck of pickled peppers.' 'How much wood would a woodchuck chuck if a woodchuck could chuck wood?' Practice, pal, makes perfect, pal. *Practice!* Habituality conquers reality. See the athlete: every muscle a maneuver. Unused, things collapse. Occupancy is a life principle. What else explains the growth of the caretaker industry in this country? They leave rangers in the forests in the wintertime. Use. Use use! Who's talking about your creepy zippered dago shoes? This is *life* I'm talking about, friend, character I'm pushing for three dollar bills. Your shoes need practice. Let my shoetrees walk your shoes! Stuff them with my proxy feet and let them run around down there!" He shoved the shoetree into the young man's hand.

"Leather dehydrates. Did you take chemistry? Did they tell you that in chemistry? The shoetree you hold in your hand has been treated with a thin emollient possessing exactly the consistency and molecular structure of human foot oil. Save your shoes! Save them!"

"But they're locked up. How could I get them into the shoes now?"

"The guard," Feldman said.

"He'd never let me."

Feldman reached behind him. "Slip him this candy and wink." He forced a bar of the confectioners' sugar into the young man's other hand.

When Feldman had finished with him the young man had spent three dollars seventy-six and a quarter cents in prison chits. It was a goddamned shopping spree, Harold Flesh said. He had never seen anything like it.

It went on like that for days. Feldman sold things in half-dozens that had never been sold before at all. He pushed the number-four pencils, and when the men discovered that these produced unsatisfactory, almost invisible lines, he sold them ink into which they could dip their pencils like old-fashioned pens. He had luck, too, with the flower balls, which was the only thing that could neutralize the taste of the guava soda. The mauve soda neutralized the taste of the flower balls. Only the suntan lotion neutralized the taste of the mauve soda.

He told the men that the difference between success and failure lay in education.

"I know," one said, "I'm taking a course for college credit."

"College credit? *College?* Don't kid me."

"I am. European Literature in Translation."

"Then why are you here? It's Saturday afternoon. Why ain't

you at the game? Where's your pledge pin? Who's your date for the big dance?"

"Are you calling me a liar?"

"I'm calling you a fool," Feldman said. "Tell me, Professor, what is the capital of South Dakota, please? Which is smaller, the subtrahend or the minuend? Give me the words of 'The Pledge of Allegiance.' "

"What are you talking about?"

"Fifth grade," Feldman said.

"Hey—"

"Hey, hey," Feldman said. "What's the matter? You never heard of the formative years?"

"The formative years?"

"Sure the formative years. Of course the formative years. It makes me sore the way you guys are taken for a ride. Why are you here now, do you suppose? Because you stole a car, pointed a gun, beat up a grocer? You're here now because you had lousy formative years. *Mal*formative years is what you had. I won't fool you—you're a grown man. What's done is done. I can't make you nine years old again, but I can give you a tip. Listen to me, college boy. The only education that counts is the education you get in those formative years. The difference between you and the squares is that the squares *know* 'The Pledge of Allegiance.' Imagine someone pointing a gun who can tell you the capital of Iowa."

"You know, you're right."

"Of course I'm right. Go back, go back. Learn what everybody learned that you didn't learn. There's a program for men who didn't complete grammar school. Sign up for *that*. It'll be your *re*formative years. Here," Feldman said, "you'll need paste. There's no time to lose. Here's blunt scissors. Take notebook paper. A ruler. Here's crayons. Here's gummed reinforcements."

In a week all that was left was what Feldman had hidden. Gradually he began to reintroduce cigarettes, books of matches, edible candy, the toiletries. These he let Flesh and Walls and Sky sell.

"You hate these guys," Flesh said.

"No," Feldman said. It was true. He loved a good customer. Feldman himself was sometimes an easy mark for a good salesman. The formative years, he thought.

"It's as though they had to spend money," Sky said.

"That's right. That's *right*, Sky." Feldman felt expansive. Without fear, the mood of his safety still on him, he had begun to miss his life, to feel a sort of homesickness for the habit of being Feldman. He was tempted to talk to them as he had sometimes talked to his employees. (Gradually he had begun to think of the three as his employees. Criminals. The best staff he had ever put together.) "Anticipate the consequences of desire, and you'll be rich. All things are links in a chain. All the things there are. Objects take their being from other objects. A salesman knows. This is the great incest of the marketplace." This *was* the way he spoke to his employees—after hours, the store closed, before a weekend perhaps, or a holiday. There was something military about it. He might have been an officer who had just brought his men through a great battle. There had been blood. Money and blood. All shoptalk, all expertise had a quality of battle about it, of exultation in the escape from danger. Something was always at stake, every moment you lived. No one could ever really afford to tell the truth. Even after hours, when the store was closed. But sometimes the truth was so good you couldn't keep it to yourself.

"Unless he's enormously wealthy a man puts out just about what he takes in. Some people get behind and a few rare ones get ahead, but for the most part accounts balance. This is so no matter what a man earns. There's something humorous about the plight of some young fellow struggling to get along on five thousand a year still struggling to get along on fifteen thousand a year ten years later. It's because desire's built into the human heart. Like the vena cava or the left ventricle. It's there from the beginning. You never catch up. When I found this out I wanted to be in on the action. I asked myself: if all things are links in a chain, what must I do to control the chain itself? The answer was clear. I must own a department store! Did you know that in England, where they were invented, they used to be called 'universal stores'? So that's what I worked for, because the possibilities are unlimited in universal stores. There's everything to sell.

"I'm telling you what's what. That's usually a mistake, but I don't see right now how it can hurt me. I'll surprise you. I've always been very fond of my employees. The boss usually is. He loves a man who works for him, who furthers his ends . . .

"What was I talking about? Yes. I like to wait on trade myself. Sometimes I try to see how far I can take a customer, if I can wrap him in the chain. Once a woman came to buy some gloves when I was behind the glove counter with my buyer. She spent four thousand dollars and had been on every floor in the store and in almost every department before she left. Admittedly that was unusual. The woman was wealthy and had almost no sales resistance, but wealthy or not, she got in over her head. *That's* the test.

"Listen, it's like odds and evens, men and women, Yin and Yang. I discovered—I had help, my father was moving toward this before he died—that there are casual items and resultant items. An object can be both, but usually it's one or the other. Ice cream is casual because it generates thirst. But chewing gum is resultant. That's why they put it by the cashier's counter in an ice cream parlor. A hammer is resultant, but a two-by-four is casual as hell."

"Tables and chairs," Flesh said.

"That's only the beginning," Feldman said. "Cloths for the tables and silver for the cloths and plates for the silver and bowls for the plates and soup for the bowls and napkins for the soup and rings for the napkins."

Ed Slipper was standing outside the cage of the canteen, watching.

"And what for the rings?" Manfred Sky asked.

"Fingers for the rings," Feldman said, and stepped outside to greet Slipper. "You're out of the infirmary," he said. "I'm glad to see you."

It was the first time he had seen the old man in daylight, and he felt doubts. When he had gone to his room to bribe him with the chocolate cherries, he had seemed in the dark commendably greedy, someone who could be dealt with. Now the light clarified the old man's age, stunted his appetite, and he seemed in his infirmity a wanderer, someone loose, virtuous as the sick are virtuous. Feldman wondered if he had made a bad deal, if Slipper even remembered what the deal had been.

"I have something for you," Ed Slipper said. "You have to come."

Feldman was surprised to discover he was disappointed. He had sought an advantage, but since then he had not felt the need for it. He had been comfortable recently. Suppose the warden had sent the old man. If so, he was no longer safe, he was being threatened again. Something was always at stake.

The old man moved away from the canteen and through the corridor into the main part of the facilities wing. The fact that they were in the recreation area added to Feldman's annoyance. Here were the classrooms, the chapels and dining and assembly halls. The gym was here and the TV rooms. The rooms had an air of having been donated. He looked for the brass plaques citing the givers. He stayed away from this area as much as he could, rarely spending any of his free time here. Indeed, nothing about the prison made him feel more a prisoner than its salons. Watching a movie with a thousand men who had not paid to get in made him feel terrible. He had always been uncomfortable if he could not ask for his money back. His cell, at least, despite its being shared and barred, was *his* cell; his cot; despite its discomforts, *his* cot. If anything, the very fact that the cell was locked added to his sense of being in possession there.

"This way," the old man said. He moved down another corridor, and Feldman followed. They passed a guard, but luckily they were not challenged, for he had forgotten to get a pass. The old man bothered him; he seemed too clam. Sure, Feldman thought, he's on Warden's Business. He's got the flag in his pocket.

They came to a chapel. "Wait," Slipper said, "I have to sit down a minute." He pushed open the door and found a seat on a back bench.

"Listen," Feldman said, "I forgot to get a pass."

"It's all right," Slipper said, "if you see a guard, pray." He was referring to the privilege of sanctuary which the warden had introduced. If a prisoner could get to a chapel, he could remain there indefinitely—so long as he was praying aloud.

"Maybe I'd better go back and get one," Feldman said uneasily.

"No," the old man said, "we're almost there. We already passed the guard. You don't need a pass."

Feldman was positive Slipper was working for the warden. The man had changed. Despite his obvious frailty and need to rest, he seemed very much in control of himself. "I thought for a while you forgot about me," Feldman said.

"No, I didn't forget."

"I thought for a while you had. I gave you six days to get my file."

"I was in the infirmary, Leo," Slipper said.

He calls me Leo. "Sure, Ed. How you feeling?"

"Well, you know, I got some bad news when I was in the infirmary."

Feldman looked at him.

"They took some tests."

"Yes?"

"I've got diabetes."

Feldman felt relieved. "They can control that," he said. Perhaps the old man's manner was only concern for his health.

"Certainly they can. But it means something else."

"Yes?"

"I'm off the chocolate cherries."

"Oh."

"Poison," the old man said.

"Oh."

"Rat poison," the old man said. "I might as well swallow deadly rat poison."

"I see."

"I don't need your five dollars a month. There's nothing I want to buy except candy, and I want to live more than I want a sweet."

"That's right, Feldman thought. Slipper had *two* obsessions. They conflicted. That warden. "A deal's a deal," he said. "It still accumulates."

"Well," Ed Slipper said, "I'll have an estate."

"You're still in my debt. You're still my man," Feldman said half-heartedly.

"Sure."

"You don't seem to mind much, being sick," Feldman said. "I'm surprised."

"Well, I got some good news too. I'm the second oldest con now, Leo. I moved up two guys. That bird in Atlanta died in his sleep a week ago, and the fellow in Baton Rouge, Louisiana, was sprung when someone made a deathbed confession to his crime."

That warden, Feldman thought. He knew I went after him with chocolate cherries, and invented chocolate-cherry disease. I exploit obsession; he instills it. "Listen, Ed, I have reason to believe you might not have what they say you have. The night I came to you, the warden—"

"Shh," Slipper said, "I hear someone."

"—saw me in the corridor—"

"Shh, it's the guard." Ed Slipper fumbled to his knees. "Dearest God, strike down that old bum in Leavenworth in his tracks. Restore my health and hold down the sugar in my blood and urine. Grant me a peaceful, wise old age." He turned and tugged excitedly at Feldman's sleeve, pulling him down beside him. "*Psst.* Pray. *Pray!*"

Feldman could think of nothing to pray for. He felt immensely stupid, but the old man was poking him in the ribs. "And God bless Mommy," he suddenly blurted in a loud voice, "and Poppy and Uncle Ned and Aunt Stephanie and Uncle Julius and Cousin Frank and Dr. Bob and Baby Sue." He reeled off fifty names. Who the hell *are* these people? he wondered, amazed at himself. Suddenly he was conscious that the old man had stopped praying and was looking at him.

"You got a big family, you know that, Leo?" Slipper said respectfully. Then he began to laugh, and he seemed greedy again. Avarice boomed out of his glee.

"Okay," Feldman said. "I get it. There was no guard."

"Leo," Ed Slipper said, wiping his eyes, "I *swear* I thought I heard him. Anyway, I knew what you were going to say. The warden warned me, but I saw the results of the tests myself. I got it, Leo. I got it, kid. I *think* I got it. Anyway, can I take the chance? I want to live. I'm second oldest con in the country now if the warden didn't lie about that. What would you do in my place?"

"What about my file?"

"Oh sure," the old man said. "Come on, I'll show you. That laugh was terrific."

Feldman stood.

"Better brush your blue suit off," Ed Slipper said. "Floor's dirty. You got some dust on your knees." He was still chuckling.

"Yeah," Feldman said. "I pray sloppy." Some shape I'm in, he thought. I make him laugh, the second oldest con in all the prisons. Relax, he told himself, life is ordinary. Nothing happens. "Rested up, old-timer?"

"Oh yes," Ed Slipper said, "just give me a hand up, please."

He has a buzzer, Feldman thought. I touch him, ten thousand volts of electricity go through my body. A *practical* joke. You live, you die. Nothing to it.

He helped the old man up.

"Your file's just down the hall," Ed Slipper said, leading Feldman out of the chapel. "come on."

Feldman felt like someone walking into ambush who knew what was coming but not when. It wasn't too late to turn back, but somewhere along the way his duty had taken over. He had to see it through to the end now. Comic obligation had to have its way. Life was ordinary. He was going to have to step through some door into a pitch-black room where suddenly the lights would snap on. A thousand killers would be singing "For He's a Jolly Good Fellow." His wife would be there, his son. And at the instant that he started to think: Today is my birthday—all the

tenors, two hundred and seventy-five of them, would beat the shit
out of him. They would cut out his son's heart and feed it to him,
and he'd have to eat it—they'd have a way of making him. His
wife would be doing a striptease under a magenta light. And all
the king's horses and all the king's men couldn't put Feldman
together again. He groaned.

They passed Bisch in the hall. Bisch nodded. "What's new?"
he said.

"What could be new?" Feldman said.

Slipper took Feldman's arm and guided him to a door. The
word "Library" was painted on the milky glass.

"Beyond this one, right?" Feldman said.

"Yes sir," Slipper said.

You don't have to call me "sir," Feldman thought. Not before
a big job. "Shall I open it or shall you?" he asked sweetly.

"You open it," Slipper said.

I am going to blow up, Feldman thought. I am going to ex-
plode into a trillion billion fragments, and they will put out a
report that I have escaped. There's going to be a disaster, he
thought, looking at the old man's virtuous face. There's going to
be a disaster, and all I can do is cooperate. And if there is no
disaster there will be a disaster. Warden Fisher demands a disaster.

He opened the door. They were in what appeared to be the
library. He looked at the book-stuffed shelves. They didn't have
to go to all this trouble, Feldman thought, transferring all those
books, alphabetizing the cards, setting up the Dewey decimal system. Or did they use Library of Congress? He would never know
now. That would be the problem he took with him to the grave.

"This is it," Slipper said.

"This is it, right, old-timer?"

"Yep."

"Yep," Feldman said, "this it."

"Yep."

"My file, please, Slipper," Feldman said. He felt like a straight
man feeding a line to the second oldest and second funniest banana in all the prisons in all the United States of America and all
its territories and possessions. He felt like sticking his fingers into
his ears to muffle the explosion of the big laugh.

Slipper marched up to the check-out desk. "The file on Bad
Man Feldman," he told the trusty.

The man looked up at them. Feldman remembered thinking

he had the bluest, clearest eyes he had ever seen. "Bad men are on the open shelves," he said. "Feldman," he said, underscoring the first letter. "Is that a *Ph* or an *F*?"

So, Feldman thought. They use phonetics.

"*F*," Ed Slipper said.

"Open shelves, under *F*," the trusty said.

Uv course, Feldman thought, whut then? Liphe is ordinary, and the man's a phool who thinks it's phancy.

"Come on," Ed Slipper said. They walked back to the open shelves and there, just as the trusty had said, under *F*, between a volume entitled *Federal Offenses* and another called *Felons and Felony*, were seven copies in high stiff black covers of the book on Feldman. Slipper took down a copy, flipped through the two hundred or so mimeographed pages and then removed the card from the little pocket in the back. "This one's been checked out five times," he said, offering it to him.

Feldman shook his head. "I saw the picture."

Suddenly the door flew open. It was the warden. Two guards were with him. "Guards," he shouted, "arrest that man!" They rushed up to Feldman and grabbed his arms. "Throw him in solitary confinement," the warden roared. "I warned you and warned you! I sent you a letter. I explained how you get along. 'Life is ordinary,' I told you. But you think you're an exception. I know what you did at the canteen, how you forced items on the men they didn't need, bankrupting them, bankrupting poor men. Deliberately twisting what I told you. You're up to here with passion. Up to *here* with it. But life is simple, Feldman. Now you'll see that. Get him away. Get him into solitary. Lock him up in a cage by himself. Now he'll learn. *Now* he will. Fuck-up!"

Phuck-up yourself, Feldman thought.

11

Now I am alone.

The cell to which they brought Feldman for his solitary confinement was no smaller than the one he shared with Bisch. If anything, because of the absence of the other cot and the small table on which each convict was allowed to arrange his possessions, it seemed a little larger. Nor was it, as he expected, darker. When the warden roared the words "solitary confinement," they had suggested some black hole-and-corner of the universe, or cramped subterranean quarter the sun never touched. He had expected, really, that it would be a place bad for one's bronchial condition—a calcimined, limey strongbox locked by big keys, the bedsprings rusted and the mattress mildewed.

It ain't the Ritz.

On the other hand, it was no less institutional-looking, and thus, in a strange way, competent, functional, than anyplace else in the prison.

When he had taken in that they had not put him into a torture chamber, that he was nowhere where preceding sufferers had etched their dark dates on the walls of their cells like poems of their catastrophes, he substituted another expectation: science. That is, he began to think of himself as of some modern, poisonous by-product, a radioactive pile perhaps, which may only be handled remotely, by tube digits, mechanical arms operated from the other side of thick walls by men in lab jackets.

Or of someone forlorn, abandoned. He remembered films he had seen as a child, victims abandoned in trick rooms whose ceilings descended hydraulically, an inch an hour, or rooms inexorably flooding with some killing acid. He remembered terrified men standing tiptoe, climbing the bed, pulling a table on top of that, and a chair on top of that, and the mashed, heaped bedclothes on top of that, building a Tower of Babel with the furniture on whose nervous pinnacle they could place themselves, tottering, swaying out some sure-footed doom.

But he was wrong there too. There was no one-way mirror, so there could not have been a two-way one. The place was not bugged, not because *that* possibility was too fantastic, but because there was nothing they could learn from Feldman. He was simply isolated, avoided, quarantined, steered clear of in the jail's society, as one might steer clear of a man who always failed, or one with a contagious disease. And indeed, there were times he had precisely *this* sense of his confinement, other times when he experienced the same brief, pointless confinement that occurs sometimes during a convalescence.

What struck him at last, after those first hours when his expectations about the nature of what would happen to him failed, was that there was something faintly old-fashioned and rural about his punishment. He might have been the town drunk locked into a cell while he slept one off. Even the man who brought him his supper seemed more bailiff, more turnkey than stern guard. Feldman speculated that the man might even be more approachable than the other guards. He couldn't help himself; he had begun to notice a certain predisposition in himself to *like* the guards, to look upon them as *finer* somehow than the prisoners; to, in fact, show off in front of them: in the exercise yard to hold down the swearing, never to fart in front of one, to offer them cigarettes during breaks—hinting a sort of gentlemen's "You're one, I'm one too" special relationship. It was the way, in the old days, he had reacted to Jews he might come upon in a Howard Johnson's in the state of Nebraska, on the way West. Feldman supposed that the guard assigned to such a place, where the special enclavic sense of being in a different rhythm from the rest of the prison induced an atmosphere of things in abeyance, might have wrought in him that vulnerability toward democracy found among men working late, or among witnesses to the same accident. But when he tried to talk to the man to find out what might

be expected of him here, merely asking for the same precision of
rule that was available upstairs—he *still* felt, though he knew it
wasn't so, knew he was only in a different wing, that he was in
some old sub-basement of the penitentiary—he found that the
man was even less permissive and more reserved than the side-
armed, rifle-pointing, machine-gun-dug-in troopers on the walls.
When he asked the simplest questions the guard just stared,
frowned and walked away.

Now I am alone.

Yet for a time this remained his chief concern, after he became
accustomed to the idea that the ceiling would not crush him, that
the bed was not electrified, the drinking water scalding. If there
was nothing to resist, what was there to comply with?

He couldn't ask other prisoners. There were no other prisoners. Through the bars of his cell he could see only a long corridor of blank wall. And when he shouted for others to identify
themselves—*expecting* no answer—no one replied. Not even the
guard came by to make him shut up.

Feldman had an insight after the guard left. Of course, he
thought, he brought me dinner. *The rule of silence!* The same here
as in the dining hall. Now he had a clue about how to act. He
was impatient for the guard to return for his tray so he could ask
him if he was right. But after an hour the man had not returned.
Now the question was immense. Each time he heard a noise Feldman sprang from his cot to see if the guard was coming. There
was never anyone in the corridor.

A little soup he had not finished filmed the bottom of the
bowl. His fork was chinked at its interstices with bits of carrot,
scabs of meat. On the metal tray the scraps had become garbage.
Feldman flushed the larger remnants down the toilet and tried to
wash off the tinier pieces in his small sink, but he had no soap
and the sink would not drain properly. A rich thin scum collected
in the basin. Feldman scooped it up with his soupspoon and tried
to knock it into the toilet, but it splattered on the floor and along
the rim of the bowl. It looked as if he had vomited. He cleaned it
up with the last four sheets of toilet paper. Still the guard had not
come.

Now it was very late. He was tired, but he did not want to
go to sleep until he had asked the guard his question. He couldn't
risk lying down. Faintly, he heard the signal that meant lights out
in the other parts of the prison. Another hour passed. He sat in
the dark and no longer jumped at each noise. It was difficult to

keep his eyes open. After a while he lay down. Soon he was asleep.

When he awoke in the morning his tray was still there. It frightened him. He knew what it was all about now. They meant to starve him. He thought at once of the end a few weeks from now—how long *could* a man go without food? two weeks? three?—when he would be on his cot, delirious, deranged, hunger like swallowed knives, his head an open sore, and already he could feel it starting. That was why he was so isolated, why no one could hear him when he shouted. Science. It *was* science. The goddamned scientific soundproof walls, their scientific thickness. He was ferociously hungry. He sprang up, despising his fastidiousness of the night before, regretting that he had thrown away those scraps. His action had had the heavy renunciatory quality of an obligation. I did it to myself, I did it to myself was all he could think of, as if, his resistance surrendered, he had shamefully compounded the loss of his life. He examined the sink. A thin band of dried smutty food remained, the color and consistency of apple butter. He scraped this up, carefully collecting it in his spoon and placing it back in the tray. He began to plan how he would apportion it to himself. It was senseless, he knew, but he prayed that some small value remained in it. Didn't they say that in the peels and skins, in the cut green tufts of carrots and vitals of animals and rinds of cheese and cores of fruit and calluses of vegetables, the real nutrition lay? Why not in garbage? Why not some dear good stuff residual in *that?* See the niggers, how *they* thrived, hearty on the shitty cuts.

Just then the guard came with his breakfast.

Feldman was too astonished to ask his question. He simply took it and gave back his empty tray.

"Use the same silver," the guard said, and left.

At noon Feldman asked him. "Do I have to be silent during mealtimes?"

"What for?" the guard said.

So, the rules did *not* operate!

He had been oppressed by the prison's deflecting forms. Even in his resistance to those forms he had been deflected, his life eaten up by a concern with behavior, the appearance of behavior. All rights wrested their existence from something inimical to rights. Upstairs, the simplest thing he could will had to be meshed with the prison's routine opposition to the thing willed. This was why he assumed there would be something he could resist in solitary, because he felt his life changed. Upstairs, it was the prison which resisted. Each thing he wanted—*each* thing—the prison did not want. It should have been a relief, then, to get away from the rules of silence, permission slips, warden's flags, assigned tables, assemblies, the censuses when the prisoners froze and the pencil man came by to count them. But it wasn't.

He learned at last, then, that his punishment down here was to be himself. It was ridiculous. How could he be Feldman if there was no one there that he could be Feldman to? He thought of the garbage with which he had hoped a few hours before to support his life. He thought of all nugatory things thrown away, of vast lots blooming with junk. That's where the nutrition wasn't.

Now I am alone.

Don't say that Feldman was unwilling to go along with the program.

What *is* the program?

The clever warden didn't do things haphazardly. There was significance in the placement of each water cooler. (Hadn't he seen the bills? Eight hundred twelve dollars for replumbing, for pulling out the old pipes and settling them in a new pattern. *Why?*) He supposed he was meant to go over his sins, to parse his past like a grammarian. It was the old wilderness routine. They'd left him in this desert to think about things.

Feldman refused to think about his past. If that was the warden's purpose the man was out of luck. People don't remember what has happened to them, he thought. You couldn't even remember how you felt. Unhappiness was always neutralizing itself. Likewise joy. So that the past had no character—neither of pain nor pleasure. It gave the impression of something canceled out, a sort of eternal breaking even. It was like what happened with the leaves. In the first flush days of spring, he couldn't remember when the trees had been without leaves. Again in autumn it seemed as if they had never had them. Even this experience—if I outlive it, he thought—will neutralize itself. It was a kind of fallout. Too much was lost. Too much was lost even of his neutralized life. He knew that you were supposed to be able to store in your subconscious everything that had ever happened to you. How many slices of cake you'd had at your eighth birthday party, the names of all the people you'd ever met. That if they gave you truth serum you'd spew all this stuff back. He didn't believe it.

He sat up and pinched his arm. Remember this pinch, he commanded himself, squeezing. Remember the date and the hour and the exact pain, and on the anniversary of the pinch a year from now, five years, ten, fifteen, think about it. Try to remember to remember it on your deathbed.

He released his flesh, and instantly the pain thinned out, was absorbed, halved, quartered, sixteenthed. He couldn't have taken up exactly the same flesh in his fingers again. It was as if he had thrown a stone into a lake. In seconds he could no longer identify the precise spot where it had gone down.

"Nymph, in thy orisons be all my sins remembered." Who said that?"

If he had difficulty remembering, he had none at all imagining. On about the third day he began to fantasize. He thought much about girls and women and kept himself exhausted by yielding to every sexual impulse, building the foundations of his lust always on real women—girls who had worked for him, his buyers' wives, customers to whom he had given his personal attention. Sometimes, however, at the moment of climax, he swiftly substituted some film goddess, or girl seen on television, or a record sleeve, or a billboard, or some girl never seen, some college woman from books and imagination.

He became almost animally potent, yet remained somehow in control, cool enough to build his fantasies carefully, starting again if he made a mistake, constructing what he said to her, what she said to him. It was a more careful wooing than any he had ever done in his life, and he saw himself in a new light, gallant, charming. He held off climax and teased himself with manufactured complexities, sudden jealousies—seeing himself deep in love, smitten till it cost him. Together, he and his girl friend worried about new places they could go, and later, what they were to do about their affair, how the children were to be told, how it was to be broken to the husband, to Lilly. It was marvelous. All that disturbed him were those occasions when his carefully managed, highly organized affairs were interrupted by random, spontaneous introductions of new women—the movie star, the imaginary TV singer—as unplanned and unprovided for as a freak in nature. At these times all his cool will would be suddenly broken and as he came he groaned the erotic words, invoking flesh almost violently, spraying his sperm, fucking completely. Cunt, he thought, oh pussy, oh tits and oh, oh, ass!

But even taking into account these aberrant moments, robbed of the gentle consummation he had planned, he realized that he had never had so active nor so satisfactory a sex life.

It's a goddamned love nest in here.

He was illimitably free to plunder and profane. In his unvisited cell, with all the privacy he could want and all the time in the world, he had enough for the first time in his life. Oddly, however, it was through just these fantasies that his real past was finally evoked. Why, he remembered suddenly, it's exactly the way he had lain beside Lilly!

He could see himself—himself and Lilly—the two big people huddled in their corner of the bed. They should have had a king-size bed. Feldman had asked for one, but Lilly had said they didn't make king-size in French Provincial, that it would look ridiculous. "But they had all the kings," Feldman said.

"That doesn't matter," Lilly said.

Feldman thought bitterly of the small kings, the teensy-weensy, itsy-bitsy kings of France.

And twin beds would somehow have strengthened the appearance of their consanguinity. He didn't even ask for twin beds. He thought of Dagwood and Blondie, of the husband and wife on "The Donna Reed Show," of Lucy and Desi, and all the conjugal Thompsons and Richardsons and Wilsons and Morgans in America in their twin beds, in their rooms within rooms—each with his own table, his own bedlamp, his own electric blanket; each with his own slippers beneath the bed, the polished toes just sticking out, like the badly concealed feet of lovers in farces. Such things bespoke order, reason, calm. Paradoxically, they bespoke a sort of detached tenderness for the mate that Feldman had never felt. Twin beds were out. (But they did say that love was more exciting in a twin bed. Feldman wondered. It raised penumbral questions like what happened at sea when in the mixed company of a life raft somebody had to go to the bathroom. How did two unmarried archeologists, holed up in a cave, hiding from savages, take a crap? The shipwrecked and the archeologists and the coed Yugoslav guerrilla fighters, they were the ones who had the fun. Policemen raiding wild parties, firemen rescuing ladies in their nightgowns from burning buildings, *they* did.)

So they lay together in the regular double bed, Feldman pulling back his knee when it brushed Lilly's thigh, creating a space between them, imagining the space a distance, making that distance into a journey he would never willingly take. She could have been in Europe, in Asia, in craters on the moon. And wild. *Wild!*

As unfaithful to Lilly right there beside him as some philanderer at a convention across the country.

He waited until she slept. It was easy to tell. She was a deep breather. (She breathes for six people, he thought.) Then, silkenly sheathed, luxurious in his mandarin's pajamas, he would begin his fantasies. (Feldman picked out his pajamas like a pajama scientist. No millionaire, no playboy, no bedroom sybarite has pajamas like mine, Feldman thought.) If Lilly happened to snore at one of these moments, he experienced the most intense irritation. If she snored a second time, he poked her, jabbed her with rigid, extended fingers in some soft part of her soft body. "Close your mouth," he'd hiss. "Get over on your own side." And in her sleep she'd obey. (Lilly listened in her sleep. Sometimes he'd give her pointless commands and watch with interest their clumsy, torpid execution. It was like playing a great fat musical instrument, some giant bellows thing.)

He never permitted himself the luxury of an orgasm, gradually abandoning, as sleep encroached, his carefully arranged trysts, his logical seductions, losing his place, forgetting to touch himself, until finally his erection waned like an unstoked fire.

And Lilly never knew. (Pure kindness on his part, for in truth he didn't give a damn what she thought.) If she had ever discovered his teen-age games he would have laughed in her face at her disgust, since it was her fault anyway. Because she was unbeautiful. Because her body harbored a traitor to love which pushed up bumps, jellied her flesh, dilated the veins on the backs of her legs. She was wrapped in her skin like a bad package. Everywhere there were excrescences, tumescences, body hair, cold pale scar tissue the blood never warmed, black-and-blue marks which arose from no ever-identified origin. She gets them from drying herself with a towel, Feldman thought, from dressing, from sitting in drafts.

Because Lilly was unbeautiful. Unbeautiful. And because she didn't care. She accepted every blemish—they're benign, she reasoned, they're all benign; she was benign—forgiving herself. Because she had no vanity. None at all. (No. One. A-line dresses to conceal her big hips. And he didn't mind big hips. He *liked* big hips.) What he hated was the strange combination in Lilly of fragility and a peasant heart. When she visited her parents in the East she would sit up for two nights in the coach. Or she took a bus. "I don't mind buses," she said. She *didn't* mind buses, but the air conditioning gave her a sore throat. She didn't *mind* a sore throat. He took her to expensive restaurants. She ordered liver. Thick steaks gave her heartburn, she said. Thick *steaks* did. A play came to town. Feldman bought seats in the orchestra; she preferred the balcony. Sitting close gave her headache, she said. Feldman wished she were beside him now. He would give her one in the back with his fingers. Unbeautiful Lilly!

Aghh, he sounded like a night-club comic. But what if all the tasteless jokes were true? What if they were true? Lilly made them true. She made them *come* true. She was like a fairy. Lilly the joke fairy. Poor Lilly, Feldman thought. Till death us do part, you. And *why? Just give me one good reason!*

Because during the war, when he was putting his store together, when 4-F—the homunculus wrapping his heart—he was getting rich, he had no time: 80,000 miles in '42, 112,000 in '43, 100,000 miles in '44, 128,000 in '45, in '46, 215,000 miles and in '47 even more. Getting the stock, traveling where the goods were, riding the trains—endless, endless—riding the planes, bumping full colonels, the whole country on the take, "table" a dirty word, and under it where the action was. A United States Senator told him once, "We know what you're up to and we don't mind a bit. During a war these things have to happen. It's an abstract factor but very important. It keeps up morale. You sell your wares, and the people on the home front, the factory people and the civil servants and the fillers-in, buy them and it gives them strength. Most people get their strength from the things they own. We have to keep up the balance between guilt and strength to get them to produce. The war news isn't enough. That just takes care of the guilt. So we know how you manage and we don't mind a bit." But the Senator was wrong. Because genius went beyond mere bribery, beyond shaking hands all around on an insinuation, beyond favors and winked eyes and the inference of evil like a secret between friends—though he did all that too, did all of it, though mostly in the beginning, folding bills into hundreds of palms, using cash like a password or a message from spies. (*Cash, cash,* the whole country crazy for cash, the only thing they'd touch, wanting no records, his far-seeing countrymen, those practical folks. What the *hell*, it couldn't last forever. Nothing could last forever, not even greed.)

Because the Senator was wrong. Because genius was genius. There was something physical in it too. Feldman took risks. (What, are you kidding? All those miles in all those airplanes in the forties? The cities blacked out, radar not perfected yet? Re-

member those plane crashes in the forties?) He was there, ubiq-
uitous, making his pitch. Looking over the operator's shoulder
while she sewed the last seam; among the toys, sneezing over the
teddy bears; his feet the first ones up on the sofa when it came
from the shop. In the small-arms factory too. He was the first
merchandiser to sell government surplus on the open market. And
during the war! The first department store in America to offer a
magazine-subscription service. Food departments. Virginia Sugar-
Cured Ham departments. Setting things up. Collecting his
merchandise. Inventing it. Johnny on the spot, picking over America, the rummage champion of World War Two, hearing the rumors, getting the word ("St. Louis has shoes"; "There are baskets
in Vermont, dishes in Portland"; "Carolina has hats"). Tours
through the plants. (And not just those innocuous preserves
where they turned out the belt buckles for civilian consumption—
the other parts too, to see what he could use. His suits on those
days had holes in the lapels and over all the breast pockets from
the badges he had to wear.) And this isn't just New York City
and Chicago and Cleveland and Los Angeles and Pittsburgh and
St. Louis we're talking about. We're talking about places in Nebraska and the Dakotas and southern Indiana and Montana and
Idaho and small towns in Dixie. Places with lousy accommoda-
tions for travelers and rotten food. And you can't always get there
from here. He got there. Feldman got there.

But he was busy and didn't meet girls. Except those who
worked for him. And life wasn't exciting enough, kissing the ladies in the big black hats and black dresses, the buyers in long
black gloves, those boozers and flatterers and users of make-up
and smellers from perfume. Feldman's buyers. (After he had set
up the *possibility* of buying, established that there was something
to be bought.) Feldman's girls, who were taken to lunch. And got
fucked at the gift shows, wooed in the Merchandise Mart in Chicago, in the showrooms of the McAlpin Hotel in New York, in
motels that were no bargain along the highways on the outskirts
of those two-bit towns Feldman had rummaged. (Well, didn't I
tell you? Genius *is* more than just being able to put down a cash
bribe. Cash, cash, that's all most people know. Take a little risk,
have a little fun. And pussy leaves less record than cash. Feldman's buyers were famous.)

But he had a sense of humor and wished to parody his situation. (It is in the long sad tradition of my people to pluck laughter from despair.) And then he met Lilly in New York City in 1949

in the Pennsylvania Hotel at the wedding of the son of his hand-bag supplier. She was the kid's aunt. She was infinitely boring, but she didn't have on a big black hat, and she had never been to a gift show. Feldman had never been so excited. He needed something special or he would go mad. (The war over four years. Nothing for him to do. The way he saw it, those fools in Washington would *never* bomb Russia.) Lilly's unspecialness was spectacular. He grew breathless contemplating it. What a mismatch! The two people stuck with each other—if they married—miserable together for the rest of their lives. Miserable in some important domestic way that Feldman had never known. A mystery. They would tear each other up. That would mean something. A little grief would mean something. *Excitement, excitement, give me excitement. Give me Sturm and give me Drang. Wring me out. Let me touch bottom. I don't care how. Thrown from the rocks, keel-hauled or shoved off the plank. Let me go down, down to the depths, further than fish, down by the monsters, the spiky and fanged. God, give me monsters. Scare me, please!*

He married Lilly.

And one monstrousness was that she wouldn't go along with a gag. Nor would she pluck laughter from despair. Despair depressed her; it gave her heartburn, like steak in a restaurant.

At this time—it was before he invented the basement—Feldman was a game player, a heavy gambler. He bet the horses, the ballgames, the fights, the elections, the first early launches of rockets. And though he mostly broke even, or better—he was lucky with money—he found that to be a bettor, to deal with bookies, accepting another's odds as fixed and beyond his control as the value of a share on the market, was to make of himself a consumer like anyone else. He would have quit long before he ultimately did but for Lilly's nervousness in the matter of his gambling. It worried her and she urged him to give it up. Her anxiety kept him going, but Lilly's anxieties—her fear of bookies, the association of them in her mind with a gangster style that had ended with the end of Prohibition—were part of her character. She worried for the safety of relatives in airplanes flying to Miami, for the careers of nephews, the betrothals of nieces and cousins. She was not anxious only about her own life, assuming safety and happiness and good luck like guaranteed rights. Feldman saw that he was not getting his money's worth from the gambling and abandoned it. On the other hand, he thought, if he could get *her* involved, concerned for her own losses, that would be something.

He made up games. Lilly played reluctantly. Sometimes they played gin rummy for wishes. The stakes weren't high, a twentieth of a wish a point. Lilly was a good cardplayer, and Feldman did not always win. He sweated the games out. Even at those small stakes, ten to fifteen wishes could change hands in a single game. When he lost, however, Lilly's wishes were always insignificant, unimaginative. She might ask him to bring her a glass of water, or to sing a song, or to clap his hands five times. Feldman insisted that she try harder, that she think of more damaging things for him to do.

"You're wasting your wishes, Lilly. Do you think wishes grow on trees? Why do you want to win them if all you do after you get them is throw them away?"

"I *like* to hear you sing, Leo. You have a nice voice."

"You try harder. It's no fun for me otherwise."

They had set a time limit, twenty-four hours, in which the winner had to make his wishes. By constantly harassing her and forcing her to think of more and more complex wishes, Feldman knew that he would be able to finesse at least half the wishes he owed her. She simply couldn't think of things for him to do. (And the truth was he *hated* to sing songs for her, *hated* to bring her a glass of water, to clap his hands for her.)

Chiefly, however, he won. Then he let her have it. (Another rule he had invented was that you could never wish the other fellow to do something that the other fellow had wished you to do. It was a way of protecting himself, of course. Ah, he thought, this *was* better than playing with the bookies. It was a marvelous thing to make house odds. House odds, domestic bliss.)

"Lilly, I wish you to take a bath." It was two in the morning. And when she had come from the tub, "Run around the block, Lilly, please."

"Leo, my pores are open."

"We are not fourflushers, Lilly. We are not welshers and Indian givers."

He watched her from their picture window. She came back puffing. He opened the glass doors and stood in the doorway. "Lilly, pretend you're drunk. Stagger around in the street and make noises."

"Leo, it's after two. People are sleeping. I won't do it. I balk." It was the formula for refusal. But they had another rule. If a player balked, he had to grant three wishes for the one he had balked at.

"Come inside," Feldman said sullenly. "Bake a cake," he wished half-heartedly. (She was on a diet.) "Have three big pieces and a glass of milk and go to sleep on the sofa."

Then he lost a close game.

"Leo, I wish that you wouldn't shout at Billy today."

"I balk."

"I wish you'd be nicer to me."

"I balk."

She sighed and had him count from a hundred backwards, say a tongue twister; read her the funnies, wind the clock, open the window, shut it.

Eventually, of course, she refused to play with him. It was the result of a fight. They had finished dinner, and Lilly was in the kitchen, fixing blueberries and sour cream. She still owed him a wish. Feldman saw a man on the sidewalk. "Lilly," he called, "there's a stranger outside. I wish you to go out and ask that stranger what he's doing in this neighborhood."

She didn't answer and Feldman walked into the kitchen. Lilly was spooning blueberries into a bowl from a basket.

"Didn't you hear me? I made my wish."

"No, Leo."

"He's right outside. You can see him through the window."

"No, Leo."

"Are you balking?"

"I'm not going to do it."

"Then say it. Say 'I balk.'"

"I'm not going to do it."

Feldman was furious. "You know the formula for refusing," he shouted. Billy was in the kitchen, wrapping rubber bands on the doorknob. The sight enraged him. Billy was six years old and took sides. He would whisper to his mother that he loved her most and that Daddy was bad, and to his father that Mommy wasn't very smart. Feldman pulled him away from the doorknob and told him to hide in his room. "A boy loses respect if he sees his father kick his mother's ass," Feldman said.

Lilly, saying nothing, continued to spoon the blueberries. She patted them around the sides of the bowl and fluffed them up with the spoon.

"When you finish there you can do the rest of the rubber bands," Feldman said.

Lilly said nothing.

"What's wrong with you?" Feldman demanded. It was one

of his questions. He asked it when they were doing something together and he was having a better time doing it than his wife. He asked it on complicated occasions like this one, when his head hurt and there was a sourness in the air, unsortable wrong, rife and general as a high pollen count. "You be careful, Lilly. I am as fed up as a revolutionary, as righteous at this moment as a terrorist. You better watch out."

Lilly was dipping sour cream onto the blueberries.

"*You're a shitty sport,*" Feldman screamed, and went for her. When he tore the spoon out of her hands some sour cream got on his shirt. He stared at it as if she had drawn blood. "Oh, you *will*, will you?" he roared. In his room Billy was crying. Feldman thought of all the times she had refused him. In the car, nothing on the radio but static, he might suggest that they both make speeches. Inaugural Addresses or nominating speeches at the Republican National Convention. And she would refuse. She didn't even want to hear *his* speech. Why couldn't she say "I balk"? What would *that* cost her? More sour cream got on his shirt, and Feldman made a fist and punched her in the behind.

She overturned the blueberries in the sink.

"You son of a bitch," Feldman screamed. "*Those are out of goddamn season!*"

"We shall never play gin rummy again," Lilly announced softly. She had tremendous self-possession at this moment, superhuman dignity. She seemed as calm and studied and smug as a circus performer holding acrobats on her shoulder. It was too much for Feldman. The sour cream burned holes in his shirt. He pulled her from the sink and spun her roughly away from him. She went turning and twirling across the kitchen, rapt as a blind woman in a dance, concentrating on her injuries as if they were already memories. She fell back against the refrigerator, and Feldman imagined the black-and-blue marks, proliferating on her back like stains.

"Oof," she said demurely.

"I can't stand it," Feldman roared. He stooped down and opened the cabinet beneath the sink. He pulled out the garbage pail. He reached inside it and scooped up great handfuls of garbage—ovoid clumps of wet coffee grounds, the pulps of oranges, eggshells, pits, bones, fat, the shallow rinds of honeydew melon like the hulls of toy boats. He flung all this onto the kitchen floor. He might have been sowing seeds.

In the distance Billy cried uncontrollably.

Lilly folded her arms across her breast, a look of mock indifference on her face like that of someone who has just done a turn in a challenge dance. Feldman stopped short and dropped the rest of the garbage. He folded his arms across his breast. "You serve, Lilly, I think," he said.

"Billy," Lilly shouted, "come in here."

Feldman was delighted. "What are you calling him for? This is between us," he said.

"Billy," she shouted again, "I've told you once. Come in here right now."

"Leave the kid out of it," Feldman snarled. He could have hugged her. Something magnificent was going to happen.

Billy appeared at the entrance to the kitchen, his face a smear of snot and tears. He seemed blind, breathless, choked as a child in a polyethylene bag.

"Go back to your room, Billy," Feldman said.

"If you do I'll follow and beat you up," Lilly said.

"If she does I'll kill her, Billy. Don't you worry, son."

Billy wailed.

"Pick up the garbage your father threw down. Every piece," Lilly commanded.

Billy, crying insanely, moved toward the garbage.

"What is this?" Feldman said. "What is this?"

The little boy bent over a piece of lettuce coated with cocktail sauce and picked it up.

"Give me that," Feldman cried. He pulled at it. The lettuce tore, and they each held a piece of it. Feldman turned to Lilly. "Is this how you raise a child?" he said angrily. Lilly's arms were still folded. Billy, terrified, was on his hands and knees, pushing the scraps together. Feldman pressed the point of his shoe into the rind of an orange that his son was trying to pick up. "I had not realized, Lilly, that the boy is so terrified of you," Feldman told her.

"Let me pick it up, Daddy," Billy said. "Let me pick it up."

"Get up, Billy," Feldman said with great, deliberate compassion.

"I'll do it," Billy said. "Please. I'll do it."

"He's hysterical," Feldman said. "He won't listen to me. You win, Lilly. You win. Tell him to get off the floor. I'll pick it all up."

"Get up, Billy," Lilly said, "your father will do it."

Feldman got down on his hands and knees. He breathed heavily. His palm slipped on something, and he fell forward awkwardly. His cheek lay in the wet coffee grounds. He got clumsily to his knees and put his hands on the boy's shoulders. "Listen to me, Billy. Make me a promise, son." He hung his head down a moment, apparently trying to catch his breath. He rubbed his eyes, then put his hand back on Billy's shoulder. "If she ever touches you, I want you to tell me, darling, and I'll break her bones, sweetheart. You tell Daddy, honey, if Mommy bothers you, and Daddy makes you this promise, adorable, that he'll smash her nose and pound her heart and crush her skull, pumpkin. You're Daddy's darlin', chicken, remember that. She's a great rough pig, angel, but Daddy will protect you. If that bitch ever bothers you—I don't care where I am or what I'm doing—you get to a telephone, lamb chop, and call me up, and I'll come home and put her in the hospital. Do you understand that, Billy? Do you understand that, dumpling? You're getting to be a big boy, watermelon, and you've got to understand these things. Give Dad a kiss now and promise that you'll never be afraid of her any more." He put his hands behind the boy's head and brought him up close to kiss him. "Now run and play, son," Feldman said. "Poppy will pick up the garbage for you."

Lilly's arms had come unfolded. They hung down like untied laces.

Feldman looked at her through an eggshell and smiled and splashed in the garbage and thought: Your serve, Lilly, I think, your serve, Lilly, I think. It's a regular second honeymoon, it's a second regular goddamned honeymoon.

Although he had not touched himself in two days, the jerking off had taken it out of him and he was exhausted. Now he would be continent. It would be a new phase. He lived by phases, like an artist with a blue period, a green one, a red. Seeking some ultimate violet. Did others do that? Lilly didn't; no one he knew did. Others had homogenized lives. Not Feldman. Feldman had periods.

How do you do it, Feldman?

This is how I do it, kid. I live by phases. Full Feldman. Quarter Feldman. Half-by-full three-quarter Feldman. Feldman waxing, Feldman waning. The astrological heart. Down through time to high night's noony now.

*　　*　　*

The homunculus, little stunted brother of his heart, stirred. The homunculus, stony, bony paradigm, scaled-down schema of waxing Feldman, flexed its visey brothership.

"Ouch," Feldman said. "You again."

"Move over, O greater frater. Give a toy twin space."

"No, pet. What can I do? I'm in solitary confinement. O solo mio."

"Have a little consideration, please. I feel terrible. For days I've been riding your passionate bronco heart. I'm seasick. I must look a fright, Leo."

"Are you sure you're my brother? You talk like my sister."

"Leo, please," the homunculus said.

"O steak-knife soul in my heart's bloody meat, leave off."

"Listen, brother," the homunculus said, "we have to talk. Watch your step. You forget you're living for two. Why can't you remember that? You specially. You're your brother's keeper if there ever was one."

"My little brother," Feldman said, giggling.

"To think," the homunculus said, "I might have been alive today but for some freak in the genes. Alas the blood's rip, alack my spilled amino acids, my done-in DNA. Woe for the watered marrow and the split hairs."

"Don't get clinical, you fossil."

"Oh, Leo, I would have done things differently. I would have taken better care. You have no right—"

"*I* have no right? *I* have no right? Didn't you ever hear of primogeniture? You're out of the picture, short division."

"*Leo,*" his homunculus said sharply, "you stop that. All your cynicism—that's just our father speaking. You insist on siding with him."

"I never knew our mother," Feldman said. "She was your department, death."

"Don't be sentimental either. Really, Leo, I'm surprised you try to pull this stuff with me. I *know* your heart. I've been there. I've been lying on it for years. It's a rack, buddy, a desert, some prehistoric potholed thing. It's a moon of a heart. It will not support life, Leo. So don't start up."

"You don't happen to have a deck of cards on you, do you?"

"We have serious things to discuss, Leo."

"I won't listen."

"Leo, you owe me. As a businessman you have always paid your bills."

"I owe you? What do I owe you? What have you done for me?"

"Like Wilson," the homunculus said slyly, "I kept you out of war."

Feldman admitted grudgingly that this was so.

The homunculus smiled; it pinched. "What do you make of this bad-man stuff?" it asked confidentially. "Anything to it?"

"Why ask me?" Feldman said sourly. "You know my heart."

"Only its terrain," the homunculus said.

"My heart hurts."

"Is that why, Leo? Is that it? Do you suffer much?"

"I *never* suffer. *Never*," Feldman said. "Tell me something. What's it like down there?"

"What's it *like?*"

"Is there an odor?"

"It's a butcher shop, Leo."

"Then you don't have it so easy, do you?" Feldman touched his chest. "Me, I never suffer," he said. "Things hurt once in a while. Like my heart just now, but I can stand a little pain. I can stand a lot of pain. I've the pain threshold of a giant."

"You can stand other people's pain," his homunculus said.

"Everybody's," Feldman said. "Pain disappoints me finally. How do you know I'm telling you the truth? Or does a good angel just know?"

"I'm not a good angel."

"An alter ego."

"I'm not an alter ego."

"Who you?"

"I'm a homunculus, a fossilized potential."

"What might have been," Feldman said.

"Not to you. To me."

"This is my interview, you sit-in sibling."

"Go ahead," the homunculus said. "Enjoy yourself."

"Enjoy myself," Feldman said. "Listen, sidecar, let me tell you. One summer I went East with Lilly to see her family. They have this place on the Sound. They call it a summer place, but it's terrific. It's like a hotel. They've got a band shell. They have tennis courts. A swimming pool. All the styrofoam toys—you know, chaise lounges that float around beside you in the water, tables with drinks on them. They've got boats. Lilly is a water-skier, did you know that? Your sister-in-law is a water-skier. They've got all this stuff. The very best. If you like that sort of thing."

"Don't you?"

"No. Fun's fun, but it always turns out to be some new ride. It's onanistic, if you want to know, because what counts is what's going on in the pit of your stomach. Sin ought to involve other people too. I don't see the point. It's a question of risks and balanced thrills. In a roller coaster the risk is relatively small, but the thrill—the fright and the queerness in the belly—is large. On water skis the queerness is much less but the risk is greater. Do you know what I'm talking about? There's nothing to do. I can take a lot of suffering because I can take a lot of pleasure too. There's nothing to do."

"Don't tell me you're bored."

"No. I'm not bored."

"I don't see how you manage to avoid it then, O solo Leo."

"There's a pleasure that never disappoints. It comes from setting other things in motion but not moving yourself."

"Ah, Leo, you've the soul of a model railroader."

"You forget yourself. I'm your host."

"I'm sorry. How does one manage this?"

"Sell," Feldman said.

"Cell?"

"Yes," Feldman said, "sell."

He was going nuts. It was a new phase. He became desperate. It was a new phase. He felt a need for exercise and dreamed of learning to water-ski. It was a new phase. He defined physical health as a flexibility of posture and imagined himself a scientist. It was a new phase. He defined unhappiness as a flexibility of mood and imagined himself a philosopher. And the ground kept shifting on him and he thought again of those rooms where the walls close in and the floors move up to meet a descending ceiling. And he had to take his hat off to that warden, which was an old phase. And for a while he was afraid. He wanted to be able to stretch his legs, *really* stretch them, slide into third base or climb some high mountain or run the mile. And he felt this rapid alternation of the soul, and he commanded the homunculus to sit still, but *it* wasn't doing it, it said, and as far as it, the homunculus, was concerned, solitary confinement was something it was used to, what with being a shut-in and all.

Feldman didn't know what to do, so to steady himself he decided to try to sell the homunculus a little something. He tried to sell it some of the soup the guard had brought him for lunch—

it was a cold day, and soup warms the heart, Feldman said, and it would do the homunculus good—but there was absolutely no way the little fellow could pay him. Feldman offered to extend credit (he remembered fondly that he had done some marvelous things with credit), but no, the homunculus could *never* pay him. It was a pauper, of course, a spread-eagled parasite riding the heart like a surfboard. It couldn't help itself. It had no money. It had never had money. It was born without pockets. Since it was against Feldman's principles to give anything away, he ate the soup himself.

"Want to buy back this empty tray?" Feldman asked the guard.

"Watch out," the guard said. "You don't get out of here until I can report to the warden that there's been a significant change in your behavior."

"*You?*"

"I'm a trained psychologist," the guard said.

Then he entered a very bad phase. It was the one he had the most faith in because it was the one he had the least to do with. That is, he had not invented it as he had invented the others. Instead, it was visited upon him, as a disease might have been, or seven fat years, then seven lean ones.

He was low, as low perhaps as he had ever been. With the clarity of an insomniac, he saw—and so striking was the impression that he could not remember when it had been otherwise—the inferior quality of his life. Most of the acceptable lives he could think of were lived by strangers. He thought of the warden. How would it feel, he asked himself, to be the warden? Not so hot, perhaps. The man was too much like himself. It was not acceptable, finally, or respectable, to have to deal with those who were not your equals. He and the warden had never dealt with equals. Feldman lacked respectability, the clubby regard of peers. (It was funny, because most people were respectable. All the clerks in his department store were respectable, all the cousins at a wedding.) It was the serenity of the franchised, and Feldman had always lacked it, and because he lacked it his life was without the possibility of consolation.

Where, he wondered, are Feldman's peers? Nowhere. Then where are his customers? All gone, taken away, and the salesman locked up in a cage. Then where's his life? Here's his life, here in the cage.

*   *   *

This phase did not soon pass—he had some hope that it might; so sly was he, so long had he lived with aces in the hole, that he thought they must be there always; superstitiously he thought they grew there—but when it finally ended he lay back on his cot, returned to a condition of an earlier phase. He was again the man who could not remember, forced into some narrow channel of the now.

He was like a sick man, had just that sick-man sense of languid withdrawal even from his own symptoms, and even the sick man's vague unthrift, his sporty indifference that he existed in an ambience of letters which had still to be answered, appointments which had still to be canceled, invitations which had still to be withdrawn. Deprived of detail, he was brought back into himself and was surprised to learn that this was possible, for he knew that as a selfish man he had never lived very far away from himself, had hedged distance and all horizons like some twelfth-century mariner. The idea that there were pieces of Feldman which could still be recalled gave him a sense of his own enormousness.

It was just this awe of himself which gave him his first hope in days. He marveled at his spinning moods, his barber-pole soul. And again he found himself praying. "Give me back constancy," he prayed, "make me monolithic, fix my flux and let me consolidate."

"Listen," Feldman asked the guard, "are there any letters for me?" He hadn't the least idea why he had asked the question. He had told Lilly not to write him, and he was still so turned in on himself that it would have been impossible for him even to read a letter. (He had noticed lately—with some alarm—that without any work for it to do, his will proceeded in its own direction.)

"You should know that you're not allowed to receive letters while you're in solitary confinement," the guard said.

Feldman nodded.

"They hold them for you, of course," the guard went on. He was looking at Feldman intently.

Feldman nodded.

"They keep them in the census office, *where my friend works,*" the guard said. He was staring at Feldman now.

"Say," Feldman said doubtfully, "would it be too much trouble for you to find out if any are being held for me?"

"I could find out if any are being held for you," the guard said. "Would you like that?"

"I'd appreciate it," Feldman said.

'If you like, I might even be able to tell you who they're from," the guard said.

"Would you do that?" Feldman asked.

"No trouble," the guard said.

"Do you think you could check the postmarks?" Feldman said. "I'd like to have an idea when they were mailed."

"Sure."

"And if you could make a notation of the station they were sent from," Feldman said. "Sometimes a person drops off a letter downtown, or on the way to the movie in the shopping center."

"Certainly," the guard said. "The rule states only that mail may not be received by a prisoner in solitary or opened for him."

"I see. Then could you check the color of the envelope and the kind of stamp that's been put on it?"

"The stamp?"

"Well, these things could reveal the sender's mood."

"Say, that's right. I'll check the color of the envelope and the kind of stamp."

"Could you smell the letter for perfume?"

"Well, I'll try," the guard said, "but I have a cold."

"I'm sorry to hear that," Feldman said.

"Thank you, I'll be all right."

"Thank God for that," Feldman said.

"Would you like me to look for little instructions on the front?" the guard asked. "Sometimes it says 'Personal' or 'Please Forward.' "

"I'd be grateful," Feldman said. "Could you look at the back too? Often the flaps are scalloped."

"No trouble at all."

"I miss my people very much," Feldman said. "I see that," the guard said.

The guard brought his lunch. "There weren't any letters for you," he said.

"Then how we doing in the cold war?" Feldman asked.

"I'm sorry," the guard said. "You haven't any newspaper, TV or radio privileges in here. It would be a violation of the spirit of the rules for me to tell you."

"I see," Feldman said.

The guard winked broadly. "I don't suppose my cousin Dorothy will be taking that trip to Berlin this week," he said in a voice somewhat louder than the one in which he normally spoke.

"That's too bad," Feldman said, winking back and raising his voice too. "I can imagine how disappointed she'll be. But maybe she can go someplace else. They say the *Far East* is nice this time of year."

"Well, they say *most* of the Far East is nice, but they don't say it about *Thailand*," the guard said. He was practically shouting.

"Don't they?" Feldman yelled.

"No, they don't," the guard yelled back. *"And they don't say it about Formosa or the offshore islands either."*

"I see," Feldman said. "Is your brother Walter still doing the shopping for the family?" He held a wink for five seconds.

"I beg your pardon?"

"*Wal*ter. Has *Wal*ter been going down the *street* to the *market* recently?"

"Oh, *Wal*ter, the *market*. Yes, indeed. *Wal*ter's been going to the *market*. He sure has." The guard winked, touched his temple, clicked his tongue and nudged Feldman with his elbow.

"Yes? What has he been bringing back with him?"

"Missiles, chemicals, utilities," the guard said.

Feldman nodded. "How's your friend Virginia?" he asked after a moment.

"Virginia?"

"You know, Caro*lina*'s sister. The sports fan. The one that's so interested in *races*."

"Races?"

"Vir*ginia*, Caro*lina*'s sister, *Georg*ia's roommate."

"Oh, *Virginia*. The one that was a *riot* last summer?"

"That's the one."

"Very quiet," the guard said, roaring.

Feldman suddenly began to whistle a popular song of a few weeks before. The guard stared at him as Feldman whistled it all the way through. The guard shook his head, and Feldman whistled another song from the same period. He winked one eye, then the other, and began a third song. Before he could finish, the guard brightened and began to hum a tune Feldman had never heard. When he finished that he hummed another song to which he performed in accompaniment a strange shuffling dance Feldman had never seen. Feldman leaned his head against the bars and listened and watched raptly.

* * *

"How are the rest of the fellers?" Feldman asked the guard when he brought his breakfast the next morning.

At lunch the warden was with the guard. The guard handed Feldman his tray without a word and stepped outside the cell to stand beside the warden. Feldman placed the tray on his lap primly and began to eat his lunch. He took a bite from his sandwich and looked out at the warden. "How did the men enjoy the movie this week?" he asked. The warden didn't answer, and Feldman ate his pear. He wiped his lips with his napkin. The guard and the warden continued to stare at him. "Have they completed the construction of the new wing in the infirmary?" Feldman asked. "Have the boys at the foundry met their quota this month?" The warden frowned and turned to go. As the warden started off, the guard shook his head sadly and shrugged. "Is Bisch all right? How's Slipper? What's going on at the canteen?" Feldman called. The warden looked back over his shoulder for a moment and glared at Feldman. "I'll never forget," Feldman said, "one time—it was on a Sunday afternoon—I had just awakened from a nap and my son Billy was in the room." The warden turned around, looked at him for a moment and came back toward the cell.

"Yes?" he said.

"It was on a Sunday afternoon," Feldman said. "I'll never forget this. Billy was about six or seven. Six, he was six. I had been sleeping, and when I woke up, the first thing I saw when I opened my eyes was my son."

"Go on."

"He was beautiful. I had never seen how beautiful he was. He was sitting on the floor, cross-legged. You know? He had on these short pants, his back was to me. He had come in to be with me in the room while I slept. He pulled some toy cars along in wide arcs beside him and made the noises in his throat, the low rough truck noises, and the sounds of family cars like the singing master's hum that gives the pitch. He had fire trucks and he did their sirens, and farm machinery that moved by slowly, going *chug chug chug*."

"Is this true?" the warden asked.

"Yes," Feldman said.

"What did you do?" the guard asked. "Did you kiss him?"

"No. I was afraid he'd stop."

"How long did your mood last?"

"Something happened," Feldman said.

"Yes?"

"I started to cry. It frightened him."

"Did you tell him why you were crying?" The warden had come into the cell. He was searching Feldman's face. Eternity was on the line. What did he have to come into the cell for? "Did you tell him why you were crying?" the warden asked again.

"Yes," Feldman said. "I told him it was because he woke me up."

"I see," the warden said.

"You want the truth, don't you, Warden?"

"We'll see what the truth is."

"Here's what the truth is," Feldman said. "Billy *wasn't* in the room when I woke up. A couple of feathers had come out of my pillow, and I had this idea. I pulled a few more feathers out and I called the kid. 'Billy, get in here. Come quickly.'

"He was standing in the doorway, and I told him to get his mother, that my feathers were coming out. I held one up for him to see and then I stuffed it back with some others which I had pushed into my bellybutton. He came over and stared at my stomach. A few feathers were on my chest, and he picked one up. 'Don't touch that feather. It's mine. Put it back in my belly, where it belongs.'

" 'You're fooling me,' Billy said, and I started to scream as if I were in pain.

" 'Get your mother,' I yelled, 'I need a doctor.' I told him that if you lose fifteen feathers you die."

Remembering it all, Feldman became excited. " 'Wait,' I told him. 'Count them first so your mother can tell the doctor and he'll know what medicine to bring. Can you count to fifteen?'

" 'Yes,' Billy said.

" 'Well, don't make a mistake now, for God's sake. You're a pretty stupid kid, and I know how you get mixed up after twelve. Hurry, please, but don't touch the feathers or more will come out.' So he started to count the feathers, but they were all rolled up together and it was impossible. 'Hurry,' I shouted. He started to cry and got all mixed up and had to count them all over again. He couldn't do it. He was in a panic. Finally I told him I had felt about eleven come out and that he'd better tell his mother that. As soon as he left, I pulled three more feathers out of the pillow and called him back. 'Billy,' I shouted, 'three more feathers just came loose. If I lose one more I'm a dead man.' He rushed over to see. Listen, he was sobbing, he was hysterical, out of control, but do you know what he managed to ask me? 'Daddy,' he said, 'do I have feathers too?' Don't tell *me* about love. His daddy is dying of feather loss, and he wants to know if it's contagious. *I am what I am, Warden.*" Feldman moved away from him and went to the sink and splashed cold water on his face. "I blew it, right?" he said. "I stay here forever."

"We are *all* what we are," the warden said angrily. "Jackass, we are *all* what we are. What's so terrific? 'I am what I am,' the hooligan says, and hopes by that to lend some integrity to his evil. To be what one is is *nothing*. It's easy as pie. The physics of least resistance. What appealed to me in your story was the regret in your voice just now when you asked if you blew it. 'We'll see what the truth is,' I said. And we shall. Think, Feldman. Think before you irrevocably indulge what you are. Did you tell him why you were crying?"

"What?"

"Did you tell him why you were crying?"

Feldman, astonished, stared at the warden. The guard laughed. "Hush," the warden said, and turned back to look at Feldman with a bland indifference. "We have no time. Make your reply at once."

Feldman had to. He had to. "I told him—" But he didn't finish. He couldn't talk. "I told him—" He held out his hands helplessly.

"Yes?" the warden said. "What did you tell him?"

"I told him that I thought he was beautiful. I told him I loved him. I lifted him up next to me in the bed. I held him in my arms." He was sobbing.

"Good," the warden said, "not only what you told him but also what you did. Good." He turned to the guard. "Guard, I think we can let this man join the others." Feldman was on the cot now, his head in his hands, and the warden gripped him by the shoulders. "There, there," he said, "it's all right. Everything is all right. You'll be back in your regular cell in a jiffy." He looked back at the guard. "Make the arrangements, Guard, please." He slapped Feldman on the back. "Well," he said, "I think this calls for a celebration. As a matter of fact, I usually give a party in Warden's Quarters when a man is reclaimed from solitary. Let's say Friday night. About eightish. Will you be able to come to dinner?" He leaned down and whispered to Feldman. "Stop it.

Stop your crying. Get it out of your head, you fool, that you've been mortified by the devil. You think you're rid of your soul and now your comfort comes, but it isn't so. I'm not the devil, and you've still got your soul. Your passion's on you like perfume. Undream your dreams of fuck and freedom. Your warden warns you. Stop it. Stop your crying. You'll need your tears."

12

Feldman, behaving, sold his quota of toothpaste and shaving articles and filter-tip cigarettes in the canteen—no more, no less—and tried to feel the virtue that is the reward of the routinized life. He thought with dread of the volumes in the library that bore his name, and guessing what might be in them, tried to act in such a manner that others might think him some other Feldman. He made small talk with the guards, just as the others did, warming to their crude kidding like some old yardman. (It was true. Each time they addressed him he felt as if he had just come from trimming hedges, pulling weeds, growing roses. He felt soil on himself and the small sharp plunge of thorns, and thought comfortably about baths with brown soap and worried about frost, about drought, about flood and the blight of beetles.) He looked for them to kid him, encouraged it in small ways, offering himself like a sparring partner or the bandaged man in a first-aid demonstration. He had it in him, he felt, to be a favorite, like a fatty, like a baldy, like a loony, like a spoony. Like a dummy. Like a guy with clap, with lush, beautiful daughters, with a small dong. He envied the loved, classic fall guys and thought with jealousy of the libeled butts in the prison paper: the "Nigger Lips" Johnsons and "Pigface" Parkers and "Beergut" Kellys and all the others.

"Give me gland trouble," he prayed. "Treble my chins and

pull back my hairline. Make me a farter, a stutterer, a guy bad at games. A patsy make me. Amen."

He was afraid of the warden, afraid of his party, afraid in particular, afraid in general. It was as if he were a traveler unused to the currencies of a new country. He was reminded of all queer special units used to fix values: the score of butter and the proof of booze, the carat of gold and the pile of a carpet and the line of a tire. The way of a warden, he thought.

A memorandum came down from the warden that the dinner would be semiformal and that Feldman had permission to request the pre-release of the suit of clothes the state had made for his discharge. Feldman took the note to the tailor shop and showed it to Bisch. It was still months until his release. "Is this ready?" he asked Bisch.

"Sure," Bisch said, "it was ready a week after you came. I'll have my apprentice get it."

The apprentice brought back a dark suit of coarse material. There were stiff tickets pinned to both sleeves of the jacket and over the breast and stapled across the creases of the trousers. Faint chalky marks, like military piping, were soaped around the seams at the shoulders.

"Try it on," Bisch said.

Feldman took off the blue fool suit Bisch had made for him and struggled into the new clothes. It was as if the suit had been made for someone of exactly his frame but twenty or thirty pounds lighter. "It doesn't fit," Feldman said. "It's too tight."

"Where?"

"Where? Everywhere. Across the shoulders, in the back, around the arms, the waist, the crotch, the seat. Everywhere. There's some mistake here."

"Take it off," Bisch said. "I'll check."

"You'll check? You don't have to check. You can see it doesn't fit."

"I want to see the measurements on the tickets." He turned to his apprentice. "Get the body book."

The man came back with an enormous ringed notebook. Bisch took the book from him and spread it open on a sewing table. "Here's your page," he said, peering at the figures on the page and then at those on the tickets. He took a tape measure and measured the different planes of Feldman's clothes. "Every figure checks out perfectly, Leo. It's a well-made suit of clothes."

"Well, where did you get those figures? Nobody measured me."

"They come from the physician," Bisch's apprentice said. It was the first indication Feldman had that they expected him to die. These were to be the graveclothes of a wasted Feldman.

He refused to wear the suit and sent a message at once to Warden's Desk. (It was a prisoner's only recourse to direct appeal and was rarely used. The petition had to be framed as a question backed up by a single reason. If the response was negative, the petitioner was subject to a heavy fine or a severe punishment for "Aggrandizement.")

Feldman waited nervously for his reply. He had it inside of half an hour:

> *Yes. A guest should be comfortable. If you're uncomfortable in the suit, don't wear it. Get your old suit from Convict's Wardrobe and have it pressed. W. Fisher.*

When it was ready Feldman put it on. It was enormous, almost as big on him as the other had been small. He sent another note to Warden's Desk. The reply came:

> *Yes. Suit yourself. Come as you are. Warden F.*

Feldman, released from his cell at 7:45 by a guard with a machine gun, went to the party in his blue fool suit.

The guard led him down passages he had never seen. Every hundred feet or so there were abandoned directions—narrowing converging walls, crawl spaces, oblique slopes. They might have been traveling along the played-out channels of a mine, tracing prosperity's whimmed route. They came to locked doors, barred gates. Bolts shot, tumblers bristled, plopped, falling away before the guard's keys and signals. Feldman had the impression he moved through zones, seamed places, climbing a latitude—as once, in winter, driving north from the Florida Keys, he had come all the way up the country to the top of Maine, feeling the subtle, dangerous differences, the ominous botanical shifts and reversals of season.

They came to a last steel door. The guard moved Feldman against the wall with the muzzle of his machine gun. "Fix your tie," he said, "or I'll kill you."

Feldman looked back along the dim passageway through

which they had just come. He felt like a bull in the *toril* before a
fight, a bronco in the chute. The sunlight will startle me, he
thought. I'll be confused by the day. Men will thrust capes at me.
Cowboys will scrape their spurs across my sides. Not a mark on
me till now, he thought sadly. He mourned his ruined flanks.

The guard inserted a key into the door, and a buzzer buzzed
somewhere on the other side. As the door slid back into the wall
an enormous butler stepped toward them, pulling his huge formal
silhouette through the lighted room behind him. "Hands up," he
said quietly.

"The butler's a bodyguard," the guard explained. "He has to
frisk you in case you bribed me on the way over."

"He's clean," the butler said gloomily.

The guard tilted his cap further back on his head with the
barrel of his machine gun and leaned casually against the wall. "I
guess I'll hang around the kitchen till it's time to take him back,"
he said. "Who's supervising?"

"Molly Badge."

"Molly? No kidding? I haven't seen old Molly since I was
with the Fire Department and she catered the dinner dance. Good
old Molly."

"Come inside," the butler told Feldman. "No tricks tonight.
Some of the guests are plainclothesmen. Follow me."

He followed the butler through the doorway. He was conscious of the brightness; he had not seen so much light since his
arrest months before. He wondered where they were—outside the
walls, more deeply within them? Coming here, he'd had a sense
of tunneling, of a Chinesey-boxish progress. The warden lived
well, but there was about the place an air of exile, as if, perhaps,
he were someone bought off, bribed to live here. Taking in everything, he had an impression of wells sunk miles, a special flicker
in the lights that hinted of generators, a suggestion of things done
to the air. The wood, so long now had he lived without wood,
seemed strange, extravagant. The upholstery and drapes, though
he suspected no windows lay behind them, were almost oriental
in their luxury. He moved across the carpet as over the fabricked
backs of beasts in a dream. Apprehension was gone. Here the blue
fool suit, loose on his body, no travesty, was a robe, exotic, falling
away from his chest like the awry gown of a seducer. Will there
be women? he wondered. He hoped so. He rubbed his hands together and turned to the butler. "I'm a sucker for civilization," he
told him.

The butler pulled back the heavy doors to the library and motioned him inside. Feldman found himself on tiptoe, leaning forward, his eyes darting, in the eager posture of a host. The room was empty. The butler left him.

The library was ship-in-the bottle, oakey. "Oakey-doakey," Feldman said. Wing-chaired. Beamish. Rifles over the mantelpiece, a clock with a visible movement, dark portraits of the founders of banks. "Generations of gentiles," Feldman said. There was a big desk behind which a landlord with a *schmear* in his integrity could kill himself. "After brandy," Feldman said, "a silver bullet in a silver sideburn." The will would be read here to out-of-towners in black suits.

There were decanters of whiskey and silver bottles of soda. He fixed a drink, drank it off quickly and made another. When he turned, the warden, in carpet slippers and a red silk smoking jacket, was watching him. Feldman raised his glass. "To crime and punishment," he said.

The warden motioned Feldman to go ahead. "I'm pleased you came," he said, "and glad you've made yourself comfortable, though I doubt the sincerity of your ease. I wanted the sergeant to show you this room first. Do you like it?"

"A showcase, Warden," he said.

The warden smiled. "I'm being urbane," he said. He sat in a wing chair and crossed his legs smartly. Feldman saw the bright bottom of a carpet slipper, like the clean soles of the shoes of an actor on a rug on a stage. He stared at the light that slipped up and down the smooth stripe of his trousers. "Say what you will, Feldman," the warden said, "but urbanity is a Christian gift. Rome, London, Wittenberg, Geneva—*cities*, Feldman. The history of us Christians is bound up with the history of the great cities. I mean no offense, of course, but yours is a desert sensibility, a past of pitched tents and camps. Excuse me, Leo, but you're a hick. Have you held canes? Have binoculars hung from your jackets?" He indicated a portrait in a gilt frame. "Just a moment," he said, standing. He moved to the portrait and pulled a small chain, turning on the light in an oblong reflector. "Where would you buy one of these? Tell me, merchant. You see? You don't know. You've seen them, but you haven't experienced them. I've stood beside sideboards and spent Christmas with friends. There's leather on my bookshelves, Feldman. I've been to Connecticut. I know how to sail. What are you in our culture? A mimic. A spade in a tux at a function in Harlem.

"I make this astonishing speech to you not out of malice. It's way of life against way of life with me, Feldman. I show you alternatives to wholesale and retail. I push past your poetics, your metaphors of merchandise, and scorn the emptiness of your *caveat emptor*. I, the least of Christians, do this. Come, the others will have gathered."

They went to the drawing room, where, as the warden had said, the others had gathered. They must have collected suddenly, but as he and the warden entered they were already lounging in a stiff, suspect sereneness. Feldman recognized none of them, but their ease was familiar to him. He was reminded of his own casual duplicities, the petite infighting of maneuvered-for advantage and self-control. They were people one step ahead of other people, he thought, like schoolchildren whose teacher has come back to find them all studying. Or spies who have rifled drawers, suitcases, the seams of pillows. As he preceded the warden, who had turned deferential, he had a sense of the queer, sedate violence of entering a strange room. He thought with wonder of all the times he had arrived early for appointments, guiltily examining the instruments in doctors' offices, a lawyer's framed degrees, family photographs, of all the times, left alone in hotel rooms while others shaved and apologized through closed doors for their lateness, he had picked candy from boxes open on the table.

Though he no longer cared, there were women. Men in dinner jackets stood with ladies in cocktail dresses. "Excuse me," the warden said, abandoning him, "I have to see to some guests." Feldman stayed nervously where he was, smiling back tentatively into the remote stares of the others.

A tall graying man came up to him. "Tell me," he said, "which is worse for you, the day or the night?"

"*That* old chestnut," another said, slowly wheeling from the margin of a small group to which he had attached himself. "Paul's still espousing those malfeasant ideas. As Chargé de Disease, I couldn't permit his theories to become operational in any institution in which *I* had an infirmary."

"I believe, Chargé de Disease," the tall man said with much dignity, "that I was addressing the thief here."

"I'm not a thief, sir," Feldman said shyly.

"There's only one crime," the man said. "It's theft."

"A dietary approach to punishment," the second man said. "Paul, it's medieval."

"Please, Chargé, let him answer." He turned grimly back to Feldman.

"The day is worse," Feldman said.

"Morning or afternoon?"

"Afternoon."

"Early or late afternoon?"

"Early afternoon."

"You see?" the tall man said. "He means that dead center of a waking life fifteen minutes past lunch, three hundred forty-five minutes before dinner. My techniques would extend that desperation. Stretch the fabric of his hopelessness—all crimes are wishes, Chargé—over an entire day, and you've returned his aggressions to his dream life, where they belong. Let him writhe in bed. Cut out this fellow's lunch, remove the water coolers, make the water in the sinks as nonpotable as on European trains. Forbid him cigarettes. Abolish his coffee breaks and canteen privileges, poleax the penny gum machines as if they were gaming tables, Chargé, and you've denatured him. Nullify his oral gratifications, and you've stripped his hope, I tell you, and made his imagination as incapable of crime as of epic poetry."

"Well perhaps—"

"Not perhaps, Chargé—certainly, absolutely. It's historical, Chargé. When was the golden age of obedience in this country?"

"Historical, Paul? Historical? Pooh pooh, tut tut."

"When was the golden age of obedience in this country?" Paul insisted.

"Well—"

"It was the *sweatshop* age, Chargé. It was the *piecework* age. It was the twelve- and fourteen-hour-day age. The simultaneity of those hard times with the flourishing of the city park system, when parks were safe, was no coincidence. Where were your Coca Cola machines then, Chargé? Where were your *refreshment* stands? Sweat and hopelessness, Chargé, is our only hope."

"Well, I agree with you in principle, of course, Paul, but do you really think you can keep hope down? 'Hope springs eternal.' "

"Hope does not spring eternal *forever*, Chargé," the tall scholarly man said.

Feldman excused himself and went up to a servant who carried a tray of drinks. He had already had three in the library, but they had not been enough. He removed a glass from the tray and nodded his thanks. The servant looked at him blankly. A plainclothesman, Feldman thought. He finished it quickly, and the servant handed him another. Flatfoot, Feldman thought. I'd better not get drunk here. Keep me sober, he prayed. He reminded himself merely to sip the next drink, but in a few minutes the servant was beside him again, extending the tray. "No, no, I'm fine," Feldman said. The servant did not move, and Feldman drank the rest of the liquor in his glass and took another from the tray. Watch your step, he thought. Watch my step, he prayed.

He remembered an empty, comfortable-looking couch he had seen on first entering the room, and now he looked for it again. There were no empty couches. He was very puzzled. That's funny, he thought, they must have taken it out. There was a couch just where he remembered the empty couch to have been, but five people were sitting on it.

It was essential that he make himself inconspicuous, so he went up to the couch and squeezed in. Because it was already crowded, he had to place the edge of one thigh in a woman's lap. He had not had this close a contact with a woman in months, and soon he had a hard-on. In those close quarters his erection was pretty apparent, but he reasoned that because of her age—she was about seventy—the woman might not mind.

"Recidivism's not important, Julia. What counts is that we catch these guys," the man on Feldman's left said. "The very fact that we have statistics on recidivism demonstrates the efficacy of our policework."

"I don't contest that," Julia said. It was the old lady. She had a gentle voice. Feldman fought off a vagrant impulse to blow in her ear. "It isn't that at all. It's the older parolees. Men who've done twenty and thirty years. It annoys me that *they* don't behave."

"You think age quiets those old thieves down?" the man asked. "Infirmity? How thick is plate glass? How heavy is a watch? A diamond bracelet?"

"The inspector's right," said a man at the other end, half of whose body Feldman's presence had forced far over the arm of the couch. He supported himself with his right arm extended on the floor, so that he looked like a downed boxer waiting to rise. Feldman hoped someone would step on his watch. "And I'll tell you something else. Science in its development of transistorized equipment has made our problem tougher. A thief's armload today is worth more than a thief's armload was yesterday, and a thief's armload tomorrow will be worth even more. I foresee a time when the thief's armload will be approximate in value to the thief's truckload of yesteryear. *That's* what science has done with its vaunted miniaturization!"

With the strain on his arm the man had spoken louder than he had perhaps intended, and Paul heard him. "And not only that," Paul said, "but improper diet—the snack-food industry is a three-billion-dollar-a-year business today—has made his thief's arms longer." He saw Feldman. "Which it worse for you, the day or the night?"

"The night," Feldman said. He got up quickly and moved away from them. Across the room he blew a kiss covertly to Julia.

Behind him the warden was standing with two men. "Keep them under," one was saying.

"But there's no need to keep them under," the second man said. "You've changed the goal," he objected. "Hasn't he, Warden? Hasn't he changed the goal?"

"Well—" the warden said evasively.

"What's the goal?" Feldman asked, turning around.

"Order," the second man said.

"Acquiescence?" I'd say," said the first man.

"Acquiescence?" Feldman said.

"Well, silence," the first man said.

Feldman nodded. He joined another group. He was afraid he was drunk. The Lord has failed me, he thought miserably. On his own he avoided the servant with the tray, turning his back whenever the man approached. In a while, though, he could no longer remember his reason for wanting to remain sober. What am I afraid of, he asked himself—that I won't be invited again? He giggled and sought out the fellow with the drinks. "Thanks, gumshoe," he said, taking another drink from the cop. They were all cops here. It was the Policemen's Ball. He could smell rectitude. The odor of ordinance was in the air.

Suddenly he felt compassion for his fellow inmates. It was a shame, he thought. They talked about the underworld—"Keep them under," someone had said—but what about the overworld? They talked about organized crime, but Feldman couldn't think of two hoods who could stand each other. If one had a gun, sooner or later the other was a dead man. The real organization belonged to the overworld. Did cops shoot each other, horn in on each other's territory, beat each other's time? No, the cops had their cop cartels, their FBI's and state troopers and Policemen's Benevolent Associations. It was the poor crook who was alone. The crook had no ecumenical sense at all. For one Appalachia Conference, and he could just imagine the screaming and backbiting that must have gone on, there were hundreds of parties like this one. He was consumed by a truth, sudden and overwhelming. He had to share it at once or he would burst. He rushed up to someone. "There isn't any," he told him passionately.

"What's that?"

"There *isn't* any. It doesn't exist."

"There isn't any.what?"

"There isn't any Syndicate. There isn't any Mafia. There isn't any Cosa Nostra. You can all go home."

"Try to eat something," the man said. "Would you like some coffee?" he asked solicitously.

"No," Feldman said glumly. He found a chair and sat down. They'd probably have to shut him up, now they knew he was on to them. Already the man was conferring with someone; together they were staring at him. It was all a fake. Maybe even evil was a fake. He'd better keep his ears open and his mouth shut. (The thought nauseated him.) He had to focus, concentrate. There were things to learn he could bring back to the boys. He thought fondly of the boys. Good old Bisch. That grand old man Ed Slipper. And Hover—fine, maligned Hover. Sky and Flesh and Walls were the best pals a guy ever had. He thought of his friends asleep on their cots. They might be thieves and murderers, but they were good old boys. He had a duty to the guys to sober up, to tell them what he'd learned: that they were a myth. He imagined a youthful eagerness in his voice as he told them. It was news to make a tenor of a man.

Concentrating, he was astonished at the enormous varieties of cophood there were in the room. In addition to those he had already met, the sheriffs and marshals and constables and private detectives, there were insurance investigators and high officials in the National Guard. There was a man who trained German shepherds and leased them to department stores and warehouses. Another man was in charge of an army of crowd handlers at ball parks and arenas. There was a chief of house detectives for a large hotel chain and a woman who headed up an agency of store detectives. There were polygraph experts and fingerprint men and a police artist who was introduced to Feldman as the Rembrandt of his field. There were prison chaplains and expert witnesses for the prosecution at murder trials.

He felt as if he had been caught in the guts of an enormous

machine. As he had noted before, there were no windows, and he
rushed instead to the door to get some air. Outside stood the
deputy who had brought him to the prison. The man passed him
by, smiling. "It's ten thirty-seven," he said, waving his wrist with
Feldman's watch on it.

When he was calm enough Feldman went to the buffet table;
his new knowledge had made him hungry. He was surprised at
the meager character of the food. Perhaps there was something in
the make-up of good men that subdued their tastes and deadened
their appetites, something surly in their hearts that made them
trim their lettuce and chop their food, as though matter had first
to be finely diced and its atoms exposed before they would eat it.
Feldman almost gagged on the liquescent potatoes and minced
loaves of meat and could not even look at the colorless gelatinous
molds with their suspended chips of pimento and halved olives
and thin, biopsic bits of carrot, like microbes in a culture.

He toured the room, a spy among spies. There was an element
of nervousness in their talk, which surprised him. They spoke of
men still at large, public enemies who were armed and dangerous,
their very vocabularies reminding Feldman of news bulletins that
interrupted dance music on the radio in old films. They could
have been residents of some storm-threatened outpost on the
mainland. But there was smugness too, a basic confidence in their
cellars of guns and stacked riot helmets and cases of tear gas.
What was Armageddon to these guys?

"All the borders were closed," one said. "It was the tightest
security net in the history of the state. They used three hundred
squad cars, for Christ's sake. They *couldn't* have done any more."

"I know, Chief Parker was telling me," another said.

"Still," someone else said, "I see Commissioner Randle's
point. They didn't take the mountains into account. One call to
Lane Field, and they could have had fifty helicopters over that
area in twenty minutes. They could have dropped troopers with
infrared gun sights. They could have lit up the entire state with
flares. It doesn't make any sense for a manhunt to fail when you
can get that kind of cooperation."

"I'm glad you brought that up about the mountains. We'd
improve security a thousand percent if the borders were rede-
fined. Take Wyoming and Montana, for example."

"Flanders and Labe have a tough one there, all right. I
wouldn't want to be those two lawmen."

"Well, sure. They've got it tough, but it's not much different

for True in Tennessee or Wright in South Carolina, or even Grand
and Nobel in Massachusetts and Connecticut. I could give you a
dozen examples. The mountainous common borders of those
states offer the criminal a million places he can hole up. We've
simply got to recognize that sooner or later the frontiers have to
be moved in this country. The natural border is a thing of the past
anyway, since four-wheel drive. Place your state lines far enough
away from your mountain ranges—create a twenty-mile belt of
flatland around the high country—and when they come down
from those hills they fall right into our nets without all this crap
about extradition."

"I don't know, Jim, it sounds pretty idealistic to me."

"Hell, Murray, we've been doing it in our penitentiaries for
years. What's your yard between your outside walls and your
main buildings?"

We're surrounded, Feldman thought. We're lost, but we're
surrounded.

He took a cup of coffee with him into an empty room. Even
normally he moved around a lot at parties, but tonight he had
covered miles. He was looking for a place to hole up, but what
he really wanted was to go back to his cell, to be with those who
knew him. I'm Feldman, he thought; my book is in the library.
He longed to be with anyone who had read his book, who knew
about his life. What was this party all about, anyway?

Always an invitation had meant to him something more than
it was: a secret message, a signal, a declaration of love. And
though he was not a public man he had gone to all parties open
to the regard of others, to their attention. It was all that he would
ever do for anyone—show them his moods, demonstrate himself.
I should have been a late-model automobile, he thought. But these
people, these cops and armored-car executives and czars of baseball and auditors of books, wanted only to be protected from him,
and to have the right of protecting others from him. His blue fool
suit was as heavy as armor. Ah, he thought, I'm such an amateur.
He despised his clumsiness, his bad balance. He knew himself for
a stumbler in the dark, a stubber of toes, a snagger of pockets.
The insurance companies wouldn't touch him.

Once—it was the year his father died—he had sent himself to
Boy Scout summer camp. Joining on a whim at the last moment—
he had seen a poster of some boys around a campfire, Negroes,
Asians, white kids, all of them strangely Caucasoid—he'd had to
go as a Tenderfoot, years older than any other boy of that rank,

and as a pauper, with none of the equipment that the others had. He hadn't understood why he'd come. He couldn't tie the knots or make a fire or pitch a tent. He didn't know the pressure points and was clumsy in the canoe and didn't recognize the plants. He couldn't find the North Star. He suffered much from the taunts of the other boys and from the commands of boys much younger than himself; yet for the two weeks he was there he had been convinced of his happiness. He remembered one clear, cool evening of a three-day portage when they had slept in the open. He had no sleeping bag and lay in his town clothes, his only protection the few rubber rain slickers the others had lent him and would take back as soon as it rained. He recalled looking at the sky, knowing none of nature's names but smelling its woods and feeling its earth, sensing himself there in it, who knew no cloud formations nor the shapes of leaves. He was too excited to sleep, and he began to talk to a thirteen-year-old boy who lay near him, telling him about himself, speaking as someone younger might have spoken to someone older but rarely as someone older ever spoke to someone younger. And the kid listened. Then it rained and that kid was the first to ask for his slicker back. Best pal I ever had, Feldman thought.

It's the liquor, he told himself. It makes you sentimental. Hell, he thought, *something* has to.

A woman came into the room and sat down in a straight chair a few feet from the couch where Feldman was sitting. She slumped backwards, her behind sliding down inside her clothing, so that her body appeared to be lowered from her dress, exposing thigh, straps, the top of a stocking like a vase of flesh. Her position might have been something the Red Cross recommended as a specific against a certain kind of respiratory attack. Feldman waited for her to speak, then realized that she was tipsy and hadn't yet noticed him. He watched her underwear, soon imagining shapes in it, lumps and shadows and stains. It made him nervous to stare, and he wondered if he should cough or scrape his feet. He looked at her face. He knew nothing about people's eyes, couldn't tell character from facial planes. People were young or old, dark or fair, fat or thin. This woman seemed to be in her thirties, a brunette, an inch or so taller than he was, though perhaps it was only the way her legs were extended in front of her that made her seem tall. (He thought of her posture as Lincolnesque.) He found it pleasant to be there with her, their accidental intimacy and her apparent ignorance of his presence enormously sexy. She looked up once and still didn't seem to notice him, and he settled into a comfortable contemplation of her. He let his hands rest in his lap.

"I read about *you*," she said suddenly, and Feldman jumped. "I read about *you*," she repeated, her voice shriller than Feldman would have guessed. He allowed himself a stiff, frightened nod in her direction, only then realizing the danger of his position. There were many things that he, their prisoner, could do to earn their anger, and knowing this, he had had any disadvantaged man's low-souled regard for his own prerogative. His contempt for his captors had been modest, abased, and he had moved only reluctantly around their rules, all the while unconsciously—doing superstitiously the personality's special pleading—trusting in miracle to save him in some final pinch. Now he was furious with himself. He had been about to commit the great sin: to have been at ease with one of their women. And *that*, he understood at last, was what the party was all about.

Of course, he thought, seeing everything. Guest of honor, life of the party. His first thought, his *first*, had been to wonder if there would be women. He thought of the omniscient Fisher. How that man worked him! He had wanted a maudlin Feldman, a Feldman sorry for himself—Boy, oh boy, Feldman thought, he's yours, you've got him—and had scared him into self-pity with the shilled routines he had been suckered into overhearing. Then they had softened his fear, using forgotten comfort as an aphrodisiac, turning him into a yearner for tenderness and solace, off balance as a man on tiptoe. Even now, as he looked at the girl, he found it difficult to resist, and he longed to touch her, to pull at one of her straps as at a ripcord. He considered rape, though even as it crossed his mind, he knew she would know judo, know karate, know Burmese foot fighting, and he contemplated his sensuous, bone-shattering comeuppance, the intimate complicated smells of the hammer lock and bear hug. But all that she could do to him would be nothing; it was what the others—he thought of them as of her older brothers—would do. He could see a creosote-and-spit-on-the-floor doom, some blunt-instrumented humiliation, steamy clouds of race hatred, rage, righteous anger, an edge-of-the-bread-knife ruin. He understood how they felt. In a way, he was even on their side.

"My name is Mona," the woman said.

"Mona. Well, well. How do you do? Mona, is it? Nice weather, Miss Mona. Well, well."

"Why are you so nervous, a tough guy like you?"

"Me? Tough? say, that's rich. Yes sir. Kind of chilly, don't you think? Feels like rain."

"You just said it was nice."

"Nice for some, not nice for others. Me, I like it. I do, I like it. Suits me."

"Hey, where are you going?"

"Got to be running along, got to be skedaddling. It's been a real pleasure, Miss Mona. *Yes.*"

"Ooh, I *love* you tough guys. You killers kill me."

"Pshaw, Miss Mona, I'm no killer."

"Well, you wheelers and dealers then, you big-time operators, you behind-the-scenes guys who can get someone killed by picking up a phone."

"Heck, miss, I wouldn't know what number to dial."

"Sure, sure. *I* know. Tell me something, will you? Will you tell me something?"

"I'll try," Feldman said. "I'll give it a try." I'll kick it around, he thought. I'll see what I can come up with.

"Well, a thing that's always fascinated me is why when you people are arrested and step out of those cars at the courthouse you always hold your hats over your face. It can't be you're afraid of the publicity. Everyone already knows what you look like. Why do you do it?"

"Our hats, is it?" Feldman said.

"Yes. Why?"

"Yes, well, we like the smell, that's why we do that."

Mona looked at him. Now she blows the whistle, Feldman thought. Now she taps the glass with the little hammer. Mona to Warden, Mona to Warden, come in, Warden. "That's cute," Mona said. She came over to his couch and sat next to him. She put out a finger and touched his arm. Don't touch me with that, he thought. "I liked the part," she said, "in the basement, where you did all those terrible things for people."

Feldman couldn't move. He was frightened, but now that she was close he could smell her perfume, the odor, he imagined, of cunning poisons. Her hand on the sleeve of his jacket made a complicated gesture of petition and restraint; it was as light as air and weighed forty-seven pounds. He could feel the warm tickle of her fingernail beneath the cloth of his suit.

"I liked the part," she said hoarsely, "about Dedman and Freedman—and the other one, that other man."

"Victman," Feldman whispered. Her hand was on his neck,

the long nails grazing gently against his skin. The area about his ear prickled with a soft malarial chill. I love you, Miss Mona, he thought.

"I liked the part," she said, placing her hand on his leg, "where you make Lilly play those games." She touched his chest inside his shirt.

"I liked the part," he said, "where your hand was on my leg."

"That's cute," she said. She put both her arms around his neck. Now he could not sit still. She bent to kiss him. I'll pay for this, he thought. So I'll pay for it, I'm rich. They kissed.

Seduction's suction, he thought. He wanted action. He wanted tearing, room-defiling. He broke her hold and regrasped her. *My* way, he thought. He wanted the pillows on the sofa at lewd angles, the pictures askew, rape-happened furniture and the stains of love. *"Awghrrh,"* he roared, and pushed the girl back, shoving up her dress, up to his elbows in it, getting a fugitive image of someone rolling someone else in a blanket to put out a fire. He fumbled around inside the blue fool suit.

"Aren't you going to take your clothes off?"

"A tough guy like me?"

"That's cute," she said.

Feldman rampant, roaring, amuck. Tumbling the world, rising, falling. He pummeled. He tummeled and tunneled. Aroused, he browsed and caroused and roamed and caromed. He smashed and crashed. "THAT WASN'T BAD AT ALL," he cried in climax. It was a lyric scream.

"Shh," she said. "Shh, shh."

"That wasn't bad at all," he chopped out. He started to cough and laugh at the same time.

"You'll bring the others," she said.

"You *are* the others," he said.

"I'm not," she said, as if she knew what he was talking about.

"Say, give me a cigarette. Wow, I'm some tough guy. Wow. Wow. Look at me, I'm gulping like a kiddie. My heart says, 'Gosh.' Everything goes on. This goes on too. What a place, what a world! My heart says, 'Golly.' "

"Shh," she said. "Shh. Shh."

Feldman got off her, but she made no effort to move. He had done some job on her. Through the girdle. She lay, hobbled by her dropped, ripped pants, like a fallen sack-racer. Her stockings were collapsed at her knees. Straps and buttons, clasps and wires loose on her thighs made an opened package of her legs. He stared

at her thighs. They were red. They fascinated him. He took his
time, bent forward and touched one. He pinched it hard, drawing
no white marks. The redness goes all the way through, he thought,
swallowing. It excited him. She might have been some ur-colleen,
some boggy, seaside lady in black linen, shawled, a keener at ship-
wrecks and storms. A coffinside wailer. The real Catholic hot stuff.
"Look at that," he whispered. "How about that!"

"Pull my dress down."

"Psst, Leo, what's going on out there?" It was his homunculus.

"It's terrific," Feldman said. "It's fabulous."

"Pull my dress down. What is this?"

"No," he said, "please. Wait a minute."

"I will like hell," she said. She sat up, tugged at her underwear and pulled her stockings taut. It was the old story. Disarray
inspired him, and as she adjusted her clothing Feldman felt his
energy drain off. "I think I've been taken," he said quietly. "I'm
over a barrel in some new way." He sighed.

"*You've* been taken?" Mona said.

"What I don't understand are the elaborate processes. The
technicalities of your justice. Why do you have to have me dead
to rights?"

"I don't know what you're talking about."

"All right," he said. It was true. He didn't understand the
trouble they went to. Why didn't they fake their photographs, rig
their lie detectors? What difference did it make?

Mona finished dressing and turned to face him, sitting on a
leg, flexing her big knee toward him like an enormous muscle. He
recollected her red thighs. There was something terrifying about
them, something powerful and secret like those biological myths
about the angled cunts of Asians and erogenous palms of Ne-
gresses. There were rumors about the tough, horned nipples of
Russian girls and the queer asses of squaws. Were these things
true? They must be. Everything goes on. The forms of life were
infinite—look at himself, his homunculus, old Short Ribs—as
were the forms of death. You were nuts not to acknowledge
power, whatever its source. Mona smiled at him. She must love
me, he thought, she *must*. Otherwise—a flick of those red thighs,
and he would have been done for, sent flying. He prayed silently
to the red thighs, while one spur of his imagination conjured speculatively the thighs of his *schicksa* mom. Were they red too? Nah,
he thought. She'd be alive today.

One of Mona's earrings had fallen on the carpet, and he picked it up. It was for a pierced ear; you could have hung drapes on its hook. "Here," he said.

"Hey, thanks. I didn't feel it fall out."

"Listen," he said, "can I put it back?"

"What's that?"

"May I put it back?"

"Go ahead." She shook her head, and her hair swung. Feldman, failure in forests and catcher of poison ivy who never knew the planets or found the North Star and couldn't remember which were the months with thirty days, gingerly held red-thighed Mona's milky ear lobe. He bent his neck to see the hole, and then on impulse, arranging carefully his lips and tongue, precisely as a musician's mouth at a flute, he blew through the aperture.

"Don't fool around," she said.

Feldman, who had already made several connections with the universe in the last half-hour, leaned back gratefully. He handed the girl her earring. "I might hurt you," he said.

"Not a chance. The skin's tough in there. I can't feel a thing."

He took back the earring and threaded it through her ear, deliberately clumsy. He felt marvelous. How many points, he wondered, for *that* sweet basket?

"We've been in here too long," she said. "What about the others?"

But he had forgotten the others. He was interested now in what he might do with Mona. He saw himself at her controls: combing her hair, going through her purse for lint; then if she'd let him—always remembering the power of those red thighs, those tough pierced lobes—putting her toes in his mouth, her nipples in his ears, sitting in her lap and exploring her teeth with his fingers. "What about the others?" she repeated. "Is this smart?" It was hard to reconcile her anxiety with her red thighs, but then, he thought, he didn't know what kind of thighs the others had. Maybe theirs canceled hers, bleached them in blood's bright pecking order. Or maybe he was right the first time: she had done a job on him, and time was up. He stood reluctantly, nervous again, and said that maybe it would be better if they weren't seen going out together.

"It's too late to think about that," she said.

"Why?"

"Don't you know where we are? This is the warden's bedroom."

"It's not," Feldman said. "It can't be. It doesn't even look like a bedroom."

"The couch is a hideaway. The wing chair's a bidet."

"Oh," Feldman said. And the sofa pillows are sprinkled with Spanish fly, he thought. And the lamp is a camera. And the coffee table is a plainclothesman. Everything goes on, he thought. *Why do you let everything go on?* he prayed.

"Come on," she said. "Let's face the music." She tried to take his hand, but he wouldn't let her have it. At the door she passed through first, and he followed sheepishly.

They were all gone; the room was empty. Mona went to the sideboard and made herself a sandwich. Feldman stood beside her as she spread mustard on a roll. "Where is everybody?" he asked.

"I don't know," she said, her mouth full. "Gone home, I guess. Tomorrow's a working day."

"Tomorrow's Saturday," he said.

"Are the jails closed?"

"Well, what do we do now?" he asked.

"How do you mean? Have a sandwich."

"They're all *gone.*"

"Well, I know that. They're all gone. They're a bunch of party poopers. Have a sandwich."

"I don't want a sandwich," Feldman said. "Listen, how do I get back to jail?"

She shrugged. Feldman left her impatiently and looked into another room. No one was around. He went into all the rooms he could find, and it was the same. The idea of being alone in Warden's Quarters terrified him; somehow it seemed to be the ultimate defilement. There *wasn't* a more serious crime. He sat down in the library and put his head in his hands. Then he remembered that the guard had said he would be waiting in the kitchen. He found Mona again. She had finished her sandwich and was making another. "Change your mind?" she asked. "Want a sandwich?"

"Where's the kitchen?" Feldman demanded.

"What do you need the kitchen for? There's plenty of stuff right here. Look, here's some meatloaf. Here's eggplant. What do you want? Shall I pour you a glass of Vegemato?"

"Where's the fucking kitchen? Tomorrow's Saturday. I have to get back to jail."

"Well, listen to him," she said. "Oh, all right, follow me."

They went down a service hall Feldman had missed. Mona stopped at a wide white door. "In here," she said, and pushed open the door.

"Look," Feldman said, following her, "I'm sorry I'm late. I was off by myself and—"

The warden was counting desposit bottles and arranging them in neat rows.

"It's me," Feldman said softly.

The warden looked up and saw them, and Feldman whimpered. The warden's face seemed momentarily to fall, as though some symptom he had not felt for months had suddenly recurred. In a second he had recovered, but when he opened his mouth it was to Mona he spoke. "You know each other," he said. Feldman noticed her ring for the first time.

Mona nodded nervously.

Were they married? Oh Christ, was she his wife? The thief's armful, he thought awfully. His mouthful. How do I get back to jail? he wondered. Crime and punishment, he thought. Punishment and punishment. Suddenly he felt compelled to offer the warden a confession, to admit everything, sign papers. He did not exactly feel moral obligation, but a necessity to flatter the warden with his crimes. It was what the man thrived on, what he deserved. The urge to plead was strong, but he did not yet know what he should plead to. He shrugged helplessly and smiled and tamped down a yawn. "Late," he said.

"Your guard has been dismissed," the warden said. "The prison's closed."

"Closed?"

"It's sealed until morning. A warden's danger is at night," he said, and looked at Feldman.

"I drank like a pig," Feldman blurted.

The warden nodded, bored.

"I drank like a pig, and I hated the food. It was too wet."

"Was it?"

"It was too wet. There wasn't any delicatessen. I hoped there would be delicatessen, and there wasn't. If there was I would have had six sandwiches."

"I see," the warden said.

"You do?" Mona said.

"He's copping a plea," the warden said.

"No," Feldman said, "I'm not."

"You're copping a plea," the warden said.

"I coveted my neighbor's wife."

"What else?" the warden said.

"Everything else," Feldman said. He saw that it made the warden wince to look at him, and he felt like someone with no nose, with reamed hollows where the eyes went. He stared out from behind the holes in his face, beneath his singed queer brows. "What happens now?" he asked.

"You can't stay here," Fisher said.

Feldman nodded. He understood. Fair was fair.

"Come with me," the warden said.

He was comforted. People said "Come with me" to him, and he followed them down long, twisting corridors, through crowded rooms, a content sense of irresponsibility in his trailing footsteps, of abeyance, things held off. You climbed stairs and went to doom by degrees. You waited for elevators at the end of hallways; you crossed bridges that connected buildings. Then, at the end of it all, there were comfortable chairs; you could smoke; there were magazines to read. It surprised and disappointed him then when the warden merely walked across the kitchen to a narrow metal doorway and took some keys from his pocket. "Go in," Fisher said. Feldman had seen the doorway when he had first come in, and thought that it must be some kind of freezer. He hesitated, then saw that the warden had produced a gun. "*Go in,*" the warden commanded. Feldman walked through the doorway; the door slammed behind him, and he heard the key turn in the metal lock.

Automatically he began to stamp his feet and rub his arms. He still thought he was in a freezer. "I've got to keep moving," he said, but saw at once that the words had produced no visible breath. "I'm not cold," he said, testing to make sure. Then he saw that he was in a kind of areaway and that a few feet in front of him was an arch and a stairway leading down, probably to the basement, though he had never gotten over the impression that Warden's Quarters, like the solitary-confinement cells, were already below ground. "I can't stand here all night," he said, but that was an excuse. He knew that he wanted to go down the stairs and that the warden probably expected him to. He stood at the head of the stairway and looked down. The stairs declined at a rude angle. He could not see the bottom, although a line of naked bulbs—incredibly dim, like those drained lights before the curtain rises in a theater—hung from the narrow, curved Conestoga ceiling that canopied the stairway. I'm a fool, he thought, and began to descend the stairs.

There was no rail, and the rough stone walls felt damp, a thousand years old. A bad smell covered the walls like a tapestry. The lights overhead were spaced further and further apart. Soon he had left the last light behind him and entered the darkness. At the bottom he could see nothing, and stepped off the last stair as into space. The underworld, he thought.

He stopped where he was and listened, afraid to go further. He might be on a narrow stone apron, above water perhaps, although he couldn't *hear* water. Perhaps it was a pit he stood over. He imagined enormous drops, plummets of miles. He took a cautious step, holding one foot in place and sliding the other carefully forward. Then he brought the other foot up. He tried to stand with his feet together—he imagined himself on a small platform about the size of a man's handkerchief—but the strain of keeping his balance in so constricted a space was too great for him and he fell. He hit the floor abruptly, and because he had expected to tumble forever—"Come with me," the warden had said; he recalled the leisurely fate he had anticipated—the impact knocked the breath out of him. He lay on the stone floor until he got his wind back, and then stood up slowly. Again he put one leg out, sliding it forward along the ground and then bringing the other leg up with it. In this way he proceeded for about five minutes. He had lost the stairway. He decided to throw something to see if he could judge from the sound if he *was* above a pit. He looked in his pockets for something to throw. He had nothing. What a poor man I am, he thought. He tugged a button off the jacket of his blue fool suit and threw it in front of him. It clattered on the floor. That doesn't prove anything, he thought; I might have thrown it too far. He tossed the next button gently, and heard it drop a few feet in front of him, roll a foot or so and stop. He removed another button and flipped it to his left. It fell heavily. The remaining buttons, which he took from the sleeve of his jacket, he threw all around him. One rolled up against what was possibly a wall off to his left. The last button he threw behind him; it hit almost at once. "Well," he said, "no pit." Boldly he did a little dance, finishing with a daring leap in the dark.

His eyes could not get accustomed to the darkness, and since it seemed unlikely that he could find the narrow stairway again in this pitch, he decided to try for the wall which the button might have bounced against. He put his hands out in front of him to grope with the darkness. Momentarily he expected the tips of his fingers to smash against a wall. He was so conscious of them that they seemed wet, as if he had licked them and thrust them out to test the direction of the wind. Without realizing it, he had slipped back into the sliding, skatey progress he had adopted earlier. Again he had a sense of all the strange rooms he'd ever been in.

He moved his left foot forward, but it hit bluntly against a solid barrier. The sudden contact, slow and cautious, sent something like an electric shock through his body. He leaned forward and found the wall. The same bad smell of the stairway met his nostrils. He slid his hand over the rough, grainy wall and felt the metal panel over an electric switch. He flicked it on, and instantly the place was flush with light. Just to his right was an arch and the stairway he had descended. He had traveled in a circle. He turned around.

Across the room—it was enormous—thrust out from the wall, was a narrow wooden platform like a low stage. On it, stiff, its rigid form and strict ninety-degree angles already suggesting its function, was the electric chair.

"*Aiiee,*" Feldman shouted. "*Aiiee, aiiee!*"

He turned off the lights; then, afraid to be with that thing in the dark, he turned them back on. Shielding his eyes with his arm as though he moved through a sandstorm, he approached the chair. It looked, on the platform, like a throne. Its high straight back and stiff thrusting arms suggested the stern posture of pharaohs. Two straps rose on each arm, and at the back, attached at the level of a man's chest, a huge leather strap, the color of a barber's strop but bigger, hung down, curling on the wooden seat like some mechanical snake. He reached out as though he would stir the leather coils, but pulled his hand back at once. Jesus, he thought, what if it's turned on? He leaned forward and examined the chair closely. How did it kill you? He spotted a thick black cable that ran from the wall behind the chair and climbed its ladder-back into a queer device at the top, a soft puffy collar like something on a dentist's chair. Two metal nodes—electrodes probably—protruded through the sides of the collar.

"Oh boy," he said. "Oh boy oh boy."

A notice was scotch-taped to a corner of the platform. CAUTION, it said. "This penitentiary, like comparable institutions, operates exclusively on DC (Direct Current) current only. Electrocution, however, must be performed using AC (*Alternating*) current, or the condemned's body will be charred beyond recognition, making *legal* identification of the corpse impossible. Also, because of the high-body-heat factor in electrocution—the electrocutionee's body temp. will normally rise to 140 degrees F. (Fahrenheit)—even under a jolt of the more humane Alternating (AC) Current, care must be taken to avoid administering DC current, since two to three thousand volts will immediately raise the body temp. to 400 degrees F., or sufficiently beyond the kindling point of human flesh to create a fire hazard. This chair is equipped with AC/DC conversion facilities. Make sure that the following procedures are carefully followed." Then there was a complicated list of directions that Feldman found impossible to follow. The electrical schema was incoherent. How is the guy supposed to know what to do? he wondered. They even have to tell him what AC and DC stands for. He read the sheet again, then a third time. Finally the letters seemed to blur and the arrows on the schema to move around.

He clapped his fists rapidly, excitedly, just under his chin, pantomiming a kind of classic vaudeville distress. "I've got to get out of here," he said moving away from the platform, and he began to tour the room in great rough circles. "The last mile, the last mile," he said, still knocking his fists together. Out of breath, he paused at the far edge of one of his circles. He could still see the awful chair, and he turned his back to it and sat down cross-legged on the cold floor.

"All right," he asked himself, "where do I stand? Where do I stand, what did I do? I didn't do anything." Adultery, he thought. "Adultery," he said, "I committed adultery. Two victims I made tonight. Lilly. Lilly is a victim. And the other one—her husband. Her husband is a victim. Now, are they married? She's married, Mona's married. But are *they* married? She knew about the bidet, she found the kitchen. So let's say they're married, where do I stand now?

"The unwritten law is that the husband has the right to kill the man taken in adultery. *Or* the woman. It's his choice. There have been cases where the unwritten law has given him the right to kill both. Taken in adultery. I'm a dead duck. *Taken* in adultery. But I *wasn't* taken in adultery. Hey, what is this? I *wasn't* taken in adultery. I walked into the goddamn kitchen. The guy was counting deposit bottles. It was the furthest thing from his mind."

He got up and rushed to the stairway. *"What is this?"* he roared up the stairs. "What do you think you're doing? I wasn't taken in adultery. You'll never get away with it." He started up the stairs. "Do you hear me? *I was not taken in adultery!* It doesn't count twenty minutes later. The unwritten law says you've got to kill the guy immediately. And it means bare hands, or a blunt instrument, or a handy knife. Electric chairs are out. Do you hear me? They're *out*. *I don't have to be anybody's electrocutionee!"*

He sat down on the stairs, exhausted. "What the fuck am I talking about?" he said. He shook his head. "That's not where I stand. That has nothing to do with where I stand. He hates me. *That's* where I stand." It's the unwritten law, he thought. Sure, power liked to play by the rules. But power was arbitrary. It changed its mind. It killed you with its alternating current. There were ways to get rid of Feldman—he thought of his discharge suit carefully made sizes small a week after he'd arrived—and they didn't even have to be clever. They could shoot him, stick a shiv in him, beat him up, run him over—anything. The thing is, he thought, I don't really understand why the warden hates me. It was very puzzling. He could not honestly say that he hated the warden. He wondered if that was what was wrong. Really, he thought, I don't hate enough. It's a weakness. He had never hated the Communists. He had not even hated the Nazis. Nazis were nuts, but they had been good for business. Did the warden know he had not hated the Nazis? He was a little sorry now. Not hating was *bad* for business, but to tell the truth, he didn't even hate what was bad for business. Then he remembered that he didn't give a shit about his neighborhood and always voted No on bond issues. Once he had rejected a referendum which proposed to merge the population in the county with the population in the city, lifting the city into seventh place in the nation. The campaign slogan had been "Seventh in America, Seventy-fifth in the World." It hadn't appealed to him. Well, that was too bad, because they could kill him for that. They could kill him for his lack of support, for his indifference to having a National League team in the town, for not getting behind the United Fund, for his public indifference and for his private indifference. For not signing petitions, and rejecting their projects. And for his ambiguous status: not partisan or loyal opposition, not anarchist, not anything. Simply inattentive, mealy-hearted. They could kill him for that.

He looked around wearily. Only then did he realize that there was no one to put him in the chair. He was alone. It was out of the question that he would die. He climbed the rest of the stairs and stood before the metal door.

"Ha, ha," he said, "you think I'm going to volunteer for that? What's the matter with you? Ha, ha. Fat chance, you hear me? Big fat chance." He put his ear to the door to see if he could hear the warden. Nothing. It was probably too thick. He might be out there and he might not. Still, he felt better about his position now that he realized he could save himself from electrocution by the simple expedient of not sitting down in the chair. And if they had decided to starve him—that would be ironic, he thought, starved to death with the kitchen just on the other side of the metal door— he would take his shoe off and pound it against the door. Someone would hear that. A trusty. Or Mona, if the unwritten law had not taken care of her and she was still alive, raiding the icebox. Someone would hear him. God would hear him.

"Dear God," Feldman prayed, "dear Jesus and Buddha, Jehovah and Love, Mind, Spirit, Soul and Guts, dear Yin, dear Yang, Allah, Father, Son and Holy Ghost, Jupiter, Zeus, Thou and Almighty Dollar—blast and cream them, wreck their plans, rip them for Feldman."

What in the name of all that's holy am I praying about?

Calmly he thought of his fears. Tonight he had feared death by freezing and death by falling. He had feared death by frying and death by being left alone. And each he had hoped to forestall: by refusing to sit, by ripping his buttons, by pounding his shoe. But those deaths, far-fetched as those salvations, had not happened. They had not happened because the warden had not meant them to. They were not the Warden's Deaths, who could have him shot or beaten or run over, who could have him thrown into machinery or dropped from walls. They were his own, Feldman's Deaths. Feldman's death was Feldman's doing. His imagination was the murderer, and the deadly plans and bloody businesses and the doom schemas had been all his own, everything his own. Him the killer, the assassin in trees, him the waylayer.

It was true: he wanted his death. He wanted his death because it was coming to him and he wanted everything that was coming to him.

He turned again, went down the stairs, entered the room and rushed to the platform, scrambling onto it awkwardly. Maybe it was converted to AC and maybe it wasn't, but it was turned on all right. He picked up the leather strap and flung it aside so that he could sit down. He sat well back in the chair, excited by the idea of the two or three thousand volts that would course up his ass. "All right," he told the warden, "we both get what we want."

Nothing happened.

"Tch tch," he said. "I don't do anything right." Of course, he thought, he had to be strapped in. He reached around and grabbed the great leather strap and fastened it to the metal buckle attached to the other side of the chair. He pulled it tight. He could hardly breathe. He slipped his fists and wrists through the leather loops on the arms of the chair. Still nothing happened, and he realized that he was not making the proper contact. A curved metal band like a leg shackle was connected to the right front leg of the chair, and Feldman kicked off his shoe and tried to push his foot through it. Restrained as he was by the leather strap across his chest, he could not get the correct leverage. He pulled his hands out of the loops, undid the buckle at his side and forced his feet into the hoop. It was like stepping into a boot. Then he refastened the chest restraint and put his wrists back through the loops. They needed adjustment, but he could only tighten one. He chose the right, since it was to his right leg that the electrode was attached and the probability was that that side would take the initial jolt. He imagined his loose left arm, involuntarily escaped from its bond, waving in electric death.

He was ready. Now he would die. Last words? Nah. He wondered if there would be time enough to know what it was like. He hoped so, or what was he doing in the damn chair? Here goes, he thought, the big one. "It is finished." He giggled and leaned his head far back into the headrest at the top of the chair, his neck scraping against the metal plates.

He lived.

This too, he thought. I'm a lousy conductor.

He undid all the straps, rose and stretched. His foot was still in the leg manacle. *I* didn't know, he thought. I supposed it was turned on. What he had felt about his death was perhaps all he would ever feel. If that was so, then now, in a way, he didn't have to die. Ever.

It is finished, he thought. But he was very sleepy. He got his foot out of the hoop, found his shoe, sat back down in the chair and made himself comfortable. Soon he was dead to the world.

13

A Warden's Assembly was called. Feldman filed into the hall with the others and sat down.

Maintenance trusties unfolded the Gothic sidings and fitted them into place along the walls. Seen from close up in the still lighted auditorium, they had the cartoony aspect of painted flats in old burlesque skits. Scalloped apertures, cut into the cardboard and covered with sheets of colored cellophane that might have been torn from lollipops, were aligned with the auditorium windows. Bits of sequins embedded in the siding gave a quartzy effect to the granite blocks. Here and there little painted gargoyles frowned down from the moldings. They had the faces of the bad men. Everything had a livid cast, quickening the eye as though it were perceiving under strobe light.

The workmen finished and the warden entered from the back of the auditorium. The first to see him began to applaud. Those up front, without even turning, clapped lustily. One man stood, then another, and soon everyone was on his feet. There were shouts of "Bravo! Bravo!" "Hurrah" called a man near Feldman and was immediately echoed by one next to him, who seemed peeved that he had not thought of it first. "Hurray for the warden," another invented, and "Three cheers for Warden Fisher," yelled someone else. "Two-four-six-eight," a voice rose triumphantly, "who do we appreciate?" And the thunderous answer. "*Fisher! Fisher!*"

The warden climbed the steps leading to the stage and looked out calmly over the cheering men. The applause was brutal. He smiled and glanced down shyly and they screamed. He raised his hand, and the men cheered louder. Piercing whistles shrieked through the room like the announcement of bombs. Again the warden looked up and raised his hand, but the applause raced on. A trusty fitted a collar microphone around his neck, and the warden raised both hands and faced the men. "Civilization is forms," he said. "It's also doing what you're told. It's knowing when enough is enough."

The men began to shush each other. Some in the rear pounded each other's shoulders, admonishing silence. "Shut up, you guys," someone near Feldman said. "Warden Fisher wants to speak." "That's right," another added, "we won't hear him if you're not quiet." Feldman's neighbor nudged him and pointed to a convict down the row who was still applauding. "Some guys ruin it for all the others," he whispered. A man pointedly stifled a cough.

" 'The Parable of the Shoo-in,' " the warden announced. A few around the auditorium began to applaud again, but they were effectively squelched by those next to them.

"A guy had worked for a large corporation for seven years," the warden said. "He'd had the whole bit: the interview in college in his senior year, the junior-executive training, the tour of the plant in Milwaukee, the couple of moves to branch offices around the country. The works. The guy was a quick study, very diligent, and his superiors were duly impressed. He made it apparent almost at once that he had what it takes. Some of his suggestions saved his company thousands of dollars, and he came up with some fresh new ideas for promotions and campaigns that were substantively reflected in the annual profits.

"Gradually he came to the attention of the higher-ups, the big boys, and whenever they were in his city they made it a point to look him up. Always they came away impressed and delighted.

"When the lad had been with the company five years a job opened up in the home office that they thought he might do well in. It wasn't the biggest job, but it was a good one, and for the right man it had a future that didn't quit. When they told him he could have it he didn't hesitate a minute, and the company liked that too. This was a difficult post, very sensitive, and some of the men they had put into the spot in the past, though they looked terrific on paper, just hadn't worked out and had jeopardized their careers with the firm. Most fellows would have thought twice about making the shift. The money was about the same, and it was more expensive to live in the town where the home office was situated. But the guy took it, and just as the big shots expected, he did very well. In fact he was the best man they'd ever had in that particular slot.

"It soon became apparent, however, that if anything he was *too* big for the job. Oh, he didn't complain, you understand. He wasn't arrogant and didn't even seem particularly aware of the sensation he was making in the organization, but the men at the top saw that he was being wasted, and when a vacancy opened up on the board of directors of this internationally famous company, they immediately thought that the young man would be a perfect choice to fill it. They discussed this among themselves and decided to propose him formally as a candidate.

"The next day the chairman of the board called him into his office and told him about it, and just as the man had anticipated, the candidate wasn't flustered at all, though it was perfectly clear he was grateful. There wasn't anything snotty about it. 'One last thing,' the chairman told him before he let him go, 'the company has an official policy for a prospect at your level. We need the names of four top men not connected with our organization whom we can write to request letters about you. It's just a formality, of course. The board never announces a man's candidacy to him unless they mean to confirm. Nothing ever goes wrong when you get this far, but it's standard operating procedure, so if you'll give me the four names I'll see that letters are gotten out at once, and you'll be confirmed at our next meeting. You're a shooin.'

"Well, to the chairman's astonishment the candidate seemed a little flustered at this, and the chairman asked him what was wrong.

" 'Nothing,' the guy said. 'What sort of letters?'

"The chairman saw that the young man didn't understand and tried to reassure him. 'Just the usual stuff,' he told him. 'About your character, that you're honest, that you're not likely to embezzle our funds or get us into trouble with the SEC. A little about your personality. You know.'

"He saw that the fellow still had some misgivings, and he began to get suspicious, but just then he realized what it was probably all about and he broke into a big, friendly smile. 'I get it,' he said. 'It's because you're so young and don't yet feel you know four top executives well enough to ask them to write letters for you. That's your problem, isn't it?'

" 'Well—' the young man said.

" 'Look,' the chairman told him, 'they don't have to be the biggest men in the country. You've been with the firm seven years. You've had important posts. When you were out West and handled that government thing for us, didn't you have to work with major men in smaller companies we subcontracted to?'

"The shoo-in nodded and the chairman said well then, he could use *those* names. 'Come on,' he said, 'let's get this over with. You sit down here at my desk and write me four names of people we can get in touch with. You don't even have to know their addresses. My secretary will look them up.' With that the chairman rose, and the shoo-in sat down behind the desk and quickly wrote out four names. He left the list on the blotter under a paperweight and got up to go. 'There,' the chairman said, 'now that's done we'll be approving your candidacy in no time.'

"The shoo-in left the office, and the chairman read the list. What was his surprise when he saw that the young man had written down not the names of the presidents of *small* organizations, but of men at the head of *the biggest companies in America*, companies that dwarfed even the chairman's own! Four key captains of industry, man in the vanguard of corporate America! And not just their names, *but their Grosse Pointe and Virginia-hunt-country addresses as well!* He couldn't leave *this* to his secretary, and he decided instead to take up his own stationery and write out the notes himself in longhand and pen.

"The responses came back quickly, and the chairman had them reproduced and took them with him to the next board meeting. He told board members of his interview with the shoo-in and about how nervous the young man had seemed when he had asked for the names. 'But what puzzles me,' he said, 'is what could have been in the fellow's mind. Here, look, you can see for yourselves. The letters are marvelous.' And with that he distributed copies of the letters all around the big mahogany table.

"Just as the chairman's own had been, these letters too were handwritten by the executives and owners of the companies themselves, and frankly it was a little while before many of the men could make sense of the contents, so interested were they in the turns of phrase and styles and patterns of thinking revealed in the letters. Each was a rare industrial document. One member who had been with the organization since its beginning and was regarded by the others as the most solid and conservative among them grew so excited he had to hold up a letter and wave it. 'Here,' he said, 'this one. You know I've only seen his signature before on the product. Why, it's just like the stylized signature on the trademark!'

"Then the chairman gave them time to assimilate the contents and suggested a vote of confirmation, saying that he had left the shoo-in in his office and that if they finished their business quickly, they could all enjoy a celebration lunch together before some of them had to catch their jets.

"At once the vice-president offered a motion to confirm, and before his motion could even be repeated by the chairman two voices were heard. The chairman called on the man furthest from him, the organization's chief counsel, a man famous for his careful evaluations, expecting that he wanted to second the motion, and by thus giving *his* blessing, preclude any merely routine discussion. When the man spoke, however, he surprised them all. 'I don't know,' he began. 'Perhaps I'm being arbitrary, but I think we ought to take a closer look at these letters.'

" 'What do you mean?' the chairman demanded. 'The letters are genuine. Are you making the monstrous suggestion that they've been forged?'

" 'Not at all, not at all,' the lawyer said. 'Of course they're legitimate. I'm not suggesting otherwise. All I mean is that we ought to examine the substance. This one, for example.' He held up a letter. 'This one says—let's see if I can find it; yes, here it is—this one says that what the writer is chiefly struck by is the candidate's good humor, that he's had him out to the farm and found him "convivial, gay, charming, an indefatigable social catalyst whose jokes and anecdotes enlighten as well as entertain." He mentions "his dancing, his tennis, his universal good manners and courtly display of wit to the least of the other guests and to the staff," as well as to himself.'

" 'What's wrong with that?' the chairman asked. 'The man goes on to vouch for his brains and efficiency too. What's wrong with that?'

" 'Nothing, of course,' the lawyer said, 'but then we have *this* testimonial'—he picked up a second letter from the pile—'where the writer remarks on being impressed with the candidate's seriousness of purpose, his levelheaded and even solemn approach to a situation. He's been our candidate's host too, it seems, and claims that he considers those weekends when the candidate was a guest in his home to have been "philosophical mileposts, times for meaningful contemplation and the dignified reappraisal of goals and values." The young man has been an inspiration, this man claims, and "has redirected and subdued the frivolous and cynical vitality of others into more worthwhile channels." '

" 'But the fellow talks of his perspective also, of his balance and good sportsmanship,' the chairman said.

" 'I know that,' the lawyer said, and began to read from a third letter, but at this point was interrupted by the board member next to him, a man who had opened up vast new customer areas in Asia.

" 'I see what our colleague is getting at, but I like the part in this letter—'

" 'That's the one I was just coming to,' the lawyer said.

" '—where the young fellow's foresight and courage are praised, ". . . his willingness to take a big risk and then back up that risk with everything he's got." He says he can almost smell the fresh young blood in him. I like that. That sort of thing could stir some of the rest of us up around here.'

" 'Certainly,' said the man who had spoken up at the same time as the lawyer, the member the chairman had not called upon when the vice-president made his motion to confirm. 'Yet in this last letter the writer speaks of the boy's "prudence, his steady imperturbability, and reluctance to seek an advantage when the percentages are against it." He goes on to comment that this is rarely found in someone the candidate's age.'

"Now *all* the board members began to discover inconsistencies, calling them out to each other like people who want their songs played on a piano. The chairman, who had risen out of his seat to oppose the lawyer when he had read from the letters and who had remained standing through it all, now sank back wearily. 'I hadn't realized,' he said. 'The letters were all so enthusiastic. I hadn't realized.'

" 'None of us realized, Joseph,' the vice-president who had proposed confirmation said.

" 'I hadn't realized myself,' the organization's chief counsel said. 'It was only when I remembered what you told us of the fellow's being nonplused when you asked him for the names. Then I thought of certain phrases in the letters and I became concerned. I'm sorry, gentlemen, but the candidate is devious.'

"The chairman thanked him and asked if there was now a

second to the vice-president's motion. There was no one to second it. Reluctantly the vice-president rose, asked that his former proposal be withdrawn and suggested that the candidate be disqualified from further consideration. This was quietly seconded and somewhat sadly passed by all present.

"Now the chairman had the responsibility of returning to his office to tell the shoo-in he had been rejected. Before he left the young man, he had urged him to sit in his chair at the big desk, assuring him that the joke was standard ritual for a shoo-in like himself. When he opened the door, however, he saw that the fellow was still standing where he had left him. He came in and smiled, not knowing how to begin. 'Something came up,' he said at last.

" 'I know,' the young man said. 'The board of directors has denied me.'

" 'It was astonishing to me. Naturally as chairman I did not exercise a vote. Objections were raised. I'm sorry.'

" 'May I ask what the objections were?'

" 'These meetings,' the chairman said, 'they're confidential.'

" 'Never mind,' the young man said, 'perhaps I already know.'

" 'There was no animosity. And if you like, of course we want you to stay on in your present job. The letters—'

" 'The letters were thrilling,' the young man said.

" 'They were very enthusiastic,' the chairman said.

" 'But they contradicted—'

" 'They presented a picture of four different men,' the chairman said.

" 'Yes,' the shoo-in said.

" 'Naturally the directors were confused. They felt that since each letter carried equal weight, they weren't competent to determine which estimate was the one . . . And someone suggested afterwards that his own enthusiasm for your character and work lay in different directions entirely from the ones he had seen represented in the letters. My reactions too are . . . You see how it is?'

" 'Yes.'

" 'A man should be fixed,' the chairman said. 'The board felt that a certain firmness was lacking—'

" 'That one ought to know his necessity and bow down to it?'

" 'Yes,' the chairman said, 'that's it.'

" 'One is what one is?'

" 'Properly so,' the chairman said, 'yes.'

" 'No,' the young man said. 'What you call character is the mere obstinacy of the self, the sinister will's solipsist *I am*. One adjusts his humanity to the humanity of others. Not *I am*, but *You are*—there's the necessity. Love cooperates; it plays ball. I hate a chaos. Does the company need me?'

" 'I beg your pardon?'

" 'You said I might stay if *I* wished it. What does the board wish?'

" 'Well, of course, we talked mainly of your candidacy, but your work's been splendid and I get the feeling that all of us would regret your going.'

" 'I shall stay on then,' the young man told him.

"He is there today," the warden said. "The firm has prospered. It has built new plants. Thousands are employed. It pays enormous taxes to the government, and the government uses the money to build ships and planes that defend us all. That is the parable of the shoo-in. Beautiful, isn't it? Isn't it beautiful?"

"Yes, Warden," a man said.

"Yes, Warden," some others chipped in.

The cry went up throughout the hall. "Yes, Warden. Yes, Warden."

The warden raised his hands for silence. *"But he didn't get the job*, is that what you're thinking? Is it? You bad men, is that what you're thinking? No 'making warden's mouths' this time. Answer in your hearts. Well, you're wrong. He got the job. He *got* the job. And when the old man died, he got *his* job too. He got everybody's job. And he bought out other companies and deposed the chairmen, and he got *their* jobs too. Today the men who wrote those letters work for him. That's what flexibility does. Right there, *that's* what it does! That's what it does, you guys stuck in your casings of self like pure pork sausage! *There are no piker saints!"*

The warden paused, then stepped forward. When he spoke again his voice was soft. "There's some prison business," he said. It was what he always said before announcing policy changes, and the men, who had seemed confused during his parable, now looked more confident. A few had brought pencils to take down whatever he said. This was a prisoner's privilege, since it was the warden's custom frequently to introduce new rules or to abridge old ones during a Warden's Assembly. The changes would affect them all, but they were never written down by the administration. The warden preferred that there be a sort of oral tradition in the penitentiary. Indeed, it was his boast that the prison did not even own a mimeograph machine. But, thought Feldman when he heard this, an electric chair they've got.

The warden's reasons for denying the men any codified regulations were perfectly apparent, Feldman thought. Since infractions were met with severe punishments, it became the responsibility of the men themselves, as well as their best interest, to try to understand the warden—in short *to listen*. Nevertheless, they were allowed a certain latitude here. The most literate of the convicts were appointed by their fellow inmates to catch the warden's words on the tips of their pencils. Later their notes were checked, double-checked, collated against the notes of the other scribes. (In this way a certain respect for scholarship was induced too. Feldman had never been anywhere where there was a more genuine admiration of those who knew facts, though a scholar's mistakes earned him beatings.) Discussion groups were formed to resolve inconsistencies and to interpret what had been said. Indeed, the warden had created in effect a hard core of penal Talmudists, men who parsed intention and declined nuances like lexicographers, men adept at shorthand, good punctuators and spellers who wrote with a strong, legible hand. Now, as he glanced about, Feldman saw their strained attentions, their lick-lead alertness; they seemed passionate, fools leaning forward.

"I have this day sent to all administrative personnel," the warden began, "formal notification of my intention to introduce a policy of remission in this institution. Early next week I shall be forwarding to the appropriate officials a detailed schedule of indulgences, which will then go immediately into effect.

"Now, as you know, paroles have, in the past, been based upon projections of a convict's ability to adapt to the workaday world. Among the documents he has had to include in the dossier he builds for the parole board are letters from a prospective employer, character endorsements from members of the clergy, character endorsements from members of the secular arm, statements of reconciliation from members of his family and, if he's to return to his old community, from his neighbors. It is on the basis of these, taken with his own pledges of good will, that the board makes it prognosis about the prisoner's chances on the outside. I need hardly point out to you that such sentimental evidences as these would be of little consequence in a court of law. Of course the parole board also considers a convict's record, his behavior during confinement, and makes, from hearsay, what it can of his present attitudes. But the poverty of these techniques is illustrated by the dramatic statistics that there is only a twelve-percent difference in the incidence rate of recidivism among parolees and those who are discharged only after serving their full sentences. *Twelve percent.*

"As you should be able to infer then, there is a distinct *tense shift* between the philosophy of punishment and the philosophy of pardon. A man is punished for a *fait accompli*; yet that same man, up for parole, is forgiven his past and granted his chance largely on the basis of a prediction—say rather a *hope*—about his actions in the future.

"It is this—this schism between past and future—which my policy of remission and schedule of indulgences seeks to adjust. Henceforward *my* recommendation to the parole board will be based upon my personal observation of a man's *virtue.* 'Warden's Approval,' formerly automatic like the principal's signature on a diploma, now becomes the vital element in the parole process. The jerry-built letters of recommendation will still be required, of course, and sappy-hearted priests and social workers and wives who forget and sons whose hope exceeds their expectation will still be found to write them, *but these will be meaningless without my own recommendation.*"

The warden stepped forward onto the apron of the stage, at the length of the wire on his collar microphone. He took another step and must have broken the connection, for he tore the microphone from his lapel impatiently and dropped it to the floor. When he spoke, however, his voice still seemed amplified. "Now I would solicit your honor," he said. "Now I would urge your virtue. Now I would inspire. You—" he called, "men with pencils, scholars of this place, ministers of my administration—hear me. Explain to them. Speak what I tell you. The tongues of Pentecost are upon me, and I would teach you prison business.

"And we shall prove here again, together, what crusaders traveling armed and East once proved, and what the old popes knew, and the hooded saints who stretched the rack, who turned its wheel, getting God's awful leverage, and all those who once tied hate-knots on wrists behind backs and then tugged at the strappado, hauling at the lousy heretic's flaggy self: *that virtue is as active a principle as evil, that cruelty is written off in a good cause, that there is no violence like an angel's violence.*

"Let us pray."

The man bowed their heads uneasily.

"Lord God of hooked scourge and knotted whip, of sidearms and sidecar, of bloodhound and two-way radio, vigilant God of good neighborhoods and locked Heaven—lend us Thy anger. Teach us, O God, revulsion. Remind our nostrils of stench and our ears of discord and our eyes of filth. Grant these men a holy arrogance and instill in them the courage to expose all bad men, to divulge their plans for jailbreak, their schemes of dirty escape in the back of a laundry truck. Give them the will to betray all wicked confidences, to publish secrets right and left. Bestow on them wakefulness, God, to collect the broken-talk dreams of their cellmates, and give them the memory to report *verbatim* whatever is spoken in anger behind my back or the backs of my guards. Move them to mar a friend's plot, and to sing like canaries the hymns of their blessed betrayals. Instruct their tongues in delation and denunciation, and arrange it so that all charges brought against anyone anywhere may be made to stick!

"Transubstantiate now their prison garb into their chrisoms, for they would be Thy paracletes, and their very cells become as benefices in Thy penal see. Call on them to abjure and recant all blasphemy, in the *murus strictus* now and here and in the *murus largus* then and there. Admit them as successful spies to all infamous councils, and sustain the *endura* of their reputations, the ordeal of their betrayed confidences. Strengthen all stoolies to Heaven, O Lord, and make them to turn state's evidence. Marry them to whores that they may correct them, and give them wicked children that they may chastise them. Have them to live at the scene of crimes near telephones.

"*But let their compurgations, if they would make them, fail in their mouths! Strike down all extenuators!*

"Amen."

"Amen," said the men.

"This isn't part of the prayer now," the warden said. "The rest is off the record." He winked. "We're moving against the bad men."

Feldman shuddered.

"Sometimes," the warden said, "it isn't enough merely to bring charges or to make sermons. There are—well, *you* know, you aren't stupid—things that are done and there's no recourse. There is . . . latitude. There are great nasty areas where one is still within one's 'rights,' *legal, snug as a bug.* Ask yourself. *How much time can a man be made to do for being himself?* Well, you see the problem. The bad men . . . Suppose—get that word, 'suppose,' I said—suppose they were *relaxed* to you? Listen to me." He paused and wiped his forehead with his hand. Then he looked down at his shoes. "It's embarrassing," he said at last. "I'm no hinter, no intimator. Let's not crap around with each other.

"I am calling for the infusion of the sacerdotal spirit! I need inquisitors' hearts! You must be—you must be *malleus maleficarum*, hammers of witches, punishers and pummelers in God's long cause. You must be warden's familiars. We shall share the power of the keys. Despoil, confiscate, make citizen's arrests. You know what needs to be done.

"We must invent terrible penances together. Rebuff the bondsman along with the bailee. Seek the alkahest of perfect punishment to dissolve the stony-hearted men. Bring your charges, bring them, please. Say 'I know not whom to accuse, but here are the names of those I suspect.' Imply. Implicate. Indict. What would you? Torture the witness? Force the confession? You've your immunities. I give you carte-blanche souls. Charge even the dead. *Yes!* Let us have exhumations. Bones to scatter. Visit plagues, visit poxes. Zealously, zealously, flagellate, spank. Interdict and preclude. Exorcise the *lamiae*, rout the *mascae*, bury the *incubi*. Ignite the dark conventicle. Hate heresies. Kiss not the toad on its posteriors nor lift the dog's tail to make love. Don't chew the Scriptures, nor piss on private property. Go straight, goddamnit! *Tapas. Tapas. Tapas.* If you would live forever, then think on sin until all scores are settled. *Talio. Talio.* Push them in cesspools. *Accusatio! Denunciatio!* Trust dreams, bad tastes in your mouths, hunches, first impressions. Bet long shots. Tribulations of the flesh. Trifle their hearts. Bread and water them. *Durus carcer et areta vita.* Be impeccable. You shall know them by their *kosti* and *saddarah*, their thread and shirt. *Haereticus indutus or vestitus. Poena confusibilus.* Crush the tergiversator, the vitiator, the equivocator!"

You got all that down? You got all that down, you good punctuators and spellers? Feldman wondered.

"Well," the warden said cheerfully, "*well.* That felt good, I have to admit. It clears the lungs. A shout clears the lungs. Ah, there's nothing like rage, men. It tones a man. But I tell you criminals, until you guys go straight you'll never know what it feels like. Oh, you've your anger, I suppose, but you've never peaked to wrath or felt a fine fury. Guilt waters your whiskey and niggles your righteousness. Pikers, pikers, you nickled-and-dimed. Well, it stands to reason. You're all debtors to doubt, uncertainty. There's vacillation's dreary falsetto in your tantrums. It amateurizes you, men. Try as you will, how can you hate a man with your gun in his ribs? Is a shooter e'er sore or a mugger e'er maddened? God damns and makes decisions and denotes, but the devil's all contingency and connotation. There's something listless in a crime of violence, something pale in a prisoner's pique. So you lose wrath and make do with a lousy bitterness, settling for slurs instead of curses. Petulance, bitterness and the soured heart. Dyspepsia and low dudgeon and never the high decorum of an injured outrage or the sweet reason in a rich reprisal.

"Why, look around you! Who blooms here? Who's got the health? Is the charlatan cheerful or the robber robust? Only your cuckold thrives, your murderer for morality. Sure, sure, only your criminal of passion, your redresser, your reparator—your strangler, your stabber—only your gut-ripper and your castrator. There's nothing like their strength unless it's the fine fettle of the framed. Innocence. Innocence does it, self-defense does.

"Well, I'll let you get back to your cells in a moment. I'll lock you up. There are some night-shift personnel and their families outside that I've still got to talk to, but before I let you go I want to urge you again to think about what I've told you. I wish I could imagine that your malice toward bad men were predicated on your own good will, that you won't just do what I ask merely to assure your paroles, but . . . well, I'm not naïve. I wasn't born yesterday in a cabbage patch, I tell you, and I think I know the score. So I'm making it attractive, sweetening the pot.

"Yet—yet—yet a still small voice within me whispers that the time may come when you won't be in it for the money, when you'll vie for vengeance and strive for spite, your hearts swept by a lust for havoc and the will to afflict. You'll get the hang of it, you hangmen. Trust me. Think—think—a journey of a thousand miles begins with a single step. In the meantime you've your own motives. So go back and size up your fellows. Don't let them out of your sight. Take notes. Be suspicious. Watch in the foundry, in the print shop—*in the canteen*—the laborer's labor. Does he love his work? When he whistles, is it a stirring march to set himself a fine pace, or is it a dreamy love song he hums to distract himself? The perfect crime's imperfect. Sin leaves clues. Open your eyes, be alert. Stop, look and listen, for the world's unsafe still. Earn your paroles. Time off for good behavior, everyone. Leave me with a remanence of corrupt men, I ask only that. Remember— rat and do worse, but leave no visible bruises. *Connote* injuries and stop short of murder, or we'll both be in trouble.

"That's that," the warden said.

"That's that," the men said.

The warden nodded and they rose to leave. Guards came to prod them toward the doors. Someone shoved Feldman, but it was not a guard. It was his neighbor, a quiet convict from his own cellblock, stepping on his heels, jabbing him in the back.

They were marched to the rear-center door but then jammed together into the last few rows in order to let the night-shift personnel and their families pass into the auditorium first. While they were halted, the man behind Feldman leaned toward his ear. "You shit," he whispered. "You mother-fucker kike bastard. Son-of-a-bitch cocksucker," he told him softly. "Prick, fartass, scumbag, jerk. Fairy." Feldman determined to ignore him, but the man's mouth was almost in his ear. Once he felt the fellow's lip brush against his lobe. He pulled his head away, but the man became bolder. He pinched Feldman's back, first surreptitiously, then openly. Feldman moved forward and bumped into the man in front of him.

"Stand still there, you," a guard said angrily, and smiled his sanction when the one Feldman bumped shoved him back roughly. Feldman stood still, enduring their pinches and shoves, the small talk of their marginal violence.

Meanwhile, the warden, still on the stage and able to see the temporary bottleneck at the doors, had begun to speak again, shouting a sort of recessional to them. "Not enough of you have been using Warden's Forest in your free time," he said. "I set this plot aside for your benefit, not my own. Yet when I look out on it from my office window I rarely see anyone in it. It's not enough to reason that it's winter and that the trees are all bare. Much can be learned from the cold. Much. What good does it do, men, to see the spring but not to suspect its sources? Little credit redounds to the gazer on fall's fat spectacle.

"This is *your* copse, you robbers, and I want to see it used! Is that clear? All right, then. Move on out back there." He began to clap his hands. "Virtue, virtue, virtue, virtue, virtue," he cried. "Virtue, virtue."

They started to march again, Feldman sliding out in a long first step to elude an anticipated shove or at least reduce its force. As they went up the aisle, he saw that his face had been the model for one of the gargoyles on the last panel of the Gothic siding.

Virtue, virtue, virtue, virtue, virtue, Feldman thought. Virtu, virtu, virtu, virtu, virtu, Vertigo!

14

Elegant Feldman, mandarin-robed, tasseled, the silken fringes of his belt like a very soft cat-o'-nine-tails—"To beat down grime. To punish all ordinary life's shabby shit"—came up to the satinwood sideboard—"Get me breakfast, Innkeeper. See to the horses. Feed the postern, feed the coachman. Wenches, farewell. Here's your health. Hey, nonny, nonny, with a hi and a ho and the rain it raineth every day"—and raised heavy silver lids; ladled, as if giving breakfast a downbeat, from the still-steaming chafing dish, goldenly scrambled eggs onto a thin white plate, smooth to the touch as cake icing. He picked, to go with the eggs, a sprig of lush mint, like a flower for a loved one, or a ceremonial herb for the gown of a bride, and carved a slice of ham, ruddy, scorched beneath its luscious glaze. He poured his coffee—black, for he admired the way it looked in the light cup, and loved to see the way it set off the steam. He brought his prizes to the table, already laid, and set them beside a napkin furled in its ring. He returned to the sideboard and hefted the viscous cocktails of jam and crystals of bright sweet jellies. He chose his toast, dark brown and crisp as bark, and took up a dish of butter pats jammed in a frozen choke of crushed ice. He lifted down a halved melon in its silver ring, its green meat pale as money.

Seated in the high white leather chair, squat as a jolly king in the polished-lensy side of one bright brim-to-cloth goblet, he tucked himself into the broad twilled napkin and smoothed his damasked lap, comfy as a man in a deck chair. Beside his plate, in three smart folds, Lilly, as she did every day, had placed the front section of the *New York Times* (air-mailed, but more than a day old anyway. Wednesday's paper mailed Tuesday night and read Thursday morning, so that he had come to think of all facts as tentative, subject to change, *already* changed, all bulletins stale, all remarks by all spokesmen revised by now or framed in clearer contexts, all outbursts toned down, apologized for, corky with loophole—so that gradually he conceived of most truth as of something even the air could change, set to spoil like standing milk or the browning oxidized flesh of halved apples, and learned to view the world and everything in it with a comfortable hindsight, and thought of wars and strikes and uprisings as fictions).

Feldman loved his solitary breakfasts, loved his own corpulent sense of them, and enjoyed, in the dark smoked mirror, seeing himself eating them, turning the pages of his paper, tapping at egg in the corners of his mouth with a thick, linen-wrapped finger, lighting cigarettes. Although he usually ate alone, Lilly—in an old beltless raincoat she used as a bathrobe, in damaged high heels, the counters broken—sometimes came in while he drank a second cup of coffee (in this one he took cream, two spoons of sugar, high, rounded as dunes).

He finished and scraped his nail absently on a piece of toast. He allowed himself to think of the store, and his mood changed. He did not even remember to enjoy the opulent ruin of his breakfast—the dark toast crumbs on the thick table linen, the stains of coffee and the greased plates and smudged tumblers and the jellied, sticky handles of the silver, the tiny bits of stiffened egg in the creases of his napkin like clots of rheumy eye matter. The store is not doing well, he thought. Things must pick up, he thought; they must.

He didn't grieve for his condition so much as for the effort it would take to improve his condition. This he dreaded, as he dreaded all revision. He had discovered long ago that he did not enjoy competition, or even "business." The truth was Feldman had no feel for patterns. Trends bored him. He hated even to be controlled by the seasons, the holidays, thought of Christmas as a violation of free enterprise, of the climate—summers, say, when he sold no skis—as a restraint of trade. He endured the nation's economic crises impatiently, was indifferent to predictions of boom and angered by warnings of bust. He scorned even the empty optimisms of designers about a certain color or a length of skirt. Yet adopting an attitude toward the competition that was vaguely laissez-faire, coming, as it were, to Christmas as he came to the obsolete news in his thirty-six-hours-old newspaper—his store did the biggest volume in the state in *post*-Christmas selling—he had prospered, acquiring over the years a reputation for flair which had less to do with deliberation perhaps than with a certain looseness of timing. And of course he demanded good salesmen. Many of his people were old pitchmen, who—behind their counters, talking with their hands; their voices slightly raised, faintly nasal in high pressure's elliptic twang; pointing, quick and graceful as men doing card tricks, to the features of a shirt—knew how to "build a tip." ("You know, Leo," one of them once said, "half us guys ain't used to working indoors yet.") A handful of men in departments like Furniture or Housewares had once sold on television. Others had sold over the telephone or door to door. There were barkers, men who'd owned shooting galleries or Pitch-a-Penny booths in carnivals.

What hurt him now was a shift in the structure of the city: the decay of old neighborhoods and proliferation of suburbs, the incursions of Negroes, the lousy parking and all the rest. Feldman's city had held its shape into the postwar years, and he had not had to face the problem of discount houses, or—to show the flag—had to build, shopping center for shopping center, the murderous big branch stores. (It was the new Diaspora, the Diaspora of fat cats, the whole middle class in flight.) Now, belatedly, he had to do something. He had been paralyzed by conservatism—not fear, not even caution—just a strange Feldmanic inertia when it came to expending any energy on the merely remedial and makeshift. It was as if he were impatient with time itself, forbidding flux as he might have forbidden, if he knew it was happening and he had the power, a change in the structure of his cell tissue.

He heard Lilly before he saw her, the timid *clack-clack* of her heels and the lungy, wheezy chuffing of her feet as they moved over the broken counters and deeper into her shoes. "My dear?" he said, not looking up.

"Billy needs a tutor, Leo." She carried a bowl of cold oatmeal in one hand and half a hardened fried egg on a plate in the other. It was their son's unfinished breakfast. She would sit down now and finish it, wiping the egg into her mouth with Billy's discarded crusts. Feldman appraised her. In her open raincoat she looked like a disaster victim. Lilly, the mailman's treat, he thought, the paper boy's first young love. "Billy should have a tutor, Leo. You saw last night."

He had. A revelation. They had gone to "open house" at Billy's school, and Billy's second-grade teacher, Mrs. Blane, who looked to Feldman like an aging whore—it was the trenchcoat draped over the top of her desk; he knew those trenchcoats: $45.95, a big item with the singers in piano bars—had tried to give them an orange card with the words "Billy F.'s Father" printed across it. He had no intention of pinning the thing to his suit. (Billy F.'s mother already wore hers. Billy F.'s mother would pin on anything anyone gave her. She regarded her breasts as a sort of vast field bordering the highways and byways of her lapels and collars, the superhighway that was her cleavage. Around all this she would hang great shining pins like the blazing signs of motels.) Trampy Mrs. Blane's own bosom was bare except for the pointy warheads of her nipples puckering her sweater. Feldman shoved the card into his pocket, pricking his finger on the pin.

"Goddamnit," he said.

Mrs. Blane, who liked that kind of talk, smiled broadly and stroked her trenchcoat. A whore certainly, Feldman thought, and had an idea. Why not a sort of Show Biz Board, something like the board of college girls he used in the store during the summer? He could aim it at "26" Girls, Go Go dancers, burlesque queens, waitresses behind the bars in bowling alleys, the wives of army sergeants. A whole new line: satin stretch pants, brassieres like spider webs, half-bras like the pouches of kangaroos, panties with a quilted male finger at the crotch; rubber butts, foam tits; gratuitous garters. *Marvelous*, he thought.

Lilly had found Billy's desk and was reading a note he had left for them on the top of his workbooks. "Leo," she called, "look." He took the sheet of paper from her and read:

dear mothar nad fothar, Hi. Lok arand my room hav a nice tiem.
your Son billy F.

There were two words on the other side: *"Lok taebl."* Feldman didn't understand all of it, but since he hadn't known his son had started to learn to write he was rather pleased by the note. He gave it back to Lilly and smiled. "Not bad," he said. Then he noticed that there were notes on all the children's desks, and he leaned over to read them. "Welcome to our open house," the note on the next desk said. "We have been working hard all week on the projects you see tonight. I hope you enjoy everything. Please look at my workbook before you leave and be sure to see the 'city' the class has been building on the table at the back of the room. It should amuse you. Certainly it has been a lot of fun to make. I made the fire station. I love you both and will see you at breakfast tomorrow before Dad goes to work. Your son, Oliver."

Feldman looked around the room for Oliver's parents. Standing next to a striking woman in tweed, he saw a tall, handsome, successful-looking man wearing a card that said "Oliver B.'s Father." He didn't like their looks.

"Leo," Lilly said, "look at this one. These are really charming."

Feldman bent over the tiny desk and stared at the paper.

Dear Mom, Dear Dad,
Your being here makes me glad
Please look around and see our work,
I hope you like it,
Your son, Burke.

"Beautiful," Feldman said, and glowered at Burke's mother. He read all the notes, sneaking up to seats only moments after a parent had vacated them.

"You'll eat your heart out, Leo," Lilly said.

"Not at all, not at all," Feldman said, waving her off. "I've been meaning to ask you, sweetheart, was there much idiocy in your family?" He went back to Billy's desk and opened one of the workbooks. "Why," asked the box beneath the story, "did Tim's grandfather make Tim promise to keep the calf a secret until Sue's birthday?" Below there was a sentence with the last word left blank: "Tim's grandfather wanted the calf to be a—." Billy had printed the word "apple" in the blank space. Feldman closed the book.

He went to the table at the back of the room and looked at the city the class had made. There was a water tower made from half a Quaker Oats box painted silver. It was supported by four black pencils stuck into the bottom. There were cigar-box schools and skyscrapers fashioned out of cereal boxes. Tiny windows had been cut into the cardboard and glazed with Scotch tape. There was an elaborate City Hall, a jail, a railroad station. The names of the builders had been worked into their buildings, and Feldman stared glumly at Oliver B.'s cunning little firehouse with its shiny brass peashooter for a fireman's pole. He tried to find his son's contribution but couldn't see it anywhere. Then, behind the city, he noticed a small vague area with two crumpled-up wads of paper and a few loose pieces of gravel and clumps of dirt. He smoothed out one of the pieces of paper. "Grabage dunp. Billy F.," it said.

Furious, he looked around for Lilly and saw her talking with Mrs. Blane. The teacher nodded and compressed her lips sympathetically. He watched them bitterly. He was going to march up there and pull his wife away from the woman, but his eye was caught suddenly by a series of charts and graphs tacked to the walls. Examining them, he saw that thinly disguised as games and contests, they indicated a kid's standing in a particular subject. There were charts for spelling, reading, arithmetic, social studies, science—other things. By the name of each child was a tiny paper automobile pinned to a mapped track that led toward towns on a kind of West Coast called things like "Scholarsville" or "Goodstudentberg." On the spelling chart Billy's car had never even left its garage, and he had barely made it to the city limits on the reading and penmanship charts. On the arithmetic chart Billy had no automobile at all.

Next to these charts were others that were more advanced: arithmetic became mathematics, reading became literature, penmanship art, and so on. Only those children who had made it to the West Coast were represented on these new charts. Here they boarded little paper steamers and began a journey that led out through the Gulf of Graduation and took them across the University Ocean, past places like the Savant Islands and Curriculum Reef to seek port in the Bay of the Doctorate. Many of the children were just getting seaborne, although several were fairly far out, and some, like Oliver B., were already breasting the international date line. Feldman could find Billy's name only on the goodcitizenship chart, but he couldn't locate the boat that went with it. Probably it had sunk. He shook his head and stared sadly at a series of launching pads that bloomed along the width of a blackboard. Feldman guessed that the rockets, in various stages of loft, represented the grand prospectus of each child's achievements in the class. Billy's hovered weakly over its launching pad like a thin flame just above its wick.

"It looks like the goddamned Stock Exchange in here," he told Maurianna Q.'s mother, standing beside him. "Like the goddamned Big Board."

"Are you one of the fathers?" the lady asked. "I don't see your card."

He looked quickly around the room and turned back to the woman. "I'm little Oliver B.'s daddy," he told her softly . . .

Feldman tapped at his mouth one last time with his napkin and pushed back his chair. "Get him a tutor, Lilly," he said. "Finish your oatmeal, Lil, and get him a tutor, kid. Money's no object. None of your three-buck-an-hour graduate students, honeybunch. Get him a Nobel Prize winner. If he doesn't shape up soon, we may have to institutionalize him."

Because he couldn't bear to enter an empty store, Feldman always tried to wait until twenty or thirty minutes after the doors opened before going to work. Sometimes, if he was early, he would stand outside, feeling ceremonial, beside the big brass plaque that bore his name and the date of the store's founding. Seeing the plaque, and on it the solid, memorial letters of his name, he often had a sense—though the store, in an old building once a warehouse, had not yet been in existence twenty-five years—of ancestors, a family business, and had to remind himself forcibly that *he* was Feldman.

He pushed the big revolving doors, feeling, as he always did, heavier, and waiting, as he shoved slowly on the door's metal rung to feel himself thicken with opulence, to become wider, gravid. The door spun him out onto the main floor, and he smelled at once the perfumes and face powders, the mascaras and polishes bright as sodas. By the high glass cases he knew himself some glamour mogul; by the lipstick cartridges like golden bullets a grand armorer, love's field marshal among those shiny warheads. Art, art, thought Feldman, impresario of deep disks of rich rouge, pastel as flesh, of fine-grained dusting powders like soft, fantastic sand, of big plush puffs and cunning brushes. He stood by lotions in bottles, by cylinders of deodorant in a female climate of balmy aromatics, in a scent of white gardens, thinking of dreamy debauches in palatial bathrooms, of comic blows, cutie-pie spankings with the big fluffy puffs. Here, where other men might have felt intimidated, Persian Feldman lingered, feeling the very *texture* of his wealth, his soft, sissy riches, the unctuous, creamy, dreamy dollars.

I am the master of all I purvey.

(In the old days, new to ownership, he would take things from counters, filling his pockets with toys, wrist watches, cuff links, pulling a tie that had attracted him, stuffing it into his jacket; more attracted by his merchandise than any customer, unreluctant as an assured guest at a feast, and feeling just that, his own reflexive hospitality—knowing ultimate freedom, the last man on earth, nimbused with luck. There had been complaints, his own people had not known him, thought him a thief, a madman; some customers even, driven by an abstract loyalty to the ceremony of sale, daring to pull against him in ludicrous tug of war, to collar him, to call a cop. But it had not been these fools who had been able to stop his raids, nor even the complex decorum of inventory. Bookkeeping could not deal with him; it knew profit and loss, credit and debit, and made allowance even for pilferage that struck as malice or arrived as need. But it was helpless to explain what *he* did. There was no place on the ledger, no word for it, unless it was this: "Feldman." It wasn't any objection at last but his own: not surfeit finally, but surfeit's mild adjunct, superfluity, his idea, grown to a principle, that things—*all things*—were just gewgaws, and that nothing, *nothing* could ever excuse a disturbed profit. A lost sale was lost forever, something gone out of his life. So he doubled the guard, was ruthless with shoplifters, prosecuted until it cost him thousands and the word got out: that his place was no place to get away with anything, that you might as well try to hold up a bank. And all this, the expense of prosecution, of tight security, was reflected at last in the books. Meanwhile, he had packed in six big boxes and stored in his garage all those things he had taken during the enthusiastic year of his spree, a monument—an objects lesson—that nothing, nothing, *nothing* was ever lost, that all was recoverable and advantage lay where advantage lay: *everywhere*, available as atmosphere. And one day he sent a truck to take it out, to bring it all back to the shelves and bins and counters to be *sold* this time, only keeping one thing back, a wallet, to remind him.)

Now he moved past the cosmetics and began his morning tour—he had not outgrown this—of the main floor, his reviving stroll through an acre of artifact. No one dared address him. They thought it *business*, some trick or formula he had, some private, infallible rule of thumb. "Nothing gets past that one," they told each other. Nothing did, but he walked there only because it was refreshing, because the department store's ground floor offered a panorama of his possibilities. For it was thus that he had come to view his merchandise: as possibility, chance, turned risk, all of it latent with purchase and profit. But it was dreadful too: dreadful to see the high heaps, an infinity of the on-hand, dreadful to know that there was more on the floor above, and more on the floor above that, on up the full six floors, more, more—and across town, more in warehouses, more in trucks even now arriving in the city or just starting out from a dozen distant cities, more in railroad cars and more in the holds of ships and bellies of planes. Feeling the full responsibility of the risks he took for profit, terrified by the threat of ruin, of their not being customers enough in the city or time enough left in his life to sell it all, but made bold by his very fright, comforted by the magnitude of his terror and the slimness of his chances.

He was obsessed by it, the merchandise laid out like a city, patterned, zoned as neighborhood, and missed nothing on the fluorescently tubed yellow wood and glass horseshoe counters. He knew without touching them the feel of the glass, greasy as plastic from the precious contact of shoppers, their leaned, open-palmed surrenders on the countertops, smudged from their groped investigations, their excited jabs at the glass: "There, *there*—next to the white one." (The counters, washed each night, bore a now intrinsic blur, ineffaceable as the cloud on an old watch crystal.) And could almost have told which belts had been sold from the tiers mounted like coiled snakes in their clear oblong boxes. And even which ties, perhaps, hanging thick as a curtain before some gay vaudeville.

He stopped to look at the big brown cash registers, complicated as console organs, and to peer at the figures in the windows at their tops, seeing sadly against the broad black strip that ran from one side of the register to the other the rows of white, thick, squarish zeros, the icy decimals big as hailstones. He was released by the sound of the bell registering a sale, and moved on, restored as a prince in a legend.

Trailing his hand comfortlessly through the heaped, dark piles of socks, he looked out over the open rectangles of distant counters and cases and racks, and went toward Men's Ready to Wear to stand among the mountains of slacks, aware as always of the faint, sweet, oily smell of the massed cloth. He pulled at a rack of suits built into a wall, dollying it effortlessly forward on its big tracks, turning it soundlessly on its thick, greased shaft. He drew in one last deep lungful of the pleasant odor and moved on, the tweeds and herringbones giving him, as he glanced at them in passing, a faint illusion of speed.

In the broad center aisle, between vast counters, he paused

before a display table covered with a red moiré satin, grainy as wood, on which expensive gifts had been arranged at random: a captain's cabin barometer at Fair and Very Dry, the pressure 31.01 and rising; an enormous obscure brush with bristles the color of aluminum; a black leather casket with four drawers like a jeweler's trays. He scratched at a drawer but failed to open it, and could not locate the key which fit into the bloated, classic keyholes. He handled a carelessly spread tent of printed silk which looked like the master sheet from which ascots were cut. Considering it, Feldman had a sense that it had been there forever, that it would be there always in its wicked obsolescence. He left the table.

Passing counters high with prim stacks of ladies' blouses—it occurred to him that he was probably losing money on the men; fitfully he regretted their larger bodies, the additional cloth that went into their clothes and ate up profits—he came to an area of domestic, personal hardware (A MONTH O' SUNDRIES, the sign said) and moved among cigarette cases, boxed wallets like open books, ganglia of leather key rings, lighters, umbrellas, zippered sewing kits, the bright aligned spools of thread like fantasy ammunition. In the aisles were pastry carts of handbags. (Maze, he thought, the tempting obstacles of possession.) There were tables of slippers, step-ins, bootie socks, sequined moccasins, scuffs, woolen hip-length stockings. There were ladies' belts rising on successively diminished wheels, sweaters and white blouses you could blow your nose in, sheerish scarves as rough to the touch as a human heel, chandeliers of hats, stoles like folded flags, monogramed sachets, crocheted shawls, muliebrial hospital bed jackets that made a ploy even of death. He bent to examine a display case of men's coinlike jewelry, fashion's mintage, the small change of cuff links and tieclasps and studs. And peered closely at the stacked octagonal hatboxes, Dickensian, Bond Streety, the grayish cardboard shaggy, linty as money.

Entering Yard Goods, he had to pick his way past bright throw pillows like big candies. There were reels of ribbons, cards of lace, buttons, piping, upright bolts of flannel, wool, silk, horizontal rolls of cloth, packages of zippers, big pattern books thicker than telephone directories. (He was excited by the clutter here, and in the luggage department next to it, the big grips and steamer trunks thickening space as in a crowded customs.

In the Specialty Shop he briefly rummaged among the wicker baskets with their foreign chocolates and hams and sardines, their dry, queer pods and briny rinds. He paused to read the legends on the colored tins of biscuits and the Balkan, closely printed labels—medaled, decorated as some prince's chest—on the bottles of dark steak sauces. He stared at the jars of caviar and salad dressing, at the curious bottled gems of pimentos, artichoke hearts like preserved organs. He browsed the anthologies of strange cheeses and the glasses of rare jellies with their suspended slivers of fruit like motes in thick light, and thought hungrily of all turned, vexed appetites, soured and satiated by the normal vegetable and the ordinary meat, lusting himself to taste the canned worms and chocolate ants, to savor the snake, coiled as twine in the clear jar, to gorge himself on grasshoppers and make a feast of the lizards' tongues, tender, sinewless as fish.

He crossed to the large glass tanks of candy, staring at them as at treasure: the mint lentils and nonpareils, the dollhouse bricks of jelly and licorice boats, the chocolate stars and strings of pectin marjels, wafers, candy canes, the huge almond-pitted blocks of scored chocolate—all the sweet, hard crystals, all the fondants. He placed his fingers in the trough of a scale and lifted out a sugary residue, a kind of candy gravel, succulent dust.

And this is only the first floor of it, he thought.

He turned, stumbling, passionate, and got onto the enormous chiseled X of the sculpted escalator, having more than a king had, having everything. Rising slowly above the plains of goods, seeing it all at once now, the customers ringed and lost in his wilderness of product. Desperate with his untellable risk, his inventory heavy as the planet. This was the last time he would see it today, and though he wished he might never see it again he knew that tomorrow morning he would have to look once more.

By the time he had risen two or three more floors, however, he was an altered man. His spirits, oppressed on the main floor, became higher the higher he rose. This often happened. There was something hospitable in danger. He began impatiently to climb the moving stairs. Barely glancing around him, he rose above China, above Appliances, above the children's department, the men's, the women's, climbing toward levels of the store which were insular and half deserted. Here's where the real trading's done, he thought, standing in the furniture department among its scatter of dining- and living- and bedroom suites. He saw a woman testing a chair, a man at a desk, pretending to type and making imaginary compensations for the height of his typewriter, an engaged couple sitting aggressively on a bed. They all seemed unconscious neighbors in some odd, enormous house. Feldman was undiscouraged by the quiet here. If it had been noisier below, much of the stir had been aimless, a buzz of browsers, a falsetto, idling rasp of wills in abeyance. Here, though, he sensed purpose, the pious silences preceding high purchase, almost a condition of privilege when money changed hands, like those moments a family has alone with its dead before the coffin is closed. (In these regions he had sometimes fired people on the spot if they lost a sale. "If they get this far," he said, "they want it.") Now he paused, caught by something sanctified, basilican. He sniffed the air. A sale—the man at the desk. Observing him, Feldman saw the ceremonial poses, the last bemused, executive glance into the empty drawer. ("Have them try it on," he told his salesmen. "Whatever it is. Have them act it out. Pull them to the mirrors. Let men who've never hunted see themselves with guns in their hands.") The sale would be made; it was money in the bank. He smelled decision, impulse—the guilt that went with every yielding. (There were days when the store stank of all the accreted, powerful discharges of submitted-to temptation; other days when the place smelled of resistance as of stone.)

Feldman did not wait for the salesman to write up the order, but rushed away, almost as if he needed to be unaware of something good happening to him so that when it came to his attention later, it would carry a special increment for having been delayed. He rarely thought of his character, but took a certain comfort from such measures, seeing them as respectable evidences of his soundness, a willed humbling that qualified him for fortune.

In his effort to hurry away, Feldman took a wrong turn and found himself on a descending escalator. Feeling exactly like one drifting earthward in a parachute, he saw the looming women's-wear department and was seized by an old idea.

There had been, in his adolescence, a spate of films about department stores—comedies about stern old merchants who found it difficult to understand their carefree rakish sons. Sometimes it was the fathers with the eccentric good will and the sons who were serious. These films had been Feldman's literature. They embraced, he thought, everything that was possible in human character, and watching them, he had glimpsed the irreducible polar concepts of human existence—stodge and lark, duty and holiday, will and sense. Inclined to the one or the other, he was sympathetic to both, the good arguments of reality and the good jokes of hedonism. He saw that life could betray decent men and that beauty took beatings. The comedies were turned into torments for him. In the darkened theaters, biting his nails, seeing the tragic implications of either alternative, he felt himself the most vulnerable human in America. His own father was obliterated; his own self was. (It sometimes occurred to him that in modeling himself in those old days on those characters' character, he may have slipped his own. Perhaps, he thought, Feldman was all artifact now, supposititious, and the real Feldman, meant for one fate, had found another.)

With puberty, however—Feldman's puberty had been late, his drives unserious; perhaps in serving two personalities, he had actually stalled biological time—he discovered something else: that the conflict between the father and the son had been only a natural irritation, the personality of the one demanding the personality of the other, imposing a petty distance that wrote no one out of anyone's will and generated no avenging codicils; discovered, well, the girl. And because the people he had become loved her, he loved her too. Loved her helplessly.

He had never seen anyone like her and never would perhaps, but it was enough, as it would have been enough for some knight of old time, for him simply to have an idea of her. Now he named all those girls Jean Arthur, and he loved her still, looked for her still, listened for her funny squeaky voice, seeking her feisty intensity. (He recalled her as a girl Communist, someone trying to organize the help in the store; other times he saw her in a Salvation Army bonnet, adorable with her cheeks in mumpy, musical pout, filled to bursting with trumpet *geschrei*. He loved her tics, remembered how cute she was in men's pajamas, or when she was drunk and mispronounced words. He loved all her irrelevant passions, her tough—cutest of all when making a tiny fist, throwing things, huffing and puffing, her hair in her mouth—working girl's integrity.) She defined innocence for him at a stage in his life when everyone else his age was falling from grace into a despair, so that for Feldman, who had come from a despair—his years as his father's captive, his inability when embracing the style of the one son to annihilate ultimately the style of the other—it was like awakening to a grace, like an infant angel smothered in his crib. In this way his timing had been thrown off, and he left moony and smitten—not catching the joke, actually believing such women existed—and all love was love fallen short of itself, doomed through his credulity, and himself given over to an unwilled but permanent adultery, made to serve like the forced slave of Amazons.

Perhaps the department store itself—the real one, the one he owned, that terrified him—was only a sort of the creating of the conditions in which his dream might be realized, a fatuous placation like that of the New Guinea cargo cults which constructed bamboo airplanes on the tops of hills in the hope that they would attract real planes with their heaven-launched gifts. Idiot! Lovestruck! he thought. So this is what lies at the source of my will. So this is what my profit motive rests on. He felt like a sucker, comic as a cuckold. In fact he *was* a cuckold: where is she anyway? who has her? "I wonder who's kissing her now," he thought, "I wonder who's showing her how." But despite what he knew to be the reality, he held on to a helpless hope that he might yet find her.

"Somewhere I'll find you," he sang in his head. "Someday my prince will come," his heart answered. (That was another thing: even his ballads were old-fashioned. Most of them came from operettas. He didn't even adjust the lyrics to his condition, but hermaphroditically sang for both sexes. It was a vestige of the old schism in him between the stuffed shirt and the prodigal.) "I am calling you—ooh—ooh—ooh—ooh—ooh—ooh," he sang mutely, soul seeking soul, love's sonar. "Someday he'll come along," he rendered, "the man I love."

Now, looking for Jean Arthur in earnest, he roamed the store, loped it—Feldman striding, darting, squinting, peering. There was a labored, frantic quality now ("Through the dark of night," his head sang, "I've got to go where you are"), exactly like one partner to a comic appointment just missing the other in a revolving door, or losing her behind a pillar or a potted fern. "Some enchanted evening," he warbled silently, "you will meet a stranger."

He sat down to catch his breath in front of a tiny vanity table in Ladies' Hats. He had not made his search in several months and he was rusty, unused to the strain.

He looked at himself in the table's oval mirror. The tricky glass—hat sales up fourteen percent since it was installed—gave back a thinned, lengthened Feldman. Aware of the ruse (he had commissioned optical specialists in Baltimore to do his mirrors), he compensated by filling his cheeks with air. Too much, he thought, and let out a little. There, *that's* what I look like. But he couldn't be sure (only the mirrors in the employees' toilets were accurate), and he stood up and gave himself half an hour to find his true love.

Picking girls who wouldn't know him, he approached their counters in disguise. Now he was one sort of son, now the other. In Ladies' Nightgowns he grinned shyly at the young woman behind the counter. By holding his breath for a minute and a quarter, he was able to bring a blush to his face.

"It's a shower gift for my secretary," he gulped. "She's just about your size, ma'am. I guess I could get a better idea if you could sort of hold it up to your—to your—if you could sort of hold it up to yourself. Gee," he said, "wow. I mean that's very beautiful, isn't it?"

"Its washable," she said wearily, "it's wrinkle-resistant. It won't stain." She took up her order pad. Feldman hesitated. "You throw it in the washer same as you would a bedsheet. It's one of our sexiest items," she said, looking at a point somewhere above his left shoulder. "Is that a charge, dearie?"

"Do you know who I am?" he asked.

"I do not," she said.

"I'm Leo Feldman, and you're fired."

"I need this job," she recited. "I've got to have an operation on my internal female organs. I'm saving up."

"Out, dearie," he told her. "You're washed up, same as you would a bedsheet."

He went to the toy department—he should have looked there first; hung up on kids, she'd be, the darlin' angelface—where he spotted a gentle-looking blonde with a cute, snub little nose he associated with figure-skaters. The girl he had in mind would be soft-spirited, her female internal organs ripe and luscious as the top strawberries in a basket. He hung back a moment to form a plan, then went up to her.

"I need about a hundred toys," he began. "They're for an orphanage. These kids have had tough lives; most of their parents are in prisons or asylums. A lot are from broken homes where neither the mother nor the father was deemed morally fit to retain custody. Many of these children were with their folks when they were killed in auto accidents and train wrecks or burned to death in fires. You can imagine what it's like for them."

"Yessireee," she said flatly. "Have you seen our new war line? WW Two?" She scooped up some metal tanks and pieces of artillery and placed them on the countertop. "Everything's scale," she said. "There's a bomber that drops artificial napalm. We've got a model of the atomic bomb exactly like the one that killed seventy-four thousand people in Nagasaki."

Feldman tipped his hat.

"There's a terrific special on rubber knives."

"I'm Leo Feldman," he said.

"This is interesting," she said, and lifted down a sort of chemistry set. "It's the new germ-warfare kit. It's perfectly harmless, but if you dust this powder on a wood, stone or metal surface, it grows a fungus. There are gases too. They don't do any damage, but the smell is terrible."

"You're transferred to Lingerie," he said curtly.

Mooncalf, he accused himself. Stargoose! Comet-shmuck! He walked away, shaking himself to remember who he was. But by this time he knew, and what he looked like without a mirror. Not the wiseguy, not the dullard; he was the old man himself, the stern paterfamilias of damn fools and creeps—the loveless grump of the world.

In this mood, in his office, Feldman read his messages and opened his mail.

There was the usual number of charities. At his level they did not always ask for contributions but invited him to join committees. He set these aside for Miss Lane to reject with the excuse that while time did not permit, etc., etc., they could use his name on their letterhead (although to a few he had her fire off righteous declarations of opposition in principle). On one letter he recognized his name on the list of sponsors printed down the side of the stationery. My second notice, he thought, and threw it in the wastebasket.

He had become a sort of public spirit. So prominent was his name on so many letterheads that the real community leaders had no idea of how little he actually did. They embraced him, welcomed him warmly to their executive class, and once they had almost made him Man of the Year. Where, Feldman wondered, was the vaunted anti-Semitism in the upper reaches of his society; where was the famous aloofness and coolness he had counted on? He couldn't, he supposed, rise to the presidency of an insurance company, a railroad, a steel mill, a utility, and there was no real future for him in Detroit, none in the north woods—he worked in softer fabrics—but the gray-haired ranks of all philanthropists remained ready to open for him. Money talked: it talked to money. There wasn't a country club in the state—not a hunt club, not a horse club or a talk club or a fuck club—that was closed to him. He could drink bourbon over ice in any of them. He could part his hair in the middle, and no one would laugh. He could wear a vest, a pocket watch, retire behind steel frames. But there was something tame and flat in wealth. He knew there was nothing he could buy, except his comfort, that would please him. He knew more: there was nothing he could give. The thought of sponsoring museums where people came to look six seconds at a given work of art and took home a deeper impression not of beauty but of all the things in the world that did not belong to them depressed him. It spoke ill for wealth if all that one could usefully do with it was give it away. There was something repressive in money finally, something inhibiting. Rich men used it as a lesson to poor men, dispensed it—whatever the sums; he had seen the restrictive clauses in those grants, the ironclad regulations—cautious and painstaking as chemists doling out the proportions of a boring formula.

An executive—what was that? That was nothing to be. He had no heart for empire; only for the day to day, hand-to-hand, rough-and-tumble of imperialism, of which, sadly, empire was the single issue. But already, failing the Diaspora, he was dug in. Poor little rich boy, he mocked himself. Don't mock *me*, he stormed. Only the damn miser counts his blessings. Pain has degrees. There are numbers on thermometers. Gloom isn't staved with reasons. Look, he thought, clinching it, at that department on the fourth floor, for God's sake, with its gifts for the man who has everything: personalized cue balls, solid gold zippers, framed thousand-dollar bills. Why, that, in his life, was what *he* had been reduced to: gestures gestured by the man who has gestured everything. He got by on joyless *joie de vivre* and forced life force.

Last week he had made a speech in his book department, introducing Vice-Admiral Marlow ("Sea Power") Bellingstone, USN Ret. He had read the man's autobiography and wired his publisher, promising to split expenses if he could get the Admiral for an autographing party. He took out a half-page ad and called the local naval-recruiting office for a color guard. (The Navy would have nothing to do with the Vice-Admiral, and Feldman had had to settle for Billy in a sailor suit.) Standing on a raised platform draped with bunting, Feldman had addressed the crowd.

"It is my high privilege," he told them, "to pipe Admiral Bellingstone here aboard the *Feldman*. Many of his provocative views are familiar to you. His idea about extending the twelve-mile limit until sea mass exactly displaces land mass and each nation has its mirror image in the water—do I read you right, Admiral?" The

Admiral saluted. "—is already known to most Americans. His career-long fight with the Pentagon to recognize Britain, rather than Communism, as the real threat to this nation is equally well known. So, too, are the Admiral's efforts to restore our country once again to its rightful place as leader in the world's whaling community. 'It just doesn't make sense,' as the Admiral puts it in his book, 'to let foreign Denmark put one over on us in this department.'"

Feldman lifted one of the Admiral's books off a tall stack. "An admirable work, Admiral," he said, and touched his forehead in salute. The Admiral saluted back, and Feldman turned again to the crowd. "Less familiar, perhaps, but gone into here in careful detail is the Admiral's fascinating proposal to form a team of naval historians and sea geographers to try to establish once and for all the historicity of Davy Jones's locker. The Admiral's belief that if we find it we'll probably also rediscover the lost city of Atlantis could be one of the brilliant serendipities of the twentieth century." (Even as he spoke, Feldman took the measure of his own outrageousness and disapproved. There was a lot of talk about the poor man hanging while the rich man got off scot-free, but there were other inequities. How much nonsense a rich man could speak!) "I am reminded, as just in passing I peruse the Admiral's useful index, of his frightening warning about the danger of salt leakage from the ocean through the St. Lawrence Seaway. In the Admiral's phrase, we are 'bleeding the Atlantic.' In just seventy billion years—do I have these figures right, Admiral?—the Great Lakes will turn saline. What are we supposed to do then?

"Friends," he said in conclusion, "I don't want to keep the Admiral too long from his *pensées*, so I'll turn him over to you right now, but I must just mention one more of his ideas that was particularly exciting to me. I'm talking about his research regarding the dangerous integration of the Atlantic and Pacific oceans via the Panama Canal, what the Admiral calls 'The Mongrelization of the High Seas.' Maybe he'll tell us a little more about that one himself. Ladies and gentlemen, let's welcome aboard Vice-Admiral Retired Harlow 'Sea Power' Bellingstone, USN."

The madman blinked, talked crazily for twenty minutes about his theory on mermaids—they were not good swimmers—and Feldman sold three hundred books.

Or the bananas. From time to time Feldman had noticed news stories about merchants who, through misplaced decimals and literally interpreted metaphors in incautious ads, had been forced to part with valuable merchandise. A woman in Hartford bought a used car for four hundred potatoes. In Idaho a furniture store had to let a dining-room set go for "only a very little lettuce." It was always big, good-humored news, and worth a picture even on the front page: a housewife, bent, smiling under a one-hundred-pound sack of potatoes; a gag photo of the Boise furniture man staring glumly—"That's one on me"—at a shriveled garden lettuce, one browning, crumpled leaf of which protruded from his lips; a woman with her mouth open, and a beefy fellow with his hands over his ears who had just sold an air-conditioning unit for a song. It was as if a real bargain, things being what they are, were a blow for the underdog, from which all might take heart. The lucky seemed to give the unlucky hope, cheer, a belly laugh.

A year before, Feldman had given his TV salesman a day off and run an ad for a floor-sample color television set with a twenty-five-inch screen. The price was three hundred and fifty bananas, and he had arranged for someone from his photography department to stand by with a camera. When the store opened, Feldman was behind the counter, waiting. In ten minutes there was a man before him, holding his ad. "You advertise the sale on the twenty-five-inch color TV?" the man asked.

Feldman looked at the ad closely. "Yes sir," he said, "but that's just a floor sample."

"I know that," the man said.

"Yes sir," Feldman said.

"You still got that set?"

"Yes sir."

"I want to buy it."

"Don't you want to see it demonstrated first?" Feldman asked. "The first color show doesn't come on until ten this morning."

"No, that's all right. It's guaranteed, ain't it?"

"Yes sir," Feldman said.

"That's good enough for me," the man said. "Three hundred fifty, right?" he asked cagily.

Feldman smiled. "That's right."

"Okay."

"Okay," Feldman said. "Let's have them."

"It's a charge," the man said.

"A charge?"

"Here's my charge plate."

"What is this, buddy?" Feldman demanded. "Are you trying to get away with something? That ad says bananas!"

In the end he had to let the set go for three hundred and fifty dollars, but the photograph of him making out the sales slip was uninspiring.

A month later he tried again. In a prominent ad in the Sunday papers he promised to sell an electric typewriter for "peanuts." He was shooting for the wire services, and in fact it was a reporter and his photographer who showed up first. The reporter claimed the machine and handed Feldman the peanuts.

"What," Feldman said, extending the peanuts in his outstretched palm and turning toward the photographer, "peanuts? Where are the lawyers? Will this stand up in court? Well, well, that's one on me."

His heart wasn't in it. But he did it.

As he did everything. "That Feldman," anyone might have said, "there's a man who's *alive*." As if eccentricity and a will set to scheme like a bomb to go off had anything to do with life. As if aggression and the maneuvered circumstances did.

Look at him, his ringed, framed concentration like a kid seeking a lost ball in high grass. An aesthetic of disappointment, a life of wanting things found wanting, calling out for the uncalled for. But the shout down from the mountain was always the same— that the view wasn't worth the climb. It was what one heard: "War is hell," says the General. The movie star quoted: "All those retakes. Always on a diet. The lies about you in the columns. The crank mail." Or the truth about spies: "People don't realize. Mostly it's just boring legwork. It's dull, routine. I don't even carry a gun." *And* the loneliness of the Presidency, *and* the endless ceremonial obligations of the King, *and* the brief, doomed flare of the athlete's prime, and all the small-print, thick-claused rest. People *didn't* realize. That it wasn't who one was, or even *what* one was, or if one made an effort or only took what came. What counted, finally, was whether you were lucky or not, whether the gods, the stars in their ornate sequences, had given you timing. There *were* lucky men. How often—this seemed strange now— had he had occasion to say, "I am one. *I* am."

So he kept up his ersatz enthusiasms and redoubled all efforts, like some gambler letting it ride, and just yesterday he had called all his stock boys and shipping clerks and maintenance men together for a meeting in the back of the store.

He smelled glue and string and rope and wrappings and postage and saucered sponges the color of erasers on pencils. In the shipping room he felt a physical disgust. He heard scales click, whir, a solid, metallic tattoo of postage meter. He saw the open rate books, the thumbed, greasy timetables. A telephone was out of its cradle. He lifted the receiver to his ear. "That you, Simon?" a woman's voice said. "I see you tonight, honey. I tell my husband Mrs. Shicker want me for a dinner party she giving." He hung up. Oppressed, he saw the pink third copies of bills of lading and wandered through a maze of senseless shipments with crayoned messages: "#7 of 10," "3 of 9," "1 of #4." He felt a thick sense of half-point signatures, a smudged, bewildering spiral of unfamiliar initials and names: R. L. and J. H. and Herman Shaw. (They were his proxies. They signed for him. Who were they?)

He opened a heavy door. A man lay sleeping on a wide loading platform. Feldman saw his shoes—thick, high-topped, like blunt weapons. He closed the door and continued through a warehouse whorl of bagged lunch and paper cups of gray coffee. Everywhere were the smooth, dark cardboard rails of open packages of candy. (He made a profit on the machines: here a profit, there a profit, everywhere a profit profit.) He saw the safety signs, the conserve-electricity signs, the turn-off-faucet signs, the absenteeism signs: all the crazy placard pep talk of management to labor. It was the landscape of time clock, and he plunged still deeper into it. He breathed the whelming dinge, the hostile, grimy fallout.

They were all waiting for him in the locker room. There were high school boys in tan linen jackets and women in the blue uniform of maids in hotel corridors. A few of the men wore the thick wool of lumberjacks, or wide bright ties down the front of their denim shirts. Feldman paused beside a young boy and held his elbow. "There's a man sleeping on one of the loading platforms. Get him."

He climbed up on a long bench. "I like it back here," he told them. "You're the backbone. The fortunes of this store rise and fall because of what you do here. Listen, just because you don't get the medals and the hurrahs of the crowd, that doesn't mean you're not appreciated. You're behind the scenes, you folks on the bench, you understudies. You're unsung. Permit me to sing you." They looked up at him, and he saw their pastiness, the abiding solemnity or causeless joy beneath their waxy pallor. Suddenly he had a sense of his own presence and was touched, seeing himself not as someone beyond them, out of their lives, but as someone close. He whiffed their hatred and sensed himself their caricature, demonized by them, stuffed into monogramed white-on-white shirts, dappered for them, given a thin mustache, his fingers fattened, pinkened, softened, remembered as one who wore rings. (Looking around, he recognized a boy who had delivered a package to his office once, while he was having his hair cut. What a story that must have made: "Fat-assed Feldman in a Big Silk Sheet." And the hair on the sheet—stiff, curled shavings, the association made forever in the kid's mind with ruthlessness, strength. Passionate hair. Showy, shiny sprigs of it, waved, tufted, patent-leather clumps of it by the large pink ears—a dancer's tufts, a pitchman's, Mr. Big's.) He imagined their projections of his green felty drawers of clothes, their lustful thoughts of the cedary scents, the smooth piping on his handkerchiefs, of where he kept his cuff links, his Broadway agent's jewels. He was part of them now, food for all their false anecdote. Adding up his curt hellos, his Jew's indifference. How dare they? he thought. How dare they?

"Who straightens stock on five?" he asked suddenly.

There was a greasy flash of a pompadour as a young boy looked up.

"It's a pigpen," Feldman said. "The fucking suits are out of line. Nothing is sized. I counted nine jackets loose on the cases." The boy stared down at his shoes. "All right," he demanded, "what's holding up the deliveries? Why can't the orders go out faster? Customers are calling up for their merchandise and I see half-empty trucks going out." They shifted uneasily. "What's the matter with you? Do I have to get new people back here? I will, goddamnit. Your union isn't worth boo, and I can hire and fire till the cows come home. You're breaking things. We're getting too many returns."

A man in a red-checked shirt put up his hand.

"What is it?"

"Sir," he said, "we never have enough excelsior."

"Balls," Feldman shouted back. "Excelsior's twenty-five dollars the ton. Bring newspapers from home. Use the goddamn candy wrappers, the paper cups. Do I have to tell you everything?" He harangued them this way for twenty minutes while they shifted under his gaze. "You've been using the postage meter for personal mail," he said. "That's stealing stamps. I'll prosecute, I swear it. I'll be back to see you in two months. If things aren't shaped up by then, I'll fire your asses all the hell out of here."

They turned to leave, and something in the soft, bewildered shrug of their shoulders suddenly moved him. "Wait," he called. "Wait a moment." They turned back, and he descended from the bench. "Life is not terrible," he said. "It isn't. I affirm life. Life is not terrible." They stared at him. "Get back to your duties," he said roughly.

Ah, but how tired he was of his spurious *oomph*, of all eccentric plunge and push and his chutzpa only skin-deep, that wouldn't stand up in court. "I like your spirit, boy," the skinflint says, surprised by brashness. "I need a man like you in Paris." Feldman didn't. He was exhausted by his own acts of empty energy. Unambushable he was, seeing slush at spirit's source, reflex and hollow hope in all the duncy dances of the driven. He was helpless, however. He had been born without a taste for the available. "No more looking askance at reality" had been his fervent prayer. But ah, ah, there was no God.

It occurred to him that he ought to knock off and go to a cocktail lounge and sulk. He could drink liquor and listen to the jazz they piped in. It might be pleasant. But then, he thought, he couldn't hear the melodies without thinking also of the words, the college-kid love poems. Not for him. For him there should be new songs, new lyrics. "I got the downtown merchant's blues," he sang softly. "My heart is lower than my bargain basement—all alone at the January White Sale." Stirred, he buzzed for Miss Lane. "Will green be the color this season?" he sang.

Victman was in Feldman's office with him. He was excited. Eight years ago Feldman had been proud of Victman—his New York man, his Macy's man. (Today everybody had his Neiman-Marcus man, his May Company man, but Victman was the first.) He had been a hot shot, in department-store circles a wonder merchant. (He had invented the shopping center, and the suburban branch store, and was in on the discussions when the charge plate was only in the talking stages—in department-store circles a household word.) Now Feldman could not look at him without wincing. He looked at him and winced for his $287,000 winced for his failed campaign. (Three columns and a picture in *Woman's Wear Daily* when he came with Feldman, articles in the *New York Times*, and the *Wall Street Journal*.)

"Leo," Victman said, "you ought to listen to this."

Feldman's irritation was such that he began to scratch himself.

(If he could get just some of his money back, it would be goodbye Victman.)

"Please, Leo," Victman said.

Feldman looked at him. He winced and said, "Victman, where you going to command a salary like the one I pay you?"

Victman groaned and Feldman winced again.

"*Where*, Victman?"

"You ruined me, Leo," Victman said.

"Ruin is relative," Feldman said. (A picture of this man had been in *Fortune*.)

"You ruined me, Leo," Victman said again.

"I'm the more injured party," Feldman said. "I can't look at you without wincing."

"Yes. I meant to say something about that," Victman said. "I wish you'd try to control that, Leo. It embarrasses me."

Yet he was sorry for Victman. He *had* ruined him. If he left tomorrow, though it was impossible that any major store would have him now, there would be nothing in the *Times*, nothing in the *Wall Street Journal*. Mum would be the word from *Woman's Wear Daily*. Looking at him, Feldman was often reminded of those "Where are they now?" features in magazines. Question: "Whatever happened to Norman Victman?" Answer: "He's with Feldman. He's sitting on his ass for many thousands of dollars a year."

"Victman started talking again, but Feldman wasn't listening. Victman stared at him. "You can't stop thinking about it, can you?" he asked.

"You're on my shitty list," Feldman said weakly.

Eight years ago Feldman's fortunes had been at their apogee. He had come up and up, the upstart, and in the last few years had outtraded and outdealt all of them, his store neck and neck with the largest ones in the state. Movie stars in town for personal appearances carried home his shopping bags on airplanes.

And his demon told him that it couldn't last, that prosperity was short-lived deception, that at last Red China and The Bomb and Civil Rights and The Russians would take their toll: that the world was turning a corner, the blue sky was falling. He saw a terrible fight for survival in which America—white men everywhere—backed against a final wall, would have to scrap its style. (Hadn't he been there himself, a passionate Jewish guerrilla fighter on the beachheads of the Diaspora? Hadn't he, the little terrorist, thrown his bombs and Molotov cocktails, and didn't he understand ardor, zeal, impatience, all the harassing, importuning passions? Wasn't he, by analogy then, an expert on the little yellow men, the little brown ones, the big black ones?) He foreknew the failing markets and the finished fads, anticipated in some sweeping, dark, Malthusic vision America's throes, this very city's—saw it choking on its fat. When others spoke warmly of progress Feldman kept his troubled peace, but he knew they were wrong.

Then he saw Victman's picture in *Fortune* and read his articles: "The Suburbs: America's New Market Towns."

He made the phone calls, sent the wires. Then the flights to New York and the wining and the dining and the feeling him out, and finally the secret meeting between the two men in the motel outside Chicago. "What can you expect from Macy's, Mr. Victman? You know their setup. Their echelons. Think of those echelons. Think of your distance from the king. How many princes and dukes and archdukes and barons and counts stand between you and the throne?" "That's true," Victman said, "that's true." "America is West, Mr. Victman. The whole world is, the whole universe is. Dare to dream. I'm talking future with you tonight— empire, dynasty, destiny. Neiman-Marcus, Norman. Consider, conjure. Soon Hawaii will be a state. Guam. The Philippines. Dare I suggest it? Come closer. Formosa. Quemoy. Matsu. Quemoy— keen; Matsu—mmnn. Shh. Shh. Are you the passionate man I think you are? Did you mean what you said in 'The Suburbs: America's New Market Towns'? Then get in on the ground floor. This is foundations, first principles. Make a wish on the stars, on the blue horizon. Climb every mountain, Mr. Victman. Pioneers, O pioneers, sir. Come West, young Victman."

He came, Feldman talking so fast Victman didn't know what was happening. Of course he came. Expecting perhaps to find mud streets, plank sidewalks, boomtown—assay offices, burlap sacks of nugget and dust, old-timers leading packmules. Finding instead only Feldman's somber city, a place of half a million looking older and more settled than New York. Then held in check: allowed to fiddle, seek sites, arrange for surveys, market-research reports; consult till the cows came home sociologists, city planners; even consulting architects at some predecision, top-of-the-tablecloth level, positioning goblets, inclining forks. Seen everywhere, overheard everywhere, egged on by Feldman himself, spilling his dreams in restaurants near the tables of men Feldman recognized as competitors and he didn't. His enthusiasm daily primed, each scheme encouraged, Feldman himself squaring his plans, complicating, flourishing, until the man thought he dealt with some merchant Midas and that on this rock would be founded some new commercial Rome. Until the casual chitchat of millions made even this city slicker's head spin: "Invest at a hundred dollars a man. That's the best rule of thumb, I think." "But that's fifty-five and a half million dollars!" "Today. I don't *mean* today. What were those population projections you got from the university? Let me see them, please. But this is only for two generations. It's a mistake to plan for under three. That's house-of-cards thinking, pigs who build with straw and sticks." "Wow!" "Wow indeed. *Indeed* wow."

Only gradually disappointed, held off for eight months by Feldman's ploys: Feldman dutifully inspecting Victman's sites. "You know your business, Victman, or you wouldn't be working with me, but I thought we were speaking about three generations. Can you see this place in even *two* generations?" (They were standing in a green pasture eight miles from town.) "It'll be a slum. Women unsafe on the street after eight o'clock at night, men unsafe after nine." Held off some more by his ploys for backing ("We don't want our capital from American sources"). Sent once to India, another time to Dutch Guiana ("That's where the money is, Norman, in your underdeveloped nations. Among those old Dutch planters"). And one time actually coming back with a pledge for twenty million from a man in Mexico ("No, Norman, I want thirty million from him. Either he's willing to show some good faith in this or we don't want to have anything to do with him").

And then, in a year, the disappointment growing in leaps and bounds: "I don't understand, Leo. Let's not sit on this. It's been eighteen months. We should break ground this winter so we can start building in the spring. The competition has its sites already." "Give them their rope, Norman, please." And then, later, after he had obtained additional pledges and pushed the Mexican up to thirty million: "Leo, we could have the capital investment tomorrow if we wanted. Let's move already." " 'Let's *move* already'? We *have* moved. We *have* moved, Norman, you silly man. What else do you think we've been doing for two years? And don't talk to me about having the capital investments tomorrow, when I have them today, when I've had them for two years. *You're the capital investments, Norman.* Don't you see what's happening? They've taken the bait! They're *overextending!* Those stores will be open in a year. Built in the sticks. Who'll go? Who'll go? And not just the double maintenance, but the double staff, the double advertising, the double trouble. We've thinned them out, we've spread them thin. You did, Norman. With your table talk, your reputation, your picture and the three columns in *Woman's Wear Daily*. You believe in progress? Progress is irreligious. Read your Bible. Seven fat years. Seven lean. And the seven lean shall be seven times leaner than the seven fat are fat. Seven lean, Norman, and all it takes is two—say three. No, Norman, no, they're tough, these guys. Say four. Say five, and have a margin of two. So don't speak to me about capital investment, nor prattle of progress. Checkmate is the name of the game. Not moving forward: standing pat when all about you are losing theirs."

"Don't you *believe* in progress?" Victman asked, shocked, shattered, who had based his life and staked his reputation on that principle.

"I believe," said Feldman softly, for they were in a restaurant now too, and he recognized faces and the walls had ears, "I believe in smearing the competition, survival of the fittest, cartel by default. I believe in the disappointed expectation and the harpooned hope, and that the best-laid plans of mice and men often gone astray. The tire with the plumpest tread has never moved an inch. Norman, Norman, consider the man in the club chair. That bulk comes from exercise's opposite: if you'd increase, decrease and desist. The proud falsetto of the castrate, the fat lap of the dowager, the banker's big ass—seats of power, Victman. I believe in ploy and stratagem and maneuver and conspiracy. I believe in espionage, the coup d'état, assassination, the palace revolt, guerrilla attacks and the cheaper revolutions. No more parades, sir. No more expensive reviews and costly May Day brags. No more shopping centers, no more sites, no more branch stores. Think me up commando schemes!"

He'd been had, poor man. When the other stores had their grand openings Feldman would have fired him, but he had invested $150,000 in him in the past two years and could not consider the deal closed until the stores had gone under. In the third year, having thoroughly discredited him, he lowered his salary to a more wieldy $30,000. (Two years, and not one coup to add to his score. No one knew, of course, how Feldman used him.) And the next year his salary was lowered again, by five thousand dollars. "The laborer is worth his hire," Feldman told him. "That's the best rule of thumb, I think."

Only one thing. And Feldman now considered it.

The stores had *not* gone under. There had not been seven fat years and seven lean ones, but fourteen fat. Disastrously, there had been no disaster. Red China had not laid a finger on the competition. "If you're so smart," he sang, "why ain't you rich?"

"They're taking us off the charge plate, Leo," Victman said.

"They're what?"

"What they threatened. When the new plates come out in the fall, we won't be on them." Feldman stared at him. "We haven't kept pace," Victman said shyly.

"Why? How can they do that?"

"I've been trying to tell you. There isn't any one reason—pressure from the retail clerks' union."

"I pay a straight commission."

"Hiring policy—"

"The first store in the state to hire a Negro?"

"Token, Leo."

"*Tahkee* token," Feldman said.

"They claim we run phony sales."

"Phony sales? *Phony?*"

"Who celebrates Arbor Day today?" Victman asked tragically. He was inconsolable.

"Some irony, hey, kid? It must be tough for you. You practically invented the charge plate."

"I was in on the discussions."

"Sure you were," Feldman said. "Come on, Victman, cheer up. It's not so bad. Smile once for me. Grin and bear it. Say 'cheese.' We've been there before, you and me. Back to the wall. Listen, try to look at it this way. You've had your back to the wall ever since you came here. I put you there. I made you stand in the corner with your back to the wall. What, you've forgotten all the lousy tricks I've played on you? The underhanded deals, the way I've used you, all the dirt I've made you eat? I've been hacking away at your salary for years. Why let a little thing like this get to you? *I* know. It's symbolic, your being in on the discussions and all, but frig them, I say. Listen to me. Please take heart. You've got Feldman back there against the wall with you now. That's my territory, the landscape I know and love.

"So they've taken us off the charge plate, have they? Well, who needs them? Say that with me. '*Who needs them?*' The charge plate is new-fangled anyway. It's against nature. We'll put out our own charge plate. We'll do better. We'll make the customer bring a note from home. Come on, we'll show them, Victman. Are you with me on this? The ammo's running out and winter's coming and there's nothing between an enemy bent on rape and our helpless, sleeping women and children but you, me and the token niggers. *Never say die*, I tell you. Rally round the flag, pal. Stomach in, chest out. Five, six, pick up sticks and beat hell out of them. What do you say? *Never* say die. What do you say?"

"Leo, the property I told you about—why don't you look at it? Won't you look at it now? This is no joke. Our volume is down. We *haven't* kept pace. Come this afternoon. I'll get the developer to meet us. What do you say?"

"I say die."

"It's a beautiful site, Leo. When the projects go up, there'll be ten thousand middle-income families within a twelve-block radius."

"Die," Feldman said.

"Parking for fifteen thousand cars. At least talk to the developer."

"Die."

"You can't avoid it any longer. The handwriting's on the wall. Leo, I warned you a year ago. It's no joke, being dropped from the group charge plate. It's a slap in the face. *What do you keep me for if you don't listen to me?* I don't sell for you, I don't wrap packages or wait on trade. I'm an idea man, Leo, a merchandising-concepts man. I see ways to bring this all off. We can get financing. My home-shopper plan, Leo—"

"Die," Feldman said. "I say *die*."

"It could be terrific. We put the customer's size on IBM tape, we code his tastes, his needs, then we keep him advised what we have for him and send it to his house. They'll go for this big, Leo."

"Die."

"Leo, you don't listen. My franchise plan. What was wrong with my franchise plan? It's only logic. If the little name can't absorb the big name, let the big name absorb the little name. *Merge*, Leo."

"Die? *You say die?*"

"All right, forget that, but at least look at the site I have in mind. This charge-plate business is only a first step. If the big stores put on the pressure, the papers won't accept our advertising. It could happen. It happened in Mobile to Blum's. Our volume is down eight percent. We let go sixteen people this year. Gerard Brothers took on fifty, Llewelyn's thirty-seven. At least *look* at the site."

"All right," Feldman said, "I'll see the sites. Die. Die."

"Listen to what the developer tells you. It's important."

"Die," Feldman said.

Feldman with his buyers—there were more men than women now (the war over and no more shortages, it being everywhere a nineteenth or even twentieth fat year, Feldman's girls had been replaced, no longer traded away in his name their ultimate quiff pro quo, happily married for years, raising kids; really, he thought, it was astonishing how many of them had married the very men who had once been their clients, the boys stirred to sacrament by the premise of unvirtue). They were in a private dining room of the best hotel for the Quarterly Lunch. Back from the Coasts, returned from the factories and showrooms and warehouses for the ceremony, they felt, he supposed, in what was after all their home base, somehow even further than the miles they had traveled, because they were all there together, like correspondents returned from the fronts, knowing some special sense of *colleague* that lent distance. Specialists, authorities, one big happy family with private knowledge of the skies over Texas, Twin Cities' economy, what's moving in Portland. Today their mysterious brotherhood even deepened by a still unconfirmed report of a brother downed, Chester Credit of Furniture, alleged to be aboard a plane that had crashed outside of Charlotte, North Carolina. *One of our aircraft is missing.*

Feldman taps the cut-glass water goblet with the edge of his butter knife, rises to speak, their gloomed attention making him cozy, snuggish, solemn-comfy in the orderly business reality, actually at home, and them too—you couldn't tell him otherwise— in the reserved room, reassured by the deep brown walls and the dark carpets and the white tablecloths and black waiters and, oh yes, this too, even Credit's empty chair. He waves off the white sleeve of a waiter offering a dish of ice cream. He speaks to him in a soft voice, making an arrangement. "Don't bother with that now, Waiter, please. I have to speak to these people." The waiter looks at him. "If it melts, it melts, pal, okay? My responsibility. Thank you very much." He clears his throat, a joy rising in it with the phlegm. He loves saying something important. "Ladies and gentlemen, my dear associates," he begins formally, pleased as always by the rhetoric he brings to these occasions (his Secretary of State diction, as he thinks of it). "In private conversations just prior to this luncheon, I have already given some cursory briefing to a few of you regarding the absence of Chester Credit. I did not intend that my unfortunate news be imparted to some rather than all, and if I may be permitted a rather bitter paradox, it pleases me to see all of you so solemn. No one likes to be the bearer of bad news, least of all myself, and I take it that the seriousness of your composure is an indication that you have all been apprised of my fears for Chester.

"Regarding the crash itself, I have very little additional to report at this time. During salad I was in telephone contact with our Miss Lane, and she tells me the situation in Charlotte is still indefinite. Let me emphasize that there has still been no official confirmation of the crash—repeat—there has still been no *official* confirmation of the crash. All we know for certain is that a check with the tower in Pittsburgh indicates that Coast Airlines Flight Number Eighty-seven is seven hours overdue. My informants tell me that an airliner's instrumentation, and that would include its radio apparatus, frequently kicks out during the traumatic jar of a forced landing. But this ought not to comfort us very much, as none of the control towers between Charlotte and Pittsburgh report having had any communication with Flight Number Eighty-seven. The reflex s.o.p. for a pilot forced to bring his ship down is first to declare his intent over a special emergency frequency. Additionally, the weather throughout the East has been almost preternaturally clear for the past eighteen hours with an unlimited ceiling. Thus, unfavorable climatological murk can have nothing to do with the plane's disappearance. For all these reasons, we can only conclude that the 'fireball' reportedly discerned by the two farmers fifty miles from Charlotte probably *was* Coast Airlines Flight Number Eighty-seven. I can extend no reasonable hope that these men may have been mistaken.

"Half an hour ago, during meat, Charlotte Airport was still unwilling to release its passenger manifest for Flight Eighty-seven. Coast Airlines was quite as adamant. I'm not blaming them for their reticence. Indeed, as I understand it, they are bound by law to maintain silence until it is positively ascertained that there has *been* a crash. Frankly, they have been most cooperative, and I for one am proud as hell of both of them. I've obtained their promise to release the manifest to us as soon as it's made available, even before the agonizing rituals of positive identification and notification of next of kin, which, strictly speaking, they are obliged by law, though not, I gather, so stringent a one as the other, to observe. Their cooperation here could save us literally days of anxiety, and so, even under the oppression of our feelings, I don't think we ought to let this occasion of still another instance of the mutual courtesy and respect between one American industry and another go by without acknowledging it. Whatever happens, I am tomorrow sending my personal letter of appreciation both to the executives of the Charlotte Airport and the executives of Coast Airlines.

"I want at this time to commend, too, Mrs. Beatrice P. Lisbon, secretary to Herbert Kronenberger of Dixie Chair, for her untiring efforts during this crisis. Not everyone knows this, but it has been chiefly Mrs. Lisbon with whom we have been in communication in Charlotte, and Miss Lane apprises me that the woman has been unstinting in her efforts to keep on top of the situation. I understand that she has put in numerous calls to the Coast Airlines people and the C.A.B. people and the Charlotte tower people, some of them during her lunch hour at perhaps her own expense. From what Miss Lane tells me, I am thoroughly satisfied that we could not have had a more selfless anchor man in Charlotte, and I mean at some not too distant date to formalize our appreciation with a small token from one of our departments.

"Now I don't mean to extend to you here something which might ultimately turn out to be a deluded hope. We're adults, and we must accommodate ourselves to adult reality. *However,* I would be finessing my responsibilities and would perhaps irretrievably undercut any future claim to candor, or claims on *your* candor, did I not acknowledge now one tiny morsel of possibility that Chester *may not in fact have been aboard Coast Airlines'*—let's face it—*FATAL Flight Number Eighty-seven at all."* Feldman paused. "Would you close the doors please, Waiter? Very good. Thank you very much." He leaned forward. "What I am about to tell you must go no further, ladies and gentlemen. Should it turn out to all our infinite relief that Flight Number Eighty-seven did not crash, or that it did crash but that Chester was not aboard it, the information I shall impart must remain privileged. I wouldn't bring it up at all, save that in matters of life and death, those concerned, even only peripherally concerned, are entitled to all the facts, that they might more intelligently apprehend the dangers. Not even Chester himself—if he's alive—must ever know you know this . . . Very well, then. Here's the situation.

"On first hearing reports of the alleged crash, I had Miss Codlish in Payroll research Mr. Credit's expense sheets. This was a routine measure, intended merely to provide us with the name of

Chester's Charlotte hotel. Many things can happen, people over-
sleep, people miss planes. I wanted it confimed that Chester had
or had not checked out. Well—and this struck me as peculiar—
there just *is* no record of a Charlotte hotel, not a single voucher
for the last five years. I had Miss Codlish double-check—with the
same result. His dinners are accounted for, mind you, his *lunches*
are, and there were even some significantly costly breakfasts, but
not a single hotel or motel bill. It was upon discovering this that
I first contacted Mrs. Lisbon, or rather had Miss Lane contact her,
to find out if Chester had divulged his plans for the evening. You
all travel. You know the small talk that goes on between a buyer
and a secretary. Evidently she at first denied any access to Chester's confidences, but from a certain tone she took, Miss Lane suspected she was concealing something. She pressed her on this, and
several things came out. It seems that on one of Chester's Charlotte trips *five years ago* Mr. Kronenberger gave a party. I know
Herbert Kronenberger and have always found him to be a gra-
cious, hospitable man, not one to stand idly by while a lonely
buyer fends for himself in a strange city. He *would* invite Chester
to his party. It would be a typical Kronenberger gesture. Mrs.
Lisbon was at the party too—perhaps as innocent company for
Chester; that part isn't clear. What is clear is that evidently Chester
had quite a lot to drink. Let's not mince words: Chester was
drunk. Rather than let him go back to his hotel by himself, one of
the guests—*not* Mrs. Lisbon, and it's chiefly this which leads me
to suspect that Mrs. Lisbon had been invited to the party earlier
and not merely as the extra woman to Chester's extra man—volunteered to take him back. He left with a Mrs. Charlote DeMille,
a prominent Charlotte divorcée, and there is some reason to believe he spent the night with her. What happened, evidently, is
that in the car on the way home, Chester vomited all over himself.
(Many of you will remember his behavior during the store's tenth-
anniversary celebration some years ago.) You can appreciate
Charlotte DeMille's position. She could not enter the hotel with
him, and he was in no condition to negotiate the lobby by himself.
Even to discharge him into the custody of a doorman would be
to compromise herself irrevocably. (Charlotte is not the biggest
city in the world, and this woman is, as I say, a prominent person
there.) All evidence points to the probability that she drove him
directly to her own home. There, from what I can gather from
Miss Lane, who pieced it together from the discreet Mrs. Lisbon,
Mrs. DeMille helped the helpless Chester to the bathroom next to

her master bedroom, there being only a half-bath on the main floor, and a tub, in which she must have feared he might drown, in the guest bathroom on the second floor—helped Chester to the bathroom next her master bedroom, and undressed him and put him under the shower. Then, perhaps seeing that he was still helpless and that the vomit was not coming off, she found it necessary to lather him herself, and one thing led to another and she began to lather his penis and testicles. (Mrs. DeMille is a healthy woman, ladies and gentlemen, a healthy divorcée with the appetites and needs—I say *needs*—of any healthy woman.) All indications are that the warm water, the creamy lather, the concupiscent silences and darknesses of the divorce-lonely house created in Chester an erection a foot and a half long, and to make a long story short— no pun intended—Chester and Mrs. DeMille have been lovers for the past five years.

"Now, I had Miss Lane urge Mrs. Lisbon to call Mrs. DeMille to check about Chester's sleeping arrangements last night, and although she manifested some reluctance, as they are no longer friends and such a question breaches the proprieties of estrangement, she did at last agree to have Mr. Kronenberger himself make the call. I have every confidence in Mr. Kronenberger's delicacy in such an affair, but the fact is that Mrs. DeMille hung up on him, and we know no more now—unless one interprets outrage as guilt—than we did before. Even if Chester lives, I feel that a permanent strain may have been put on the Kronenberger/ DeMille relationship. But I say *this*. I hope he lives. Although I better understand the real justification for those exorbitant breakfasts I have been paying for for the last five years, and although he was committed to return to our Quarterly Lunch, and although in the light of these developments we must soon undergo a searching reexamination of our furniture requirements—I must say that up to now I have never fully understood Chester's insistence on using the products of North Carolina when other, cheaper merchandise is available elsewhere—I hope he lives. I hope, in sum, that it was a lovers' quarrel, or some happy passion, some newly discovered refinement of shower love, that has kept him from us. And while I am not of course in a position to guarantee his job, I hold his life of value."

At this point the maître d' approached Feldman and whispered in his ear. Feldman straightened. "Thank you very much Maître d'," he said. "See what else you can find out, please." He turned back to the table. "Ladies and gentlemen," he intoned, "I

have just been informed by the maître d' that Charlotte has confirmed the crash. Fragments of the plane and the main fuselage
have been discovered in a woods thirty-five miles from the airport." Again the maître d' approached the table, and Feldman
heard what he had to say. "Yes," he said, "I see. Thank you." He
sighed. "A headless body that fits Chester Credit's description,
and in the suit pockets of which have been discovered some
singed identification papers belonging to him, was one of the first
recovered. Under the circumstances, I have suggested to the maître d' that we probably don't want dessert, but if I have been
unduly presumptive in speaking for all of you, I would want at
once to be told about it, and in that case we could call the fellow
back."

The developer turned out to be little Oliver B.'s father.
Feldman went with him to the site, an ovid valley three miles
from the western edge of the city, where the developer tried to
explain what the scarred, bulldozer-bruised area would look like
in a few months, with its facilities in—the spanking planes of
cement and intricate ramps and the cunning approach of the access road from the new interstate. But Feldman, who had no imagination in these affairs—he could not read blueprints or conceive
how furniture would look rearranged—and for whom there was
a terrible inertia in things, had difficulty following the developer's
explanations.

Instead, he found himself fascinated by the man, saw something terribly virtuous in him. For all the developer's slim, distin-
guished appearance, his large eyes scholarly behind glasses, and
odd, ruminative quality as he talked, the muscular mounds of
cheek rising and falling comfortably with his words, Feldman
sensed in him a fearful, optimistic energy, and found himself re-
senting what he knew would be the man's good luck with machines—he was positive the developer got better mileage than he
did—and skill with nature. He looked into the developer's white,
fierce teeth and knew at once that they were teeth that had sucked
blubber and jerky—is that jerky on his breath now? he wondered—as easily as his own had scraped the pulp from an artichoke. He had a mouth that had saved lives. Feldman imagined
its ardent kiss on a snakebite, or slipping over the blue lips of a
man dragged from the sea. Listening to him, Feldman grew oddly
comfortable, easy, and found that he had to move about to shake

out the warm sensation in his extremities, the sense he was beginning to feel of melting into the universe.

Frequently, as Feldman spoke, the developer smiled, inclining
his head in an attitude of listening and judgment, his mood not
of attention but of nostalgic concentration and courtesy and patience. At these times Feldman looked over the teeth and into the
mouth and throat at the healthiest tongue he had ever seen, choice
and red as a prime cut. You could drink his bright juices, his saliva
clear as a trout stream. He could feel the man's immense, beaming
tolerance, concentrated as heat from a sun lamp, and had actually
to shuffle his feet to dodge bolts of the chipper good will.

Then the developer, making a point, smiled a wide one, the
biggest Feldman had yet seen, and Feldman stared deep down
the man's eyes, past good wishes, deeper than good hope, past
faith itself to the sourcy bedrock of the developer's vision, where
he thought he saw the basic mix—the roily vats of molassesy
premise that worked the circuits of his phoenixy will and gave
him his feel for reclaimed land, for swamp and ashpit and trashy
field where rats lurked and mice skittered. Feldman had seen
enough. He interrupted him. "Excuse me, but that's some smile
you've got there."

"I beg your pardon?" the developer said.

"You make jumping rabbits for Oliver out of an ordinary
pocket handkerchief. Am I right?"

"Well, yes—but . . ."

"Sure," Feldman said. "You do an admiral's hat and a paper
airplane from the war news. You make a tree from rolled-up
newspapers, and forest animals from the shadows of your fists.
Right?"

"The developer nodded slowly.

"I know. And a flute from a reed, and a kite from the wrappings around your shirts from the laundry."

"What about the property?" the developer asked coolly.

"The property? I don't want it."

"Mr. Victman said—"

"I don't want it," Feldman said. He was very excited. "I won't
have it. Fuck your virgin land." He looked at him narrowly.
"We're in the homestretch of a race: your energy against my en-
tropy. The universe is running down, Mr. Developer. It's bucking
and filling. It's yawing and pitching and rolling and falling. The
smart money's in vaults. Caution. Look both ways. Look up and
down." He picked up a beer can one of the workers had discarded. "Here," he said, pushing the can toward him, "get yourself a string and another can. But don't call me, I'll call you!"

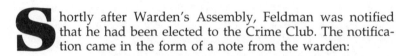

15

Shortly after Warden's Assembly, Feldman was notified that he had been elected to the Crime Club. The notification came in the form of a note from the warden:

Your name has been placed in nomination for membership in the Crime Club. Lest you get any funny ideas about your popularity, let me tell you right now that I do the nominating and the electing. I nominate and elect people to the Camera Club, the Model Airplane Club, the Literary Club—all the clubs. That's what it means to have power, Feldman. Also I have made you president of the Crime Club; you will conduct your first meeting this Tuesday week. (Room 14, W. wing, 7 o'clock. Sharp!)

Your Warden,
Warden Fisher

P.S. The other members do not know that you have been accepted as a member or that you are their president, so you will have to wrest your leadership from the incumbent. He is a man that the others have nicknamed "God," and you will have no difficulty recognizing him, as the underside of his tongue is tattooed. (It is my understanding that his armpits are also tattooed, so it's my guess that he probably isn't ticklish.)

Feldman decided to ask for Official Respite, making his request formally, in a document witnessed by a guard from another cellblock (he had to waste a permission slip and a pass) and by a prisoner in sick bay (another permission slip, another pass). In his petition he asked the Director of Prison Labors that he be permitted to absent himself from the canteen during a portion of the workday on which the Crime Club was to meet.

He wanted the extra time because the warden had underscored the necessity of being punctual, but the terms of Respite were difficult: three hours of labor for every one of Respite, the labor to be accomplished in shops in which the Respiter was a stranger. What made the conditions even harder was that mistakes were to be paid for on a strict retail basis. Thus, if a Respiter were to fudge, say, a license plate, he was charged the full sum the state would have received for the perfect plate. Moreover, this sum was repayable only in work—again, exclusively in shops in which the prisoner had had no experience—at a rate just *one third* the convict's already low rate of pay. An inept man could conceivably add months to the end of his sentence by accepting even one hour of Respite.

Feldman worried fitfully about his decision, changing his mind at least a dozen times. He considered the other avenues open to him—Warden's Desk, for example, a prisoner's single opportunity to petition the warden directly. But because no "sweat"—the prisoners' term for intense effort, the cost to him of favors—was attached to it, it was unreliable. A refusal at the level of Warden's Desk was binding, and Feldman rejected this option. Nor could he see how he might have restorted to simple absenteeism from the canteen, even if he had been willing to accept the additional day tacked on to his sentence. An absentee was required to "freeze" within one hundred yards of the area where he had declared his absenteeism. As a last resort, he considered the Buddy System. The term was misleading. It meant that any prisoner could at any time ask for and *have* a privilege belonging to another prisoner, but since favors could not be paid back in kind, the borrower became, in effect, the lender's slave. Here was a loophole big enough to drive the entire system through. "Only show restraint," Feldman had urged the convicts in the informal discussion groups on prison regulations. "Give the privilege and ask for nothing in return. Don't make a slave of the borrower. Then when anyone needs something, he can have it with immunity." They had agreed in theory, though some scoffed and called him Red, but in practice, the temptation to assert power when it was so infrequently available was always too great. So he was forced at last to ask for Respite. (Nor, once the decision was made, did he easily determine how many hours of Respite to ask for, rejecting the three that would probably serve, to settle finally on the five which if they did not serve could only mean that fate and circumstance had been against him from the start.)

After his written request he was called up before the Respite Officer (a revolving role, but always taken by some minor functionary—usually a cook, or one of the tuckpointers in constant service around the prison—to dramatize, Feldman suposed, the absolutely rigid and binding force of the Respite obligation). The "sweat" was again explained to him, and he indicated that he understood and even, as part of the ceremony, asked a few questions so that there could be no objection later that he had been railroaded. Then he raised his hand to take his solemn oath.

"I, Leo Feldman, understand the nature . . . of the contract . . . that I have entered . . . into here," he repeated, in the familiar halting rhythm of all tandemly sworn oaths. "I understand the obligations imposed on me by accepting Respite and deriving the benefits . . . thereof . . . I undertake to pay back . . . fifteen hours of duty . . . to be worked out . . . however . . . the Director of Prison Labors . . . sees fit . . . but in some capacity . . . foreign to . . . and differing in kind from all my past performances. I further concede . . . my willingness . . . to pay back to the state . . . for all my mistakes . . . resulting in loss of revenues . . . at the fixed retail price . . . through labors . . . again foreign to past performances . . . and recompensed"—here the Respite Officer slowed down the pace of the oath—"at . . . one third . . . my . . . nor . . . mal . . . dai . . . ly . . . rate . . . Now," he concluded, "I accept Respite"

He was impressed by how deep an oath could go, and had an impression of commitment extensive as the root of a tooth. He had given his word, and recognized for the first time the serious implications of having a word to give. It was as if he and all men walked around always under bond, a burden of treacherous feasance. It struck him, too, that such obligation was onesided, the dangerous cutting edge toward himself.

And all this simply to guarantee that on the following Tuesday there would be time enough to obtain a permission slip to get a pass to go to the west wing for the meeting of the Crime Club.

It was possible that he might have done without his elaborate preparations, that things would have gone smoothly, but he had lost his nerve in a way, though another kind of nerve had taken its place. Here he was, spending permission slips, passes, Respite, taking on tiers of obligation, confronting a jeopardy of consequences that he could not possibly foresee. It was like living in a boom town whose primitive facilities and difficulties with supply forced the prices of even those ordinary commodities one took for granted to skyrocket mercilessly—like paying two dollars for toothpaste or five for milk. Necessity made for a sort of obligatory sportiness.

So he had the Certificate of Respite in the breast pocket of the blue fool suit. He touched it at least a hundred times that Tuesday. After lunch he did not return to work in the canteen, but went back to his cell to wait for the pencil man. Disappointingly the man didn't question what he was doing in his cell—despite himself, Feldman was itching to show him his certificate—and after getting his permission slip, he brought it to the Fink to trade it for a pass.

He was relieved when the Fink, one of his enemies, questioned the legitimacy of the slip and had him taken back under guard to check it. The pencil man had left on a break, and they had to wait for an hour and a half.

"Yes, this is all right," the pencil man told the guard, glancing casually at the slip, when he returned.

Feldman was brought back to the Fink, who searched his face for signs of triumph. It's good I planned ahead, Feldman thought. It's good I had the foresight to anticipate all this.

He was disturbed, however, that he took no real pleasure in his justification. For one thing, he couldn't be sure that the Fink had really doubted him. Perhaps he had been pretending merely to cause him trouble. But wasn't trouble exactly what he wanted? he wondered. And then, saddened, he realized that if it was, he had been trapped into wanting it by the warden. What of the generosity he had seen in his thriftless preparations? Wasn't that all undermined if he wanted to use up all the security-to-spare that he had purchased by asking for five hours of Respite when three would probably have served? It was difficult to know which was better—gratefulness for things gone smoothly, or delight that his pains had been really necessary. Had the warden *intended* all this? Feldman was numb. He suspected it had been the warden's objective to bring him to just this state of stymied feelings. Call the police, he thought wearily. I've been robbed.

With the pass to the west wing secured, he went to dinner at five and still had time to return to his cell for a half-hour's rest before starting for the meeting. He was exhausted, but so worried that his precautions had stripped him of the energies he would need that evening that he saw it was useless to try to rest. He set out for the Crime Club.

He was early, but several members were already there and he wondered if they had had to make the same preparations. They— many, like himself, wore special clothes; he supposed these were bad men, and he thought *Flair*, thought *Style*—herded together on folding chairs in a strange, tight grouping. Feldman went up to the small stage at the front of the room where they were stacked and took one down, feeling curiously depleted. It seemed odd to him that no one had attempted to make rows or to line up the chairs around the walls. The members were bunched together in a random arrangement, so that despite the fact that it was still early and probably not everyone was there yet, the room seemed crowded.

As others came, they went up to the stack of chairs and continued the odd pattern Feldman had observed. The back of one chair was at an oblique angle to Feldman's shoulder; another began to describe a rough arc a couple of inches to the right and slightly forward of his stomach; someone else sat facing him, so that their knees touched. It was like coming to life in a Cubist sketch. This is some bunch, he thought sorrowfully, guessing the implications of the seating arrangements.

"Who the hell are you?" asked the convict facing him.

Feldman moved his chair a few inches, bumping into one behind him and feeling what was almost certainly an ear against the back of his neck. "Excuse me," Feldman said, but the convict ignored him.

"I said, 'Who the hell are you?' " the first prisoner repeated.

Rather than answer, Feldman reached inside his jacket to pull out the warden's letter. The man unfolded the paper and read it. "This is a Certificate of Respite," he said.

Feldman looked at it again. Already the five hours were up, and he had a heavy, sudden sense of uselessness. The official seals flared obsoletely on the certificate like great gilded nipples.

"All right," a voice announced, "it's seven o'clock. I call this meeting of the Crime Club to order."

In the close quarters it was difficult to know who spoke. The voice might have been tough and husky, but was marred by a faint lisp and, at the other, deeper end of the man's speech, a difficulty with *l*'s and *r*'s. The result was a peculiar effect of retardation, of the frictionless speech of monsters in films. The tattooed underside of the tongue, Feldman remembered. My God, it's God.

"Old business?" the voice asked. "All right. New business?"

"I have new business," Feldman said. He had decided to assert himself at once.

"Who's that? Who's there?" the voice asked, and Feldman saw a man stand up not far from him. Seated, he caught a quick glimpse of the flowered underside of the man's tongue.

Feldman rose. "I have new business," he repeated.

"State your new business." The man was huge. He looked like all the dock-wallopers and bodyguards who had ever lived.

"You're out of order," Feldman said. "I'm the new president of this club."

"Who the hell are you?"

It was disconcerting to Feldman not to be known here. Troublesome as his notoriety had been in the other parts of the prison, he had always been able to take from it a kind of reassurance, reading the prisoners' contempt (and perhaps fear) almost—he knew this was insane—as a sign of their *culture*. Now their ignorance of him deepened his impression that they were corrupt. There was no telling what such men might do. As yet, however, he had no real fear of violence, taking comfort from the man's very size, trusting in a big man's admiration for order and due process.

"My name is Feldman," he said.

"Credentials," the incumbent said calmly.

"I have credentials." He took out the warden's letter and read it to them, leaving out the postscript.

"Check the signature, Forger."

The man seated at Feldman's knees held out his hand and took the letter. "It's legit," he said after examining it.

"I have a letter saying I'm the new president too," one of the other convicts said.

"Sure you do," said a man on the outer edges of the circle. (They formed a rough circle, Feldman saw now.) "We all have letters like it. As the son of a bitch says himself, he's the one does the nominating and electing." The men laughed.

"That's right," Feldman said. "That's right. You all *would* have similar letters."

"It's a goddamned banana republic, we got so many presidents," someone else said.

"What are we going to do?" Feldman asked.

"What the hell," the big convict shrugged. "You be the president." He sat down.

"Installation of officers," a convict called mechanically. "Let's get on with it."

They swore Feldman in at once, the outgoing president administering an oath that he seemed to compose as he went along. (It wasn't a bad oath, Feldman thought, considering it had been made up on the spur of the moment.)

"Well, what do we do now?" Feldman asked. None of the men said anything. "Old business?" he asked, remembering the formula of the past president (not, despite appearances, a bad officer, all things considered). He tried "New business?" with the same results, then looked around the room at the Crime Club membership. "Let's steal something," he suggested, giggling. He stared out at them for a few more minutes and then sat down, no longer uncomfortable. Gradually he felt even more at ease, and despite the physical closeness in the room, he began to grow sleepy and once or twice actually caught himself nodding. He wondered what they were doing over at the Model Airplane Club.

It was strange, another of the endless rituals and counterrituals he had met with here. Some time ago he had begun to think that he saw a design. It had to do with the nullifying of energies, as though the warden's final intention were to keep the men quiet by having them perceive just what Feldman was slowly perceiving, that they were caught up in a treadmill rhythm of opposing impulses. It seemed too simple a theory perhaps for the elaborateness of the rules and ceremonies, but he was relieved by its very simplicity. It humanized the warden. Not that it made him kinder or easier to get along with, but it stripped away some of the mystery. If the mystery was unearned he was glad to know it. And now, hoping that they knew it too, he felt suddenly closer to his fellow convicts. Surely they shared his perceptions and accepted them. (After all, they all stood to gain from passivity, stood to gain from the saltpetered food and the worked-off violence and the deflection of their intentions. Let us all take the cold shower together, he thought. Let everyone behave: no prison breaks, no complaints about the food, no misspelled petitions for the redress of grievances.) Expansive, he felt not their good will, but the clubby chill of their sophistication. Their discreet indifference was attractive. Something could be said for superior sales resistance, for sulk and moroseness of spirit, and suddenly he felt like congratulating them and being congratulated by them. "We'll pull through," he would have said, "it's not so bad." Before he could speak, however—and why, anyway, did he want to? why had he tried to comfort his personnel that time in the soiled back rooms of his department store? what had he meant to tell them? why did he still feel a necessity to respond? was his own sales resistance not so superior after all?—he heard a stirring of the chairs and someone rising.

"I'll tell you something about crime," a convict said, startling him with the unexpectedness of his speech. "It's too indoorsy. Why's your average con doing time today? Shit, look at the terms used to describe him: he's a *breaker and enterer*; he's a *second-story man*; he's *on the inside*, he says of his jail, *behind the walls*. It's all inside jobs, I tell you. What's his own term for the world but *the outside*? Never Chicago, never Detroit.

"His pallor. His plans made in pool halls! All that messing with locks, that struggle with safes. And *rape!* Breaking, entering and the airtight case.

"What, I ask you, is the highest act of crime? The one that takes the most planning, the greatest research and preparation? It's the bank robbery—the *bank* robbery! All that snuggling in cozy vaults down among the safe-deposit boxes. He *asks* for it. Your crook *asks* for it. He loves his handcuffs, worships his bars, his restraints. Give him balls and chain, give him ringbolts, straw in a dungeon give him. And don't talk to *me* about escape. That's all it is, my dears—talk. Why, these jails couldn't hold us a minute if we really *believed* in escape. Twenty to one? Thirty? Fifty to one? One hundred to one in many places. What odds are we waiting for? It's a sickness. Most of your crime is a sickness.

"I became a sluice robber, and I remained outdoors. I breathed real air in my lungs. And the sun. Three years I've been here, and I've still a piece of my tan. That's how deep it burns you. The bones themselves are browned by now. And there was never any skulking, any stooping, any crawling. And I never hid in hallways or crouched behind the stairs.

"The troughs I robbed, like great wooden Babels up the

mountain. The tumbling nuggets, oh, that skittery wealth. It wasn't robbery. You couldn't call it robbery. Just a man on a line on a mountain with sense enough to reach. And first on line too. First. To cut the theft if there was one, and give a sporting target. (I was caught on a mountain.) All I ever needed was to make a fist. I made tools of my palms—as God intended—found a use for my opposing thumbs. God's will in a handful, you guys. (And testing always my prehensileness, growing a grasp.) Palming more than magicians palm, than basketball players."

His eyes shone, glittered with memory. Feldman felt he should say something, call for order. Though no one made a sound, it was as if there had been a sudden displacement of passion in the room, like the pressure of the first thighs against a barricade.

"Nevada is right," a convict said.

"He's wrong."

"No, he's right. Only he's got too narrow a sense of it. I'm a rustler—horses, cattle. The feel of flesh is what I like, the mass of beast. All that muscle. All that meat. Like an appointment at the source of things. It was nothing for me to steal a hundred tons, two hundred, three. Think of the weight of such a theft."

"Booty is bulk and bulk booty," a convict heckled.

"The nostrils," the rustler said, raising his voice above their laughter, "that wild gristle. The rheumy eyes, their mucky silts. Those dreadful genitals and those steamy hides."

"I don't understand any of that," another prisoner said quietly, "but if it's the wide-open spaces that Nevada was talking about, or that Tex here meant when he said he agreed with him, I can see the reasoning."

"I'm a poacher," a prisoner said. "In my time I've fished other men's rivers and killed the deer in other men's woods. There's nothing beats nature, men. I'm a bit of a squatter too. I've done some squatting. I nick myself off a piece of their land, and they never miss it, don't know it's gone."

"Kentucky, you piker, you make me ashamed," a fourth man said. "I'm a sooner. I steal land. Vast tracts in Alaska. In Hawaii vast tracts. Land, steal land. I jump the gun and beat the bell and move before the whistle. I've made a living out of always being offside, and I tell you there's nothing like it. The race is always to the swift."

"I know about that," said a fifth convict. "I trespass too. But deeper than you boys. Down, deep down in the mines. I jump other men's claims. I move in and take over. It's work, but rewarding. I hate the sluice robber. He's meager. I tell him to his face."

I'm in Hell, Feldman thought. I'm the president of Hell. How had he ever imagined these men to be indifferent?

"Well, you're all out of touch, it seems to me. You live in the past. The mines are played out. There's detergent in the rivers and streams. Tourists in the forests pose the bears. Myself, I'm an artist." The forger was speaking. "There's got to be some art to crime. It's show biz. Catch *me* with a gun? The rough stuff is out. Jazz and pizzazz are what's wanted today. Me, I forge license plates. I'm a sort of a sculptor."

"He's right."

"He's wrong."

"No, he's right. I dress up as a cop. I impersonate dames."

"I make my own moon."

"I fake petitions, a nickel a name. A dime for addresses. It's very satisfying to make up people and where they live. Listen to this: Wilma Welfing Pearsall, 7614 Carboy Street, Marples, Ohio. Jerome Loss, Rural Route Two, Clegg, New York. Ed and Naomi Baird, Apartment 404, the Sinclair Apartments, 160 Clipton Drive, Archer Hills, Oregon. I don't mess with the zip code. Federal offense."

"I give false measure," a convict said.

"And I was a dentist who short-changed on teeth. I'd water the silver, adulterate gold. Delicious my fillings; they'd melt in your mouth."

"I worked for a real estate firm. I seeded treasure in vacant lots for the suckers to see. I buried coins and statues and place settings for twelve—that sort of thing."

A very small convict stood up. "I made the stock certificates that the con men sell," he said. "Suitable for framing, they were. On a thin parchment, very expensive. The paper around the borders like the rough edges of the pages in old novels. Painstaking. I tore it myself. And a seal like a sunset or a harvest moon. A great wheel of a seal. Very official. Barbed at the circumference, the full three hundred sixty degrees.

"And the types. Hand-lettered. Glorious stuff: roman, italic, old-style roman, old-style italic. Cursive and minion. Sans serif, nonpareil. Brevier, bourgeois, and brilliant and canon. Columbian, English, excelsior too. And what we call the stones: diamond and pearl and agate. And primer I did. And great primer. Pica, of course, and small pica and double pica, and double-small pica as well. And much of this, you understand, in condensed and even extra-condensed. (To discourage the reading, I guess. I didn't ask questions.) Only the great fictive companies themselves in extra-bold black letter. But almost illegible. Like a sketch of chop suey.

"But what I liked best were the pictures I drew. Spidery, thin as a watermark, of old engines, old cars. And a hotel in St. Paul, Minnesota, I took off a soap wrapper. And a factory after the one on the box of Shredded Wheat." He sighed.

"Yes," said a distinguished-looking convict. "I know the feeling. I was a quack. I worked with machines. I had an electrodynathermy machine, a honey. And an adgitronic nucleosiscope, cost me two thousand dollars. Also a honey. And I had this vibrating wooden box with insets for the patient's hands. He'd wear coated rubber gloves and press down hard for fifteen minutes at a time for an advanced cancer. Less for something not so serious.

"I loved to watch the colored lights. There was no special sequence. I liked to hear the hum it made, the whiz and whir, the crackles, and crepitations and thuds. I don't see the harm. I did a lot of good and may even have effected some cures, I think."

"He's wrong."

"No, he's right. Doc's right."

"He's wrong. Two thousand dollars for a piece of equipment? Seeding all those miles of vacant lot? I don't care how shallow a man buries that stuff, it's backbreaking work. Or all those hours over a draughtsman's board. Just take a look at the glasses that guy wears, not to mention the condition of his lungs from breathing those inks.

"*No*. Get in and get out. That's what *I* say. Who needs all those props? Sure there's satisfaction in the artist's life, but we live in a practical world. Profit margins and overhead and cost per unit have got to be thought about. My money's on the middleman. I'm a suborner myself. I can give you statistics. It costs me anywhere from five hundred to twenty-five thousand dollars to fix a judge today, depending, of course, on the offense and the defendant's prospects of being convicted. All right, let's take a closer look. We'll take a relatively modest case: a white kid accused of a car theft. A first offense, and the kid's from a nice middle-class family, say. It costs three thousand dollars to get that boy off. Of that three thousand I take home a grand, the judge fifteen hundred, and the rest is divided up between the officers of the court and expert witnesses like the social worker or the arresting officer. Notice that the judge gets more than I do. That's important. I do that on purpose. And I'm pretty careful to let him know it too. Something like the same principle holds for the law clerks and the others. *I* know the judge's unlisted number. *That* isn't the point. I could reach him *direct*. The thing is, I try to implicate as many people as I can. I bring in the middlemen. If a conspiracy is wide enough *no one* gets hurt."

"Me, I'm a fence. I receive stolen goods I might never see. I buy up a thousand transistor radios and never lay eyes on a single one. I don't *want* to see it. I make a few phone calls, tell the trucks where to go."

"Did you ever hear of champerty?" another man asked. "That's what I do. I'm a party to law suits that don't concern me. I bankroll a plaintiff. I buy him his x-rays. We split on the judgment. Some grievances I invent, I make up offenses. It goes back before Coke, the old common law."

Feldman wondered why he had thought he should call for order before. There had been order. It was as ordered in here as a pageant or masque. Even the chairs made a circle.

"Yo ho ho and a bottle of rum," a man said.

"The chair recognizes the pirate," Feldman mumbled. Pegleg's wrong, he thought. No, he's right. He's wrong *and* he's right.

A prisoner rose and spoke of hijacking the big rigs, of ambush at crossroads and hazardous tailgating through the mountains, broadside duels on dangerous turns at sixty miles an hour. Another agreed and told of how he put up false lights in treacherous waters to lure the shipping and then scavenged the wrecked vessels. A third was a rumrunner, a fourth the leader of bandits in caves in the hills who stole from the tourists. There was a bartender who worked for a ring of white slavers on the waterfront. He slipped Mickey Finns into the girls' drinks. He showed how he winked a signal to a man at the jukebox when they collapsed on the stool. The appeal, they agreed, was in the strategy, the sense of maneuver, of logistics, the idea of government itself perhaps, some rich, loyal, aggressive joy taken in gangs and bands and mobs and rings.

A sour-looking convict got up to speak. "Crimes of anger," he said. "Crimes of rage. What else is motivated? Give me spiters, men with grudges." He told of barns he had burned, ricks he had put to the torch, the pets of enemies he had poisoned.

A young man stood up. He rolled the fairies, he said. He beat up the drunks. Another beat his wife and children. Someone else exhumed the dead; "I hate the lousy dead," he said.

A man rose shyly. "I tried to kill myself and botched it. Suicide's against the law, you know, although you don't hear much about them putting a failed suicide in jail. I guess I'm an exception—an example to people. The psychiatrist says I probably didn't really want to die if I couldn't make it stick, but that's not true. I want to die, I think, but that's beside the point. What attracts me is the violence, the prose of the notes I leave behind, the halting syntax and the confessions and the passionate accusations. But even that isn't the real point. It's the other thing, the violence. I love the feel of the gun butt, the hard, quilted iron. The handles of knives too. Clubs. Whips. There's a packed solidity in weapons, a center of gravity. You get a sense of lumps of power in your hands. The force is terrific. A hangman's knot in a rope—like a full gorge—is the same. And poison. Discreet. The pills seem to weigh eighty pounds. And then there's the pain you feel. All that power to inflict injury, and all that capacity to absorb it. That's all there is. You know?"

"I bugger sheep," a man said. "I give it to sows and dogs. How do you like that? A man and his dog. I ride horseback on the bridle path in the park, and I come in my pants. What do you think about that? How low can a man get?"

Then there was a reckless driver, and another man whose pilot's license had been taken away because he had buzzed his own home for three hours, until he was out of gas and had to make a forced landing on a ballfield where his own kid was playing.

One last convict stood up. "I shouldn't be here at all," he said. "What I did was an accident. It couldn't be helped.

"I was a laborer. I had a job in this factory in my hometown. We made switches for an outfit that turned out radios and television sets. Half the people in town worked there, maybe more. Then the home office decided to close down the plant. It wasn't economical, they said, to have the switches made in a place a thousand miles away. They relocated the engineers and a few of the foremen and let the rest of us go. There wasn't any work in town. I did odd jobs, but everybody was doing odd jobs. All the men. The competition was fierce. I had my family to support. We all did. It got to where I wouldn't lend my tools to my own neighbor for fear he'd find some way to use them that would do me out of a day's work. And I couldn't borrow his paintbrushes. I only wanted to touch up the woodwork, thinking maybe I could sell my house, but he figured different. He thought I had this paint job somewhere. He begged me to tell.

"We lived like that six months. A summer, a fall. And always the money getting harder and harder, and the kids so hungry you could see their hunger happening. Then, in the winter, I heard there was work a hundred miles away. A plant was hiring and I figured to go. I saved for the gas and couldn't make it, and had to beg it off a guy I knew in the one station in town still open. Out on the highway? He gave it to me and I was all set to go, and a storm come up. A terrible storm. The worst I've seen. It rained so you couldn't see to drive, and my wipers was bad. I waited for it to stop, but it didn't. Three hours later it hadn't let up. And they was only hiring for five days. One had passed when I heard, three more while I looked for the gas. I only had hours. I had to try.

"So I drove in the rain. Maybe ten miles an hour, and it come down harder, and even harder. I couldn't see, it was as if I was blindfold. And straining my eyes. I had to pull up. I had to stop. I moved to the shoulder and waited again. Lord, I was tired. Up before dawn. Straining my eyes. Worried like that. Lord, I was tired. But I didn't dare close my eyes. If I slept and it stopped? So I waited and watched. Two hours, three. And I prayed: God, make it stop. Make it stop, please.

"Then all of a sudden it did. It stopped, it was over. Do you know what I saw? What I saw up ahead? It was *clear*. It was *dry*. It hadn't rained there at all.

"I started my car and got stuck in the mud. I heaved it and hauled, I *pulled* it away. With my rage, with my strain, I was tired as hell. As weary I think as a man's ever been. I got in the car and stepped on the gas. Two hours I had before the plant closed. My God, how I drove, how I flew down the road. But my tiredness grew, enormous it was. And just for a second I rested my eyes—

"The accident happened but ten miles from town. Doing eighty and ninety, the witnesses said. I swerved from my lane and hit them broadside. His family was killed, but I was thrown clear. How does that happen? Was it my prayer?

"I landed unconscious, or maybe asleep, but here is the miracle: *I woke up refreshed!* Mind clear, alert, fresh as a daisy, I guess you could say. And only for minutes had I been out.

"I saw what had happened and sent for the cops. I waited and helped, but there was nothing to do. A baby, a daughter, a wife and a son. The father alive but damaged real bad. Crippled for life and can't move his arms. Can't pass his water or chew his own food.

"He sued me, of course. Took me to court. I had no insurance or he would have been rich.

"Well, that's about it, but there is something else. *Refreshed*, I keep thinking, *I came to refreshed*. After the guilt, after the grief. After all that, the fear that I felt, the being in trouble and down on my luck, there's *still* something else. The impact, the bang, the damage I did. The crippling, the terror, the spilling of life. The *joy* I keep feeling, the excitement, delight. The sense that I have of some final deed done. The cleanness I feel, the absence of stain."

The convict sat down, and the rest of the prisoners were silent.

"He's right," one said at last.

"Yes," murmured another.

"Yes," still another added, "he's right."

"He's right, he's right." They took up the call.

"He's right," said the poacher. "He's right," said the fence. "He's right," said the ghoul. "He's right," said the quack and the man who set fires for spite. "He's right," the hijacker agreed and the man who screwed pigs.

President Feldman rose and they all looked toward him. "No," he said. "He's wrong." He told them about his basement.

16

Feldman invented the basement by accident, a great serendipity. But afterwards nothing was an accident. He
meant every word, every move. So, in a way, the flukish-
ness could be written off. It can almost be said there was nothing
accidental about it.

When he had rejected the developer, that kind guy, that gentle
jerk and nonbarbarian, he was pretty blue there for a while. He
didn't know where to turn. Very low. Rock-bottom. Feldman, the
felled man. Who found himself—what, so down was he, was accidental about this?—in the basement of his store. On holy
chthonic ground. And there one day in the record department,
scolding a kid who had undone the perfect plastic envelope in
which the album had been sealed, he was approached by a nervous young man in a tweed overcoat. "Excuse me," said the
young man. "I'm looking for a record."

Feldman was about to tell him to ask the clerk—do you *see*
how low, how miserable?—when something about the young
man made him stop. His manner, apparently halting, was not
really timid at all. It was as if his shyness had been assumed as a
courtesy. Feldman listened. "Do you have the records of Mildred
Eve?" he asked. Was *that* all? Feldman wondered. He went to the
catalog to look her up, but she wasn't listed. "She wouldn't be in
the catalog," the young man said. "She sings party songs."

Feldman called his distributor. "Why haven't you been sending me the Mildred Eve records? Do you know how many sales I've lost because I don't have them?"

"Mildred Eve?" the distributor said. "She sings filth. Her stuff is sold under the counter."

Feldman ordered all her releases and put them on top of the counter. He had the records played on the stereo equipment so that they could be heard all over the basement.

A strange thing happened. Whether because of the music or for some other reason, the tone of the store gradually changed. This was his sense of it, at any rate. There began to appear in the basement certain listless men who seemed to be on lunch breaks, well dressed enough, and carrying briefcases, many of them, but giving off an impression of loitering. There were boys too, wiry and underweight, who seemed to have stepped from morning movies at the downtown theaters. They strolled the aisles of his basement, the rolled sleeves of their tee shirts making pockets for their cigarettes, and dropped their butts without stepping on them. The women seemed to have changed too, to have become faintly aimless, like people killing time in bus stations.

His first thought was sales. He kept a careful check on the figures, lest the new music—he attributed the changes to this—should wind up costing him money. His research, however, did not indicate that the basement was doing less business, although, and this might be something to look into, the *kinds* of things that people bought seemed to have changed considerably. Formerly, his basement had done a substantial business in family dry goods. The back-to-school sales and the volume in sportswear (a little out-moded, perhaps, the basement of Feldman's store being a place where a sort of mercantile sediment tended to collect; it was, for example, one of the few places left in America where a man might still purchase hobby jeans, or fur-collared car coats) had been among the most impressive operations in the city, and almost by themselves brought in enough profit to justify the existence of the basement. Now, however, domestic clothing gradually ceased to move at all, and housewares fell off. But these losses were made up for by a sharp increase in the sale of fetishistic automobile accessories, stereo phonographs, color television, transistor radios and, in the basement's small Toy department, those miniature roulette wheels and baccarat decks and dice cages that had once done little but collect dust. His personnel were hard put to maintain supplies, and Feldman had, over the long-distance telephone, to wheedle and lean heavily on old relationships, reminding more than one jobber of forgotten favors. The record department itself was apparently unaffected. Mildred Eve's records did well, of course, once people learned that Feldman was offering them at list price—a fiction, since there was no list on her recordings—but fell off a little when the other stores began to feature them.

Feldman could not get over the feeling that the basement had metamorphosed. This was all the more dramatic when he realized that in the main store nothing had changed at all. That is, business there continued to fall off, but at a rate so imperceptible that apparently nothing could be done. Feldman wrote it off as his personal lean years and had no energy—audacity? it took audacity to go against the whim of God—to try to change it. Instead, he concentrated on the basement: what could be made of the strange changes he sensed? how could he capitalize? he wondered, staring at the people down there, observing each with a commanding curiosity as if they were foreigners wrapped in saris or the queer robes of chieftains.

One of the strangest things he noticed was the peculiar decorum of his personnel. Perhaps it was owing to his frequent presence (something was up, they may have thought, and been put on their guard), but their dignity—they could have been salesmen in Tiffany's—was jarring when contrasted to the rather blowsy bearing of the customers. He played with the idea of finding more lively types elsewhere in the store to change places with them, and experimentally he brought down some glad-hander from his hardware department. But observing the fellow in action, he was astonished that his presence was somehow even more jarring than that of the solemn salesman he had replaced. Hurriedly he had the hearty, peppy Hardware man reexchange places with the solemn salesman. Somehow, discrepancy or no, the serious man seemed more at home, better for the counter and more appropriate, than the flashy fellow from upstairs.

He was convinced there was a clue here, but try as he might, he could get nowhere with it. Increasingly he sent for sales figures—*sent* for them, not daring to leave his vantage point near the solemn salesman, pulling salespeople from behind their counters to get almost hourly totals from the various departments in the basement. These he checked against yesterday's figures, looking for clues and, because he found none, to see at least if the trends had held. Only two weeks had passed since the young man had asked for the recording, yet he was convinced the trends were genuine, and he had the feeling that here in the basement was the true pulse of the store, the true pulse, perhaps, of the economy itself.

Preoccupied, he had no time for any monkey business at home, and for the first time since his marriage to Lilly, their relationship took on at least the appearance of a normal one. He picked no quarrels, played no games, and at night, exhausted from the day's labors, simply forgot to invent his lusts. He even lay more easily in the bed, shifting his limbs when they cramped, unrestrictedly turning his pillow, and occasionally rolling over to make an accidental contact with his wife, unthinkable before—and even, occasionally, maintaining it.

Lilly, meanwhile, mistaking distraction for détente, became more natural too: that is, more *un*natural, for her attitude, except for those few times when she openly resisted his domestic games, had always been solicitous and conciliatory. But under the influence of his own apparent relaxation, she too changed. Though she did not fight with him, she became more peckish, expressing her discontents, as if now it might be safe to do so. On the occasion of one of Feldman's neutral rolls to her side of the bed, she misread his intentions, and thinking he wanted to make love, declined gently. "No, Leo," she said, "not tonight." It was the first time she had ever turned down a fuck. Later she herself, dreaming whatever dreams she dreamt, maneuvered herself into his arms, and it was the first time she had ever initiated one. Still preoccupied, he accepted.

The solemn salesman began to appear regularly in his dreams, conducting his transactions (Feldman could not tell what merchandise he sold, though in real life he sold loose cutlery, odd-lot glassware, tumblers and small sets of Melmac such as bachelors buy) with that nonsense dignity Feldman had noticed in the store, at subdued odds with the uneasy, shifty customers.

Still he was unable to account for his effectiveness, until one day—was this only the Thursday after the Monday that he had first noticed the man? was that possible?—happening to be in the old bus depot near his store, where he sometimes ate a solitary lunch at the fountain, he passed through the arcade. A woman was playing a pinball game; another was buying a horoscope from a vending machine. A teen-ager had his driver's license laminated in plastic, and a Negro with a stocking over his forehead recorded his voice. A soldier took four snapshots of himself for a quarter; and another man peered through a thick, greasy collarlike device at a one-minute dime movie of some ancient stripper. The man at the booth, leaning down from a high stool to dispense change, reminded Feldman of his own salesman. *Of course*, he thought, recognizing the expression at once. And requesting change for his dollar just so he could obtain a closer look, he perceived in himself the same shy shamble, the same odd, crablike sidling of the customers. He felt the two-mindedness of a delicate shame, the ambivalence of a regretted decision freshly made, and thought he sensed what the customers sensed—an uneasy submission of embarrassment to desire. (But what were their reasons? What were his? Just being there? Having to submit to a kind of moral muster before this distant, disapproving godlike man? *Of course!* And since the music, they had not come in any honorable, aggressive pursuit of bargains. Money was no object. It was as if their needs had been subverted, and they had now the aspect of people who knew they had been worked but could not help themselves.)

Feldman installed Foot-Eze machines in the basement. He had heard somewhere about vibrating contour chairs and ordered one. He had a coin device attached—fifteen cents—and learned a great deal from studying the guilty, rapt faces of the women and men who sat in it. He did more than ever with vending machines, positioning a whole bank of them against the unused spaces between his elevators. Here could be bought condoms, combs, lucky coins, magnetic dogs, leaded capsules that behaved like jumping beans—all those nervous little purchases of the lonely and poor. Elsewhere there were scales that told your weight for a penny and your fortune for a dime, and a special machine where you signed your name and wrote key words ("wealth," "death," "sex" and "God") on a sensitized IBM card. For fifty cents the card was processed, and a printed letter analyzed your handwriting and your character. There were machines dispensing term insurance covering every imaginable contingency. (Women bought as much protection as men, children as much as adults.) He installed soundproof booths were people could record their voices, but added a new wrinkle. Inside the booth a phonograph played a one-minute-fifty-second instrumental version of "Golden Earrings." The words were framed on the wall just above the microphone, and for a dollar the customer could activate the phonograph and sing with the orchestra. (Many, he noticed, spent five, six or even ten dollars rehearsing.) This machine was so successful that almost at once he had to add another and then a third.

There was a contrivance that created abstract paintings by centrifugal force, but Feldman removed it after only a few days. A certain larky kind of exhibitionism attached to it. Crowds gathered about the artist/customer to observe him squeeze his paints from the bright plastic ketchup and mustard containers. Inevitably he would perform, cheering them with clowned genius or the burlesque grace of some master chef dispensing herbs. Who needed that?

There were devices of petty torture. For a quarter you could send a small charge of electricity through the rubbery, bell-wire toes of a chicken. (It was too easy to think of the next step, intensifying the charge and allowing the shoppers actually to electrocute the chicken. That would have brought the cops perhaps, but more, it would too blatantly have advertised what was going on down there. The small, "harmless"—and so labeled—charge was quite enough to sour the ambience.)

Meanwhile, the songs of Mildred Eve filled the air. (Feldman wondered what she looked like; her album covers, which were flat statements of the sinful primary colors, contained no picture of her.) Her voice, once one got past the lyrics—lust anthems and the throaty hums of orgasms—was good. For all the low profundities of supper-club sensuality, she had a robust, sexual flair, and Feldman was reminded of the young girl lifeguard at the pool where he and Lilly had rented a cabana. A superb, broad-shouldered, powerfully legged girl in a white bathing suit, the dark vertical of her behind just visible under the wet white suit like the vein in jumbo shrimp. Once he had witnessed several of these girls rehearse a water ballet, horny in the chaise lounge at the flashing flex of rump, his heart pounding at the full pull of their strokes and skipping a beat at the last gratuitous twirl of their wrists and fond slap-spank of their hands on the water. It was all gestures like these, caricatured flourishes of style, faintly military—gunfighters fanning the hammers of their guns, commandos shooting from their hips, the smart exchanges of crack drill teams, and the airborne deep knee bends of drum majorettes—that Mildred Eve's voice called to mind. It was stirring as a bright enormous flag, and Feldman yearned. Mama, he thought, erotic and primed, red-hot, low-down, wild-hipped, fat-titty-juiced mama.

Yet all this was beside the point. The machines were beside the point; so was the daily more tawdry shooting-gallery atmosphere of the basement, and Feldman had a sense of baited traps set by an explorer in some jungle no white man had ever penetrated. What monsters would come? he wondered. Looking at the shoppers, he thought he could perceive tracks, gored remains of meals eaten hurriedly, the bent-twigged, crushed-leaved evidence of violated water holes. (And indeed, he had just this sense of doing time in the wilderness, the waiting and nervous patience he exercised a preparatory ordeal.) All he knew was that he was on the threshold of something big, and the basement might have been some secret subterranean laboratory where ultimate weapons came into being. He would not even discuss it with Victman, who repeatedly pressed him for information.

It was odd though, wasn't it, that what was going to happen—and he *knew*, didn't he, though he hadn't yet phrased it?— would come about, *could only come about* through the intercession of these same shady customers, cautious, crabbed from dispossession, whose unfrocked presence was the very essence of the shabby. Feldman imagined, when he looked at them, successive routs, long histories of trials and errors. It was the absence of the romantic, or of anything having to do with the romantic, that betrayed them chiefly. Unfrocked perhaps, but never drummed out of any corps, never failed rich men, or prodigies burned out at puberty, or writers on a lifelong binge of block. Their failures somehow precluded their successes. Looking at the women, he imagined they all had names like "Marietta Johnson" or "Juanita Davis," the irresolute monikers of practical nurses.

What was strange was that they never went above the basement. Despite their characteristic air of loitering, the pressure Feldman sensed in them of a piecemeal, building nerve, like that of lovers unsure of their influence, they came there directly and stayed there. Feldman waited for them to make their move.

Lilly, who had no notion of what was going on, who tested her husband's intentions with a growing irascibleness, as if could she but have his indulgence she could have anything, continued to flex her will. Liver, which Feldman abhorred, appeared on the table. Whole-wheat toast, which had been forbidden in their house, found its way onto the napkin-covered salver at each breakfast. She threw margarine into the fray, and he drank skim milk in his coffee. Saccharin and the diet colas became staples. In a way, she was like someone who had just lost her orthodoxy and, in the first flush of independence, serves only the forbidden fruits. Feldman knew she must be feeling guilty, and wordlessly spread his margarine on his whole-wheat toast, poured skim milk into his Sanka and stirred the saccharin in it with the same single spoon she had given him for his grapefruit.

Billy, on whom these domestic shifts had not failed to make an impression, laid low. He couldn't read and he couldn't count; he couldn't tie his shoes or tell time (he used his own incomprehensibly complex system: "It's fifteen minutes," he would say, always rounding off the odd minutes, dropping them out of his life to the next convenient lower number, "before twenty-five minutes past six o'clock . . . It's ten minutes past five minutes before twenty minutes after fifteen minutes to eight o'clock"). He had always been a very Indian in the forest of their household moods, but now he was clearly scared stiff, and it was he—who had *thrived* on ersatz foods, who would rather eat a handful of barbecued corn chips or a slice of flecked luncheon meat than a piece of pie or a bit of beef—who could not touch his food. He did not trust his father. Obviously, Feldman thought, as close to paternal pride as he had ever ventured, he's a lot smarter than that great rough pig his mama.

The thoughts he allowed his family were vagrant, however. He resented them; they diverted his attention from the store. It was odd. In the past, since, that is, the time that his department store had become prosperous, he had been indifferent to its success. Not corresponding to the myth sometimes associated with businessmen, Feldman had not lived for his work—had not lived as much for it, for example, as some of his own employees may have for theirs. He had, despite his having written them all off, sought his life at home, with his family. Not a devoted man, and largely bored by his wife and son, he nevertheless found it unique to be so closely associated with other beings. They took car trips together, Lilly sharing the driving. It never failed to astonish him, as she showed her credit card and signed the slip the attendant handed her when she bought gas, that they would send him the bill and that he would have to pay it.

Similarly, Billy's report card, which either parent was authorized to sign, always went back with Feldman's signature. The notion of his son's accountability to him, and his—in the state's eyes, at any rate, since they accepted his signature—to his son, was stunning. That he had been so long a bachelor might have explained it, but he had long been a married man too, and had never accustomed himself to what other men take for granted. He could not get over the feeling that he had gotten hooked up with strangers, and it was just this sense of things—that he would have felt closer to cousins if he'd had them—that permitted his abuse of them. For he was not, damn it, a cruel man—just, like others on the Diaspora, a xenophobic one. Even his bedtime fantasies about other women were understandable if one granted that Lilly was essentially a stranger somehow, only temporarily linked to him. (Well, they would both die someday. It was as if, through the prospect of their deaths, they were already divorced.) But these were thoughts which he scarcely had time for now. Until he got this other thing straightened out, his family would remain submerged and he would be mild, benign, whatever courtesies it cost, let them read into it whatever incipient affection they wished.

For some while Feldman had considered that the time was ripe. He was unwilling to install any more machines or to make any additional shiftings of stock (he had had brought down to the basement certain items of sybaritic indulgence: rich levantine garments luxurious as the costumes of despots; gigantic celebrational cakes so painstakingly sculpted that their showy frosting could no longer be eaten; jeweled, tropically feathered fishermen's flies on platinum mountings), afraid that he had achieved an ecological balance so exquisite that any further adjustment would destroy it. Thinking ahead to the time when whatever was to happen would have happened, he congratulated himself. (Accident? What accident? Opportunity knocks. I'm prepared. Feldman's prepared. I know it will come. I make it come.) So he watched and listened and waited, unexposed even as he paced the basement, primed as a gent in a blind or some bad man in ambush.

Then one day a man stopped him in the aisle. Wealth, death, sex and God, Feldman thought. He knew it had happened.

"I want," said the man, "to buy a gun."

He meant, Feldman knew, a rifle, some antiqued walnut thing, sporty as its trophy prey. But seeing the man—he had observed him before: the dark orbit of his felt brim pitched low, crowding an eyebrow in wrought, posed suspiciousness, the thin murderous nose as though pressed by swimmer's clamps, the pearl-mooned buttons like the medals of gangsters, and gray powerless hands that had choreographed their own goofy, spooky rituals—he understood that the rifle would never be used for sport, save that fancied one of this fool's imagination. And why did it have to begin with a madman, some jeopardizing clown who would purchase the rifle as he must have purchased each item in his costume (the fedora, the long dark coat with the pearl buttons, the white silk scarf), as he would buy the next (the black leather gloves, if he could just give up the fancy handwork or convince himself that it was even more threatening in wraps), one thing at a time, like a collector? Why did it have to be such a person? Because it had to be. Because the time was only mildly ripe. Because in any new enterprise it is the madmen who step up first. Watching him, Feldman knew that the man had not yet selected a victim. The hatred in his eyes was unspecified, in love with its own posture, an emotion seeking itself in mirrors behind Feldman's head. One day it might focus, but perhaps not. If it didn't, it would do its damage anyway, but with its heart not in it.

"I want," the man repeated, "to buy a gun."

"Yes *sir!*" said Feldman.

He let the word get out that he wanted to see all persons with strange or unusual requests, explaining to his personnel that the only way anyone in charge of an operation like this could develop new markets or make intelligent suggestions to the designers and manufacturers was through experience in the field. He wanted *no one* turned away, he said, no matter how exotic or even out of the question the inquiry might be. These, he underscored, were *particularly* the people he wanted to see.

He had his carpenters build a small office for him near the basement stairwell; a desk and two chairs were moved in and a telephone installed. He established fixed office hours, selecting an hour in the morning on Mondays, Wednesdays and Fridays, and one in the afternoon on the other days. On Monday evenings, when the store was open late, he let it be known that he would be in his office from seven P.M. until closing.

He began a discreet advertising campaign—small, vaguely worded notices in the Personals column of the morning and evening newspapers. He phoned the ads in himself and told the girl that they were to run beneath those ads that sounded like trouble; in fact, they were not to appear at all on days when the paper did not carry these condensed telegrams of grief. Similarly, he had signs put up in the rest rooms of cheap hotels. A sign with the same vague message, but larger than the others and more decorative, appeared in the bus depot and the penny arcade. All right, Feldman thought, call me sentimental, say I'm a softy, but that's where it all started.

*   *   *

The first ad ran on a Saturday, and there were already people outside his door when he came in on Monday morning. If the people he had watched in his basement seemed reluctant or shy, these were direct, as if they had long since taken a professional attitude toward their troubles. Like sinners proclaiming their salvation or drug addicts their cure, they spoke of their weaknesses proudly.

"I come up pregnant," this high school girl told him, "the first time I ever let a boy. It's my blood. It's my big pelvis. A womb like a hothouse, my ma says. But that don't mean I want to have his kid. I need to be cut or whatever they do."

Feldman nodded agreeably, and while she was still sitting there, called Freedman, already, even as he dialed, giving the small signals and high signs of success, the winks of private joke and communed confidence which even on this first outing he had adopted as his cheery style, letting the sun in on sin and discovering something useful to do with his hands.

"Freedman? Feldman. How you doing? Listen, Doc, I need a favor. I won't beat around the bush. Time, essence, and what are friends for? The name of a specialist, please . . . I'm looking for an abortionist . . . I say an abortionist doctor, Doctor . . . That's right. Nobody scabby, no dirty rubber-gloved drunk. Somebody who shaves. No names, please—too shameful at this juncture, but trust me. I wouldn't ask if I didn't need this favor . . . Okay, all right, check. Spare me the righteousness . . . Okay, all right, check. I appreciate your reluctance. All I can say is I'll never implicate you. That's a promise, kid . . . All right, my back's to the wall. It's Lilly . . . That's right. She's been unfaithful. It's hard for me to say this, Doc, even to you. A *schvoogy*, a *schvartz* . . . Well, hell, maybe some of it's my fault, but I can't stand by and accept some pickaninny bastard . . . Right. You will?" Here (to the girl) a Morse code, both eyes blinking like signals at a railroad crossing, the arm going down like a gate, the mouth and tongue in elaborate, exaggerated silent conversation that had nothing to do with Freedman. "You will? What are friends for, indeed? And, Doctor, I hope to God in Heaven above that Medicare is wiped out. That's what I think of *you*, sweetheart. Wait, let me get a pencil." (One was already in his hand.) "Is that last letter an *m*? Is it an *m*, I say, or an *n*?" (He had already written down the name.) "An *m* as in 'miscarriage,' or an *n* as in 'niggerbaby'? . . . What's that? Must be this connection . . . An *m* as in 'miscarriage.' Doctor, I gotcha. I'll never forget. This is what they mean when they talk about the relationship between a doc and his patients. You don't get this sort of thing in England. Listen, Freedman, listen to me. I want you to come into the store and pick out a suit . . . No, I mean it. Promise me, promise me now. Is that a promise? . . . Right, good. I'll look for you, Doctor."

Feldman gave the girl the name of the abortionist but would accept no money. "It's a service of the store," he explained. "We're building good will." He allowed her to fill out an application for a charge account.

Although he had many opportunities to use the abortionist's name during those first weeks—later he would ask Freedman for the names of others, it being a matter of curiosity, as he would frankly tell him—something about his new business was disturbing to him. The world had begun to smell pregnant to him, spermy. He came to distrust all virginal appearance and thought of himself as love's piker. Love was everywhere. It was June in January, April in May. Before long, he thought nervously, he would begin to make passes at the prim little fuckers himself. (Prim, they *were* prim, white-gloved, white-shod, their gynecological beings underscored by the graduation-dress packages in which they wrapped themselves, like gift-wrapped horrors in boxed practical jokes.) Indeed, he felt they *expected* his advances, that in their eyes his profitless continence made him more perverse, and he was careful not to touch any of their tokens, refusing even their fountain pens when he had to write down a name or a direction, calling them back to retrieve the forgotten purse, never touching it himself or daring to smell the cloudy, steamy face-powder-cum-chewing-gum odors of their open bags. To protect himself, he was short with them, scornful, encouraged them to think of him as of an agent, an advance man, someone who would later be cut in by the abortionist himself.

He went further, and by stripping his office even of memo pads and desk calendars and blotters and paper clips, he managed to create an atmosphere of the guarded discussion, a place where deals were made while no tangible product, even money, was ever allowed to show; there was an overall impression of records self-consciously not kept and of a deliberate, guilty respectability. Still, he regretted his celibacy and found himself with a developing predilection that fed on his copious sense of the availability of these one-time losers. He was in love with their country-girl, milkmaid—in a way, they were already mothers—underdog sexuality, and with their flat-chested, smooth-thighed, stick-limbed, straightassed boyish bearing. He was in love with adolescence, in love not with the blatant statements of brassiered and pantied organs, but with all the invisible code machinery of their insides, the clear, young, clean-as-a-whistle tunnels of their bodies. As smitten by their invisible treasures as any dirty old man his gray heel bending the counter of a lady's shoe and a garter band trebled around his wrist, with the cheats of fetish.

It was no joke: for the first time in years Feldman had a mixed feeling—anxious for excitement, thrilled and annoyed when it came, irritated and relieved when it didn't. Finding no one there when he came for his office hour, he would shrug fitfully. Nothing ventured, he would think, and nothing gained, and only quits at that.

Beyond this, something else bothered him. It hadn't ever been profit that had driven him, but the idea of the sale itself, his way of bearing down on the world. Now, however, he had become a mere order-filler, no better than the kind of salesman he had always despised. He strove to counter this. "You seem oversexed," he told one pregnant teenager, "hot-blooded. Come here. I'll show you something." He blew the fair, fine hairs along her arm. He put his mouth next to her ear, and without touching it or moving his lips, kept it there until she squirmed. He kissed the back of her neck softly. She sighed. Her flesh rose in goose bumps. "You see? You'll always have trouble with that," he told her. "Five minutes of this treatment and I'd be inside your blouse, ten more and my fingers would be strumming your crotch. In a quarter of an hour we'd be screwing. And mind you, I'm a stranger—fat, homely, older than your pa. You've pronounced erogenous zones, sweetheart. One out of a hundred suffers. *Sure* suffers, *certainly* suffers. Are you Catholic? No, not even Catholic. Then why pay for some biological quirk not your responsibility? Fertility goes with your disease like night with day. You can't help it. There's sex cells on your pores thick as peanut butter. I tasted them when I kissed your neck. Listen. I say go ahead with your plans, have your abortion. But afterwards—listen to me—afterwards have this operation. Be sprayed. Come on, who winces at a scientific term? Be made infertile then, become sterile. Whatever you want to call it. A small love knot in the Fallopian tubes." It was the sort of terminology which made him lustful, though now he used it dispassionately, throwing it in to make his case. "We can't operate on desire yet, dearie. The lust glands are contiguous with the synaptic neurons. Excuse my talking dirty to you, miss, but we're both adult, *n'est pas*? If we destroyed your neurons it would be too dangerous. You wouldn't feel pleasure, but you wouldn't feel pain either. A neuronectomy is out. I couldn't permit it. You'll *have* to be sterilized. I'll bring in the biggest man. As if you were my own daughter. Could I say fairer? Wait, where are you going? Sit down, where are you going? All right, smartie," he shouted after her, "it's your funeral."

He was wringing wet when he sat down again. Have I gone crazy? he thought. He closed the office, canceled the appointments of two people and did not come in at all for a few days.

It was only that he had been overanxious to make the sale, he was able at last to reassure himself. He had to accept it: abortions were closed circuits, dead ends. Though it was stimulating to do business with anyone with a private shame, he was coming to resent the distinctly medical emphasis of sin. The doctors had a cartel, he saw; businessmen were just their errand boys. But, he thought, what can I do? Love makes the world go round, damnit.

He had five full weeks of this. Only then did he realize that he never saw a man in his office unless he was there with the girl, or by himself on the girl's business.

He began to wonder about the fellow to whom he had sold the rifle. Had he killed anyone yet?

Then he had a break. A young man came in alone one day. Feldman expected that it was more of the same and greeted him without interest. The man's uneasiness—usually these fellows were as matter-of-fact as himself—might have provided a clue to his difference, and perhaps it was an indication of his flagging faith that it didn't. He accepted the boy's halting quality as sincerity, and told himself that it was refreshing to come upon a fellow so unused to the feel of his compromise. To make it easier for him to begin, he said, "You're not married?"

"No sir."

"Not in a position to marry, I suppose?"

"No sir."

"Though it sticks in your craw to do something like this, you see no alternative."

"I'm sorry?" the young man said.

The customer's bashfulness was a waste of time, but Feldman understood it. To the man he must have seemed someone unlicensed or lightly so, like a tip-off man to the cops perhaps, paid with taxpayers' money, or a prostitute, or the man who sells fireworks out on the highway.

"I say you see no alternative to the abortion."

"I'm sorry?" the young man repeated.

Then he realized that they were speaking at cross-purposes. (Ah, it was no piece of cake. The customer was always right in this business.) He held his tongue and let the young man tell it, ignoring his own last statements as if they had been part of the room's packed silences.

"I saw your ad in the P-Personals column—" he began falteringly. (My, the dignity, Feldman observed, as though truth required an imperfect delivery, the boy's faint stutter like the riddling of an oracle.) "I didn't know. I mean—about this p-place. I've come by. I've s-seen the g-girls outside. They seemed f-frightened to me. Then I rec-recognized one from my b-block who got into trouble with a guy. I s-saw *her* here." Feldman enjoyed the cave style; he actually folded his hands at one point. There could have been diplomas behind him on the walls; he could smell the diced breath that comes through the grills of confessionals. His face fixed in a mask of stern encouragement. But when would he get to it? Were there no gestures? The boy was too coltish, yet he dared not risk a single sepulchral "Yes?" "I thought you could h-help me." A good sign. You could see light with a good sign like that. (These people actually have to *want* to be helped.) Soon they would both be all over the kid's needs, taking their greedy draughts, travelers at a well.

"I'm not an addict," the boy blurted. "I don't even have a habit." Now the rush of his speech muffled his impediment. Feldman wondered where it had gone, then tuned in on the spurious, jazzy scat of his tumbling speech. The kid could be a fake.

Feldman interrupted him. "What is this? What are you pulling here? What do you mean you're not an addict? What's all this? What's going on? What are you driving at?"

"Oh," the boy said, "oh. I'm sorry. Maybe I had the wrong idea about this setup."

"Setup?"

"I heard talk."

"Talk? What talk?"

"That you do f-favors."

"Yes?"

"That you d-do favors. I need something. I'm too listless. I need a prescription."

"A prescription? What prescription?"

"I don't know. I don't even know the name of the stuff. But I had it once and it h-helped."

Feldman picked up the phone and began to dial at random. The young man jumped. It was all the test he would ever take, Feldman thought prophetically, seeing his alarm as the sign of his legitimacy, that single reflex the springing of his addiction. He remembered for him what the boy would forget: that instinct did him in, that he had been hooked at such and such a time on such and such a date by nothing more palpable than his brief alarm. "Busy," he said curtly. "I'll try again in a minute." The boy settled back, and in a moment Feldman dialed Freedman's number.

"Freedman? Feldman. What do you say, Freedman? . . . Listen, I meant to thank you about Lilly, but I've been a little queasy about the whole thing . . . Well, it's a bad business all around . . . No. Lilly's all right. He was a first-rate man. But what I called you about—well, she's depressed. I forgave her, but the whole thing still doesn't sit right with her. I tell her a thousand times a day, 'Lilly, it's all right. Everybody makes mistakes.' I've even confessed to fictive infidelities of my own, but the girl's ridden with guilt . . . Tranquilizers?" He looked at the boy in the chair; the young man shook his head. "No, Doctor, she's been on tranquilizers, and they just don't seem to do the job. As a matter of fact, your man prescribed them himself as a precaution. I'd call him back to ask for something stronger, but Lilly doesn't want to have anything more to do with him. Too ashamed. She ripped his name off the label first thing. I've never seen anything like that girl's shame. You know Lilly, she's a ball of fire when she's herself . . . Won't stir out of the house, doesn't even want to get out of bed. I wanted to bring her over to see you, but she doesn't know you gave me that fellow's name, and she's afraid she'd blurt out the whole story in the consultation room. She's in terrible shape, Doctor. I'm really worried this time. I'm thinking maybe I should have let her have the kid. She's so *listless*. I'll tell you the truth— I'm afraid she's going to start seeing him again . . . *Him*. The nigger. Well, he's our dry-cleaning man. Big *black* brute he is. I think of that nigger's cock in my Lilly's pussy, and I want to cry. I need some help on this, Doc . . . Her bowels? How are her bowels?" The boy nodded agreeably. "One thing, Doc, her bowels are right as rain . . . A fever?" He looked at the young man. "No. No fever." The boy imitated a sleeper. "It's just this listlessness. Sleeps around the clock . . . What? What's that? The superamphetamines?

. . . What they give the advanced catatonics, you say?" He looked at the beaming boy. "Well, that sounds all right to me. Why don't we just try that? Tell you what, call the pharmacist in your building, and I'll send my boy over to pick it up. And say, Doc, I want you to come by for that suit. Hear? . . . I mean that . . . Much obleeged. Really, Doc, much obleeged to you."

He scribbled an address and handed it to the young man. "If you run out we can have it renewed," he said.

And still he was at their mercy, riding passenger to their driver's seat. He undertook to teach himself the pharmacopoeia—much as, weeks before, he had pored over the illustrations in medical texts, learning the uterus like the parts of speech—and in a week had a junkie's knowledge of all soft anodynes, and thought in ampules and capsules and decimaled grain. The *pusher*, he thought, *there's* a salesman. But it was hopeless, he reflected bitterly, with a wishful pitch, like the acceptance speech of a dark horse, already half formed in his head. "Shit! Shit for sale! Shit for shooting, for snuffing and smoking. Swallow it with water from the tap or stir it in lemonade sweetened to taste. Imported shit shipments. Domestic shit grown in our own vacant lots. Airplane glue for the kiddies and Dad's war-earned morphine and Demarol for Grandma. Psychedelics for the whole family. (The family that prays together stays together.) Why toss and turn another moment? Throw away those sleepless nights. Shit here. Shit for pain and shit for pep, shit for languor, shit for gloom. (Thank you, and will there be anything else, sir? A hypodermic, sir, a syringe? Needles? *Have you thought of everything?*)" Too bad he would never make it. To wheel and deal in ultimate products: ah! oh! me oh my! Hangmen's rope, warheads, heavy water and the life of Christ. (Judas, *there* was a salesman!) Damn, he thought. Damn the ICC, damn Food and Drugs and SEC. Damn the board of health and the FCC and the fire and boxing commissions. Damn all rulings of the Supreme Court in restraint of trade, and the laws that keep my help from going naked in the aisles. Damn the timers of the stoplights, and those who license, and those who make the rules for the safety checks of airplanes. Curse the up-to-snuff thickness of rails that support such and such a weight at such and such a temperature. Damn, too, the snoops who oversee the construction of bridges and insist on precautions before letting a single worker go into a mine or a tunnel. Damn that measly conspiracy of the civilized that puts safety before profit and makes hazard illegal, and damn finally, then, those at the top who would extend longevity by requiring dullness and who this morning reduced almost to absolute zero the possibility that when I left my house after a handsome breakfast that followed an eight-hour restoring sleep, I would see one man come after another man with a knife.

That's that, he sighed, a realist who surrendered quarter where it was due and would never be a pusher, but merely sin's friend downtown, a doer of favors, crime's wardheeler, transgressions's lousy legman, wrong's cop and felony's cabbie giving directions to the conventioneers.

But seeking to cover all markets, he needed to know the names of the pushers. He dialed Freedman. "It's me, Doctor . . . Not good, Doc, not good. Sad and downhearted. Got the blues you know, old time, sunk-spirit funk. The fantods, Physician . . . No no, nothing you could call a new wrinkle. It's Lilly again. We hooked her, Doc. Lilly's hooked. She come up a dope fiend. Flaming, raging addict, Lilly is. She'd kill for the stuff, Doc. Yes sir, she'd lie and steal and murder and cavort. We did it *this* time. Freedman. We sure did a job on old Lilly. Good thing I'm rich, a habit like she's got. Only thing keeps her off the street this minute's my money, I guess. Have to appreciate small blessings, way I look at it. But Lilly, well sir, Lilly's got a monkey on her back like King Kong . . . No, no. You know Lilly, *her* character. A cure's out of the question. Only way to make her stop is tie her up and sit on top of her. A cure's out. Lilly's system just couldn't stand up to cold turkey. No, Doc, I look down that lonesome road, and all I can see is doom in that direction. We're just going to have to accept it, I'm afraid, and that's why I had to call my family physician . . . No, hell, *I* understand your position., *I* know that as a medical man you can't just go on prescribing these drugs for her . . . I *know* about your Hippocratic oath, and I want to tell you I respect you for it. . . . *Ab*solutely not, out of the question, *I* appreciate that. I wouldn't have it otherwise. But still and all, Doctor, you're the one got her into this, ruined her health with an abortion, then prescribed narcotics to bring her round again . . . No, of course I'm not blaming you. Of course not. You did what you thought necessary. But, well sir, we're decent people, Lilly and me. What do *we* know about the underworld and the syndicate and those plug-uglies? I was hoping I could get the names of some pushers from you so's I could keep Lilly supplied, so's the cupboard's never bare . . . Sure, pos*itively*, that's all I want . . . How's

248 ~ **Stanley Elkin**

that? . . . You will? Well, I appreciate it. Here, just let me get a
pencil and a sheet of paper. Okey-dokey, I'm ready . . . Uh huh.
Uh huh. *Him?* Tch tch . . . Uh huh. Uh huh. Fine, I got it all down.
Thank you . . . But I do have a bone to pick with you, Dr. Freedman. Can you guess what it is? . . . That's right, the suit . . . All
right, now that's a promise. That's a promise from a man that's
under the Hippocratic oath."

Replacing the phone, he thought: That Freedman is dangerous. He ought to be locked up.

With his heavy abortion trade, relieved now and then by the
public's incipient interest in drugs, Feldman managed to remain
fairly equable for a while. It was still true, of course, that he was
at their mercy and had not yet found any way to deflect their
specific demands. Once, when he was still naïve, he might have
settled for just these conditions, all sin subsumed in the body's
joy, the nervous system's reasons, but he had begun to discover
in the victims—he could not say *his* victims—a sense of prior submission, of simple yielded-to, statutory plight. Here were no fearful presences to justify either pistol in drawer or alarm button
under the rug to bring help—he felt no real harm in them, and
he was annoyed by their indulgence, bothered by the absence of
driving pride, the firmer greeds. The truth was, he was haunted
by the ghosts of those who had gotten to them first. Jealous as
some taken-in bridegroom, he heard the lies still whispering
above their heads, the wily lines of truckers in bars, cousins at
parties, guests under their fathers' roofs. Also, he recognized what
they did not, that their need of him hung on an ignorance. Why
did they need him? What did they use him for? He was merely a
distraction for them, his function a ritual, a ceremonial fiction, as
though their troubles and their solutions needed channels and red
tape to legitimize them.

In the meantime, he was kept busy with referrals from his
salesmen, listening to old ladies with some determined memory
of a particular pair of house slippers long out of stock or some
fly-by-night gadget seen at a friend's. He could have whiled away
the time running some of these down, or even had what he would
once have considered fun switching their ardor to some other object, but he dismissed them as quickly as he could, getting them
out of the way for the next white-gloved, goofy-hatted girl in trouble—with whose insides, despite himself, he was still in love.

*   *   *

A man came into Feldman's office, a tall, stern, raw-boned, sinister fellow in his fifties, his hair graying at his temples but black everywhere else. His features were sharp, all angles and bas-relieved bones, the unrecoverable Eskimo or Mongol just under his skin now Anglicized and windburned Christian. He reminded Feldman of conductors on commuter railroads, whose solemn aspect had made him fearful, or of ace pilots now alcoholic, or of investors embittered by businessmen, and of businessmen themselves as they were sometimes shown in movies—hard and ruthless and cynical, soft only on their daughters. Feldman thought of the gun he did not keep in the secret drawer he did not have.

"Are you Feldman?"

"Yes," he said. The man remained standing by his desk, his courtesy a warning. "Please be seated." The man looked at the chair suspiciously, then back at Feldman, and sat down as though defying some trap. "Yes?" Feldman said. "Yes sir?"

The man scrutinized him, and Feldman thought *Cops* even as he dismissed the idea. There was something too fastidious about the man's anger. The father of some girl dead on the abortionist's table, the sore old man of a kid junkie. But this too seemed unlikely. Something about his bearing was uncommitted, as though he were checking not for some bad quality he knew Feldman had, but for some good quality he was afraid he might have. Waiting him out, Feldman could feel himself posing. He gave him tough, gave him bold, gave him patient, gave him poker, gave him a dozen patent bravuras he did not feel, and was aware that his face was as frozen as his visitor's, that not a muscle had moved nor a hair stirred. Indeed, it might still have expressed the question of his "Yes sir?" and he settled for that.

There were several buttons pinned to the man's lapel. As he shifted in his chair he seemed to propel them forward. Noticing them for the first time, Feldman thought impertinently of all strange feats of belief, so many causes inscribed on the head of a pin. On one was an American flag, on another a sort of contemporary minuteman, for which some younger version of the man himself might have served as the model. The rest were the acronyms of unfamiliar organizations. A last badge read: "WDSG." ("Wealth, Death, Sex and God?" Feldman wondered. Impossible.)

Still the man had not spoken, though Feldman understood that showing him the pins had been a gentle act, a shy feeler like the inexpert flourish of some schoolgirl's engagement ring. He was inexplicably touched.

Finally the stranger spoke. "Feldman," he said speculatively. His voice was as arrogant as ever, as if there had been no soft overture from the lapel; indeed, that had somehow been retracted. "Feldman," he said again, turning the name over with his tongue as if it had been some gunned hood's suspicious last effect in the hand of a policeman.

"What's up?" Feldman made himself ask.

"There are some merchants," the man said, though it was clear, from the tone of rehearsal that he brought to his speech, that they had not entered conversation, "I've heard about who, not Jews themselves, affect Jewishness. They do it superstitiously, much as a smithy hangs his first horseshoe above his door or the owner of a tavern frames his beginning dollar. Are you such a merchant, Feldman? Such as I've described, trading on your Christian credit to appease some Rothschild Cash and Carry Immanence?"

In a panic Feldman tried to remember Freedman's telephone number and couldn't.

"I've asked if you're Jewish, Feldman."

"Half Jewish," he said, projecting a disparagement of the Jewish half.

"Oh," the man said, disappointed, and once more was silent. But the buttons had come out again. Observing the man closely, Feldman saw that as he shifted he raised one shoulder slightly, swelling only half his chest. It was a puzzling, schizophrenic business, and he was not sure what to make of it, save that he knew he preferred the ingenious shoulder to the rigid, brooding one. He had to make the stranger keep the badges forward.

On a hunch he boldly put out his hand and fingered one of the tin buttons, the one with the American flag. "Old Glory," Feldman said.

The man sat uneasily under Feldman's touch but did not pull back.

Feldman's finger moved to another button. "AFSAF," he said. "FAFAC." He opened his drawer and rummaged in it for a moment. "Here it is. I knew I had it," he said, handing his find to the stranger.

"This is a paper clip," the man said.

Feldman winked and took it back. "*So*," he said expansively, something settled between them. "*So!*" He nodded forcefully. He had an idea now why the man had come: for a contribution. He leaned forward and glared at him. Then, inspired, he turned to the other lapel, the one without the buttons, and stared at it fixedly. After a moment the man moved his arm across his chest in a long, slow diagonal like some mystic fraternal salute, and taking the edge of the lapel, he turned it inside out. A hidden button was revealed.

"RAFAPACALFAF," he said.

"How long," Feldman asked, "have you been, ah . . . interested?"

"I haven't seen yours," the man said.

"I don't belong," Feldman said. "I don't approve of their methods." A pain swept over the man's face. "Have you heard about my labor policies?" Feldman asked quickly. "I'm off the charge plate, did you know that?" Then he leaned forward, brushing the buttons contemptuously with the back of his hand. "I'm more comfortable with the renegade than I am with the convert. There are good words that can be said for confessed former Communists. I won't deny it, but there's something embarrassing in a new passion. Give me men who keep their instincts. The *Northern* racist, give me *him*, whose best argument is his prickling skin, his crawling flesh, his abhorrence fingerprinted in his cells. Give me snarlers who bare their teeth at the soul's *traif*. Phooey on the isometric heart, the soul like a cleft palate or unequal feet. Am I taking a chance with you? *Am I?*" he challenged.

The man was silent. Then, "They're getting away with murder," he said softly.

"*Am I taking a chance with you?*" Feldman insisted. The man looked confused. "The buttons. Your buttons. So many eggs, so many baskets. I know what those cost you, you. The garish orchestration of your politics, a tune for turncoats, fa la la. First one thing and then another."

"They're getting away with murder," the man said again.

"We agree in principle," Feldman said sharply.

"They have to be stopped," the man said, and his face went through an extraordinary change, a relaxation, giving way to a kind of gravity he had been resisting. Feldman understood that his brief rhetoric had been rehearsed. Now there was something fervid as falling about him. He might have been dropping through the air in a parachute.

"We agree in principle. Go on," Feldman commanded.

"There are movements afoot," the man said with the same blank passion. "A conspiracy." His voice *achieved* the word. "The nationhood threatened," he said so feelingly that he seemed close to tears. "Rioters. Looting. So-called civil rights." As if these phrases had triggered his message, he began to talk rapidly now. Kennedy's assassination. A signal. Their call to arms. A blood sacrifice—theirs. The Mistaken's. Pervasive moral collapse. Municipal swimming pools and city parks systems usurped, national parks next. Muggings in the Grand Canyon, rape in Yellowstone. The debilitating effect of modern music: jungle rhythms, chaos. Basement tactics of the so-called Black Muslims. Trouble in so-called Asia. Prayer in schools, together with other decisions of the so-called Supreme Court. In a blueprint—he personally had seen the blueprint.

"You've *seen* the blueprint?"

"Yes. I've seen it."

"Go on."

The Mistaken were actually three and a half months ahead of schedule, and gaining at a rate of thirty-eight minutes a day. An hour and a half on the Sabbath while the nation slept. *"Wake up, America!"* he finished. *"Oh, for God's sake, wake up before it's too late!"* Then, as if to reassure himself that it wasn't, he looked at his watch.

"Guns," Feldman said quietly. "You want guns. And ammo. Plenty of ammo."

"What?"

"Be quiet," Feldman said. "Let me think. Who's with you?"

The man blinked at him.

"Who's *with* you? What's your membership? The usual smattering of retired generals, I suppose, old ladies with cat hairs on their shawls, one of two sore losers from Cuba and Budapest. Is that the element?"

"I want—"

"You want, *you* want. I *know* what you want. You want a radio ministry. Fifteen minutes a day at six-fifteen in the morning. 'Wake up, America,' indeed. Do you know who listens to those programs? Shut-ins. People on turnpikes who drive all night to save on motels. I *know* what you want. You want pamphlets in bus stations and flags for the poor. Sit still. *Sit still.* This is important. Arm."

"What?"

"Arm, goddamn it! The so called British are coming. *Arm!* But the American way—with American weapons. Do you know what I see? A militia of deer hunters in red-checkered vests. A calvary of coon hounds. An arsenal of sporting goods and bombs in

Cokes. A Winchester in every golf bag. Poisoned fishhooks and hangmen's line. Wake up, American! *Force!* How much money you got?"

"I don't see how—"

"How much *money* you got?" He waved his hand at the man's lapel. "Don't tell me that jewelry comes cheap. Don't jew around with me. We'll need sleeping bags, canteens, plenty of canvas tents and first aid kits. Don't expect to get away without casualties. If you can't stand the heat, stay out of the kitchen. You can't make an omelet without breaking eggs. We'll need Sterno, charcoal grills, paper plates, walkie-talkies. And don't forget the transistor batteries for the walkie-talkies."

Whoopee, Feldman thought. Whoopee yi o ki yay. This is it. *This* is. "Tear-gas fountain pens," he said. "Cattle prods. And flags, plenty of flags. Let them know who we are. And the rifles! And the ammo for the rifles! Forty thousand dollars. I can equip an outfit of two hundred men and put them in the field for forty thousand dollars. You *got* forty thousand dollars?"

"I—"

"*Do* you?" Feldman demanded.

The man was blinking steadily now, licking his lips.

"Come on, come on, it's near closing. They have three and a half months, six minutes on us."

"What about uniforms?" the man asked. "You didn't say anything about uniforms."

"Bowling shirts, yachting caps," Feldman said sharply. "Do you have the money?"

"My savings," the stranger said. His decision made, he seemed relieved. "And you're right about these"—he pointed to his lapel—"just a lot of talk."

"All right," Feldman said, scribbling an order as he spoke, "take this to Sporting Goods. And I'm giving you this at cost, so I want to go into your political background to make sure the stuff isn't falling into the wrong hands."

The man nodded and extended his card. He acted as if something quite familiar were happening to him.

This encounter taught Feldman a valuable lesson: that everyone had already been tempted, that everyone had already succumbed, had had those things happen to him which he wanted to have happen, and was looking for them to happen again. Seduction was routine; yielding was; everyone had a yes to spend and spent it. And there was about them all some soft, run-to-fat quality not of knowledge but of consent and peace, the puffy eyes of the heart.

He felt better, relieved of his responsibility to satanize the world.

In the next few weeks Feldman did a land-office business in a wide variety of favors. He arranged an orgy for some conventioneers (a call to Freedman: "Lilly wants to go into a whorehouse, Doc. Figures she belongs in one after what she's done to the family. Physicians keep tabs on this sort of thing. You know a place with a healthy bunch of girls? After all, I still have to sleep with her"). He helped out a woman who wanted to fix a judge ("Doc, Lilly was run in last night. What can you tell me about Judge Meader?"). He did some business with a homosexual, fixed up a childless couple with a black-market baby, and was generally content. It still nagged at him occasionally that he was not really responsible for his clients' needs, but this was partially offset by an incident that occurred shortly after the visit of the right-winger.

A fellow came into the office but couldn't say what he wanted.

"Girls?" Feldman asked.

"No. I don't know."

"Fellas then. I could put you on to some swingers. My personal physician treats them for the biggest families."

"Not interested."

"You drive? There's this guy needs a wheelman for a bank job he's planning."

"I'm no crook."

"Say, you *don't* know what you want, do you?"

"Sure don't." The fellow sat spraddle-legged.

"All right," Feldman said finally, "I've got it. I've been waiting for someone to try it out on. It's new, an experiment. Not a bit risky, but very unusual and a lot of kicks."

"Yeah?"

"Guaranteed, but it would cost you seven hundred bucks."

"That's a little more than I'd planned—"

"Okay, then it's not for you. Forget it."

"What is it?"

"Forget it. It's not for you."

"Well, you can tell me what it is."

"No, I don't think so. I wouldn't want to cut corners on this project. We'll think of something else."

"Well, just tell me what it is. If it sounds worthwhile—"

"You'd do it?"

"Well, if I thought it was okay—"

"All right," Feldman said. "You've got to go to Cleveland. You wear disguises."

"What?"

"You wear disguises in Cleveland. I'll send you to a place where they rent costumes."

"Jesus."

"You stay in a hotel, and every day you put on a different costume: fireman, baseball player, intern—that sort of thing."

"Well, what's so hot about that?"

"Sure. Forget it."

"Well, what's so hot about it?"

"Have you tried it?"

"No, of course not."

"Then how do you know? Habit—everything's habit. Tell me, what do you do when you hear a funny story?"

"Well, I laugh."

"Exactly. That's what I *mean*. Why not hold your right arm up instead? Look, do me a favor. Go to Cleveland. See what you think."

He went, and a week later Feldman got a postcard saying it was the best seven hundred dollars he'd ever spent and that next year the man thought he would try it in Worcester, Mass.

Now things ran smoothly. Each day brought new challenges, and he derived a certain joy from the balanced schizophrenic nature of his store: the aboveboard floors, with their conventional commerce, and the queer open secret of his basement. He was even able to take more interest in the main store, discovering, now that he could again pay attention to it, that in the last months it had prospered. He reconsidered his plans for building a suburban branch, and while he had not actually made his mind up to go ahead with the project, he deemed it a serious future possibility. Though he still believed in the lean years to come, he wondered whether he might not have exaggerated their imminence.

At home his relations with his family had entered a new phase. He neither tormented Lilly nor avoided her with his neutrality. Billy, who was out of school for the summer, was by the grace of his vacation able to obscure some of his intellectual clumsiness. Lean years would come for Billy, Feldman knew, but for now he was perfectly willing to pretend that there was not much wrong with his son. Though everyday he pursued Billy with questions about why he was the last kid chosen for a team, sometimes he allowed a tone of joking to give a good-natured dimension to his scorn.

It was against this background that he found himself one night on Lilly's side of the bed. They had been watching television together, and Feldman, who always determined which programs they would watch, permitted her a movie. The grateful Lilly couldn't do enough for him.

"Play with my back," he murmured. He lay on his side and pulled his pajama tops up around his shoulders. "Use your other hand," he said. "I feel your callus." It was pleasant to lie there in the dark with his eyes closed, listening to the movie. "Lower," he said, "a little lower. Yes. There." Lilly didn't have any idea when she had overworked an area. "Keep moving around," he told her. "Try to remember where you've been. That's it." For a few minutes it was much better, but every so often she would become engrossed in the movie. Then her hand would falter and stop, and he would have to shake his shoulders to get her attention again. During commercials, however, the hand came alive by itself and fluttered hither and yon with an almost geisha attention. During the next commercial Feldman removed his bottoms, and even after the movie came on Lilly's fingers still moved expertly.

"I'm going to turn the set off, Leo," she said in a few minutes.

In the dark she groped her way back to the bed. "Play with the backs of my legs," he said. "Play with my kneecaps. Play with the nape of my neck."

She reached across his body and drew her fingers up his thighs. "Let's make love," she whispered.

"No. Play with my back again."

"Please, Leo."

"I can't."

"I'll make you. Shall I try to make you, Leo?"

"All right," he said, "try to make me." He lay on his back, and she took his penis in her left hand. The callus irritated him. She rubbed him this way for a few minutes and then began to thrash about against him.

She put her breast on his nose. "Do you have a hard-on, Leo?" she asked sweetly.

"I have a soft-off."

She put her hand back on his penis. "Take my ear in your mouth," he said. She took his ear in her mouth. "Don't suck it, for Christ's sake—you'll break the eardrum." She became gentler. "Can you now, Leo?" she asked in a little while. "Will you try?"

"All right," he said, "I'll try." He rolled on top of her. "It doesn't fit."

"Here," she said.

"I'm not in."

"Sure you are."

He moved back and forth a few times. "I'm slipping out."

"Ahh. Ahh. Oh, Leo."

"You're too dry."

"*Ahhgghhrr*," she shuddered.

"Play with my back," he said.

"Leo, come back. Leo? All right," she said, "I know. Let's stand up." They stood up.

"Stop. You're breaking it off."

"Let's sit on the side of the bed."

"No. The color television."

"Leo, we'll break it—and the tubes get too hot. Let's stand on the dresser."

"Let's sit in the chest of drawers."

"Leo, what are you doing?"

"Where's the air-conditioning vent?"

"The air-conditioning vent?"

"Where is it?"

"There, on the floor. Near the chair. What are you doing?"

"I'm sitting down. Ohh," he said. "Oh boy, *Arghhrr*."

"Let *me* try."

"Wait till I'm through. *Ahhghh*. Wow."

"Leo, you'll catch cold. Nothing's worse than a summer cold. Leo?"

"Oh boy."

"Leo, please, let's get in bed." She pulled him up and they got into bed. Feldman turned onto his stomach. "Leo," she said after playing with his back for a few minutes, "try to catch me."

"All right."

"Close your eyes." He heard her get out of the bed. "Count to fifty."

"All right."

"Don't start counting until I tell you." Her voice came from across the room; she was sitting on the air conditioning. "You can start counting now, Leo. Leo? Are you counting?"

"What?"

"Are you counting?"

"You woke me up."

"Oh, Leo!"

She got back into bed. "You're hard now, Leo. Come in me."

"All right."

"Oh, Leo, you're so hard now."

"I have to pee."

"Oh, Leo. Oh. Oh. Oh, that's wonderful, Leo. Oh."

"Where's the Kleenex?"

"Oh. Oh."

"There's only three left. How can you let the Kleenex get so low?"

"Oh, I love you, Leo. I love you."

"All right."

"I did something, Leo. It's the first time. It was wonderful."

"Been quite a night for you. First your own program on the TV and now this."

"You do something too, Leo. You do something now too."

He flipped out of her and rolled off. "Can't cut the mustard," he said philosophically, putting his hands behind his head.

"I'm sorry, dear," Lilly said. "It's been wonderful these last months. You've been marvelous to us. To Billy and me. So relaxed."

"Yes."

"Things must be going well at the store."

"Very nicely."

"See? It doesn't do any good to worry."

"Maybe you're right."

"Leo?"

"Yes?"

"Did you know that I've been worried lately?"

"No. I didn't know that."

"I tried not to show it."

"Well, it worked."

"But it's all right. I found out today it's all right."

"That's good."

"It's my callus. I went to see Freedman about it."

"Best not to play around with these things—Freedman?"

"Yes, and do you know, Leo, that man looked at me in the queerest way."

"You took your callus to Freedman?"

"It was absolutely embarrassing, Leo. He tested me for syphilis."

"He tested you for—oh no—he t-test—tee hee—tested you for syph-ha-ha-lis?"

"You'd think he never saw a callus before."

"She saw Freedman. She took her callus to Freedman." Feldman laughed. He roared. He threw his right hand up in the air and laughed harder.

"Leo, what is it?"

"F-F-Freedman," he sputtered. "Freed*man*," he guffawed. "Freeeeeeman," he sniggered. He tittered and giggled and snickered and chuckled and cackled and chortled. "*F-F-Freeeedman!*" He couldn't stop laughing, and as he laughed his erection grew. It became enormous. It was the biggest hard-on he had ever had. Lilly, astonished, pulled him on top of her greedily. Laughing, he rocked and shook himself into an orgasm.

The next morning he still had to laugh every time he thought about it. His eyes teared and his nose ran. Once, during a sales conference, he actually slapped his knee in his mirth like a vaudeville farmer. It was the best laugh of his life, persistent as the symptom of a cold. When he tried to work, the throught of Freedman and Lilly kept getting in the way and he had to lay aside whatever he was doing. The people around him, Miss Lane and some of the executives and buyers, had never seen him this way, but his laughter was so infectious that they had to join him, laughing the harder because they didn't know the joke. Possessed by his laughter, he made a decision—he would remember this laughter and try always to be happy.

Then, riding the escalator up to the third floor when he returned from lunch, he saw something that made him stop laughing. A girl he had sent to the abortionist was mulling over some handkerchiefs at a counter. And as he peered through the crowd he recognized others he had seen in his basement.

"Oh, hi," a young man said to him on the fourth floor. It was the lad for whom he had obtained the prescription.

On a sofa in the furniture department, sitting there as if the thing already belonged to her, was a lady for whom he had obtained a black-market baby. She nodded to him as he went by and fumbled with her pocketbook as if she meant to show him a picture of the child. He hurried to an elevator to take him the rest of the way up to his regular office. How had they come up? He wondered. Why weren't they in the basement? What were they doing this high in his store?

Sure enough, when he stepped into the elevator, there was the man he had sent to the queers.

17

"What would you do if a hole opened up in that wall?" Bisch asked.

"That couldn't happen," Feldman said warily. "How could that happen?"

"No, I mean it. Suppose a hole, big enough for a man to go through, suddenly opened up in our cell wall. What would you do?"

"The exercise yard's right outside, Bisch."

"Yes, but suppose it wasn't? Suppose the cell wall was the only thing between you and the outside. Suppose it was light shift and all the guards had rushed to the other side of the prison to put out a fire, and the heat traveling in waves along the wall made this cell so hot you couldn't stand it, so hot in fact that a hole was melted in the wall. What would you do?"

"What would *you* do, Bisch?"

"I'd try to save my life."

"You'd go through the hole?"

"Self defense," Bisch said.

"Then what would you do?"

"I'd go around to the other side of the prison and turn myself in," Bisch said. "And you?"

"So would I."

"Yes, but suppose the guards are so busy fighting the fire that

261

no one can get to the main gate to let you back in? And suppose it turns cold, below freezing, and you know that all you have to do to get warm is just go down the mountain a few thousand feet? What would you do?"

"I'd go down the few thousand feet," Feldman said.

"You would?"

"To the first house."

"Ain't no houses down there."

"To the *first* house. Sooner or later I'd come to one. Now then, what would *you* do?"

"I'd do the same."

"What would you do when you got to the house?"

"I'd go inside and wait until I thought the fire was out. Then I'd come back."

"You wouldn't turn yourself over to the owner and demand that he make a citizen's arrest?"

"Goddamnit," Bisch said angrily, "you wouldn't either. You made that up."

"Of course I would, Bisch."

"You wouldn't. That's unrealistic."

"Oh, it is, is it?" Feldman said. "But it's not unrealistic I suppose when you tell me you'd go around to the main gate and turn yourself in to a guard. That's *not* unrealistic. The only difference is one's a paid enforcer and the other isn't. Why, *your* notion of justice is that it's of concern only to the professional. You don't care a fig about law and order for its own sake, do you?"

"Wait a minute. I didn't say that."

"You as good as said it."

Bisch was silent. Then, in a low voice, he asked what Feldman meant to do about it. It was a trap: if he said he was going to report him, Bisch would lean on him, but if he told him to forget it, he would be admitting to exactly the sort of indifference Bisch was trying to maneuver him into confessing.

"I haven't got enough to go on yet," he told him finally, "but a few more slips like that last one, Bisch, and I'll have you dead to rights."

Bisch ground his teeth and glared. It *had* been a trap, Feldman saw, though Bisch returned to his bunk, accepting defeat.

It was the sort of conversation that was sweeping the prison. For three months—since, in fact, the strange assembly in which Warden Fisher had first articulated his vigilante policy—the talk in the exercise yards, in the shops, in the discussion groups, everywhere the men gathered, had exactly this quality of probing hypothetical situations, fussy as boys challenging each other to spend a billion dollars. Most of it was just "making warden's mouths," as even the most pious convicts conceded. The warden himself, overhearing one of their voices raised in virtue when he passed, would respond with a wry smile, knowing as the expression of a parent come into a noisy bedroom now peaceful with the counterfeit deep breathing of sleep. (Assumed zealousness became a source for certain wicked jokes daringly told by one convict to another. One story—Feldman had had to read it in the warden's column of the prison newspaper—was about a convict serving a short sentence, caught stealing food from the kitchen. Asked what he was up to, he replied, "The cook's a lifer. I don't trust him." He was caught again some months later in the visiting room, making love to the cook's wife. "How many times do I have to tell you?" he said. "I just don't trust that damn cook.")

Hypocrisy flourished and became a sort of virtue, but warden's mouths or no, the prison rules had never operated so efficiently. It was almost impossible, for example, to find a Fink who would still help you through the loopholes for a few cigarettes, although the new policy had created in effect another loophole. Because the legitimacy of permission slips and passes was seldom questioned now, one began to feel a positive virtue for being grounded in details and honorably fulfilling the small procedures of prison function. Feldman sometimes wondered if this, rather than the announced object of rooting out the bad men, might not actually be in the back of "Warden's Mind" (a branch of a sort of speculative philosophy among certain prisoners). Despite himself, even Feldman felt a certain pride in knowing the guards knew he was where he was supposed to be. But if the atmosphere was now a little freer and the prisoners had less to fear from the warden and the guards, they had more to fear from each other. The new policy had shifted the tensions from between prisoners and keepers to between kept and kept.

More than once Feldman had tried to get Bisch to suggest that they drop their pursuit of each other, but the man treated these moves as further maneuvers, and always they had to return to their silly game. Feldman had even told Bisch some overzealous convict jokes that he made up himself, but while Bisch laughed, he never offered to tell Feldman any stories of his own, and Feldman, suspecting Bisch might use these jokes against him, decided he couldn't risk telling him others. Their strategies spiraled.

Only one time, and that to his cost, had Feldman, weary of their duel, spoken forthrightly. Bisch, obviously trying to tempt him into an open declaration of his feelings, had told him that he personally knew of a conspiracy to break jail. "Oh, come on, Bisch," Feldman had said. "Grow up. If you know about a jail-break, either blow the whistle on the guys who are planning it or keep it to yourself. Don't tell me about it. I've only got four months before I get out of here. Why would *I* get involved in something like that?"

"Oh, so you admit it. You *want* to get out."

"Well, Jesus, Bisch, of course I want to get out."

"It doesn't make any difference at all to you whether you've paid your debt to society or not. I'll remember that one when your time comes."

"What do you mean 'when my time comes'?"

"Never mind," Bisch said, and from his guilty blush Feldman realized he hadn't been joking. "Never mind," Bisch repeated, "the important thing is that you're unregenerate."

"I'm not unregenerate," Feldman said.

"Oh ho, sure not."

"I'm not."

"Tell it to the Marines."

"I'm regenerate," Feldman said.

It was how, he realized finally, he had to speak, and in a way, because he dared not speak otherwise, he *was* regenerate.

With others, of course, he was equally wary. Even with the bad men Walls and Sky and Flesh, he was cautious, and with Herb Mix, the bad man who attached himself to Feldman in the exercise yard. (Where, Feldman noticed, the bad men continued to jump about erratically, just as he had seen them do that first time from his cell. He himself, concentrating on imitating the more normal walks of the other convicts so as not to call attention to himself, sometimes found the restraint too great, the sheer watchful concentration too difficult, and would often start abruptly forward, making the disturbing movement of a man bolting in sleep.) But bad men had little to hope for from vigilanteeism. The paroles such tactics might bring others would not be given them, and one might have supposed that they would have fewer occasions, since they had less need, to make warden's mouths. They made them anyway, at least in the canteen when there were convicts to overhear them. At these times Feldman, who had adopted a somewhat different approach with the bad men than the one he took with

Bisch, would go about his business, paying no heed to their absurd challenges of him. If pushed too far, he might stop and call out to the convicts in the canteen, "You men see what I'm doing. You're my witnesses. See me work. See me fill your orders and make change and keep the books and dust the shelves."

In certain respects, nevertheless, he was a real offender against the new system. An astonishing news item appeared in the prison paper:

NATION'S 2ND OLDEST CONVICT REVEALS BRIBERY PLOT

Ed Slipper, this country's second oldest living convict now serving time in a federal or state prison, voluntarily disclosed to Warden's Office Thursday the existence of thirty-two dollars and forty cents in his personal savings account at the prison. Slipper, the last of whose relatives died many years ago, has admitted that up until eight months ago he had no scource of outside income whatever for several years, and that the money has been accumulating in his account due to direct deposits by the business associates of Leo Feldman, a fellow inmate and "bad man" sentenced to one year's incarceration here.

Slipper charged that the money had been put into his account on Feldman's insistence, and that in return he was to render Feldman such services as Feldman saw fit to require of him, and to impart whatever informations affecting Feldman that he as trusty might be privy to.

Slipper, who is himself a "bad man" but who was, in accordance with prison custom and policy, declared an "ancient" and made trusty on his seventy-fifth birthday, insists that he has made use of only seven dollars and sixty cents of the forty dollars placed in his account in eight monthly five-dollar installments. He declared that he has rendered Feldman no services and that he asked Feldman to stop the checks months ago but that Feldman declined. (At present no machinery exists whereby a convict can turn down monies deposited to his account by an outside source, though Warden's Office has revealed that a rule to that effect is now being considered as a result of this case.)

Slipper has asked that the funds be turned over to the prison infirmary for the purchase of additional medicines.

An editorial in the same edition offered commentary on the affair and disclosed some surprising additional facts:

ROOM FOR IMPROVEMENT

That the moral atmosphere of this institution has markedly improved, no one who has witnessed the changes of the past few months can doubt. Yet there remain certain private pockets of pollution which, for all that, smell the worse and offend the more.

A recent fact-finding committee, charged with bringing to light vestigial episodes of corruption among the prisoners at this institution, has stated that while exact figures are unavailable, there is considerable evidence to support a conservative assertion that at least two dozen permission slips are still forged monthly, along with a like number of passes; that while absenteeism is down forty-seven percent, a check with the infirmary has revealed that only eighty-one percent of the current absenteeism is legitimate; that there are perhaps two or three warden's-flag missions subverted to private ends each month; and that there are even now a handful of convicts who do not observe the proper seating arrangements in the dining hall. All this, capped by the recent frightful disclosure of attempted bribery in the Feldman/Slipper case, demonstrates that some—if admittedly only a few—convicts still seek to exploit their position.

Some good signs are likewise in the wind, of course. The same blue-ribbon committee has reported that attendance is up in Warden's Forest and that on the whole most cons have responded encouragingly to Warden Fisher's assembly plea that they keep a closer check on each other, but these ameliorating factors are tainted by the discouraging persistence of even a "little" corruption. Once again, the few bad apples have spoiled the barrel, and many are made to suffer for the mistakes of a few self-style "privileged" characters. It is no accident, of course, that the bribery attempt, long known to Warden's office but only just now revealed by Slipper himself, was the work of a bad man. Perhaps the sad statistics in the committee's report are *largely* the responsibility of bad men. Perhaps, too, Feldman himself will be discovered to

xactly how much time he had yet to serve. He knew that
  three weeks would be added on to his sentence because
   time he had remained in his cell before asking for an as-
   ent, and perhaps he owed an additional week for other days
   nd there. He had not bookkept his year well. He was wait-
   w for the official Statement of Remaining Obligation a pris-
   eceived when he had just twelve weeks to go.)
is decision to lie low was consonant with the preparations
   s making to renew his life on the outside. He wrote some
   s to Lilly and even to Billy, though no replies came. He began
   o direct inquires to the executives at his store—most, like
   an, had left when he went to prison, while others, seeing a
   e to improve their position, had stayed on and taken the
   ters' places—but their replies, he discovered, held little in-
   for him. He had to force himself to follow the figures and
   ed reports in the letters. He began to speculate about selling
   ore outright or merging it with one of the other department
   s, and he wrote to his vice-president, asking him to look
   d for buyers. The reply came from Miss Lane:

)ear Mr. Feldman:

*Mr. Nichols is on holiday now with his family, and due to
he highly confidential nature of your inquiry, I thought it best
o keep your letter here awaiting his return, and in the mean-
ime to offer you some of my own thoughts about this matter.
f I am out of line, Mr. Feldman, I hope you will understand
hat I make these remarks out of a sense of deep loyalty to you
nd to your store.*

*I think I know how terrible this past year must have been
'or you, how very frightful imprisonment would be for anyone
like yourself, who has lived apart from violence and viciousness
all his life. I have seen a drawn gun but one time in my life—
I mean the time that detective came into your office to arrest
you—and although I am not a cowardly woman, my mind still
registers the terror of that shock. A pistol! Loaded and pointed
at a man who, whatever his faults, would never have offered
physical opposition! Surely the guns of justice are no less dangerous and insulting than the guns of chaos. That you would
never draw one yourself, I know as certainly as that there was
never any wild anger in you, but only an experimental sort of
cruelty and a will that sought resistance where there was none
to be found—in the market place. (And now I think that maybe*

have contributed even more to these statis
known. Where there's smoke, there's fire.

Meanwhile, it is only fair that we app
for his recent revelations, however belated
been. It is pertinent too, at this juncture, t
frankness of others. Only with the cooper
lant population can this prison move clos
and goals articulated for it by its administ

As yet, there have been no purges h
prisoners themselves, and while history in
climate of purge is often sticky, we would
that it has always been stickiest for the gu

Feldman flushed a greasy permission sli
while Bisch slept. He even wrote a letter to the e
paper:

> *Dear Sir:*
> *All that was almost eight months ago, whe*
> *this prison for barely more than a month. As Ed*
> *has said, no good ever came to me from the ar*
> *if I sought advantage none was realized. I hav*
> *changed greetings with Mr. Slipper for the past*
> *if my "business associates," as your reporter c*
> *continued to deposit money to the old man's acco*
> *no secret, I think, that I am a wealthy man as i*
> *that I can well afford it. Indeed, I did not stop t*
> *these last six months simply because, advantage*
> *I realized that he could use the money. While I*
> *fondness for Ed Slipper, his great age alone demar*
> *(as does his status as an "ancient" of this instit*
> *son's own term for him), and I can assure you th*
> *nothing darker than sympathy that has motivate*
> *uance of those funds. Now that I learn he means*
> *over to the infirmary for the purchase of medicin*
> *continue these contributions.*

Although Feldman destroyed this letter, he f
of the expressions in it revealed an indignation
felt. He knew it was best, however, to keep it
generally to lie low. There were only about four m
on his sentence, and then he would be freed. (Act

*you have finally found it. In the prison, in the rifles of the
guards forever pointed and loaded as in some eternal stick-up.
In the bars of your cell, in the stone and steel and lead and
leather—that vicious handful of the fierce old elements of the
civil world. Am I right?)*

I am sorry for you, Mr. Feldman, and I read your letter
offering to put your store up for sale, and I despair. Believe me
when I tell you it is not concern for my job that makes me bold
now. I know my value (if you never did: I recall with pleasure
the time you tried to reduce my salary, your suggestion when
I was still green that I be paid by the job, by the pages actually
typed, so much per letter, per envelope, per licked stamp, per
search in the files, per appointment made, per telephone call
taken in your absence, per staple driven true—oh, there were
so many. I recall all our agreements—my counterproposals and
yours. That was a combat!), and I know that I could get another
job tomorrow. (Did you know, speaking of combat, that I stole
from you? That I used my position as your private secretary to
obtain merchandise for which I never paid? I tell you this in
writing because I know that in our state a convict may not bring
suit against anyone on the basis of evidence obtained while he
was in prison. Don't worry. I said I knew my value, and all I
ever took was by way of closing the gap between that value and
what you paid me. And that at list prices, so you're still ahead,
or rather, we're exactly even because I probably owe you something for the charm of the arrangement, and even at that I may
still be ahead, for I would owe you something, too, for the se-
crecy, the thrill of the guerrilla risk, the absurdity and outland-
ishness.)

There are some around here—your "executives," your department heads, your lawyers—who say that you have marred
your image with the public, that not understanding the terms
of your crime, they will be unable to come to this store and feel
uncheated. I have heard Mr. Nichols make the very suggestion
to Mr. Ray that you make in your letter: that the store be sold
or merged, at the very least that its name its name be changed.
I hope you never agree to this. I know what went on in that
basement. (I came in clothes you had never seen, in a veil—
which, it happens, was merchandise I obtained from your store
under false pretenses. I disguised my voice and told you that to
earn money I meant to become a call girl, and asked if you
would put me in touch with any contacts you might have. You

*told me that the big money was in dirty photographs and tried
to talk me into buying an ordinary box camera and doing a
series of indecent poses for a "family album" because that was
more appealing, more intimate and dirtier than the ordinary
studio shots, you said. You even wanted to sell me the "corners"
so I could mount the photographs myself when they came back
from the drugstore in your physician's building, where you said
they'd develop them.) And I don't see the harm. (And don't you
see? You're not the only one who needs freedom, and to be kept
alive by the sense of the special. The woods are full of us.)*

*Anyway, I hope you reconsider your idea about selling the
store. The world is getting to be a terrible place, and I don't
know if it's your kind or their kind who make it more awful,
but if we must have terror, let it be gay and exciting, I say.*

*I know you may fire me for this letter, but if you sell the
store I don't care anyway.*

Yours in Crime,
Silvia Lane

Feldman fired her. He wrote Billing a confidential letter to ask
if she had a charge account at the store. She did, and he assumed
that she would continue to use it. Figuring what she had been
worth to him over the years at his figures, he subtracted this
amount from his estimate of what *she* might have figured she was
worth to him at her figures. Her figure was seven percent higher
than his; she had been with him nine years, so she owed him, he
guessed, $4,410. In a second confidential letter from Billing he
learned that on the average she spent about $640 a year in his
store. This, with her employee's discount of twenty percent, represented $800 in purchases. Now that she was no longer with the
store she would lose the discount, and so he wrote Billing a third
confidential letter, asking them to research what single girls of
Miss Lane's approximate age and income and educational background could be expected to spend with him each year. The answer that came back was $500. She would be sore at him for firing
her, of course, but he knew that buying habits, once established,
were as strong as instincts. Say she spent only $400 a year. Round
off the $4,410 she owed him to $4,400. He could get his money
back, hiking her bills at the rate of fifty percent a year. It would
take work. Sooner or later someone as efficient as Miss Lane
would wonder why she was paying $600 a year for only $400
worth of merchandise. Carrying charges. (Beautiful things could

be done with carrying charges.) Nickel-and-diming her on every bill. Here and there a really gross mistake in his favor. Occasional charges for items never purchased. Then some really flashy stuff with her credits if she objected. The rest to be done with seconds, damaged goods and the clever substitution of inferior merchandise. It would take work, all right, and patience, but the important thing was that it could be done. Of course, it meant that he could not sell his store for twenty-two years, but if that's what it meant, that's what it meant. She wanted combat? He'd give her combat.

In the prison, however, he was never more docile. He had gone underground. He tightened his belt and became a very Englishman of austerity. Realizing how close he was to being discharged—his Statement of Remaining Obligation was sent from the state capital on the same day he received an answer to his last letter to Billing—he regarded the time he spent there more bitterly than ever. He no longer speculated about Warden's Mind or the meaning behind the sytem. Nor did he seek advantage. (In a way, he was actually grateful to Ed Slipper for exposing him. If Slipper had still been under an obligation to him, even one the old man did not acknowledge, he might have felt compelled to extract it, might have done something that would get him into trouble. The trick now was to stay out of trouble.)

When one day he awoke with what he was certain was a fever, he panicked. Suppose he was wrong, he reasoned. Suppose he reported to the infirmary and had no temperature—he would be charged a day for goldbricking. Suppose, on the other hand, he reported for work and the fever cut into his efficiency. Suppose he made a mistake; why, they would charge him for that too. Weeks could be added to his term. The percentage player would report to the infirmary, but suppose the fever had clouded his reason and he wasn't reading the percentages clearly. What was he to do? In the end he decided—perhaps unreasonably; he was aware of that—that one ought not arrive at a decision and then, simply on the basis of some estimated margin for error, reverse that decision. But again, could he say he had *arrived* at a decision when he was only *inclined* toward one? What *was* he to do? What?

Eventually he went to the infirmary. His temperature was 102, and they put him to bed. Weak, feverish, feeling as if he would throw up, pains in his arms, his legs, all he could think of was that it was good time, perfect in fact, that it couldn't be counted against him: that he was safest as a sick man. He resented the medications but took them obediently, unwilling to give any trouble which could boomerang. He thought it a hideous irony that perhaps the very medicines he took to make him well enough to return to that part of the prison where the dangers were might have been purchased with the funds he had given to Slipper.

In three days he was well enough to be discharged, and was granted an additional half day of "soft duty" to be performed in and about his cell. He was as grateful for the three and a half days he had gained as some other man might have been for a long, paid vacation. But he was careful not to appear too happy, lest his happiness be counted against him.

Indeed, his expression was now one of intense disengagement. He could have been one of those stone-faced palace guards whom tourists try to ruffle for a photograph. He performed all his duties—even those which he had once found loathsome, like scrubbing the toilet bowl or, in the canteen, fetching the petty items the prisoners requested and ringing up the petty sales— with a determination that rose from the bedrock of the will. In the exercise yard he counseled his body like a fight manager, and with the effort of a trained athlete, managed to get through his now near-perfect mimes of the ordinary strolls and walks and pacings of the unmarked convicts. Only he knew how much he sweated. (Perhaps it was this that had brought him down sick before, and unwilling to risk the disease again for fear that he might not have temperature the next time—sure, immunities, antibodies and unhealth's diminishing returns—he let up a little, allowing his body those occasional epileptic leaps of character that he had formerly feared.)

He went to the movies when they were shown, and paid careful attention to the plots for fear that a disarmed answer to a guard's or fellow prisoner's question about the film might be taken amiss and register a chain of consequences that he would live to regret. He devoured the prison newspaper for the same reason, and familiarized himself with every notice on every bulletin board. (Confronted from time to time with some strange new obligation—"Prisoners not involved themselves with intramural athletics are nevertheless required to pick a sport and a team, and to familiarize themselves with the records of all the players on that team"—he never speculated as to meanings. Meaning was beside the point; only performance mattered.) He memorized his table assignments as if the numbers had been state secrets and he a spy, and because prisoners were encouraged to have interests as well as duties, he participated in a hobby club, joylessly teaching himself to make irrelevant little leather and wooden artifacts. He took special care to be in the right place at the right time, rushing to his cell long before lockup, conspicuously present at each major census four times a day and at most of the minor ones on each half-hour.

Yet for all his attention to detail, for all the assiduity which the prospect of his release provoked in him, he never became what could be called a "model prisoner." He had none of the cheerfulness of such men, nothing of their dopey good will. Even this was calculated, for he anticipated the effect that such falseness might have on others. (And by "others" he meant *everyone*.) Instead, he sought to impart a sense of performance without eagerness, a careful balance of going through motions and touching all bases. (Ironically, he behaved exactly as a good cop would who neither hated nor cared for his suspects.) This, of course, made him vulnerable too, and he was aware of the dimensions of that vulnerability, knowing that he must appear to them exactly as he was, keeping nothing of himself in reserve, his distaste for his plight obvious, the desperation behind his willingness to do his job clear to anyone. In short, his eagerness, though it was the reverse eagerness of a model prisoner, was clearly visible. Anyone could see it. Yet it was his only feasible choice: tight-faced to walk the tightrope, his discomfort and hatred public as a monument. If this were a lying low it was a lying low with his head visible, his bald spot bright as a bull's-eye.

Besides, there was still the notoriety of the bad-man crap: news items about him in the paper, editorials, the book of his life a public record in the library, his club the only one disbanded by a warden's fiat in thirty-five years, the semi-sent-to-Coventry treatment from the other prisoners, whose only remarks to him since Warden's Assembly had smacked of command, distinctly like the no-nonsense exchanges between officers and men. Why, he had not had conversation as such in months. (And now that he thought of it, when *had* he had it? When had he last listened to someone else or spoken to offer an opinion that another might take or leave alone? He had always been in Coventry. He could not remember a time when he hadn't been, though again, now that he thought of it, he had listened to Miss Lane's letter, reading it over to see what she thought. Then he fired her.) How low, then, *could* he lie? But despite their ominous interest in him, he behaved the deaf-mute, a pretended mantle of invisiblity as fastidiously assumed as ever any by some discreet serving man in the presence of his quarreling masters. *That* was it. Of course! They had turned him into a nigger, and he had learned to live under threat, a quality of last-hired, first-fired doom dogging his steps and days.

It was what had made the time fly until Warden's Assembly. And afterwards, it was what had slowed it down. When he first arrived at the penitentiary, each threat, its manifestation specific but its source veiled—the warden's early aggressions and the contempt of the guards, the appearance of the blue fool suit on the cot in his cell, the discovery of the Feldman books in the library, solitary confinement—had posed a problem for him and created an interest that rose to meet it like the love of truth rising to meet fact. Time raced. Later, when he had learned to identify the source, the episodes became indistinct, and it stood still. Yet everything had involved waiting, and everything had been exciting. But for what had he waited? For them to make good on their bad-man talk. And they hadn't. They *hadn't*. Now, he realized, they would have to get him soon or miss him forever. They would have to get him at once. (Though he didn't intend to search for meaning, it occurred to him that maybe this was what it was all about: to do him a favor, to excite him, to distract him, to *make* time race.) Now, for the first time, he realized that he had never been beaten up. It seemed astonishing. No guard had made his nose bleed, no cons had punched him! A blow in the chest, and his homunculus could dislodge, rupturing his heart. They knew that, but nothing had happened. Nothing. Only a physical disaster would have meant anything. Blows, pain counted. Death did. (Boredom would have been unbearable, but it wouldn't have mattered, and anxiety was interesting, and it hadn't mattered.) Only a physical catastrophe. Only that.

And if only that, then only at the *end* of the year, when he had served out his sentence. Only then. The sons of bitches. The fuckers. The sons of bitches. (And anxiety *did* count. It wasn't interesting after all, and terror, this kind, the fear of death, was boring. The dread of pain was. Only that.) Only then. Only *after* the year of shit. They'd had him. They'd had him all along. The bastards. The sons of bitches. The bastards. They had him now. Feldman the sucker, the supersalesman supersold. Suddenly he was very afraid. Oh God, he prayed, call the police! Get my lawyer! Call the Better Business Bureau! I want my money back!

Life had never been so dear to him. He prized his past. He knew he must write letters to his lawyers to tell them what he suspected. (Suspected? What he *knew*.) But even more urgent was his need to remember his life, to have it in some formal way. He began again to write letters to Lilly. These were different from the others, which had been merely domestic patter, bland household inquiries—devices, really, for starting his life up again. Now his letters contained minutely detailed and loving descriptions of what they both knew: an exact picture of their living room, their entrance hall, the flowers in their garden, the equipment in their kitchen, what hung in a closet, all the meals he could remember, an account of their television-viewing for a week—along with whatever he could recall about the plots and the songs or the reasons a particular guest had appeared before a panel. He described their furniture and the meaning of all the random jottings and stray numbers that lay beside their telephones. He wrote about Billy's toys and the look of their pantry, and recalled to her pieces of conversations between them, arguments, brief passages of affection. He told her he loved her, asked for her prayers and pled for her help in keeping him alive.

To his lawyers he sent dispatches outlining his apprehensions, desperately offering them reasons which seemed, on paper, always more paltry than they actually were. He told about the poor bargain he'd made, how they had extracted the last penny of his debt to society, for a year keeping him on his toes with their dark menace, only to kill him at the end, compounding the interest, usurers, fiends. Most of these letters he destroyed, but others, equally strident, he sent, hoping, in his despair, to trigger an adjustment of some powerful judicial balance. He reasoned that he had shown restraint when he had destroyed the bulk of the letters and that this entitled him to use those that remained. If the lawyers could know how circumspect he had been, they would give more weight to the letters that got through—a point he felt obliged to include as an addendum to a final letter he was sending.

He was addressing this when Bisch, studying him from where he lay on his cot, spoke out. "You sure been having yourself a correspondence lately."

"One of the signs of rehabilitation," Feldman said automatically, "is a con's interest in sending and receiving mail."

"Sure," Bisch said scornfully, "is *that* what it's all about? Rehabilitation." He laughed. Feldman thought for the first time of the censors. Of course, he thought helplessly, none of it would get through.

"Have they been reading my letters, Bisch?"

Bisch winked at him.

"But I've written the people at my store," he said urgently, as though it were Bisch he had to appease if his cries for help were to get to the lawyers, "and been getting answers. Everything I want to know."

"Is that so?" Bisch said. "Very interesting. I suppose then, now that you've taken an interest in your store, the folks back home will be expecting you."

"What do you mean? What do you mean, Bisch? Do you mean that they let those letters through just to show them I think everything's all right? Is that it? To throw them off so that when— so that if something happens to me it will seem accidental? Is that how they do it, Bisch? . . . Bisch?"

Bisch was silent, and Feldman, if anything, was grateful.

Now each moment was precious to him. Only eight weeks of his sentence remained, but he doubted he would live through them. A strange joy was born in him. He had received no word from the lawyers, save only the occasional posting of their ordinary business, and he still had not heard from Lilly. Their silence confirmed his suspicions. He was helpless, but it was this helplessness which gave him strength now. He continued his routines, behaving exactly as he had when he still believed he would be released and did not want to queer his chances by giving trouble. But now his actions came from a desire to savor those actions. Discipline acted as a sort of slow motion on his days, giving him a chance (because he knew where he would be at a given time and what he would be doing) to anticipate, to go over in his imagination exactly what such and such a motion would feel like when he made it, what a particular gesture made, say, by the pencil man when he took the census (laboriously pointing now at one prisoner, now at another with the eraser end, moving his lips as he counted, licking the lead with a thick, slow tongue) would seem like to him when it happened. He prophesied the sounds of machinery starting up and faint individual smells, then softly laughed when they occurred, like a listener appreciating a story whose punch line he has foreseen.

It went on and on like this, and the next time he looked at a calendar he had just over six weeks left, and the time after that just over five, though the time between seemed like a year. It had worked. What he had felt for his furniture he felt now for the bars of his cell, for the counter in the canteen, the lunches of cold cuts they served on Sundays, the bluish flicker of the light in the TV room. And all life, all history, what he had been, what he was now, the stars and everything in books, all the wars that had ever happened, the reason behind things he never questioned, the facts about electricity and the skeletons of beasts and the mystery of God, were contained for him in the few drops of soapy water he felt this moment splash on the back of his hand as he dipped his scrub bush into the pail beside him and scrubbed and prayed to the floor of his cell.

And the next time he looked, he had three weeks left, three weeks before they would kill him, and it seemed as if only yesterday there had been eight. Oh God, he thought, I blew five weeks. Oh Jesus, they cheated me again!

18

They nailed him in the canteen on a Tuesday evening one week before he was scheduled to get out.

Come with us, Feldman, he had dreamed. Men outside his cell, he had dreamed. *I get out in a few days. Go yourselves. Take Bisch. Go with them, Bisch. Come,* he had dreamed, *with us, Feldman. No. Your plan won't work. The warden knows what you're up to.* Then a prisoner had put his hands on the bars of Feldman's cell and drawn the door wide. *Come with us. Who left that open?* he asked, he had dreamed. And yelled he dreamed, *Jailbreak! Jailbreak!* And another prisoner came in to get him. They took, he dreamed, him to the basement of Warden's Quarters, and strapping him in, punched him to death in the electric chair.

What happened was not like this, or, rather, only a little like it. Their posse presence seemed the same, their faces and the dark look of delegation on them, of caucused principle, passionate as the decision of revolutionaries in the street. Also familiar was the queer propriety of their approach, their almost touching courtesy, so that looking at them, he could tell from their shyness, from their air of an up-the-sleeve fate in reserve, that these were merely agents, lumpish younger brothers, and that others would deal with him.

"Come with us, please," one said softly. (You knew he really wanted to shout it.) "We're putting you on trial. There's going to be a kangaroo court." (And you knew this one had already said too much, exceeded his authority. The others stared at him in shushing shock. Feldman's heart dived. Aw, shit, he thought, it's planned. If he can make mistakes, it's planned. What chance have I?)

A guard came into the canteen and shoved through the men crowding the room. "Listen, Sky," he said, "it's almost closing. Start straightening up in here. Get these guys out."

"There's going to be a kangaroo court," Feldman said. "They're taking me off."

"Did you hear me, Sky? Walls, Flesh? Start cleaning up."

"They're taking me off."

The guard looked at him. "Up yours," he said.

Just so. Up mine.

They took Feldman back to his cellblock, walking openly through the corridors, Feldman himself actually setting the pace, the outraged stride of brisk business, of one challenged, leading his accusers to the place where his side of the story would be verified (having decided to show assurance, making not warden's mouths this time but Feldman's faces).

A hundred men, it seemed, were waiting for them. Prisoners from other cellblocks stood in the cement court between the cells. Doors were open, just as they had been in his dream, and the convicts had pulled their cots out onto the apron of the cells, where, lolling on them, they seemed like sleepless tenants before their apartment buildings on a hot night. There was a peculiar intimacy of emergency about the scene, of shifted rhythms and lives suddenly changed by, say, a power failure. Even Feldman could feel the good will, the fresh democratic air of the place, the sense of some newmade first-name basis. Bags of potato chips were broken out, cups of soda shared. Only Feldman they stared at with a fixed, rote stoniness. (Now he had slowed down, letting the others lead him. He would soon be with leaders, and the thought of this was not unpleasant. He sensed them before he saw them—suspicioned before he heard it their special articulateness, imagining labor leaders, officers commissioned in the field, and counted on the edge of natural aristocracy in them.) As he went by the men in the corridor he triggered their silences, set off their concentration, so that at last it seemed only he himself could be heard, moving like fire along the fuse of their attention. They brought him finally before a dozen or so men at the end of the cellblock. It was immensely interesting to see who was in on his fate, as though his life had been a mystery or detective story, and now, just before the end, he was to be regaled with solutions, satisfy curiosity in a last sumptuous feast of truth.

But there was no time to savor the irony of his various betrayers. "Get him dressed," one of them said, and Feldman felt himself deftly turned by the young convict at his side, elbow-urged back up the corridor they had just come down, and guided to his cell.

"Put on those clothes," the convict said. "We'll stand in front of the bars." The deputies with whom he had come from the canteen lined up across the front of his cell, blocking him from the view of the other prisoners. Feldman turned toward his cot and saw neatly laid-out there the suit in which he had come to the prison, the very suit which he had got the buyer to bring him for his trial. Next to it was his white shirt, freshly laundered, and on top of that his tie.

"Wash in the sink before you put that stuff on," the young convict called over his shoulder. Feldman undressed, and standing over the tiny sink, soaped and scrubbed his body, then rinsed himself off and looked around for a towel. "Dry yourself with the fool suit," the young convict said. "Okay. Now get dressed."

He put on the fresh clothes. A bad sign, he thought uneasily. He wasn't superstitious; it had nothing to do with the fact that he had already been found guilty in this suit. The clothes themselves were ominous, as if dressing him like this were to give him everything they ever would of the doubt's benefit. All his respectability in his pressed suit, his fresh shirt mustering his innocence, his carefully knotted tie virtue. He knew that everyone out there had once worn clothes like these, trusted hopefully in their telling neatness, thrown themselves impeccably upon the mercy of the court. (It was just this that he feared about justice, its conscientiousness about small things, all its zealous, meaningless courtesies. It appointed lawyers and served up gourmet last suppers, final cigarettes from the warden's own pack and provided spiritual counsel that would meekly accept any insults. Patiently it abided last words and proffered blindfolds. He bitterly considered all its Greekey gifts.)

His captors escorted him back to the men at the end of the cellblock, and leaving him to stand before them, divided smoothly on either side like spear carriers in opera. Feldman faced his judges—he assumed they were his judges—indifferent now to their identities; his curiosity soured, how they figured in his fate, or that they did, was without solace for him. It was a random collection. He recognized two from the Crime Club, the sluice robber and the man who made up peoples' names for petitions. Bisch was there, and Harold Flesh. He saw the Fink who had given him his first pass, and Ed Slipper. Two of the men had once approached him to tell him their troubles, and two others he had oversold in the canteen. Three were prisoners with whom he had once shared table assignments. The librarian was there, and the convict who had stepped on his heels as they filed out after assembly. (But where were the folk heroes he had anticipated and depended on?) A few of these men had almost no connection with his life, the three with whom he had sat silently at meals; and to these he turned now, comforted somewhat by the exiguousness of their thin dealings.

"Well?" one of them said. The voice was loud, as if to make up for the rule of silence in the dining hall. Its surly clarity frightened him. "Well? What is it?"

Panicking, Feldman threw himself at once upon their mercy. "I did this bad thing and that bad thing," he said, raising his voice. "One bad thing and then another. Then I found Christ, and Christ saved me."

"All right, stow it," another of his table partners said, coming forward. "These are the ground rules. Court's in session till a verdict, but we've got to be out here in three days. These are the cover stories: an epidemic's broken out, and they had to shut us off from the rest of the prison. There's a riot up here, and the warden's closed off the area until it can be brought under control. We took no hostages except a few trusties, so the strategy is to starve us out. Neither story will be used unless it's absolutely necessary. We stand to lose if it is. Somebody kicks back at the capital, and Warden has to throw them a few heads. It's a risk all around, but if we're out in three, nobody has to know anything. Let's get on with it."

"Get his cot for him," the librarian said.

"Somebody get Feldman's cot up here," the sluice robber said. "Jesus Christ, why wasn't that ready?"

"All right, no sweat. It takes a minute. He can stand for a minute, can't he?" the Fink said.

"Check," said the first table partner. "More ground rules. You ever sit in on a kangaroo court, Feldman?"

"No sir."

"Well, it ain't anything difficult about it. We try you. And either we find you guilty or we don't. We make up our mind on the evidence. You remember your other trial, don't you?"

"Yes sir."

"Well, think about that one. That'll give you an idea. Except we ain't lawyers, so since you ain't being prosecuted by lawyers, you ain't entitled to a lawyer to defend you. You defend yourself as best you can. Any man here wants to speak up for you, he can. Questions?"

"Rather an objection."

"Pretty early for an objection."

"Well, it's just that you say anyone who wishes to speak up for me can."

"That's correct."

"Yes. But don't you get parole credit for bringing me to trial?"

"What's in it for us ain't your business. You wouldn't be here this evening if you'd minded your business."

"I simply wished to point out that though you say you're willing to hear testimony in my behalf, there's nothing in it for anybody who might want to give it."

"What's your question?"

"That's an objection, a demurrer."

"Pretty early for an objection, too soon for a demurrer. If you have a question I'll hear it."

"May I have a change of venue?"

"No."

"No more questions," Feldman said.

"Now about punishment," the man continued. "The law in this state don't provide for capital punishment anymore, but we don't provide for anything but. If we find you guilty we kill you. One of the intramural boxers has been practicing on a tackling dummy with a knife sewn inside it and suspended just about where that little thing-ummy lies on your heart. He punches like a surgeon this guy, like a butcher. He can trim your fats or slip a bone from your flesh like you'd pull one feather from pillow. He cuts the cloth now five slams out of seven and says he'd have an even better batting average on flesh. The infirmary would put it down as a natural death."

His cot arrived and was placed in the center of the rough circle. "Go ahead, lie down if you want," one of the men who had brought it said gently. Several other cots had been lined up along the rear wall, and many of the men were already seated on them. A few were sprawled full length. Looking behind him, Feldman saw that many of the convicts had blankets and were spreading them out on the stone floor. He glanced at his cot but could not bring himself even to sit on it.

"I'd like to suggest that justice might be better served if everyone sat up straight," he said.

"Feldman's right," the librarian said. "Everybody lying down sit up straight."

It was a small point, but he had won it.

His trial began, and Feldman saw that it was to be no more formal than the introductory proceedings had been. Several men were again lying down on their cots. At times it was difficult to hear what was being said for the conversation and laughter of the convicts behind him or, for that matter, even of some of the major figures in the trial. Feldman himself had long since sat down on his cot. He was bothered, too, by the fact that he was the only one who made an effort to employ a legal vocabulary. It became literally *his* trial.

He rose to object, to challenge relevancy, to ask that certain statements be stricken from the record, even though he understood that there was no record. Technicality, however, was his only hope—to get them to acknowledge rules of procedure so that he could maneuver them into violating them and then point out the discrepancies. He knew nothing of law, save its clichés, and was aware that he sounded ridiculous, more ignorant with his smattering of courtroom jargon than even they without it. Seeing himself as parodically professional, single-minded as a vaudeville pedant, he had a momentary hope that he could win them with that. He determined to play the fool and objected more vigorously than ever.

Bisch had risen to report that once, talking in his sleep, Feldman had said that the convicts were despicable. Feldman jumped up to object. "Sirs, Your Honors, Your Magistrates," he cried.

"What is it?" one asked wearily.

"What is it? What *is* it? Why, sirs, I object, I object, sirs. I do object, on the grounds—yes, I might say literally on the *terras firmas*—that what plaintiff is saying is inadvisable, inadmissible, irrelevant and immaterial. Moreover, as per established precedent in the case of the State of New York versus Dred Scott, and the decision of Justices Driscoll, Wyatt, Jones and Fowler, only Justice Blaine abstaining, handed down in February, 1947, for which you will find the citation in that great state's *Law Record*, volume four, section seven, article fifty-two, page seven forty-six, right-hand column, lower upper-middle of the second full paragraph: 'It is unconstitutional, immaterial, irrelevant and inadmissible for evidence to be garnered from statements made in trances, stupors, comas, deliriums, tongues and dreams.' 'And *dreams*,' my sirs and lords, 'and *dreams*.' I call your attentions to the sixth item in that little list, my judges, and *your* attentions, gentlemen of the jury, peers, twelve good men and true. 'And *dreams*,' it says. 'Unconstitutional,' ergo 'immaterial,' ergo 'irrelevant,' ergo 'inadmissible.' Not to be countenanced ergo. Ergo I humbly petition that this is an improper line of testimony and that all that Mr. Bisch has just said be stricken from the record. 'Throw it out of court, Your Peerlesses. May I come up to the bench for a moment, Your Honors?'' Before anyone could answer, he leaped forward and told them all in his loudest voice that he wished to take the stand. Turning quickly toward the rest of the men he saw that they were not amused, but went on anyway. "Raise your right hand." He raised it. "Do you, Leo Feldman, solemnly swear that what you are about to say is the truth, the whole truth and nothing but the truth? Say 'I so solemnly swear it.' " "I so solemnly swear it." "Now then, proceed."

"Bisch is lying. I do not despise the convicts. I wanted to be friends with them, but they never let me. They're stuck up."

"Sit down, Feldman," the Fink shouted.

"I have asked for a ruling, Your Honor."

"What's that?"

"I have asked for a ruling on Bisch's testimony, Your Honor, on the basis of the Dred Scott decision of 1947 and the notorious Lindbergh case of 19 and 32 and the famous *cherchez la femme* precedent in the Scopes trial of 1955, only Justice William Jennings Darrow abstaining."

"Sit down, Feldman," said one of the two men who had once told Feldman their troubles.

"A decision, please. Patent pending. A ruling, sir. Yes or no, Your Honor." But the truth was, he didn't even know which of them was the judge. The people on blankets behind him had taken as much part in the proceedings as any of the men seated on cots. "Overrule or sustain. *Ooh, I hope it's sustain!*"

"Someone knock that son of a bitch down on his cot."

A convict reached up from the floor and angrily jerked him backwards. Feldman tumbled down on the man's blanket and tried to get back up again, but the convict grabbed him by his collar and squeezed his neck. "Stay put, you," he hissed.

"Only to the cot," Feldman whispered. "I only mean to get back to my cot." The man released him, and he crawled wearily back to the cot and lay there on his back, listening to the conversation and testimony go on over his head. It echoed hollowly in the stone room, as in some indoor swimming pool, and he had to concentrate in order to make out the words. Though he resisted sleep, he could not bring himself again to rise, or to play the fool, or even to counter the lies, which were now more frequent and which, in this cold enormous room, ricocheted off the walls like the rumble of cannon.

It was like being sick, having to lie there and listen. Like being on a deathbed, and their voices were his symptoms—pain, fever, falling blood count, failing pulse, clots and despondence. Now Feldman understood what he had probably understood even at first, what even the convicts understood or they would have paid more attention to forms: that what he was involved in was not a trial, not even a parody of one—that he was here in a ceremony of denouncement, a process of judgment. The single principle was that he be there with them. It resided in his body, his Feldman frame. If he were to die they would still need that, they would keep it there before them, without movement, without heartbeat, lifeless, to give point to their revilement their hate's necessary artifact and single technicality.

He knew he slept, through not from dreams. He did not dream, and awoke to the drone of denouncement, recited into the record of their gathering in the passionless, scrupulous tones of arraignment. Nothing was omitted. They laid out his year in the prison in punctilious detail, round-robining grievance like Indians, retailing sins of commission, omission, licking their snubs like wronged wives. He was denounced for food left uneaten on his tray, or for eating too much, denounced for repulsing a homosexual who had taken a fancy to him. Somehow they had found out about his struggle with the retarded Hover in the shower room, and he was denounced for that. Though he had never tried to bribe anyone but Slipper, they invented stories of others, and pictured his every transaction as a sort of graft. It was charged that he did not enjoy the movies. Bisch testified that he resented cleaning out the toilet bowl, and the librarian that he did not read good books. Amazingly, they had been able to reconstruct his masturbatory seizures in solitary confinement. "I work down there," said the man who had once tried to get him to polish the bars of his cell. "I go down to clean up the place when they let one of these birds out, and I tell you that his mattress was absolutely brittle with dried gizz. You could have snapped it in two if you turned it over. The man's a pig." One of the prisoners he had oversold in the canteen testified to his ability to sell, calling it his "power," as if it were a form of magic. Others confirmed this and cited endless tales of deprivation they had been forced to endure as a result of their purchases, referring to their hardships as if they had been hexes. Harold Flesh told how Feldman had sought their power of attorney; again a great deal was made of the word "power." It was objected that he did not care who won the athletic competition; that if he had not known that any day spent goofing off in his cell was ultimately to be added on to the end of his sentence, he would have been content to remain there for the entire year. "He was happiest in solitary, I tell you," the man who had stepped on his heels said. "He was happier asleep than awake, alone than on line in the dining hall, sick than in health."

It went on in this way for many hours, and Feldman slept more often and more fitfully. Once when he awoke in the still lighted cellblock, expecting to hear again more of their endless, inflectionless charges, he was surprised to discover that save for the heavy breathing of sleeping prisoners, the room was quiet. He sat up, rubbed his eyes and stumbled off to his cell to pee. When he returned, one of the convicts was sitting up on a blanket, staring at him. "What are you doing?" he asked.

"You missed it," Feldman said. "I just made a brilliant defense and disproved the entire case against me."

He fell asleep; when he awoke again, the convict to whom he had spoken and who, till now, had had nothing to say was charging him with having been sarcastic.

He could get no grasp on his trail. It swarmed about him, meaningless as the random arc of flies. He had no techniques to use against them—he was *powerless*—and found everything about it boring except the outcome. But always his life had been in the present, all his means temporal as the first civil responses to an emergency, and even the outcome had no reality for him now. Had he not been so bored, he might have been gay.

At about noon the next day they had taken up a new tack. They were finished with their denunciation of his antisocial behavior and had started to charge him with what they had read about him in the book of his life.

Except for the snacks that a few had brought with them they had not eaten since yesterday's evening meal, and their breath had begun to turn foul. Feldman could not stand the taste in his own mouth and went back to his cell for toothpaste. He spread this around in his mouth and rinsed it out. Then, before returning to his trial, he looked out the window. Prisoners in the exercise yard were staring up at him. The guards followed their glances. "How's it going?" Mix yelled, and a guard raised his rifle and aimed at Feldman's head.

Back at his trial he felt a little better, and when the prisoner testifying had finished, Feldman stood up. "Excuse me," he said, "I'd like to make a comment here."

"What's your comment?"

"Well, it's about all those charges about how I've behaved in prison."

"The time to make that comment was when we were on that subject," said one of the men who had sat next to him in the dining hall. "We're on a different subject now, so your comment's out of order."

"Sure," Feldman said. "Up mine."

"What's your comment?" asked the man who had told them about Hover.

"It's that the things you've charged me with—the masturbation, the bribes, my disdain for the place, almost everything—are all things you're guilty of yourselves."

"Yes. That's so. Almost everything."

"Well, doesn't that make a difference?"

"No," the man said. "It doesn't."

"The defense rests," Feldman said, and lay down again on the cot.

They went back to the book. He had never been able to bring himself to read it, and so now he listened closely. Whoever had put it together had done an incredible job. There were things he had nearly forgotten: material about his father, some of the old spiels so accurate that he could almost hear his voice. Somewhere

they had learned how he had sold his father's corpse, the old unsalable thing, and they scorned him for it, Slipper in the vanguard
of their tantrum. There was also a lot of information about how
he had put his department store together during the war, and
much about his crime in the basement. As the convicts spoke, their
voices betrayed an envy, so that it seemed to him that they rushed
through this part. How they loathed their guns just then, Feldman
thought, and despised environment, circumstance, their own low
reasons and scaled needs like the curved extrapolations on professors' graphs. But their shame would do him no good, he saw.
They turned vituperative, and for the first time since his trial had
begun there was feeling in their accusations, dactyls of rich scorn.
But astonishingly, rather than fear, he felt impatient for them to
continue, a gossip's curiosity to hear all they said he had done.

They swept back and forth, from his life at home to his life
in the department store, making all they could of his binges of
sale, times he had overwhelmed the customers, racking up enormous profits, commanding his powers, inducing his spells with
his high, perfect pitch. They recalled the time he had campaigned
to lower the employee discount from twenty to fifteen percent,
and cited occasions—he listened with a kind of queasy pride—
when he had kissed his salesgirls, felt up his models. Here their
voices had turned calm again, recounting with easy emotion familiar greed, handling offhand sin's commonplace. Feldman listened, fascinated, watching each speaker, studying not him but
his mouth as it shaped his past, as if in the swift contours of his
deeds in another man's mouth there was a clue to the spent con-
figurations of his life. They spoke from memory, but when this
failed they sometimes referred to a copy of the dog-eared, greasy
book, browsing silently for a moment and then looking up to re-
late, in their cool words, some anecdote of his viciousness.

It was four o'clock in the afternoon. Though no one had left—
could leave, the place was shut off—fatigue and hunger seemed
to have thinned their ranks. There was little fidgeting, though men
got up frequently to move toward some unlocked cell, pee, splash
water on their faces, or just to stand and stretch or walk about
the cellblock for a few moments. The trial continued without
pause, the sense of its having gone on forever, having always
existed, emphasized by the sight of the convicts who were briefly
ignoring it. Feldman saw that a distinct mood had been created
in the place, a mood not of dormitory but of lifeboat, a last-ditch

sense of equality as pervasive as the common foulness of their breath. He could lie, sit, stand, jump, run, spit, belch, pee, fart; he could reach out for the last scant handful of potato chips in a neighbor's bag; he could cadge cigarettes or even plop down beside someone on another cot, or step with his shoes across another's blanket. But he had drawn further apart from them than ever. He had listened all along to their tales of his offenses in order to recover some scrap of his emotion, but none of that, despite their researches, had been catalogued. They had not understood the simplest things. They had seen his life from the outside, and however accurate their perceptions, they had known him only empirically.

It was this point perhaps, as much as any that might do his case some good, that he meant to make when he rose and interrupted.

"What?" the third dining partner asked.

"I object," he said wearily.

"What's your objection?"

"*My* objection is I'm starving," a convict said behind him. "What about some food?"

"They're going to try to bring over some Cokes and snacks from the canteen tonight," Harold Flesh said.

"What about the chits? I didn't bring no chits with me."

"Special credits," Flesh said. "The warden worked it out."

"I had an objection," Feldman said. He was still standing, looking at the third dining partner.

"Well, I already asked you what it was," the man said irritably. "Do you need an engraved invitation?"

"The evidence," Feldman said. He indicated with a lame backhand gesture the book that the librarian was holding.

"What about it?"

"It's all hearsay," Feldman said.

"Yes?"

"Well?"

"Well, what?"

"Well, it's hearsay."

"Yes. That's right."

Feldman shrugged and sat back down.

Once more they took up their charges, and again he was conscious of sickness, as if the dry sound of their recitations had power to stir his old fever. Even after he had lost all interest in what they were saying, he made himself listen, but he found he could be attentive only to their mistakes. Some of their statements were contradictory, and he forced himself mechanically to rise and point out the discrepancies. They heard his objections indifferently, and then continued when he had finished, no more concerned or deflected by his words than if they had been coughing spells. After a while he no longer bothered to rise when to make their case or press a point they juggled the truth, but offered his objections from where he reclined on the cot, and then, his strength declining, mumbled them to himself. At last, when even this effort proved too great, he just perceptibly moved his lips, twitching at their calumnies out of some empty but not-to-be-sacrificed form, their deceptions encouraging in him only the last bland energies of superstition, as someone too lazy to seek wood to touch accepts whatever is handy and touches that.

"How's it going?" Walls asked. They were standing by the food wagon that he and Manfred Sky had pushed into the cell-block.

Feldman shrugged. "Can I get a Coke? Do you have sandwiches?"

"Sure, Leo. Excuse me a minute," Walls said. "Hey, you guys, where you going with them cups and wrappers? The guard wants the stuff stowed in this litter can." He turned back to Feldman. "What'll it be, Leo?"

"Soda. A couple of sandwiches."

"You got the chits?"

"The warden's arranged credit."

"Well . . ." Walls said doubtfully.

"Come on, Walls. What's going on?"

"Leo . . . *kid* . . . the rest of these guys'll be around to pay it back."

Feldman nodded. Then the idea had been to deprive *him*. Psychological warfare, redundant here as the built-in scream of a bomb. He started back to his place.

"Just kidding, Leo. Here." Walls tossed him two sandwiches and marked something down in a ledger. Feldman chewed them dutifully, unable to recall five minutes later what he had eaten. Giving him credit could have been psychological too, he thought, inspiring false confidence, like the presence of enemy ministers on visits of state. Their Prime Minister dances with our President's daughter. Their field marshal kisses the hand of our First Lady. The bombs will not fall tonight, we think. Not much they won't.

The food restored them, and they brought a new spirit to their attack. No longer did they need to refer to the book or take recourse in distortion. Though they had touched on his life with Lilly and their son earlier, they went over the ground now in detail.

"Once, at supper," a convict said, "Feldman made them play 'To Tell the Truth.' It's a game on television, where three people, all claiming to be the same person, answer questions about their lives for a panel, who then try to guess the right person. Feldman made Billy be the panel, and he and Lilly were the contestants. 'My name is Lilly Feldman,' he told the kid. 'I married my husband, Leo Feldman, and came to live with him in this city, where he owns a department store.' Then Billy had to ask questions. 'Do you have a son?' he asked. 'Yes,' Feldman said, 'his name is Billy.' 'Do *you* have a son?' he asked his mother. 'Say "Lilly Feldman number two,"' Feldman said. 'She's Lilly Feldman number two, and I'm Lilly Feldman number one. You must say Lilly Feldman number one or number two.' 'Lilly Feldman number two,' the kid said, 'do you have a son?' 'Yes,' she said. 'What's his name?' Feldman glowered at her, and she knew he meant for her to lie. So Lilly said, 'His name is Charles.' Billy asked more questions, and each time Feldman told the truth and made Lilly lie.

"Finally Feldman said the time was up. 'Which is it? Lilly Feldman number one or number two?' Billy was confused and shook his head. 'Come on,' Feldman said, 'which is it? You heard the answers. Which is the real Lilly Feldman, that lousy imposter or me?' The kid finally pointed to his father, and Feldman said, 'Will the real Lilly Feldman please stand up?' and both of them feinted for a couple of minutes until the kid was crying, and then Lilly stood up and went to him."

Feldman was astonished by the disclosures Lilly had had the courage to make, and that now, though their stories were told from some opposed point of view, his life came back easily. He winced at detail. Once, during the narration of a trip they had taken, tears came to his eyes. They made their points so fiercely that he trembled.

Then, when he thought that even they must see that they had flayed him sufficiently—though it was now past midnight, no one slept; there was little of the shuffling of the daylight hours; men who had taken little interest in the trial were leaning forward, straining to catch everything in the difficult, poollike room—they discovered a new theme: his treatment of Victman and Freedman.

They dwelled at length on how he had used these two, decoying competitors with Victman's destroyed career and giving the doctor the sexless, secular horns of cuckoldry, fool's bells, the ear's body blows over the telephone. They were unrelenting. They meant to polish him off. They would bring up Dedman next.

Then, abruptly as it had begun, their attack ceased. A speaker finished, and no one rose to take his place. To this point, the trial had had a marathon quality, an attribute of palm-passed torches, sequenced as choreography. Now, in the silence, Feldman sighed and wondered: Is it over? Is it finished?

It was almost dawn. He could see the washed-out night through the barred windows of a distant cell. They sat together like this for several minutes, and he may even have bowed his head. Sent to Coventry, he thought, to die of the silences. Then someone shuffled his feet, and then another did. He looked to see if they had risen, but they were still seated. He wondered if they meant for him to stand, if he was to listen now to his sentence. He rose quietly. No one said anything, and he understood that it was his turn, that none of his objections before had meant anything, that this, now, was all they would ever give him of his chance.

Feldman drew a deep breath. "Still," he said finally, "I have not been unstirred."

"Come on," a convict said irritably, "your life's on the line. What is this?"

"I have not been unstirred," Feldman repeated firmly. "I'm accused of my character. *This* is my character: I've been moved, roused. Lumps in the throat and the heart's hard-on. I'm telling you something."

He began to list all the things that had ever moved him, all the things which might have moved them. "Anthems of any nation. Anthems do. The Polack mazurka and male Greek side step. The national dances. Ethnic stamping and the fine, firm artillery of the clog dance. A certain kind of amateurism. The abandon of drunk elder uncles at weddings. There is a clumsy rhythm in me, I tell you, the blood and heart's *oom-pa-pa*. So I have not been unstirred, that's all.

"Girls blowing kisses, cold on floats."

"Now wait a minute," said the man who had stepped on his heels.

"Overruled," Feldman said.

"Hold on a second," the man said.

"*Overruled!* I'm telling you about my heart. You asked and I'm telling you. I've been moved.

"The beards of real estate men in centennial summers," he began again desperately, "their barbershop convictions. Movie stars on telethons for charity. The sweetness of conservationists. Professors emeriti who talk about their field in the afternoon on the radio. *I hate the fire that the forest ranger hates.* What do you think? It's not so difficult to break matches before throwing them away, or to make certain your campfire's extinguished. What does it cost a person to carry a litter bag in his automobile? I am stirred that *these* should be causes.

"I saw a movie on the Late Show. It was made in the thirties, the Depression. One of the characters opened the front door of his apartment to bring in the paper and the milk. There was a picture on the front page of his ex-wife, who had just gotten engaged to his law partner. They showed a close-up of the paper, and while he was reading the story about his ex-wife's engagement, I read the headlines on the stories around it: 'Grand Jury Brings in True Bill on Gangland Slaying'; 'Shipyard Heiress Elopes with Swami, Grandpa Seeks Annulment'; 'Arctic Expedition Arrives South Pole.' This was the news. Do you understand? This was the *news.* I wept.

"And vulgarity. Spangles, brass and all the monuments of the middle class. Luxury motels—listen to me—cloverleaf highways, and the polite wording of signs along the route apologizing for construction, the governor's signature big at the bottom. The charities of businessmen. Their attentions to the blind, their fresh-air funds, and the parades of their brotherhoods. Their corny clowning and their tossed candies.

"The classic struggles of artists. The genius' rejections, but more, his first success. Hammerstein out front and the comic drunk backstage, his girl shoving coffee in him and making him walk.

"And though I am not a religious man, the windows of department stores at Christmas time.

"The cook on educational television. Likewise the dedication of weathermen and the seriousness of the officer giving the traffic conditions from the helicopter. Soldiers marching off to World War One, and singers who come down into the audience.

"Glamour, magic and plenitude, I tell you. Plenty of plenitude. High waste in restaurants. Steaks no man can finish by himself, bottomless cups of coffee and lots of butter. Balloons for the kiddies, and the waiter passing mints. Ditto the individual machinery of motel rooms: Vibrabeds and the chamois for shoes, packets of instant coffee and powdered cream—the gizmo to boil the water. The paper ribbon in deference to my ass across the toilet seat breaks my heart. The magician's shy stooges and the tears of Miss America and her runners-up. Listen. 'Happy Birthday' in night clubs and the 'Anniversary Waltz.' God bless people who take their celebrations to night clubs, I say. *Listen.* Miracle drugs, the eye bank, and the first crude word of mutes. The moment they unwrap the bandages four weeks after the operation. *Listen. Listen to me.* The oaths of foreigners for their final papers. Nightschool graduations. A cake for the new nigger in the neighborhood. Towns chipping in for anything. People cured of cancer, and the singing in the London Underground during the Blitz. *Listen, listen to me now. Listen to me!* Sheriffs shaming lynch mobs. Boys who ask ugly girls to dance, and vice versa. Last stands of individual men, and generosity from unexpected quarters."

"I like New York in June, how about you?" Harold Flesh said. "I like a Gershwin tune, how about you?"

"That's why the lady is a tramp," Bisch said.

"Once, on shipboard," Feldman said, "coming home from Europe, I was standing at the rail, looking down at the people who had come to greet their relatives and friends. There was a small band, and people were throwing streamers, confetti, pitching this bright storm of festival like a gay weather. And each person at the pier was pointing up at the great ship to see if he could find the person he had come to meet. And when he did, he would leap and make an involuntary shout. Or extend his arm and point up with one lengthened finger of welcome.

"Meanwhile, we on board were rapidly exchanging places with each other, shifting our positions along the rail, trying to catch a glimpse of whoever had come to meet us. The extended arms of those who, unspotted, had spotted the better targets of their friends would then follow the friend, all the energy of welcome confounded at the same time by the effort to set things straight, to get the person on board to stand still and look back at the person on the pier.

"*And it worked.* No one was there to meet me, and I could stand back and watch it all. Again and again I saw these great, straining magnetic fields of friendship click off contact after contact, the now mutual gestures leaping great distances, touching their loved ones with flung lines of force before they actually touched. The ship still had to dock, there was customs to clear, but they couldn't wait, and so they pantomimed love, made the signals of lovers and the heart's semaphore. No longer impatient even, already home, already in each other's arms.

"And then, after a while, everyone had found everyone else. The arms ceased to crisscross in the air, ceased to sway, and a hush had fallen over us all, and though there was no room actually to do this, there was a kind of hands-on-hips gesture of standing back in estimate and appreciation. Appreciation. Yes. Appreciation. Pride. Making the eyes' small talk that people do who have not seen each other in a long while. Feasting greedily on each change, making an inventory of differences and then discounting them, accepting the small betrayals of time in the windfall of their returns. Love moved me then.

"Do you understand? How about you, you? I'm decent. *I'm decent too!*"

He was wringing wet. His face had undergone a remarkable change—his passion visible now, open wide as the groan on a tragic mask. They had never seen him like this. Some of them couldn't look at him; they stared down at their laps or toyed with the edges of their blankets.

Now it was Feldman's silence, not theirs, as before it had been theirs and not his. A man, sighing, broke the quiet only to confirm it. There was one absolutely soundless moment of preparatory breathing in, drawing up and looking around, as if to gather up fallen gloves or paper cups on a lawn after a concert—precisely this sense of performance's end, and a calm in the room like good weather, a lowered-pressure, washed-air quality of folly wised up. He saw he might make it and didn't dare breathe, still hadn't moved but remained, posed frozen, a little uncomfortable, wrenched, as though demonstrating a follow-through, on not taking chances with a beast.

He was still thinking he might just make it when the warden spoke. "But he's *kidding*," the warden said.

"I'm not," Feldman said. "I swear it."

"He *is*. He made it all up."

"I meant it. I meant it all."

"He's selling you a bill of goods," the warden said.

"We didn't believe him, Warden," a convict said.

"It's true," Feldman said.

"Objection not sustained," the warden said sweetly. "Contempt of court," he added, smiling.

Here was justice, Feldman thought, watching him. The man's dapper, discreet power seemed to be on him like a form of joy. He had never seemed so charming; he had the look of one unarmed, a sort of chairless, whipless, unpistoled lion-tamer rakishness, or of a general in civvies.

"Take him," Feldman shouted suddenly. "*Take him!*"

But they hadn't understood. Only the warden knew what he had said. "That will do, Leo," he said softly. "Now then, men, where do we stand? Thus far I've been able to keep this quiet, but it's Thursday morning already, and if the court doesn't finish its work soon I may have to put out a cover story. It's a good thing I came in when I did. He had you going there. Well, brief me, please."

"We've heard the evidence, Warden," a convict said.

"What, all of it? About his family?"

"Yes sir."

"About Victman?"

"Yes sir."

"Freedman?"

"Yes sir."

"You've heard the evidence, and he's still alive?" the warden said cheerfully. "Have you heard about Dedman then?"

"Not about Dedman, sir. No, sir."

"Well then, that explains it. Tell us about Dedman, Feldman."

"A man can't be made to testify against himself," Feldman said.

The warden considered him for a moment. "All right," he said. "I'm Warden Fisher, the fisher of bad men. I make the rules, and what happens here happens because I make it happen or because I let it happen. You're innocent. I declare it a standoff and direct these men to ignore whatever they may have heard up to now. Feldman's innocent. I whitewash his history and make good all the bad checks drawn on his character. He stands or falls on Dedman. Is that fair, Feldman?"

Feldman stared at him.

"Good. Then it's a deal. We shall have all of it, however. You must give us all of it. All right then. Attention, everyone. Feldman gives us Dedman." The warden, who had been standing, now sat down on a cot. He folded his arms across his chest and looked up impassively, waiting for him to explain what was inexplicable.

* * *

Feldman began.

"I had a friend," he said. "Leonard Dedman."

"No one met your boat, Feldman. No one met your boat, you said."

"No. This was after . . . He wouldn't have met it. It was after I decided we could be friends."

"*You* decided?"

"Yes. I used to watch them. Boys. In the towns where I lived. I wasn't envious, you understand. It was strange to me. I grew up in small towns where boys tossed pebbles at each other's windows, where they imitated the sounds of birds, made signals." He spoke as before. There was no other way now. "I'd been in their rooms and seen them cross-legged on the bed, browsing possessions, scholars of toy, touching the gifts with a curious peace. Solaced with balls, getting their heft, rolling them off with a wave of the hand. Examining guns and aiming at space, squeezing the trigger and blowing their breath down the barrel as if to clear it—death's light housekeeping. The model airplanes, the ships and cars and toy soldiers—calmed by all the bright lead effigies of the dangerous world snug in their palms. Borrowing, trading, and a major greed. I understood this. But afterwards, after the trades, an amnesty of self, a queer quiet when the playing began. Using the toys, to be sure, but something else, something undeclared but binding—"

"Dedman. Feldman, Dedman."

"But *binding*. It was honor. In the fields, running, exercising—"

"Dedman, Feldman. Feldman, Dedman."

"—the honor still there. And even in their angers, their roughnesses, there were those who were sure to be each other's allies, doing favors in a fight, passionate to cheer or console, committed as seconds in old-timey duels. A balance in the world like a struck bargain.

"It was curious to me how they knew whom to select, how they chose up their sides so that there were teams within teams, natural combinations, feats of friendship beyond athletics, a construct of amities. One boy, in practice, who always threw a particular other boy the ball without being asked. And no one left out, not even myself, though when I had the ball I never knew who to throw it to, and had to choose, and sometimes threw it away.

"Or secrets. They told secrets, each day trusting the other with a shame or a plot, trading these as they had their toys.

"How did they *know*? How? This was the thing I didn't understand. How they made up their minds whom to like. It had nothing to do with talents, and even less with qualities, or the loved gifted and the loved good would have had it all. It was a Noah's Ark of regard.

"Was it love? Was friendship love?"

"Dedman, damnit. Damnit, Dedman. Get to Dedman. Get to the part where you betrayed him."

"I met Dedman in the city when I came there a few years after my father died," Feldman said. "He was my age and had come from the West. Like myself he had no family. We lived next door to each other in the same rooming house and sometimes ate our meals together. He had been a student, but he'd had to drop out because he had no money. He never had a talent for money. All the time we knew each other, I became richer and richer and he remained the same."

"But you gave him money," the warden said.

"Yes. To start up businesses. Dedman's businesses. They always failed."

"Yes," the warden said.

"It was Dedman who proposed our friendship," Feldman said. "He asked for it formally. It was a wonder he didn't go down on his knees."

"Was Dedman queer?" Bisch asked.

"Yes. He was queer. But not in the way you mean. He was queer. 'We should be friends,' he said, 'us birds of a feather. We should take pledges, slice flesh and brush bloods. Two people like us, like the last left alive, no kin in the kit.'

" 'Too sad, Dedman,' I told him. 'Too serious, kid. It's your America.'

" 'It's *their* America.'

"He felt it did Dedman, his condition a guilt. With a whine for a war cry he assaulted my camp. A poet he was, and two poems he had. Feldman was Dedman's, and Dedman was Feldman's. He rhymed our lives, orphan for orphan and hick for hick, and what he made of the city we'd found, I won't even say. And the rooming house, of course. He told me it was significant that we sometimes chose the same restaurant and picked the same soup. (But he had no sense about money, and what I did for budget he did for hunger.) Each evening a courting, petitions, a woo, his reasons my roses and chocolates. 'And what have *you* got to trade?' I asked him. 'And show me *your* toys,' I said. But Dedman's dowry was the lack of one. 'Bankruptcy, Dedman,' I warned him. 'Love flies out the window when the wolf comes in the door.'

"About this time I had come on the spoor of my fate. A jobber I was in those days—small-time, of course, just riding the fads and making a go. But getting first clues about a better class of merchandise. Brand names and top grade, first cut and choice and prime. Founded 1780. (This was my dream.) Aspirations of the pushcart heart, stirrings—I have *not* been unstirred—in the spieler's soul. (Grand pianos are grand. Peddler. *Old clothesman. Alley cat!*) Riddled with need I was, hunting a piece of the action like a grapple of grail. 'Shit on the shoddy,' I declared to the roomers, and scorning thread-barrenness, gave up the place. I found an apartment, and what do you think?

"Dedman, of course. It took him a week. We were neighbors again. No sense about money, no feel for the score. 'Dedman,' I asked, 'just what do you do?' He was a clerk, he drove taxis, he worked at a bench, a gardener, an usher, a pumper of gas. Caddy, orderly, *schlepper* of mail. What didn't Dedman? Dedman of the semiskill and the student duty. For understand, these were all summer jobs, Christmas rush, the small-time tasks of piecemeal pressure, timed to semesters, holidays, school dismissed because of the snowstorm. As though simply by going through a process of part-time employment, he could maintain the fiction that he was making it the hard way like orphans before him. He lived in a myth. And without the squirrel's sense of winter but only his busyness had this strange garret notion of himself, laying in his profitless, pointless struggles like grist for those plaque landmarks that honor puny origins. 'On this day, in this place, on thus spot, nothing happened, Dedman,' I told him.

"But all he gave me was the *old* business—hot pursuit and the language of romance. 'Two can live cheaply as one,' he said, and slipped me ardor and the arguments of old time's sake.

" 'Dedman, Dedman, tell no tales,' I told him. There had *been* no old times, you understand, only Dedman's hard-sold dream out of books of a Damon Dedman and a Pythias Feldman, a Romulus Leonard and Remus Leo. (And what he made of our names! 'Leonard, the Leo-hearted,' I called him once.)

"I tried to discourage him—that's the truth. The man insisted on our intimacy, giving me—met in the street, on corners, in stores, or even on the stairs or at the mailbox in the hall, gratuitous for us then as the garage in the back—the secret handshake of the heart. He was obsessed by our birthwrong. (And something just occurred to me: how did he know about mine? How did he *know*? I don't remember telling him, but I might have. Put that down to my credit. Fair's fair. Or if I never told him, then put down to my credit that it was written all over my face.) And leaned heavily on the Dedman-deemed mutuality of our lives like some old out-of-work frat man—he'd been, as I say, a student—making a nuisance of himself in his fraternity brother's office. But of course even his premise was wrong. I'd had *my* father for sixteen years, and my homunculus, if I'd known it, forever.

"It's a wonder I didn't call a cop. 'Get yourself a girl,' I said. 'Buy a paper tonight. Go through the want ads carefully. Look out for something with a future. Flourish. Thrive. Purge those gypsy grudges, Dedman. Lord,' I called over my shoulder, 'deliver this delivery boy.'

"So saying, I took hold myself. What's good for the goose is unexceptionable for the gander, is it not? And to practice what one preaches makes perfect, doesn't it? I *seized* the bullish world. What can I tell you? The war and all, opportunity, the seller's market and all—I grew rich. By 1940 I had already chosen the warehouse that would become my department store, by '41 I was already in it, and by '42 and '43 I was established, getting while the getting was good and the casualties mounted.

"I didn't see a lot of Dedman in those years. I still maintained the same apartment but was away so much, putting together my store, that I didn't see him. (Though he was there. Like myself he was four-F, and what he made of *that* I don't have to tell you. 'Our disease,' he called it.) Then, suddenly, the year the war ended, I decided to capitulate. After a siege of ten years or so, I called him in and told him we would be friends. He smiled me a smile and shook my hand, and we made the manly acknowledgments, the toasts and the jokes, and I discovered before he went back to his apartment that night that it was too late—that we were already friends, that we had been friends all along and that our friendship ended on the evening I gave in to him. That until then I'd been fonder of him than he was of me, because, after all, he'd seen in me only an analogue of himself, only some far-fetched Dedmanic Doppelgänger, while I had seen in him qualities, states of being and the hardware of character. Before that evening was over I'd had it with him, with Feldman's friend Dedman, his enemy Dedman.

"Though I didn't let on. I knew I'd get him. (Let me make something clear. I don't say I needed reasons. Maybe, at first. And maybe I had some. But what happened would have happened without reasons. So let me make something clear. What I did was not because I was acting on faulty reasons. It wasn't poor judgment or a lousy argument.)

"It was very rough, being his friend. A little Dedman went great distances—light-years. Christ, I was bored.

" 'What do we do, Dedman, now that we're friends?' And don't let him kid you—it was as new to him as it was to me. Neither of us had the hang of it. I know *I* was sorry we weren't still kids. Kids have it soft. They wrestle, they run, shout, sing, throw the ball. So we just sat around, seemly now, shy. And suddenly making telephone calls.

" 'What're you doing?'
" 'Lying around.'
" 'You want to come down?'
" 'I got my TV. Come up if you want.'
" 'Your television came?'
" 'I brought one home from the store.'
" 'How does it work?'
" 'Okay. Pretty good.'
" 'What're you watching?'
" 'Wrestling.'
" 'Wrestling is fixed.'
" 'It's all they have on.' "

"My God, the arrangements, the crabbed propositions of regard! Consideration's deflections like blindness to a wart on a pal's nose. Friendship is fixed. *Friendship* is. The dives of deference and the shaved points of solicitude.

" 'Leo, it's Leonard.'
" 'Yeah, Leonard. Hi.'
" 'Do you want to go out?'
" 'What's there to do?'
" 'There's this movie downtown.'
" 'A movie? You think?'
" 'We could go tie one on.'
" 'Well, tomorrow there's work.'
" 'You're right. I forgot.'
" 'We'd get back too late.'

" 'There's a lecture at school.'
" 'Is that so? What's it on?'
" 'The Second World War.'
" 'Sounds over my head.'
" 'Wanna come down and read?'
" 'Well, maybe. Okay.'
" 'Not too exciting.'
" 'Well, I'm tired tonight.'
" 'What time you be down?'
" 'Gee, I've still got to eat.'
" 'What time? Say a time.'
" 'Around eight? Around nine?'
" 'All right. See you then.'

"One night Dedman took me to a restaurant. I'd told him it was my birthday, though it wasn't. I'd said it to give us something to do—just as when he got a new job or I had done well at the store, I would take him out, declare a celebration, so that at this time our relationship was one of shared occasions, fictive red-letter days, spurious as the commemorative excuse for a sale of used cars. Oh, those celebrations, those pious festivals!

"And this was the night that I told him it wasn't working out—though I hadn't planned to, didn't know that I'd do it till I'd done it, so that, let me make something clear, what happened, what I did, was never what you could call a conspiracy, just as it wasn't predicated on feeble arguments—that the friendship had failed. 'Phooey on our kid-glove comity, our loveless diplomatic chumhood. My apartment's no embassy, Leonard. Tact's crap, it's defunct. Well, I take *your* line,' I said. 'No one's to blame. What, orphans like us? You kidding? Shy, sure we're shy. Us virgins in croniness, us unpanned-out pals. Oh, the roughnecks, Leonard,' I said, 'they have the fun. They're the ones.' (Let me make something clear. I've said I'd known I would get him. I've told you that. So that what was beginning to happen that night, unreasoned, not worked out, was maybe just a sort of destiny, Leonard's lot, say, or Dedman's portion, perhaps.) 'Let's really cut loose. Other guys do. Will you try? Are you game? Will you take my advice?'

" 'What do we do?'
" 'We must do as other men do. Don't be embarrassed.'
" 'No.'
" 'Don't be self-conscious. Don't get cold feet.'
" 'No.'

" 'We must do as other men do.'

" 'But what? What is it?'

" 'Dedman, I'm going to ask you to call me "Ace." It's what the roughnecks call each other. I hear it everywhere. I heard it on the campus that time I went with you to the library. "Ace," call me "Ace." It's manly. It has a fine ring. If you see me in the hallway, say "How's it going, Ace?" When you pick me up to eat, say "Let's chow down, Ace." Or "Chow time, Ace." And I'll call you "Chief." Or "Flash." Whichever you prefer. We'll work it out. I'll say, "Way to go, Flash." "Yo, Chief," I'll say. It'll make a difference. You'll see.'

" 'It will make a difference?'

" 'Absolutely. It will. Look, do me a favor. Give it a chance. When the waiter brings the check, say, "Here comes the man with the bad news, Ace." '

" 'Here comes the man with the bad news, Ace,' Dedman said when the waiter came.

" 'Read it and weep, Flash,' I told him.

"Dedman, who had no brains about money, as I say, paid the check without adding it up and overtipped the waiter a dollar. 'Way to *go*, big fella,' I said.

" 'Happy birthday, Ace.'

" 'Thanks, Chief,' I winked at him. 'Flash, how are they hanging?'

" 'Better, Ace. Really better.'

"And Dedman was into his fall now, leaning exultant into his descent like a breaster of tape. Lord, we had fun! Such times! The new-goosed Damon and piss-vinegar Pythias. Hurrah, I say! Like student princes we were, like heirs and heroes, raucous as drunks past curfew on cobble. Good times and high, Ace. And Dedman as good a man as myself. Because I had led him into the games now. Shilled and hustled him down this slow-boat-to-China garden path. Led him into the games now of Feldman's Olympic friendship. And Dedman *good* at them, you understand, skilled as an actor, no feel only for what was what. Led him into the games now. The latest thing in friendship. Damon down and Pythias perished. Long live Quirk and Flagg! Gusto and zeal and zest and joy like new soaps for the shower!

"Listen, let me make something clear—it was a classic friendship out of operetta, musical comedy, Dennis Morgan movies. I honed this rivalry with him. We played clichés on each other. Jesus, the jokes!

"Dedman bought a car. We went to a ballgame. He had a beer in the third inning. In the parking lot as he was taking out his keys, I clipped him hard as I could on his jaw and knocked him out. 'Sorry, Flash,' I said over his unconscious body, 'that hurt me more than it did you, but it would be suicide to let you get behind the wheel in your condition.'

"We pretended we were athletes in training. At night we'd each try to sneak past the other's apartment to go out and meet this blond divorcée waitress we made up, who worked in this all-night diner we made believe was on the corner. We'd walk tiptoe and carried our shoes in our hands, wearing a bathrobe and pretending we were dressed underneath it. I'd spot him sneaking out, and Dedman would feign this angelic look and begin whistling. (He couldn't really whistle, but he'd pretend to.) 'Where you going, Chief?'

" 'Who? Me, Ace?'

" 'Yeah, big guy, you.'

" 'Oh, nowhere, Ace. I thought I heard a suspicious noise in the hall, and I came out to check it.'

" 'A suspicious noise. You mean like a burglar would make?'

" 'That's right. Like a burglar.'

" *'Then why were you whistling?'*

" 'I was *pretending* to whistle, Ace.'

" 'You were off to see Trixie O'Toole, weren't you? Weren't you?'

" 'Who, Ace?'

" 'You know who. A certain cute little blond hash-slinger with big blue eyes over at Joe's all-nighter.'

" 'Come on, Ace. But that reminds me, now that you mention it, what are *you* doing out here in the hall this time of night?'

" 'Who, me? Why, uh—that is, er—well, uh—gulp—er—who, me?'

"Dedman would double up, he'd be laughing so hard. I'd watch him and smile. 'This is the life, ain't it, Skippy?' I'd say.

" 'It is, Ace. It really is.'

"It really was.

"We took these twin sisters to night clubs. We ordered one glass of champagne apiece and then went to another night club, where we ordered another glass of champagne apiece, and then on to another and another, having one glass of champagne in each place, and one dance, building the evening like a montage in films. We danced until dawn and rode home in a milk wagon.

"Once when I wasn't with him, Dedman got picked up for speeding. He gave my name to the police, and they called up and asked if I wanted to bail him out. I said, 'Never heard of the dirty rat.' Do you know, before I hung up, the desk sergeant told him what I'd said and I could hear Dedman laughing?"

"All right, Feldman, get to it," the warden said.

"Blasts. Balls and binges: We would—"

"Get to it, I said."

"We courted the same girl," Feldman said softly. "Marge. Is this it? What you want me to say?"

"Marge," the warden said. "Yes. Marge."

"We saw the same girl. We took out the same girl. Only, I didn't care for her as much as Dedman did."

"You hated her."

"Yes."

"Yet you made believe you loved her."

"No. I never told her that."

"Not her. Dedman."

"Yes."

"Go on," the warden said.

"I'd met Lilly by now in New York. We were engaged to be married. Dedman didn't know—I hadn't told him. But there was time because we couldn't be married until Dedman was married."

"What?"

"Sure," Feldman said. "Because that's part of the game, marrying off your friends. You know, the married man who can't rest until his buddy is married too, who hates the idea of there being bachelors left. So I picked out Marge for him. Scum. She was scum. A bitch. And divorced. A Trixie O'Toole, she was. She even had a kid. Dedman didn't know. Christ, she was grubby. You could smell her soul on her breath. Not Dedman.

"So I built each of them up to the other. It was easy with Dedman—romance was right up that orphan's alley—but harder with her, with Marge. I hinted of money. (I think she got the idea that I was queer on him and that I would make him rich if he married.) I told her how to speak to him. I gave her the titles of books and taught her the names of operas and the themes from symphonies. What the hell, Dedman, that dropout, didn't know much more himself. And I gave her things to say that would make him jealous and bring him around.

"One night Dedman knocked on my door. 'I want to talk to you,' he said.

" 'Shoot, Chief.'

" 'No. Listen to me.'

" 'Why so serious? What's up? Come on in and sit down.'

" 'Listen to me. I want to make something clear. It's about the game.'

" 'The game?'

" 'The game we play.'

" 'Why such a long face, Flash?'

" 'It's over, that's all. I mean it isn't a game.'

" 'What?' I was afraid he'd found out.

" 'I mean it. The game is over. I'm not playing any more.'

" 'Look, Leonard, what is it? Tell me, will you?'

" 'I'm in love with her.'

" 'Who?'

" 'You know who.'

" 'Marge?'

" 'Yes, damnit, Marge.'

" 'Oh,' I said.

" 'Look,' he said, 'I'm sorry. Really. I'm sorry. I am.'

" 'Oh.'

" 'I didn't want this to happen.'

" 'Oh.'

" 'I didn't.'

" 'Well, say,' I said. 'What's the big deal, Flash? What's so terrible? *Me?* Say, is that what you think? You feel bad 'cause of me? Now, look, don't be silly. I'll be all right. Hey, old buddy, cheer up. That's terrific news. That's swell. That's really swell, Flash.'

" 'Would you be our best man?'

" 'Your best man? You've got some sense of humor, Dedman.'

" 'I'm sorry,' he said. 'I shouldn't have asked you.'

" 'No. Listen. I lost my nerve for a second, that's all. I'm honored. You just try to get someone else for best man and see what happens to you.'

"Dedman gulped. We gulped in our games, but this was the real thing—the true-blue gulp, and no joke. 'I wouldn't have another best man,' he said. 'I couldn't, Ace.'

"And so they were married and I'd won the game. But Dedman was right. The game *was* over. But it went into extra innings anyway. It was over because it wasn't a game any more; now it was something I needed to keep me alive. Something I *needed*—betraying him and betraying him, hooked on his doom.

"I called him in to see me. He looked shitty—she must really have been working him over. Poor Dedman. I told him he was a married man now and had responsibilities; school was out for good now, and he'd better consider his future, I told him. And he nodded, agreed. And that's when I gave him the money. For his businesses. Dedman's businesses. But Dedman had no sense about money. And the businesses failed. *Because I never gave him enough, you see!* Always just a few thousand dollars less than what I knew they would need. They were timed to fail. Two years, three, and he'd be back again. What did it cost me over the years? That lunch counter? That dry-cleaning franchise? That school-supply store? Ten thousand? Fifteen? Those small-time businesses that bled him and bled him, so that he lived always in a crisis of failure. Dedman's seven lean years that kept me alive.

"He came to our wedding in New York. He paid his own plane fare and stayed in a hotel. I saw him when he came through the receiving line. Jesus, he looked lousy. She did some job on him, that bitch. He shook my hand.

" '*Que será será*, Chief?' I asked.

" '*Comme ci, comme ça*, Ace.' "

"Take him." the warden whispered. *"Take him!"*

And at first, when they didn't move, Feldman thought that they had found him innocent. "Why, I'm innocent," he said. All along, the more they had talked, the more they had made their case, pushing him closer and closer to this last closed corner of their justice, the less guilt he had felt. He wasn't guilty. He was not. He was no bad man. How I love my life, he thought. How I cherish it. It is the single holiness. My icicle winter snots like the relics of saints. How pious I am, how blessed. I accept wars, history, the deaths of the past, other people's poverties and losses. Their casualties and bad dreams I write off. I remember all the disasters that have happened and all the disappointments of the generations from time's beginning to its end, and still I am permitted to live.

But then the warden repeated his command, and they started to close in.

But perhaps the warden's anger had betrayed him. It may have been an accident, or that he had simply forgotten—the foolish warden—or had maybe never known of the expert, still in the gym, who had been practicing to kill Feldman with a single punch. And possibly they would only beat him very badly, inexpertly. The homunculus would not rip his heart. He would recover. Or perhaps such an "accident" was God's sign that the Diaspora was still unfinished, and that until it was, until everything had happened, until Feldman had filled the world, all its desert places and each of its precipices, all its surfaces and everywhere under its seas, and along its beaches, he could not be punished or suffer the eternal lean years of death.

Why, I *am* innocent, he thought, even as they beat him. And indeed, he felt so.

LANNAN SELECTIONS

The Lannan Foundation, located in Santa Fe, New Mexico, is a family foundation whose funding focuses on special cultural projects and ideas which promote and protect cultural freedom, diversity, and creativity.

The literary aspect of Lannan's cultural program supports the creation and presentation of exceptional English-language literature and develops a wider audience for poetry, fiction, and nonfiction.

Since 1990, the Lannan Foundation has supported Dalkey Archive Press projects in a variety of ways, including monetary support for authors, audience development programs, and direct funding for the publication of the Press's books.

In the year 2000, the Lannan Selections Series was established to promote both organizations' commitment to the highest expressions of literary creativity. The Foundation supports the publication of this series of books each year, and works closely with the Press to ensure that these books will reach as many readers as possible and achieve a permanent place in literature. Authors whose works have been published as Lannan Selections include Ishmael Reed, Stanley Elkin, Ann Quin, Nicholas Mosley, William Eastlake, and David Antin, among others.

SELECTED DALKEY ARCHIVE PAPERBACKS

FOR A FULL LIST OF PUBLICATIONS, VISIT:
www.dalkeyarchive.com

SELECTED DALKEY ARCHIVE PAPERBACKS

FOR A FULL LIST OF PUBLICATIONS, VISIT:
www.dalkeyarchive.com